Readers love K.C. WELLS

Make Me Soar

"I had very high expectations for this book and I have not been disappointed. In each book, the author can enrich all of the characters, and does it brilliantly."

—Three Books Over the Rainbow

"As often happens with KC Wells books the epilogue is epic and is everything the characters and the reader deserves after such a harrowing journey."

—Prism Book Alliance

A Bond of Three

"I loved this story! It was full of symbols, FEELS, passion, sexy stable boys, horses, wise advisers, ancient scrolls, centuries-old betrayals, and kisses in a summer storm."

—My Fiction Nook

"I loved the way this story was written… a joy to read…"
—MM Good Book Reviews

Damian's Discipline

"Speechless… that's the first thing that comes to mind after finishing this story."

—Love Bytes

"Another wonderful addition to the "Collars and Cuffs" series, and hopefully more to come!!"

—Hearts on Fire

By K.C. WELLS

A Bond of Three
First
Love Lessons Learned
Waiting For You

COLLARS & CUFFS
An Unlocked Heart
Trusting Thomas
With Parker Williams: Someone to Keep Me
A Dance with Domination
With Parker Williams: Damian's Discipline
Make Me Soar

LEARNING TO LOVE
Michael & Sean
Evan & Daniel
Josh & Chris
Final Exam

Published by DREAMSPINNER PRESS
www.dreamspinnerpress.com

FIRST

K.C. WELLS

Published by
DREAMSPINNER PRESS

5032 Capital Circle SW, Suite 2, PMB# 279, Tallahassee, FL 32305-7886 USA
www.dreamspinnerpress.com

First
© 2015 K.C. Wells.

Cover Photo
© 2015 Dave Ouano Photography.
Model: Dirk Caber
Cover Design
© 2015 Paul Richmond.
Cover content is for illustrative purposes only and any person depicted on the cover is a model.

K.C. Wells logo design by A.J. Corza

ISBN: 978-1-63476-600-5
Digital ISBN: 978-1-63476-601-2
Library of Congress Control Number: 2015945177
First Edition September 2015

Printed in the United States of America
∞
This paper meets the requirements of
ANSI/NISO Z39.48-1992 (Permanence of Paper).

For Jack Parton
There is so much of you in these pages.
Your experience, your insights, your humor….
Thank you for sharing it, and for bringing Mike to life.

ACKNOWLEDGMENTS

As always, thanks to my wonderful betas:
Lara, Tina, Mardee, Wulf....
But I'm going to single two out for some special thanks.

Thank you, Max Vos.
You helped me keep the American flavor of this one,
even if you despaired at some of the "Englishness" of it sometimes.

And Jason Mitchell:
Thank you for the Facebook chats, the Skype calls....
Talking about this book with you really helped.

CHAPTER ONE

TOMMY NEWSOME regarded the exterior of Jungle, his stomach clenched. "I'm not so sure 'bout this, Ben." The place looked huge, and judging by the number of guys going in there, it was going to be packed. He could already hear the steady pulse of disco music, and that was enough to make his heart beat out a military tattoo in his chest. Dancing… gay guys…. Hell, this was *way* out of his comfort zone.

His roommate laughed. "Don't tell me you wanna chicken out already? I swear, you must've spent your entire first year sitting in your room every night." He peered intently at Tommy. "Geez. I'm right, aren't I?"

Tommy knew his cheeks were burning. His throat tightened, and the words wouldn't come.

Ben's laughter died, and he moved closer. "Look, it's just a club, okay?" He patted Tommy's arm. "And don't think for a moment that I don't know what's going on in that head of yours. You're thinking 'bout what your momma would say."

Shit. Tommy's stomach did a slow roll. "No," he protested weakly, but he knew it was a lie. Momma's voice was sounding off in his head, all right. Loud and clear.

Ben's expression grew serious. "Well, your momma isn't here, and all we're talking 'bout is spending a night dancing." His eyes sparkled, and there was a hint of a grin. "Loud disco music and cute boys—what's not to like about that?"

Tommy shook his head. He'd known Benson Cardiff Wellington III since that day back in October of last year when Ben had struck up a conversation in their dorm. There was no way Tommy would've had the nerve to make the first move. Ben was everything he wasn't. Ben's upper-class upbringing was evident in his clothes and his manner, so far removed from Tommy's humble origins that they might as well have been born on different planets. Once he'd gotten to know Ben a little, it was clear there were other things about him that were outside of Tommy's sphere of experience. When Ben had revealed he was bisexual, Tommy had been stunned into silence. As far as he knew, no one in Americus was bi. They wouldn't dare.

"Are we going in or what?"

Tommy sighed. Ben had *no* idea how difficult this was for him. Places like the Jungle were "the Devil's playground" according to his parents. It wasn't easy to go against everything he'd been taught his whole life. His momma had always lectured him on the evils of dancing and alcohol. Heaven knew what she'd say about a gay club—his ears would probably bleed after her pontificating.

"I promise you, God is not gonna send down a bolt of lightning to smite you the minute you set foot inside, okay?"

Ben's words were laced with humor, but Tommy knew his roommate well enough to know they were uttered with kindness.

Enough procrastinating. "Okay." Tommy took a deep breath and stepped through the door into the lion's den, Ben leading the way.

It wasn't quite what he'd imagined—it was much, *much* worse.

Music thrummed through the floor, and Tommy hated it. The lighting was low, with colored lights that played over the club's occupants. Oh yeah—add to that the sight of all those guys, some half dressed, for God's sake, pressed together on the dance floor. And there were so freakin' many of them! The place was the size of a warehouse inside, and everywhere he looked, there were bodies: tight T-shirts, bare chests, so much skin on display.

"Isn't this great?" Ben beamed at him.

"Yeah," Tommy lied. It was so far from great it was unreal, but he didn't want to let Ben down. It had been Ben's idea to come to the Jungle, and Tommy hadn't been able to say no. Part of him had been dying of curiosity of course, but now that he was there? Yeah, he'd had enough already.

Ben waved to a group of guys on the dance floor who waved back immediately, beckoning him to join them with wide smiles. Ben turned to Tommy. "How 'bout you get us a drink from the bar? I'll have a bottle of water, okay?" And with that he thrust a rolled up magazine into Tommy's hand and plunged into the crowd, which swallowed him up in a sea of flesh.

Tommy stared at him in astonishment, left standing at the edge of the dancing and feeling more out of place than ever. He didn't give the small magazine in his hand a second glance but looked around, located the bar, and joined the throng of clubbers who stood waiting to be served. Damn, this place was loud. Tommy had never even *heard* such music 'til he'd come to college. There'd been nothing like that played on the radio at home, that was for sure. He hadn't stayed in his room that first year because he'd been feeling antisocial—he just couldn't cope with the culture shock.

Finally he got their drinks and retreated to a corner as far away from the bar and the dance floor as he could get. His senses were overloaded. He sipped his Cherry Coke and tried to relax, but it *so* wasn't happening. This just wasn't him. He watched as Ben cavorted on the dance floor, surrounded by beautiful boys—lean, smooth, and flexible. In spite of his heightened nervous state, Tommy smiled to himself. Ben was in his element.

The circular was still in his hand, along with Ben's bottle of water. Tommy placed his drink and the bottle on the ledge that ran along the wall, and unrolled the circular, glancing at the front cover in surprise at the images of Atlanta Pride. It was a free gay magazine, *David Atlanta*. Curious, he leafed through it. It seemed innocuous enough: articles and ads for gay businesses in Atlanta. Tommy took his time; he'd never read a gay publication before. He stared at the photos, heart pounding. Suddenly everything seemed that little bit more real. He took a moment to breathe, trying to inject a bit of calm.

I'm really in a gay club. He'd fantasized enough about stepping out of his tight little closet. Actually doing it was scary as hell. But he'd done it. He'd *finally* done it. The thought brought a shiver to his spine, and he quickly gulped some more Cherry Coke before going back to his perusal of the magazine. When he got to the section advertising gay bars, he scanned the page. He stared at the ad for a gay sports bar, Woofs, within spitting distance of his present location. A gay *sports* bar?

His heart raced. He couldn't walk into a gay bar alone—could he? The mere thought made him break out in a cold sweat, yet that didn't stop the tingle of anticipation that trickled up and down his back. *Do it. Just* do *it. Don't even* think *about it.*

"God, you look like you're having a heart attack. Is it that bad here?" Ben's wry chuckle brought him swiftly into the present. "I wondered where you'd gotten to. What you doing hiding out over here?" He grabbed the bottle of water next to Tommy's glass on the ledge and downed half of it in long swallows.

Tommy held up the magazine. "Thought I might go see what this place is like," he said, more calmly than he felt. Inside he was a mess.

Ben arched his eyebrows. "Well, good for you, Tommy! Want me to come with, to hold your hand?" He winked.

Tommy laughed, the sound false to his ears. "Nah, I'll be okay." He was a big boy; he could handle it. Then he had to smile. He was a *very* big boy.

Ben nodded in approval. "Well, you got your ID, right?" Tommy nodded. "Then don't get too drunk—you've got the truck, remember?" He glanced at Tommy's glass and grinned. "But I guess I don't have to worry 'bout that, huh?"

Shit. Tommy had clean forgotten about that. "How you gonna get back to your place?"

Ben waved his hand. "Hey, don't you go worrying your head about me. I'm sure I'll manage. And you got a key, right? Besides, who knows where my night will end—or in whose bed." He waggled his eyebrows. "There's this one dude over by the bar who is seriously *hung*." Ben licked his lips.

Heat bloomed in Tommy's face. He *so* didn't want to go there. It was bad enough that he knew Ben went through guys—and girls—like a starving man who'd just come off a strict diet. He didn't need any images of Ben cluttering up his head. Where was brain bleach when you needed it?

"Have a good night." He patted Ben on the arm and made his way through the tightly packed crowd toward the main door. Once outside he breathed deeply.

C'mon, pull yourself together. He took a moment to collect himself and then headed in the direction of his truck. Woofs was only a short drive away. He drove up Piedmont Road, his heart still doing a dance behind his ribs. It had taken him his entire first year at the University of Georgia just to catch up with the rest of his classmates in terms of fitting in. Talk about a fish out of water. Tommy wasn't sure he'd changed that much from the farm boy who'd arrived just over a year ago, so green, so innocent.

Not so innocent now, he mused as he pulled up outside the bar. He took his worn baseball cap from his jacket pocket and put it on. Inside he could hear roars and cheers. There was obviously a game on TV. He stood on the threshold, hands clenched tightly at his sides, knees feeling decidedly wobbly. How long he remained there he had no idea, but the sound of a truck pulling up beside his forced him into action. He pressed his hand against the white door, pushed, and then he was inside.

The bar was full of guys standing around little tables or at the bar, and there were several TV screens on the walls. His first thought was that he'd made a mistake. Everyone looked… ordinary, just guys hanging out, watching a football game, yelling at the screens and cheering. He edged his way through the crowded bar that was laid out in a *U* shape until he got to the far side where there were booths, all occupied. Miraculously, there was an empty stool at the end of the bar near the tabletop video games, and he slid onto it, pulse racing as he looked around. No one gave him a second glance, and he took the opportunity to take in his surroundings, his heartbeat returning to normal.

There were three bartenders, one of whom was circulating, taking and delivering orders, and chatting with other customers. One bartender in particular made Tommy's heart pound a bit harder. He was maybe in his late thirties or early forties, about five nine, and wide across the chest, his upper arms thick with muscle. His hair was cut short, almost a buzz cut, and he had a beard, a little gray showing there. Glasses didn't hide a pair of blue eyes that were intense, even at a distance. Just looking at him made Tommy's dick hard.

"Hey, you gonna order or what?"

With a start, Tommy pulled himself back from his reverie and looked up at the bartender standing in front of him. He was tall, with a Mohawk and tattoos *everywhere*, a bruiser of a guy with rainbow-colored ear gauges.

The bartender smirked. "You back with us?"

Tommy's cheeks were on fire. "A Cherry Coke, please."

One eyebrow lifted. "A Cherry Coke." He peered at Tommy. "You got ID, honey?" He gave him a flirtatious wink.

Nodding, Tommy reached into his pocket for his wallet and handed over the fake ID Ben had procured for him. He tried to keep calm. This was the first time he'd had occasion to use it. He held himself still and kept his eyes on the TV screen, ignoring the bartender while he inspected the card with a smile. When it was handed back to him, Tommy had to fight hard to hide his relief, even though it was plain the bartender's perusal had been more playful than serious.

"Sorry, hon, but you know how fierce they are in this town about underage drinking. I have to ask *everyone*," he said with an exaggerated sigh. "I'm sure you're used to it by now."

"Sure," Tommy lied, nodding, like this really wasn't his first time in a bar.

"One Cherry Coke, coming up." The bartender gave him a nod and grabbed a glass. Tommy sagged onto the stool and breathed more evenly. He could deal with this.

Until he watched the gorgeous bartender lean across the bar and kiss the customer in front of him squarely on the mouth, then go back to his task of pouring out a beer, grinning, like kissing a guy was nothing out of the ordinary.

Shit shit shit…. Just like that, Tommy's heart was doing its little dance all over again.

Then he began to notice things. The guy near the bar who had his arm around another guy's waist. The third bartender, shorter than the other two and nowhere near as muscular, whose manner was a good deal more effeminate. More guys with their arms around each other. Kisses, just pecks on the cheeks or lips, but yeah, there was definitely kissing going on. He'd been too out of it at the club to notice if there'd been any of that going on, but at such close quarters, it was hard to miss.

That was when it really hit home. Tommy was in a gay bar.

"Here you go." The Mohawk guy was back, placing a paper napkin and a tall glass of Cherry Coke in front of him. "You wanna pay for it or set up a tab?"

Tommy fumbled clumsily with his wallet, all thumbs, taking out three dollars and handing them over. Mohawk guy nodded and went over to the till. Tommy sipped at the drink, loaded with ice, letting its coolness take away some of the heat from his face. He pulled the cap bill over his eyes and leaned on the bar, observing his fellow customers. More than once his gaze drifted back to the bespectacled bartender, who was laughing and joking with his customers. Now and again he'd raise his eyes to watch the game, joining in the roars and groans of those around him.

Who was he trying to kid? Tommy couldn't take his eyes off him. The man was sex on legs: those muscles, those eyes, that sexy beard…. Then he caught Tommy looking and flashed him a quick grin and a wink.

The hair stood up on the back of Tommy's neck, and his breathing quickened. He felt light-headed, shivery, and hot, all at the same time. What made it worse? The bartender *noticed*. That grin widened and those intense eyes sparkled.

"Hey, Mike, can you check the pump for Blue Moon?" Mohawk guy said to Mr. Sex on Legs. Glugging noises issued from the tap as beer spattered into the glass he was trying to fill.

"Sure thing." Mike gave Tommy a last glance before disappearing behind the bar. Tommy breathed in deeply and took a long swig of Cherry Coke. His physical reaction to Mike had been... powerful, not something he'd ever experienced before. He was still trembling, for God's sake.

Well, if I'd had any doubts about me bein' gay, that *sure blew them all to hell.* There'd been no mistaking the lump of stone behind his jeans zipper or the tingle in his balls. Not that he was gonna *do* anything: Tommy was more than content to sit in the bar 'til they closed, sipping Cherry Coke and enjoying the view.

Yeah, acknowledging he was gay was one thing—*doing* anything with that knowledge was something else entirely. And Tommy wasn't ready to go down that road just yet. In fact, not for a long while yet.

CHAPTER TWO

MIKE SCOTT switched off the engine and grabbed his bag from the passenger seat beside him. The parking lot of ManFactory's studios was virtually empty, but it was only nine in the morning. Mike always preferred to arrive early; he hated being last minute. He got out of the car, locked it, and headed for the main door. The last few days of September were warm, temperatures maybe in the eighties, so he'd gone without a jacket, wearing only his worn jeans, boots, and a black cotton shirt. Bag slung over his shoulder, Mike pushed open the glass door and entered the reception area.

"Morning, Scott," Paul called out in greeting from behind the glass desk. On the walls were long vertical banners of some of the ManFactory models, all staring into the camera, thumbs hooked in the waistband of torn jeans, leather pants, or a skimpy pair of Speedos. Mike tried not to look at his own image, taken when he was in his late thirties. He'd filled out since then, most of it muscle, the result of many hours in the gym and keeping an obsessive eye on his carbs intake.

Scott Masters, adult entertainer, six years with ManFactory, nearly twenty years in the porn industry, and he still had a following. Of course these days, most requests came from companies who produced scenes that were more bears and daddies than anything else. Mike supposed he had to expect that at his age. But being forty-three didn't mean he was on his way out, even if lately he was beginning to get a little tired of it all. He only worked three or four nights a week at Woofs, but he was now in a position to be able to seriously consider cutting down the number of scenes he filmed. He'd put enough by so he didn't have to worry about money. But the requests kept pouring in, and he wasn't about to turn down good money. Except, of course, it wasn't as good as it had been when he'd first started out. The times, they were certainly a-changin'....

"Hi, Paul," Mike said with a cheery wave. "Has Dino arrived yet?" His gaze drifted to the young man slouched on one of the couches next to the desk. Dressed in jeans and a black sleeveless shirt, he looked bored out of his skull, barely acknowledging Mike beyond a quick shift of the eyes in his direction.

"Nah, but he shouldn't be long." Paul handed him the usual clipboard with its attached documentation. He grinned. "Early as usual, I see."

Mike returned his grin. "You know me." He walked through reception to the main area of the studio and into the little room with its table and plastic chairs. After slinging his bag onto a chair, he sat down and filled out the boring but necessary details that were required prior to a shoot. The studio had already received his latest test results electronically several days before.

"Scott, can you do me a favor?"

Mike glanced up. Paul stood in the doorway looking anxious, the bored young man at his side. "What's up?"

Paul inclined his head in the young man's direction. "Chad here has an interview with Rod, but he isn't here yet, and there's a call I gotta take first. Seeing as Dino hasn't arrived yet either, any chance you could maybe give him a little guided tour of the studio?" His eyes pleaded with Mike. "Pretty please? I know it's unusual, but with you having been with us for so long, I'm sure Rod and Tony wouldn't mind. I mean, they trust you, right? You're one of the family, yeah?"

Mike guffawed. "Quit digging and batting those eyelashes at me, okay? Sure, I'll show him around." He rose to his feet. "C'mon... Chad? Let me give you the fifty cent tour." He winked.

Paul heaved an overly dramatic sigh of relief. "Oh, thanks. I won't be long. I swear." He dashed off in the direction of reception, leaving Chad standing there looking amused.

"What a flamer," he commented under his breath.

Mike arched his eyebrows, back stiffening. "Oh my, apparently here's someone who hasn't read *How to Win Friends and Influence People*. That guy is your first port of call for the studio, and yet you feel it's okay to make disparaging remarks about him?" He shook his head. "Never heard anyone say first impressions count, kid?"

Chad scowled. "I'm not a kid."

Mike tilted his head. "Where you from, kid?" Like he didn't already have a pretty good idea, judging by that accent.

"Idaho." Chad stuck his chin out. "You got a problem with that? And who are you, anyway? That guy makes it sound like I'm supposed to know you."

Mike bit back his sigh. Another porn wannabe with fifty tons of attitude. He ignored the last comment and marched past Chad, out of the room, and onto the main floor, beckoning him to follow.

"This section contains all the different sets the studio uses." He pointed over at the empty sets. It wouldn't be too long before Seb, the cameraman, and Tony, the director, would arrive. "Over there is your standard doctor's office, and beyond that is the business office setup. Then we have a couple different bedrooms, hotel room, classroom, apartment, the usual…." He came to a halt and turned to peer at Chad. "You *have* seen some of the ManFactory scenes before, right?"

Chad shrugged. "Couple. To be honest, I don't watch gay porn, 'cause I'm straight."

Christ, gimme strength. Yet another *gay for pay.* "But you think you have what it takes to be a gay porn actor?" He folded his arms across his chest.

There was that chin jutting out again.

"Sticking my dick in a guy's ass can't be that much different from sticking it in my girlfriend's, right?" Chad grinned. "Think I'll do just fine."

That cocky expression on his face made Mike want to smack it.

"Okay, Chad, you can come with me now." Paul appeared behind them, slightly out of breath. He gave Mike a grateful smile. "Thanks, Scott. I'll take it from here."

Mike waited until Chad was out of sight and then shook his head once more. "Christ Almighty." He watched the departing Chad, taking in the lean, slim body. *With* your *slight looks, boy, it's not your* dick *that's gonna be seeing much use.* He went back into the small admin room to find Dino Spears already there, filling in his forms. Mike gave him a warm smile. He and Dino went way back, from when Mike had first started out.

"Hey, you got here, then."

Dino snorted. "Still the early bird, I see. How you doing, Scott?" He got up and gave Mike a brief but firm hug, those thick arms enveloping him. "I heard about you and Dirk breaking up. Sorry. I always thought you two would go the distance."

Mike's chest tightened at the mention of his ex. He'd had the same thoughts too. Unfortunately, Dirk hadn't. "Let's not go there, okay?" He was in no mood to discuss his breakup. It might have been over a year since Dirk had declared he couldn't take being the partner of a porn star anymore, but the hurt was still there. Three years they'd been together….

"Who was that with Paul?" Dino cocked his head toward the door. Mike scowled. "*That* was Chad, an aspiring porn star."

"Is it too much to hope that he's gay?" When Mike let out a derisory chuckle, Dino's face fell. "Oh hell, another straight boy." Then he smirked. "Hey, you might end up with him as a scene partner if he gets the job."

"Christ, I hope not." Mike got really frustrated every time he had to work with one of the gay-for-pay guys. There were some really sweet guys, very professional, but when it came down to it, filming with them was a nightmare. They could only film for about two minutes before they had to stop and watch titty porn for five minutes to regain their hard-on. And meanwhile there *he* was, his dick getting limper by the second. "Besides, he's not my type."

Dino opened his eyes wide in mock surprise, hand pressed over his heart. "You have a type? And here I was thinking if it had a pulse and a hole, you were in there." He snickered.

"Bitch. And yes, I do have a type, so fuck off." For a moment, there flashed across his mind the young guy who'd appeared at the bar on Saturday night. Tall, maybe six feet, possibly more, muscles, burly—just how Mike liked them. The face was pretty too. Too bad he wasn't cooked enough yet. That blush was a dead giveaway, not that Mike couldn't spot a newbie after all this time. But in comparison with Chad? Yeah, give him a shy, fresh-faced gay guy over a cocky know-it-all straight guy every time.

Mike sighed and gestured toward the door. "You know what really galls the hell outta me? That little shit could end up being the next America's gay-boy-next-door darling. And what'd you wanna bet are the chances that he's a homophobic little prick on set, completely unprofessional, but who gets away with it 'cause he makes the company a fortune?" He frowned. "Yeah, Chad there will be laughing all the way to the bank, with our *fag* dollars in his pockets." He crooked his fingers into quotation marks.

Dino stared at him. "Whoa... cynical much?"

Mike snorted. "Why, d'you think I'm bitching too much about his skinny furless ass?"

"How d'*you* know it's furless?" Dino was trying not to laugh.

"Oh, please. Gimme some credit. I'd bet my next paycheck that he's a bare little twink." He sighed. "One who'll be paid more than we are, that's for sure."

Dino patted Mike's arm. "You don't even know if they'll give him a job yet. How 'bout you and me concentrate on doing a fucking hot scene, and show Mr. Wannabe there how it's done?" He sat down.

Mike grinned. "*Now* you're talkin'." He sat down next to Dino and pulled out the scene notes from his clipboard. Dino did the same, scanning the sheet.

"Okay, so we're doing a guy comforting his best friend." He grinned. "Ooh, I'm the straight best friend, and I'm having doubts about marrying my girlfriend." The grin widened. "And I'm bottoming. Wow, what a surprise."

Mike laughed. "Yeah, right. You know you love it." Dino rarely topped, but that was how he liked it.

Dino gave a mock grimace. "Well, I'd better get the ol' butt plug if I'm gonna take your humongous dick up my ass"—he waggled his eyebrows—"unless it's shrunk with age, old man."

"Oh hush." Mike studied his notes. "How you wanna do this? I'm thinking start out on the couch, then move it to the bedroom. We could use the apartment set."

"Sure." Dino put down his notes. "So maybe a couple minutes of conversation, heart-to-heart, that sort of thing. I get up to leave and you stop me, y'know, with something 'bout how you're worried and you care about me, yeah?"

Mike nodded. He loved working with professionals, guys who gave 100 percent and who cared about their work. "Yeah, and then we should have a moment to build tension, right? Staring at each other, me hesitant, you bewildered…. And then we kiss. Make it like a dam bursting, yeah? Lots of emotion, touching." He'd been long enough at this game to know what he was doing. That didn't mean he wasn't gonna discuss it first with Tony and Seb. "Let's see if the guys are around."

They got up and wandered onto the apartment set, where the cameras were already being set up. Seb greeted them with a cheerful smile, and Tony beamed. "Yay! I get to spend my morning with seasoned performers. Always prefer working with guys who know what they're doing."

Mike bit back his grimace. *Seasoned performers* sounded like another way of saying old and past their prime. Not that he could blame Tony. Many of ManFactory's most popular models were in their early twenties or barely legal. Sometimes it seemed that experienced guys like him and Dino were only offered scenes to make sure the whole demographic got covered.

Tony inclined his head toward their notes. "You've seen what we're doing?"

Mike nodded, and the four of them spent the next ten minutes working the scene out, planning positions to build variety into it and discussing lighting and camera angles. Mike felt comfortable working with Dino. They had enough chemistry between them to make it a pretty hot scene, which would please Tony. Lord knew there was no shortage of porn out there. All the free stuff online and the piracy just added to the pressure. And these days there was also the lure of bareback sites. Thank God ManFactory wasn't about to go down *that* route. At least Mike sincerely hoped they weren't. Such a decision would signify a parting of the ways, as far as he was concerned.

Wayne, the photographer, arrived. "Let's start with the publicity photos and the cover, yeah? You two get showered, and we'll do the naked shots first. Then you can choose your wardrobe and we'll do the earlier shots."

"Sure."

Mike and Dino stood up, grabbed their bags, and headed for the showers. Mike quickly went through his ritual, Dino taking longer than him. By the time Dino was ready for his shower, Mike was already under the jets, working on his erection. Not that it needed much effort. He hadn't jerked off for a couple of days, knowing it made for a much better cum shot. Watching Dino's lean body and nicely toned arms and legs, the water sluicing down over his tanned flesh, made things that much easier too. He smiled at the sight of a fat black silicone plug in Dino's ass. Apparently he'd been serious.

"Looking good there, Dino." He gazed in appreciation at his scene partner while he stroked his dick, things firming up nicely. Dino was about his age but slighter.

He flexed for Mike, grinning, and then grabbed his cock around the base and waved it at him. Mike laughed.

"You still waxing your ass? 'Cause you know how much I love munching on a furry butt."

Dino chuckled. He turned his back to Mike, bent over, and spread his cheeks, revealing the light dusting of hair around his hole, visible beyond the butt plug. "That do ya?" He glanced over his shoulder at Mike, eyes sparkling.

Mike couldn't resist. He moved closer and ran his fingers through Dino's crease, stroking lower to cup his balls. Dino shuddered. "Like that?" He leaned in closer and brought his lips to Dino's ear. "Imagine how it's gonna feel when it's my tongue there, my fingers in your hole... my dick."

There was no missing the full-body shiver that rippled through Dino in spite of the warm water. "Fuck, Scott...." His voice quavered. Dino straightened and turned, moving as if to take things up a notch. Mike stopped him.

"Save it for the scene, yeah?" he said huskily.

Dino nodded and flipped off the shower, Mike doing likewise. They toweled off swiftly and then walked onto the set in robes, carrying their bags to where Wayne awaited them. They went through the ritual of holding up their ID next to their faces while Wayne took high-definition photos of them, their birth dates clearly legible on the camera screen. Then it was onto the couch, where he photographed them in various positions. Finally they ended up posing naked on the bed in some of the positions they'd discussed. All through it, Mike was as hard as a rock, Dino too. They knew the drill.

"Okay, I'm done for now." Wayne smiled at them both. "Right, guys, get yourselves dressed, and we can take the rest of the shots on the couch."

Mike and Dino entered the large room that served as the costume department, its walls lined with rack after rack of clothing. Then there were the boots and other footwear, along with various props. Dino dressed casually in a shirt, jeans, and leather jacket, while Mike opted for pants and a shirt. When they emerged from the room, the set was already lit, and a couple of cameras were in position. Wayne took a few shots of them on the couch and standing, before announcing he was finished.

Tony clapped his hands together. "Okay, boys, let's do this."

And then it was down to business.

Mike and Dino went through their opening scene, and Mike was delighted with that first kiss. They got the passion just right, if Tony's enthusiastic thumbs-up and vigorous nodding was anything to go by. Dino played it perfectly, presenting a very believable picture of someone discovering for the first time how damn good sex between two guys could be. By the time Mike's pants came off, his cock was still rigid, leaking precome.

They took a couple of breaks, one when they finished the oral scene and another when Mike had finished rimming Dino. It was great to be able to do those first sections in one take. With some companies, filming a thirty-minute scene could take an entire day. They came back to the bed from their break and got into the penetration scene, Dino on hands and knees, ass tilted. Mike gloved up and slowly slid into his scene partner. He let out a low moan.

"Fuck, Dino. I don't know about that butt plug. You're so fucking tight."

Dino twisted to glance at him over his shoulder, grinning. "You complaining?" He tightened his muscles around Mike's dick with an evil chuckle.

Mike shook his head. "Oh, you are *so* gonna get pounded for that."

Dino's eyes twinkled. "Bring it on. You know I love it rough."

Tony clapped his hands. "Okay, you two. Let's take that again from the top, yeah?"

Mike nodded, pulling out, only to repeat the penetration, keeping the movement slow at first, letting it go on for a minute or so before he began nailing Dino's ass, on a mission. All trace of humor vanished as Dino groaned, head dropping to the bed, pushing back onto Mike's cock. They had a short break when they changed position to lie on their sides, Mike sliding into Dino from behind, his leg hoisted into the air.

After so many years doing porn, Mike was more than capable of controlling his orgasms, able to come at will. So it was something of a surprise when he felt his climax beginning to boil. He signaled to Tony. "Getting real close here." He pulled free of Dino's body, taking several deep breaths.

"We talking an early cum shot?" Tony demanded. Mike nodded. "Okay, get into your final position. Dino, on your back, yeah, with Scott straddling your chest for a facial."

Dino stretched out, and Mike got into position, pulling off the condom. "Gonna come," he gasped out, jerking his cock with firm tugs. Seconds later Dino's lips, chin, and cheeks were spattered with spunk, narrowly missing going into his eye. When Mike had squeezed out the last drop, Dino grinned and craned his neck to lap the head of Mike's dick, cleaning it with his tongue. Mike shuddered, his body trembling as he was jolted by aftershocks.

"Nice, very nice," Tony commented.

Dino ignored him, sucking the now sensitive head deeper, making Mike shiver.

Tony arched his eyebrows. "When you two have quite finished, we'll carry on, shall we?"

Mike chuckled, as did Dino, his mouth still full of cock.

"I don't think Dino's had enough."

Tony snorted. "Well, thank God we've got *that* cum shot in the can, just in case." He regarded the two men on the bed. "Having said that, you should have no problems getting it up again, not with Dino's talented mouth as incentive." He grinned, and the two cameramen laughed. Dino had quite the reputation as an excellent little cocksucker.

Mike laced his hands behind his head. "Talk amongst yourselves, boys," he joked. "This might take a while." He gave them a broad grin, and Dino chuckled around his dick before swallowing him to the root. Mike grunted and thrust into that hot, wet furnace.

He fucking *loved* his job.

CHAPTER THREE

"Hey, you."

Tommy glanced up to find Carla Brunell standing by his table, tray in hand, laden with a bottle of water, an apple, a small container of pasta salad, and a tuna sandwich.

He gave her a brief smile. "Wondered where you'd got to." He took a long drink of his own water.

Carla slid into the empty chair facing him and deposited her tray in front of her. She dropped her bag onto the floor and sagged as she broke the seal on her water bottle. "Is it just me, or was that organic chemistry class as boring as a cold pile of dog shit?"

Tommy nearly snorted water out of his nose. "Warn a guy when you're gonna say stuff like that, okay?" His friendship with Carla had developed during their first year studying organic agriculture, not the most exciting of majors, but it was what his momma wanted. Daddy would have been happier to have him work on the farm instead of going off to college, but no, Momma wanted him to have an education. It had been her goal since he'd first started school.

"S'pose this'll be useful when you're growing peanuts an' cotton back in ButtFuck County, Georgia?" Clara inquired, her face straight, her expression innocent. Only the twinkle in her eyes gave her away.

Tommy shook his head. "Well, that's rich, coming from *you*, girl. Eatonton, Putnam County, ain't exactly a thrivin' metropolis, now is it?" He knew Carla's family background was similar to his own. Both of them had grown up in very rural locations. Even so, his hometown of Americus had to be one of the smallest towns in Sumter County. The nearest big town was Tifton, and getting home to see his folks was a good four-hour drive from school.

Carla snorted. "Never said it was, farm boy." She peered at him. "An' I saw that test paper you got handed back just now. You scored another A plus, didn't ya?" She huffed. "Ain't right, I tell ya. You come off all sweetness, shy, polite as anything, but man, you're a *demon* when it comes to studyin'." Her scowl would have been more convincing if it hadn't been for the bright eyes and the twitching lips as she tried to hold back her smile.

Tommy gave her a mock glare and folded his muscled arms across his chest. "Are you sayin' I look like I'm dumb or something?"

Inside he was chuckling. He knew his physical appearance led his classmates to make assumptions about him, same as with Carla. Momma had always warned him about not judging a book by its cover. Carla looked like a big-boned, rough-and-tumble cowgirl, affable and good natured, but talk about *smarts*. She was one of the brightest students in the class. The two of them had gravitated together early in their first semester, once they'd gotten over the rivalry bit, though that was more Carla than Tommy. He liked their easygoing friendship. Tommy had noticed quite a few of the girls around campus often regarded him with interest, their eyes traveling over his body, and he usually steered clear of them. Carla wasn't like that, thank God. Besides, she already had a fella back home.

Carla snickered. She forked a couple of mouthfuls of pasta salad and glanced around at the crowds of students who filled the cafeteria with lively chatter and raucous laughter. They always sat in the same corner. It was a good spot from which to people watch, relatively unobserved. Tommy particularly liked watching the table where the more… athletic students hung out. Yeah, muscles did it for him every time.

"So, what's your type, farm boy?"

Tommy snapped back into the moment. "Excuse me?"

Carla leaned forward, half a tuna sandwich in her hand. "Do you like the jocks? Or maybe you prefer the more geeky type? I always had a thing for guys with glasses myself, but that might not be to your taste." She took a bite out of her sandwich and sat back, her gaze fixed on him.

There was a heavy feeling in his belly. He stared at her, his hands growing icier by the second. "I… what…?" The words choked him.

Carla put down her sandwich, stood up, and took the empty seat next to his. She carried on looking out over the sea of students. "S'okay, Tommy, take a breath, all right?"

He rubbed his palms on his jeans, inhaling deeply, forcing himself to be calm.

Her shoulder nudged his. "For the record? I don't give a shit either way, okay? It's no skin off my nose if you're gay. Don't change nothin' between us." She spoke quietly.

Tommy sagged into his seat. "How d'you know?"

Carla giggled. "Oh, honey. Ain't never seen you with a girlfriend all the time I've known you. 'Course, you might have a girl back home, but I'm thinkin' no on that score. 'Cause I'm pretty sure if you had one, you'd have mentioned her afore now."

"That don't mean I'm gay," Tommy protested weakly.

Carla leaned closer. "Fine, but, honey, I have eyes. I see who you look at—or should I say who you *don't* look at."

He drew in several long breaths before trusting himself to speak. "I didn't think I'd been that obvious." Tommy took a few swallows of water in an effort to regain his composure. Only Ben knew he was gay, and he'd claimed that was due to him having excellent gaydar. Oh, and of course him noticing Tommy's distinct lack of interest in girls. And then there was that whole business about Tommy eyeing up the captain of the wrestling team—and Ben catching him in the act. Tommy hadn't worked up the nerve to tell anyone else.

Carla patted his leg. "Aw, you weren't. It's just 'cause I know you." She lowered her voice to a conspiratorial whisper. "Just tell me you don't have a thing for that roommate of yours."

This time he really did snort water out of his nose. He spluttered all over the tabletop, and Carla quickly grabbed a napkin and thrust it into his hand. She chuckled while he wiped his face and then the table.

"Well, that got a reaction."

"Ben?" Tommy said incredulously. "Hell no. Just… no."

Carla straightened her face. "I thought I'd mention it, seeing as he does bat for both teams, right? And you two *are* close?"

"Yeah, but damn, girl…. Ben? So not my type, and I am so not his."

She shrugged. "Takes all sorts." She dragged her tray across the table and picked up her sandwich. "I thought you stayin' at his folks' place on the weekends might've meant…."

Tommy shook his head. "His family doesn't know he's bi, for one thing. But he's trying to get me out more on weekends, and it's easier staying with him and his family than driving back to Athens." It was getting to be a nice routine. They'd pack a bag Friday and head off to Ben's family home in the Morningside area of Atlanta when classes were finished. Friday night was usually dinner with Ben's parents, Benson and Caroline, and his sister, Bethany, a high school senior. Ben's parents couldn't be more different. Ben took after his mom; both had bubbly personalities and loved being sociable. His dad was more serious, a real man's man. And they were a whole *world* away from Tommy's parents.

Carla looked at her phone. "I gotta go. I got a meeting of the Black Student Alliance." She held the phone out for him to see. "You seen the time?"

Tommy sighed. Like she had to remind him. He rose to his feet and collected the debris from his lunch, depositing it all on his tray. "I'll see you in class, okay?" Carla said nothing; her sympathetic expression was more than enough. He left the cafeteria and walked through the campus to the quiet corner near the library where he went every Friday lunchtime. When he reached the bench set back against the brick wall of the library, he sat down and got out his phone, staring at it in his hands for a moment.

He *hated* feeling like this. It hadn't always been so, not when he'd first arrived at college. Once a week, regular as clockwork, he'd call his momma, their conversations lasting fifteen to thirty minutes. He'd looked forward to hearing the news from home, telling her how well he was doing in his studies....

But not now.

Tommy knew his momma hadn't changed. No, this was all about him, his own feelings of guilt. Once he'd accepted he was gay, his momma's customary litanies and questions took on new meaning. He squirmed, his heart heavy, chest tight, every time she spoke of what the preacher had been talking about in church the previous Sunday. It wasn't that he no longer believed, not entirely. He just felt the Lord might be having a problem loving him like his momma said he did. Not if the pastor had it right, and all gays were going to hell for their sins.... And then there was the time he chose to call her, every Friday lunchtime when he knew she'd be in the house. That way the weekly duty was done, with less chance of her calling him over the weekend when he was out, maybe someplace he wouldn't want his momma to find him.

No use puttin' it off. With a sigh, Tommy hit speed dial.

"Hey, son. I'd got to thinkin' you'd forgotten 'bout me." There was a hint of humor in her voice.

"Aww, 'course not, Momma. How's everything? How's Daddy?" He got comfortable, knowing this could take a while.

"Your daddy's just fine, 'ceptin' he works too hard, o' course. Not that he's got much choice, seein' as help is hard to come by right now."

The words were like a knife to his heart. *If I wasn't at college, Daddy wouldn't be strugglin'.* He knew his momma would never say that, but it didn't stop him thinking it.

"Did you go to church last Sunday?"

Damn. As always the question set his stomach roiling in anticipation of the lie. "Yes, Momma." The last time he'd stepped inside a church had been back in early September before he'd left for college. He hadn't been home since then, something else to give him an attack of the guilts.

"You met any nice girls lately? I'm sure there must be someone at church who's caught your eye."

"No, Momma, there's no one I'm interested in. Besides, I think my studies are more important right now." Like she was going to pay any heed to that. He tried to change the subject. "How is Mary?" He knew Momma loved to talk about his married sister.

"Oh, she's fine. Her and Dan came by last night. And Dan's daddy made sure to mention you last Sunday durin' prayers. He asked after you when we was leavin' church too."

Tommy shivered. The last time he'd heard Dan's daddy speak, Pastor Cunningham had been telling the congregation to pray against this marriage equality evil that was pervading society. Tommy had been frozen to the spot, too scared to move in case something gave him away. The enthusiastic reception that greeted the pastor's words filled him with dismay. There were loud choruses of "Amen" and varying noises of approval, especially when he spoke of the "growing menace of homosexuality" that was "spreading through the land like a cancer, infecting the nation's youth."

It sure didn't feel like an infection to Tommy. For the first time in his life, he felt like life finally made sense. Too bad most of the people he'd grown up with wouldn't see it like that.

"How's that Carla you were tellin' me about? Mightn't she be someone you'd consider datin'? She sounds like a nice girl."

"She has a boyfriend back home, Momma," he said. "Oh, I aced my last test." *Anything* to get off the subject.

"Oh, that's wonderful, son! When might you come home next? It's been a while now."

He did a quick count in his head. They were already heading into late October, and Christmas wasn't that far off. "How 'bout we leave it 'til the winter break? After all, I'll be home for a couple of weeks then.

If I come for a weekend, that'll just mean spending money on gas, not to mention all the time it'll take getting there and back." He crossed his fingers, praying she'd be okay about that.

There was a moment's silence. "But that's weeks away." His heart sank. "I s'pose you're right, son." He could hear the reluctance in her voice. "I'll have to make do with our weekly chats 'til then."

Tommy fought hard to hold back his sigh of relief. "Yeah. We'll have lots of time over the holidays."

They chatted for another ten minutes or so, while she regaled him with stories of who was getting up to what in Americus. Little got past his momma. She and the rest of her female friends at church could gossip 'til the cows came home, something that had always struck Tommy as decidedly unchristian. He finished up the call and made his way to his next class. Now that he'd gotten the call out of the way, he felt lighter. It wouldn't be long before Saturday night arrived and he'd be in a certain bar once again, trying to blend into the background while he kept his gaze on a certain bartender. A month after he'd first laid eyes on Mike, and he was still no nearer to being able to say a word to the man. He was content enough to eat his dinner and drink his Cherry Coke.

One day he'd find the nerve, but not yet.

"I SEE your stalker's here again."

"Huh?" Mike frowned. "What are you talking about now, Kev?" He concentrated on the drink order for Dave and his friends over in the corner.

Kevin grinned and flicked his head toward the rear of the bar. "You know exactly who I'm talking 'bout. Mr. Cutie Pie over there with the muscles. Y'know, the one who's been sitting on that barstool every Saturday night for the last five weeks?" He arched his eyebrows. "Don't give me that 'butter wouldn't melt' act. I seen you looking." His grin widened. "G'on, tell me I'm wrong."

Mike wasn't about to give him the satisfaction. "You're wrong," he stated emphatically.

Kevin stared. "Hell, you're a poor liar." Then his eyes gleamed. "In that case, *you* can take him his burger, tater tots, and Cherry Coke. Maybe you could even get him to say a few words beyond 'Hey.' 'Cause I swear that's all I've ever heard out of that pretty little mouth of his."

Mike snickered. "I think if I spoke to him, he'd piss his pants."

Kevin guffawed and went off to the back of the bar. Inside, Mike was cursing himself. He'd been careful not to glance too openly at the guy. Those queens he worked with were too damn good at spotting when one of them was taking an interest in a customer. And fuck it, he *was* interested in the painfully shy but *so* sexy young man who hadn't said a word.

"And then there's the fact that every time he comes in here," Kevin continued, appearing beside him as if there hadn't been a break in conversation, "I watch him look 'round the bar 'til he sees you." That grin was still in place.

"Are you still going on about him?" Mike demanded. "Sure you're not the one here who's fixating?"

Kevin held up his hands. "I just call it like I see it. I think he's only here to ogle you."

"Well, he's gonna be disappointed if he turns up in a couple weeks' time, isn't he, 'cause I won't be here."

Kevin's brow furrowed. "Since when do you not work on weekends?"

"Since I'll be in LA, that's when." Mike returned his grin. "Remember?"

"Oh, yeah, you've got a shoot. I'd clean forgotten." He faked a sad face. "Aw, how you gonna cope without seeing that gorgeous bod?" He leered. "Then again, don't worry your head about it. I'm sure me or Patrick can take care of him." He waggled his eyebrows.

Mike groaned. "For fuck's sake, just leave the kid alone, okay? He's not hurting anyone." Mike had seen enough to know the guy wasn't going to be a problem. He preferred this quiet observation to the occasional gropings of fans when he made appearances at Hustlaball or Southern Decadence. The kid appeared to have good manners.

"Here's his order." Kevin handed him the tray containing the Angus burger, tater tots, and Cherry Coke. "I'm sure he'll be delighted to get it from you." That shit-eating grin just wouldn't quit.

Mike shook his head and took the tray. He walked over to where the young guy sat, his eyes widening as Mike approached. "Here you go," Mike said cheerfully, setting the food down in front of him.

The young guy blushed furiously. "Th-thanks." He lowered his gaze and commenced picking at his tots.

Mike retreated to a safe distance and watched him while he ate. He liked the look of those wide shoulders, the reddish-brown hair, not too short, the barest hint of scruff on his jawline and those striking green eyes. His skin was creamy where it showed, which spoke of a lot of time spent covered up. With his coloring, that was understandable. But that body was speaking even louder to Mike's dick, which was definitely interested, judging by the way it filled as he feasted on the delectable view before him.

His attention was forcibly drawn away when someone pinched his ass, good and hard.

"You are *so* busted."

Fucking Kevin.

CHAPTER FOUR

MIKE SPOTTED the guy with the *Scott Masters* sign as soon as he emerged into the Arrivals hall at LAX. His driver was a young guy dressed in a smart jacket, shirt, and pants, who nodded politely and took Mike's bag from him. They walked through the busy airport to the parking bays, the driver making small talk. It turned out he was new to the job, and then he surprised Mike by adding shyly that he was a fan.

"Yeah?" Mike gave him a smile. "That's great." He peered at the name badge adorning the driver's lapel. "So, is this all you do, Sean, collect guys from the airport? I'd have thought with your looks, you might be one of Rock Hard Men's models." He certainly had everything going for him—blond hair, blue eyes, and a killer smile, not to mention a slim, lean body.

The blush on Sean's cheeks was adorable. "You think? Wow. I don't know what to say."

Sweet kid. He had to have been barely legal.

"I'm a student at UCLA, studying for a BA in Film and Television. I'm hoping to get some experience behind the camera at the studio. At least I've asked them if it'd be possible. But seeing as I've only just gotten the job, I guess I might have to wait a while."

"Stick with it, kid," Mike told him with a smile. They reached the car, and Sean placed Mike's bag in the trunk. He went to open the rear door, but Mike stopped him with a hand on his arm. "Mind if I sit up front with you?"

Sean beamed. "That'd be great." But then he opened the passenger door and hastily began removing empty takeout cups and chips bags, stuffing them into a paper sack. "Sorry about the mess, Mr. Masters."

"It's fine," Mike assured him, "and call me Scott. Feels odd, you calling me Mr. Masters when you've already seen me naked." He winked.

Sean's cheeks were on fire. He cleared his throat. "Okay… Scott."

They got into the car and backed out of the parking bay. Once they'd driven around to the machines at the exit and Sean fed a five-dollar bill into the meter, they were out into the early evening sunshine.

Mike was glad of his leather jacket. The temperature was below average for the time of year, at about fifty-five degrees. Not that he'd have to worry about that once they got filming.

During the journey to the studios, which were located not far from Hermosa Beach, they chatted about baseball, basketball, and ice hockey. Sean was really into sports, and it was a lively and pleasant conversation. Mike genuinely enjoyed talking with him. Sean had no airs about him and asked about life in Atlanta, a place he'd always wanted to visit. It seemed like no time at all before the car was pulling into the studio parking lot. Sean switched off the engine, got out of the car, and walked around to open Mike's door for him. Then he collected Mike's bag from the trunk and handed it to him.

"Have a good day, Mr.—*Scott*." Those cheeks were still pink.

Mike shook hands with him and pressed a folded twenty-dollar bill into the young man's hand. "Thanks for the pleasant trip, Sean. I hope I get you on the return journey in a couple days' time, or even when I get taken to the hotel later."

Sean beamed. "Aw, thanks. Yeah, I hope so too." He nodded and then got back into the car.

Mike watched him drive out of sight and then pushed open the door to Rock Hard Men's Studios. It was the tenth or eleventh time he'd been out there to film for them, and it never ceased to amaze him the difference in studios. Compared to ManFactory, Rock Hard Men's studio was a huge, sprawling building, maybe twice the size, and with a look about it that spoke of money. Mike knew the company that owned Rock Hard Men also owned three more studios, two of which produced het porn. Yeah, a much bigger operation than ManFactory….

He walked up to the desk to check in. Normally he'd have been taken to his hotel before going to the studio, but Sean had told him he'd had instructions to bring Mike directly there. Mike couldn't help wondering what *that* was about, especially given the hour his plane had arrived.

The receptionist smiled at him. "Mr. Masters, you have a meeting with Mr. Marks. I'll tell him you're here."

Mike nodded, his face straight. Now he *was* curious. He'd only met William Marks, the owner of the company, once before, about three years ago when he'd first gone there. Since then he'd only had contact with the director and film crew.

Five minutes later, William Marks came through the wide glass doors beyond the reception desk, his hand extended. Mike shook it.

"Come on through, Scott. I've got some coffee laid out. I'm sure you could do with some." He winked. "I know how vile airline coffee can be." He led the way along a thickly carpeted corridor to his office. Once inside, he closed the door behind them and gestured to a leather couch to the right of a wide, polished desk with two monitors and a keyboard set up on it. A low coffee table in front of the couch was laid out with a squat coffeepot, cups, sugar bowl, cream jug, and several plates with delicious-looking pastries that Mike steadfastly tried to ignore. His waistline didn't need that sort of encouragement. He'd grab something light once he got to the hotel.

He sat down on the couch, perched on the edge of the seat cushion. Something about this whole meeting had him on edge, though he didn't have a clue why.

William poured out two cups of coffee, and Mike took his as it came, setting it down before even taking a mouthful. "So, to what do I owe the pleasure of this unexpected meeting?" Mike kept his tone light, but he felt as tense as a coiled spring. His senses were telling him something was coming right at him, and it didn't feel good.

William relaxed against the seat cushions and sipped his coffee. He placed his cup on the table and then ran his fingers through his graying hair. "Scott, I wanted a chat with you before you went on set to share with you some recent decisions that have been made."

"Oh?" Mike knew he wasn't about to get fired. They'd hardly have flown him all the way out to LA when they could easily have done that over the phone. He waited for the rest.

"There have been some high-level discussions with a view to the studio producing bareback films. I'm meeting with all our models, putting out feelers to hear their opinions on this." William picked up his coffee and drank deeply, his gaze trained on Mike.

Mike went cold, his mind racing. "Wait a minute." He frowned. "You mentioned that decisions have already been made. So what's this crap about putting out feelers if you've already decided?" He saw no use in being polite, not if they expected him to do bareback. "And if you've done your research, you'll know I'm a staunch advocate of safe sex. Hardly a likely candidate to want to do bareback, right?"

"There would, of course, be more stringent testing prior to a scene, which the company would pay for." William put down his cup and leaned forward. "We have to face facts, Scott. The adult entertainment industry is evolving, and Rock Hard Men either evolves with it or faces extinction. There are too many companies these days who are producing what the customer wants—and right now that's bareback porn. So we're setting up a new branch of the company, Rock Hard & Raunchy, which will be exclusively bareback, among other things." His gaze met Mike's. "I'm asking *all* our models if they'd like to consider working for the new company."

"And if they're not interested?" Mike awaited William's response, his stomach taut.

William shrugged. "Then nothing. We're not about to force anyone—God forbid—but we have to offer the option. If models aren't interested, we'll continue to offer them work as before in the more traditional arm of the company. However"—his eyes gleamed—"I feel I should add that such a decision might be viewed as shortsighted in the current economic climate."

Mike had heard enough. "Okay, you say you're not gonna force anyone, but that doesn't mean you're not gonna do your damnedest to get them to go with you, right? I mean, we're talking guys who want to keep their jobs." He rose to his feet. "Well, maybe *some* guys might be prepared to compromise their principles and their integrity, but not *this* guy." He didn't care if this meant the end of his career with them. The mood he was in right then, he felt like packing it all in. He was sick to his stomach. "Thanks for the chat, Mr. Marks, but I'm not interested." All he wanted to do was film the two scenes he was there for, then go back to Atlanta. It was late, and suddenly he was bone tired.

William slowly stood. "I understand. Your filming is set for tomorrow morning. You must be tired after your flight. I'll have the car brought around to take you to your hotel, and we'll see you tomorrow."

Mike nodded and shook his hand, relieved the meeting was at an end. The next morning held the promise of sanity. He was due to film with Jack, a close friend of many years and his lover at one time. It had been a while since he'd heard from his sexy friend, and Mike had been looking forward to their scene. He and Jack had starred together many times over the years, and the scenes of Scott Masters and Armando DiMarco were always eagerly anticipated. It had been jealousy over their relationship that had been the main cause of the rift between himself and Dirk.

Mike always found it difficult not to worry when Jack didn't keep in touch. It was usually a case that his former lover was up to his neck in work, but now and again Mike would receive a call to inform him Jack was in the hospital, battling some new infection. Then it was a case of dropping everything and flying to San Francisco to be with him.

"One more thing," William said as he walked Mike to the door. "Sorry to drop this on you at short notice, but there's been a change of scene partner for the first shoot. Armando DiMarco will not be filming with you."

Disappointment stabbed him in the gut. "That's a damn shame." Then a hand tightened around his heart, icy to the touch. "Is he all right?" He'd been trying not to worry when e-mails and texts had gone unanswered, phone calls too.

"Oh, he's fine," William reassured him with a smile. "In fact, he's going to star in one of the first videos for the new company. We're all very excited about it."

Mike didn't hear the rest of William's comments about who his new scene partner was to be. His mind was still trying to take on board the bombshell about Jack. *He's doing bareback? What the fuck?* Mike couldn't believe Jack would go against everything he'd ever said about doing bareback porn. *No wonder he doesn't want to film with me. He fucking* knows *how I feel about this.* There was no way Mike would've been able to hide his disappointment in his friend and ex-lover. Whatever circumstances had brought about this change of heart, it still didn't detract from the danger in which he was placing his scene partners. God knew, Mike wanted to be supportive, but *this*?

He walked out of the studios in a daze, barely registering the driver's attempts at conversation as they drove to the Marriott near LAX. His mind was a mess: a new bareback site, Jack abandoning his principles and integrity, the dawning realization that his ex had been deliberately avoiding him....

Just get through the next few days. Then it's back to normal.

It took a moment for the thought to sink in. He was a fucking *porn star*, for Christ's sake. What the fuck was normal about that?

BY THE time his scene partner, Paul, had asked for a fifth break, Mike was getting pissed. Yet again, he watched Paul slope off to the corner of the set where he'd left a towel and his tablet. By now Mike knew better than to try to attempt a conversation with the guy. His first few forays had been met with cool indifference, bordering on rudeness.

Might as well take advantage of the break. Mike went off to his own quiet little corner where he'd left his rather large dildo and lay down on the low couch to have a few moments stretching himself some more, prior to the penetration scene. He slicked it up and slowly pushed it into his ass, forcing himself to relax. He closed his eyes and focused on regaining his hard-on, as his dick had apparently decided it wasn't playing ball. Not that he was all that surprised. Paul made the right noises for the camera, but there was a distinct lack of chemistry.

This was not going to be an easy one.

"Yeah, I was gonna ask if you were ready for that baseball bat of Paul's," Terry said in a low voice. Mike opened his eyes to peer at the director standing next to him. Terry chuckled as he gazed at Mike. "Guess I shouldn't have worried, dealing with a pro like you." He craned his neck to gaze in Paul's direction. "Talkative bastard, ain't he?" He grinned.

Mike pushed the silicone dildo deeper into him and looked up at Terry, the situation not feeling in the least bit surreal. He'd worked with Terry practically every time he'd come out to LA.

"What *is* his problem?"

Terry hunkered down next to Mike's head. "I'd say your tits aren't big enough, and they're covered in hair, babe." He snickered.

Mike saw the light. "Well, fuck." That explained a lot. He pulled out the dildo and wiped off the lube with his towel before leaving it to one side to be cleaned later. He sat up and glanced over at Paul, who'd plugged in some earphones and was staring fixedly at his tablet, his free hand working his cock. "Wanna place a bet on what he's watching over there?"

Terry barked out a laugh. "That's a no-brainer." He glanced at Paul. "Oh, looks like he's ready to continue. At least his dick is." He smirked and rose to his feet. "C'mon, let's get this finished. Then you can go back to your hotel and have a few stiff drinks."

"Amen to that." Mike got up from the couch, towel in hand, and walked onto the set where the bed awaited them, sheets already mussed from their encounter so far. He dropped the towel onto the floor beside the bed, climbed up onto it, and awaited Terry's instructions. Paul joined him, standing to one side, hand still tugging at his thick, heavy cock.

"Okay, boys, let's make this the final shoot." Terry gazed at Paul. "Resume the last position—Scott, on your back, legs over Paul's shoulders—and then we'll go for the cum shot. You ready for that, Scott?"

"I will be," Mike said with a grim smile. He took up his position, and Paul slid easily into him, hands gripping his thighs. When Terry called action, Paul proceeded to pound his ass, thrusting long and hard. Mike wrapped his hand around his semihard cock and retreated into the world inside his head. He focused on a spot just beyond Paul's head and concentrated on coming. Paul huffed and growled, sounding the part, but Mike dialed him out.

In his head was a sweet, shy-looking young man with reddish-brown hair and beautiful green eyes. Those eyes were fixed on Mike while he slowly unbuttoned a white shirt, revealing those wide, firm pecs, creamy skin everywhere he could see. Mike pulled at his dick, breathing heavily as he imagined that shirt coming off, those eyes growing wider when Mike stepped closer to him, reaching out to stroke that sweet face.

"Oh yeah," he said softly, picturing the young man's mouth opening for a kiss, lips full, tongue darting out nervously to lick them. Mike's balls drew up high and tight, and he gave Terry the quick hand signal. One of the cameramen focused on his dick, and Mike held his shaft tightly as his orgasm barreled down on him. Come shot out across his chest in a wide arc, surprising him by its force and magnitude. He rarely produced that much, and to do so with such a relatively innocent image in his head was a first for him. His body jolted, thighs trembling with the aftershocks of his climax.

Then it was time to film Paul's cum shot. Paul pulled out of Mike, and an assistant handed him his tablet. He knelt between Mike's spread legs, the tablet on the bed where he could see it, het porn playing silently on it. He worked his dick, his eyes never leaving the small screen, his breathing becoming uneven. Mike left him to build up his cum shot and switched off for a while. It was far more pleasant in his imagination, picturing his shy "stalker." *Where did* that *come from*? He couldn't get the image out of his head, that young man from Woofs perched on his barstool, those big green eyes watching Mike while he worked, that muscled body hidden under T-shirts and jeans....

"Ready." Paul's signal cut through his thoughts, and Mike pulled himself back into the scene. The tablet was quickly buried in the bedsheets, and then Paul cried out harshly, pulling off the condom and shooting over Mike's belly and dick in spurts of thick come.

Mike went through the mechanics of the scene, kissing Paul as he dropped his head to Mike's, hands stroking Mike's face. Then Terry yelled cut, and Paul was off him faster than a New York minute, clambering off the bed and heading to the shower.

"Nice one, guys," Terry called out while the cameramen packed up. "We'll fix the time disparity in editing." He winked at Mike. "And now you need to clean up, go back to your hotel, and recuperate. We're shooting again tomorrow at midday." His eyes sparkled. "Think you can produce another cum shot like that one, Scott? 'Cause I have to say, that was pretty impressive." Another smirk twisted his lips.

"I'll have to work on it," Mike responded, wiping himself off with his towel. He swung his legs over the side of the bed and sat there for a minute, ignoring the hubbub around him. The force of that orgasm was becoming a memory already, leaving him once more calm and in control. But that image was still in his head.

What are you doing to me, kid?

CHAPTER FIVE

"Aw, MIKEY'S little stalker is here," Patrick said, nudging Kevin with his elbow as they stood next to one another behind the bar.

Kevin glanced up from his task of mixing a Jack and Diet Coke. Sure enough, the kid was back, walking around the bar to his usual stool, which was unoccupied.

Kevin shook his head, smiling.

"Then he's in for a disappointment, isn't he? And he ain't so little, either." The young man sat down and looked in their direction, then around the bar. Kevin waited a moment before going over to him. "Hey."

The kid glanced up. "Hey. An Angus burger, tater tots, and a Cherry Coke, please."

Kevin grinned. "Like I don't know by now what you're gonna order." Those cheeks were awful pretty when he blushed. "Coming right up." He went to the back bar to give Mitch the order. When he returned, he noticed the young man scanning the room, a slight frown creasing his forehead. Then his face fell. Kevin's heart went out to him. He could vividly remember being that young and crushing on a guy. That customary sparkle in the kid's eyes was no longer there.

"Oh wow." Patrick appeared next to him, pouring out a glass of Blue Moon. "He's sure got it bad, huh? Looks like a little lovesick puppy, don't he?" He shook his head, his expression sympathetic.

Kevin had to agree. When Mitch brought out the guy's meal, Kevin took it to him, placing it in front of him. "There you go."

"Thanks." As Kevin turned to move off down the bar, the young man cleared his throat. "Excuse me, but… where's Mike tonight?"

Kevin could hear the hesitant edge in his voice. It was that more than anything that helped him decide. "Mike is… out of town this weekend. He'll be back next time you're in, though."

The young man nodded. "Okay. Thanks."

He began to eat slowly but with none of his usual enthusiasm. Kevin watched him for a moment and then went back to pouring drinks.

Now and again he'd cast a glance in the young man's direction. He was still there, although he hadn't finished his meal.

"Oh Lord, you might need to lend a hand to Mikey's little pet," Patrick said in a low voice. "He's got an admirer."

"So? What's that to me?" Kevin retorted with a frown, handing over change to a customer.

"It's Brenden, and he's already way past tipsy."

Kevin let out a groan. Brenden had a reputation for manhandling guys when he'd drunk too much. Kevin peered around the bar. Sure enough, Brenden had taken up residence on the empty stool next to the kid. He was leaning in close, rubbing the kid's leg and moving higher up that muscled thigh. The recipient of this up-close-and-personal attention looked panic-stricken. The young man was trying to edge away from Brenden, his Adam's apple bobbing, eyes wide. Kevin moved close enough to hear what Brenden was saying, his speech beginning to slur.

"Hey, what's your name? Where you from, sexy?"

Oh shit. Kevin wasn't usually in the habit of interfering, but it was obvious from the wide-eyed, panicked stare and taut body posture that the young guy did *not* welcome Brenden's advances.

Kevin walked across to stand in front of Brenden. He waited until Brenden regarded him with unfocused eyes and then leaned across the bar with his heavily muscled arms, tattoos all the way down to his knuckles, and growled. "I think we've had enough here, don't you, Brenden? Now back off."

Brenden stiffened. "Sure… sure thing, Kev." He nodded in the young man's direction and then sloped off the barstool, heading toward the restroom.

Kevin watched him go with a shake of his head before turning his attention to the young guy in front of him. "You okay, kid?"

The young guy took a couple of deep breaths. "Yeah… thanks for that." He gave Kevin a shy smile.

Kevin couldn't resist. He reached across the bar and pinched the kid's cheek. "You are just so *cute!*" He chuckled when the lad's cheeks glowed bright red. "What's your name, kid?"

"Tommy." To Kevin's surprise, Tommy extended a hand toward him and gripped his in a firm shake.

Kevin nodded appreciatively. "Well hi, Tommy. I'm Kevin. That's a nice handshake you got there." The feel of those calluses told him plenty. Tommy was a working man, and Kevin was liking him more and more by the second. Kevin smiled at him. "Anyhoo, I'll let you finish your food." Tommy gave him a brief nod, and Kevin walked off to the other side of the bar where Patrick was serving.

The older bartender peered at him with interest. "So? Does the puppy have a name?" His eyes gleamed.

Kevin chuckled. "His name is Tommy, and don't you go calling him puppy to his face now, y'hear?" He shrugged and added, "He seems nice enough. I'll see if I can find out some more about him, seeing as he's taken a shine to our Mike." Kevin grinned. "I'll be sure not to scare him off. 'Bout time Mike got laid when it's not in front of a camera." He waggled his eyebrows and then went back to work.

The bar was packed as usual for a Saturday night, and Kevin, Patrick, and Don had to work their asses off to keep up, especially being a bartender down. When things had cooled off a little, he went around the bar to where Tommy was still sitting, observing the customers and occasionally raising his eyes toward the TV.

"You want another Cherry Coke, Tommy?" When he got a shy smile and a nod, Kevin was on it. He placed the glass in front of him and leaned forward, elbows on the bar. "So, where you from?"

"Americus, Sumter County." Tommy gave a slight shrug. "It's a real small town, so you might not've heard of it. Near Tifton."

Kevin grinned. "I had you for a Georgia boy with that accent." He loved the way Tommy's cheeks grew pink. Next to him, Kevin could hear Patrick conversing with a customer, that deep voice rumbling away. He gave Tommy his full attention. "You're not dating anyone right now, are you?"

Lord, those cheeks were scarlet. "No, sir."

Damn, but he was a polite one. "An' we know why that is, right? Seems you have a thing for older guys." Kevin winked, and Tommy swallowed, eyes wide.

Beside him Patrick snickered and then leaned around Kevin to address Tommy. "Hey, I'm an older guy too, y'know." He leered, "How about it, kid?"

Tommy burst out laughing, the sound delightful. "Er, thanks for the offer, sir, but no." It was a good look on him.

"Hey, can I get you a shot of something? On the house?" Kevin offered.

Tommy shook his head. "That's real kind of you, sir, but I don't drink. An' even if I did, I got my truck, an' I wouldn't drink an' drive."

Kevin nodded. Yeah, he was liking Tommy more and more. "Well, when you're ready, the first one's on me, y'hear?" Tommy gave him that shy smile.

Patrick leaned forward, lowering his voice. "I'll bet Mike will be sorry to have missed you, but lover boy is out in LA, working in the heat—"

Kevin gave Patrick a swift dig in the ribs with his elbow, making the older man gape at him in surprise. "Yeah, well I'm sure Mike's having a wonderful time on his *celebrity bus tour*." He gave Patrick a meaningful stare.

Patrick frowned. "What the…?" Then his brow cleared. "Oh, yeah, he's prob'ly having a grand ol' time." Nodding to Tommy, he walked off around the bar, Kevin following him. When they were out of sight and sound of Tommy, Patrick opened his eyes wide. "You think he doesn't know about Mike?"

Kevin snorted. "I'd bet next month's tips on it. Oh, I'm sure he'll find out eventually, but let's see what happens before we get to that point, okay?" He grinned. "Don't you wanna see how things go between those two? Lord knows Mike sorely needs *someone* since Dirk hauled ass outta his life." He stared at Patrick. "No sense in bursting the kid's bubble. He's obviously a sweet little shy boy. Besides, it's not our place to tell him, it's Mike's. Right?"

Patrick nodded slowly. "You're right." Then he chuckled.

"What?"

Patrick grinned. "I'm just picturin' Mike and shy boy over there in a lip-lock. Think I'd pay good money to see that." He went off behind the bar, whistling.

Kevin smiled to himself. Lord, now *there* was an image.

TOMMY OPENED the door that connected Ben's basement apartment with the rest of the house and made his way to the large kitchen. Everywhere was quiet, as it usually was on a Sunday morning. Ben was still fast asleep, as it was way too early for his ass to be out of bed. Tommy knew from habit that the only person likely to be around at that hour would be Ben's sister, Bethany.

Sure enough, Bethany was leaning against the counter, her bathrobe tied loosely around her waist, a mug of coffee already in her hands. She smiled when he walked in.

"I was wondering where my Sunday morning coffee buddy had gotten to."

She put down her mug and poured him some coffee. This had become their regular time to chat. Every Sunday morning, Bethany got up real early to play tennis at the Piedmont Driving Club, and she and Tommy would meet in the kitchen to drink coffee and shoot the breeze. He liked these times. Usually when she and Ben were together, the atmosphere was very different. Her nose was either permanently lodged in a book or in Ben's business. The siblings couldn't be more different. Bethany was the studious one. She was dead set on being an international business lawyer like her daddy. Ben, on the other hand, was the one who always completed his assignments at the very last minute, scraping through by the skin of his teeth. The number of times he expressed gratitude for having a damn good memory…. Bethany clearly disapproved of his happy-go-lucky attitude.

Bethany studied him for a moment while they drank their coffee in a comfortable silence. Tommy didn't mind her much. He'd not gotten on all that well with his own sister, Mary, who was older than him, and Bethany was nothing like her. As the months had gone by and they'd grown accustomed to each other, he'd relaxed around Bethany enough to share a joke now and then.

Tommy sipped his coffee, leaning against the counter next to her. Bethany paused, coffee mug in hand, and tilted her head, staring at him.

"So, are you out yet?"

His throat seized up, and breathing suddenly became a chore. He knew his chin was trembling—hell, his *legs* were shaking, if it came to that—and he must've looked the perfect poster boy for *shit scared.*

Finally he found words. "'Scuse me?" He was still too stunned to say more.

Bethany put down her coffee mug and patted his arm. "It's okay," she said with a smile. "I'm starting to get used to it."

Tommy took several large gulps of air. He wasn't about to deny it, all the meetings he'd attended and the stuff he'd watched online had given him more confidence, but it was still a shock to hear Bethany speak of his sexuality so matter-of-factly.

"How'd you know?" he said at last.

Bethany smirked. "Tommy, I'm standing here in my bathrobe, and you haven't even looked at my tits once." Her eyes sparkled. "Like I said, I'm getting used to it. Only, please tell me you haven't got the hots for my brother. 'Cause that there is a train wreck just waiting to happen." Her lips twitched.

Oh, this just got better. "You know about Ben?" From what his roommate had said, the family was oblivious.

Bethany burst out into a peal of laughter. "Oh, honey, most of Fulton County knows about Ben, and probably half of DeKalb, for that matter. That boy left a trail of broken hearts—male *and* female—all the way through high school."

"Do your parents know?"

Bethany shrugged. "I'd say they might suspect, Mom more than Dad. He tends to live with his nose pressed between the pages of the *Wall Street Journal* most of the time."

Tommy found her comment highly ironic. His panic had receded a little, leaving him able to regain his composure.

"So I guess that's a no to my first question, huh?" Bethany said with a half smile. She gestured toward the kitchen table, and Tommy nodded. They pulled out chairs and sat down.

Tommy studied his coffee mug. "Ben knows, of course, and my friend Carla, but that was only 'cause they guessed. I've not really come out to anyone I have classes with. But I've done some stuff that I've never done before, and that's made me feel better about myself, y'know? More confident?" Like going to Woofs of a Saturday night to drool over Mike. He'd never have done anything like that a year ago. But then a year ago, he was only just coming to terms with the realization that girls left him cold, whereas boys got him all hot 'n' bothered.

Bethany nodded. "Like what, for instance?"

"Well, I went to some meetin's, for one thing. Just alumni meetin's at the LGBT center at the university, but that was easy 'cause I didn't know those folks from Adam. People were really supportive, and I felt comfortable bein' there. And then there's the stuff I've been watchin' online too."

Bethany's cheeks pinked right up. "You been watching porn, Tommy?" Her lips were twitching again.

He sat bolt upright. "Oh *Lord*, no!" He wouldn't have *dared*. "I meant I watch videos from that site, It Gets Better." Anything that helped him to mentally explore what it meant to be gay.

"Oh." Bethany's eyes shone. "'Cause if you wanted to watch porn, I'm sure my brother could probably oblige you. Heaven knows what he has on that laptop of his."

"Now there's a scary thought," Tommy said with a shudder. When Bethany regarded him quizzically, he couldn't help smiling. "The browsin' history on Ben's laptop. I don't know 'bout you, but I ain't brave enough to look."

They stared at one another for a moment, and then they burst out laughing. Bethany got up from her chair and brought the coffeepot over to the table.

"You're okay with me knowing, then?"

Tommy smiled at her as she poured them out a second mug. "Yeah, sure. I'm glad, in a way. Lately I've been thinking 'bout tellin' my parents." Telling someone of his intentions somehow made it all that more real.

Bethany paused in midpour. "Really? How'd you think they'd take that?"

It was a question Tommy had asked himself many times during the last few months. During his first year at college, there'd been no question of telling them. He'd been too damn scared. But now? Things were different. *He* was different, especially since he'd laid eyes on Mike. Over two months had passed since that first night in Woofs, and it was getting harder to ignore how he felt when he saw the muscled bartender with the wide, furry pecs, thick, strong-looking arms, and eyes so blue Tommy wanted to drown in them. Just thinking about him sent a shiver dancing up and down his spine and a tingle through his balls.

With a supreme effort, he shoved aside those delightful images and focused on the subject matter. "I watched this one video of an Air Force guy who came out to his parents on YouTube," he said. "I'd have been terrified to do somethin' like that, but his folks were so supportive in the end, and it worked out all right. An' watching all these people who hid how they felt, dreadin' tellin' their friends an' family…. When it came down to it, it wasn't half as bad as they'd anticipated."

Bethany's brow knitted. "Yeah, but, honey? I hear what Ben tells me about your folks. God-fearing people, he says. Now, he must've gotten that from you, right? In my experience, limited though that may be, God-fearing parents and gay kids just don't mix all that well." She laid a hand on his arm, the touch gentle. "You sure you want to do this? 'Cause once you open this particular can of worms, there's no going back. You need to feel pretty sure that they'll be okay with this."

Tommy sighed. "I can't live like this, Bethany. In one of those videos, I heard one woman tell her son that at first she'd thought he was just goin' through a phase, and that he'd grow out of it. When it became clear this was no phase, she had to accept this is how he was, a gay man. Well, I *know* this ain't no phase. I am *gay*. This is how I was born. I don't believe the Lord would have made me this way if this wasn't how I was meant to be." He grabbed hold of her hand and squeezed it. "An' I don't believe my momma and daddy would turn their backs on me. They love me." Didn't his momma tell him that, every time they spoke on the phone?

"I don't dispute that, really I don't," Bethany said quickly, her fingers tightening around his. "I'm just saying that when faced with something like this, your parents are gonna have to make a choice between their love for you and what they believe the Bible says about you. None of us really know how we would react in any specific situation until we find ourselves smack dab in the middle of that situation."

Tommy knew what she was getting at. Hell, he'd worried about it many a night, tossing and turning in his bed. Even going back a couple of months, he'd had his concerns. But everything he'd seen so far, everything he'd read, was telling him that it was all going to be okay.

He had to see it like that. The alternative didn't bear thinking about.

"I'll see how things are at Christmas," he told her, "an' if it's looking positive, then I'll tell them." The holidays were always a good time to be with his family, everyone happy and looking forward to the New Year.

He couldn't think of a better time to tell them.

CHAPTER SIX

THE HOUSE was peaceful again, not that Tommy had minded the last couple of days. As far back as he could remember, Christmas had always been a time of noise and laughter, carols and the crackling of log fires, and this year had been no different. The day itself had been wonderful. Mary and her husband, Dan, had spent it with them, and it had turned out to be a joyous occasion when they'd revealed their news. Tommy was still grinning about the prospect of becoming an uncle. As for Momma, she was already phoning all her girlfriends, spreading the news that she was gonna be a grandma. Daddy'd just chuckled quietly to himself when he'd seen her on the phone, and then he'd gone up into the attic to search out the wooden crib he'd made for Mary's birth. He wasn't as vocal as Momma, but it was plain to see he was delighted too.

It was almost nine o'clock, and Tommy was feeling as full as a tick on a fat hound dog. Momma was constantly pushing food at him: thick sandwiches filled with slices of her glazed ham and a layer of mustard; turkey casserole with slick, tender dumplings; the brownies Mary had brought, rich and decadent, with pecans and juicy raisins in them. Tommy felt sure he'd put on at least five pounds in one day, he'd eaten that much. But damn, it sure was good. *No one* cooked like his momma.

He stood in front of the Christmas tree, letting the scent of pine fill his senses while he gazed at the ornaments and garlands that adorned it.

"You sure I can't tempt you to some of my peanut butter cookies?" Momma was at his side, her hand at his back.

Tommy chuckled. "Are you tryin' to say I need to put on some weight, Momma? 'Cause it sure feels that way." He rubbed his belly. "I couldn't eat another mouthful, honest."

She leaned against him, just coming up to his shoulder. Tommy got his height from Daddy but was under no illusions. In spite of her diminutive size, Momma ruled the roost.

"What you lookin' at, baby?" The softly spoken words felt warm and cozy.

"There's a whole lotta history on this tree, isn't there?" He gazed up at the angel perched on top, its wings looking sad and a little tired, its painted features faded. "How old is that angel?"

Momma turned her face up toward the tip of the tree and smiled, the skin creasing around her eyes. "That angel came from your granddaddy's family, so I guess it's gettin' on nearly fifty years old now. They gave it to him when I was born." She pointed to a little wooden rocking horse. "An' your grandma got that for your first Christmas."

Tommy pointed to a little glass teddy bear, its arm missing. He knew the story behind it, but he loved asking about it, if only to get his Daddy's reaction. "Why'd you still put that bear on the tree? Ain't it time to retire him? He must've earned his disability pension by now." He grinned in anticipation.

"That bear will always have a place on *any* tree in *my* house," Momma declared, eyes flashing, "as a permanent reminder not to let your Daddy have anything to do with wiring Christmas tree lights."

"For goodness' sake, Charlene, you still goin' on 'bout that?" Daddy lowered his paper and shook his head. "Anyone would think I'd burned the house down. It was just a little fire." He glared at her. "An' it was fifteen years ago." He disappeared behind the paper, but Tommy could hear him muttering something about, "Make one little mistake an' they never let you forget it, but mention some of her cookin' disasters an' suddenly it's World War Three around here."

Tommy tried to hide his smirk, but Momma caught him and whacked him on the arm.

"Ouch!" He rubbed it briskly. "Aww, c'mon, Momma, you know Daddy loves your cookin'."

"*Now* he does" came the muttered comment from behind the local paper. "'Specially if he knows what's good for him."

Momma glared at his daddy, who wisely kept hidden.

"Remarks like that will *not* have me rushin' to make your favorite turkey, stuffing, and cranberry sauce sandwiches when you next ask me with those puppy dog eyes." She huffed. "Like those work on me anyway after all these years."

Tommy wasn't fooled for an instant. He could hear the love in her voice.

He left the tree and went over to the fireplace to kneel on the worn rug in front of it. Something *else* that was battle scarred—there was a hole in the rug from when Tommy had tried to poke the fire rather too vigorously one year and a burning chunk of wood had landed on it. He knew there was no way Momma would've thrown it out. Grandma had made it when Momma and Daddy had gotten married.

Momma went into the kitchen, and Tommy half listened to the noises that drifted in from there. He was relaxed and happy. It had been a really good visit. His parents had been so happy to have him home. He'd arrived four days before Christmas, and so far it had been great. Even Mary seemed to have mellowed a little since he'd seen her last, but maybe that was due more to her impending motherhood. She'd been talking about having a family since she and Dan had gotten together when they were high school sweethearts.

It was the love that had permeated every second of his time at home that had finally helped Tommy come to a decision. The moment had arrived. Once he'd made up his mind, it was simply a question of when.

No time like the present.

Momma brought in three mugs of hot chocolate on a tray, and after placing them on the coffee table, she settled back on the couch, feet propped up on a little padded footstool. Tommy reached for his mug and wrapped his hands around it, inhaling the aroma. He closed his eyes, ignoring the fluttery feeling in his belly and the dryness in his mouth. Tommy drew in a couple of deep breaths and then opened his eyes.

"Momma, Daddy? Can I talk with you for a minute?"

Daddy lowered his paper instantly and regarded him, brow furrowed. "Sure. Anything wrong?"

Momma put down her mug and sat up, back straight.

"No, sir, it's just that there's somethin' I need to share with you both." Tommy's heart was pounding so hard, he was surprised they couldn't hear it.

Momma's green eyes, so like his own, were fixed on him. "Is everythin' all right at school? I thought you were doin' real well."

"Oh, I am," he hastened to tell her. "It's not that." The gentle fluttering in his belly had developed into a rolling ocean. He set his mug on the table and sat crossed-legged on the rug, facing them. "Before I start, I just want you to know that the only reason I feel able to share this with you is that I know you both love me and support me." He smiled at them.

Momma's expression softened. "Of course we do, son." The love in her voice filled him with warmth. "But you're worryin' me now."

Tommy nodded. No use putting it off any longer. He took a final deep breath. "Momma, Daddy, ever since I was a little boy, you've taught me how important it is to tell the truth."

They nodded.

"Well, I've been doin' a lotta thinkin' 'bout my life, and I figured it's about time I shared it with y'all. Like you always say, Momma, 'the truth will set you free.' So this is me, sharing that I… I'm gay."

The silence that fell was so sudden, it descended with the swiftness of his daddy's axe chopping wood.

Daddy stared at him, eyes wide. Momma gaped, so still he'd have sworn she'd been turned to stone.

Momma was the first to speak. "Gay," she repeated heavily. Then she squinted at him. "Gay, as in homosexual?"

"Yes, Momma. I'm gay." Tommy swallowed, heart hammering.

She glanced at his daddy, whose expression hadn't changed one jot, then back to Tommy. "I see," she said slowly. Her hands fidgeted in her lap, and she frowned. "Well, I… I don't rightly know what to say. This is… unexpected." Her gaze traveled once more to his daddy, who nodded.

Tommy breathed a little easier. He hadn't known what to expect, but this decidedly low-key reaction definitely wasn't it. The tightness in his chest abated.

"I think you should go to bed now, son," his daddy said suddenly, his voice low.

Tommy blinked. It wasn't even nine fifteen.

Daddy nodded. "You sure have given us somethin' to think about, and we can talk more 'bout this in the morning. So why don't you go on up to your room and get some sleep, huh?"

Momma nodded in agreement.

"Okay, Daddy." Tommy rose to his feet, legs trembling slightly, and picked up his unfinished hot chocolate. He went over to his momma and kissed her cheek. "G'night, Momma, g'night, Daddy."

They both gave him a quick smile, and then he left the room. He climbed the wooden stairs, his head in a whirl. In his worst moments of panic prior to this, he'd imagined his parents ranting at him, getting out the family Bible and reading passages to him, maybe even wanting him to pray with them. Of course he'd always hoped they'd react calmly, but even he was amazed by this quiet… acceptance.

Tommy got ready for bed with a considerably lighter heart. He pulled the covers up around his shoulders and turned onto his side to stare out his window at the velvet night sky, strewn with stars.

It really is gonna be okay. For the first time in weeks, he fell asleep almost instantly.

THE NEXT morning Tommy awoke late and stared at the clock in surprise. *Since when does Daddy let me sleep* this *late?* Not that he was complaining. He'd slept like a log and felt fine. Noises filtered from downstairs, the hum of low voices. Guiltily, he sprang out of bed and pulled on his jeans and sweatshirt before hurrying into the bathroom to wash his face and brush his teeth. There was a whole list of chores that had to be done in the mornings—feed the chickens, horses, pigs, dogs, and cattle; milk the cows; collect the eggs—and Tommy was expected to help out. Holidays or not, there was a farm to run.

He came down the stairs and straight into the kitchen in search of coffee. To his surprise, the large room was empty, but there was the buzz of voices coming from the living room. The absence of his parents was suddenly clear. The living room was reserved for when there was company.

"C'mon in here, son," his momma called out.

Tommy rapidly combed his fingers through his hair, making sure he looked respectable before pushing open the oak door—and coming to a dead stop in the doorway.

The room was full of family.

Momma and Daddy sat on the two-seater couch in front of the window. To their right on the largest of the couches sat Mary, Dan standing at her side, his daddy, Pastor Cunningham, beside him. Next to Mary were Tommy's grandparents. The armchairs were taken by Tommy's Uncle Ned and his cousins, Jake and Bill, both older than him.

"What...?" Any words died in Tommy's throat when he gazed around the room at the group of people assembled, their faces set as they regarded him in stony silence. And in that moment, any optimism Tommy had been feeling packed its bags and left the building. The quietly oppressive atmosphere in the room made his heart sink fast.

This is not gonna be good was probably the understatement of the year.

"Tommy," his momma began, her voice even, "your daddy and I have spent all night prayin' an' thinkin' 'bout what you shared with us yesterday, an' we feel there are some things *we'd* like to share too."

"Okay," he said slowly, swallowing. His scalp prickled, and his belly quivered. The cool scrutiny of his relatives was unnerving. *Why are they all here?*

"Since you've seen fit to choose this… lifestyle and stray from the path of righteousness, we—"

"Now hold on a minute," Tommy butted in, his heart racing. "This isn't a choice, Momma. This is how I am, how I was born."

An angry buzz rippled around the room, and his throat grew tight. Mary stared at him, wide-eyed, Dan's hand upon her shoulder, looking for all the world like he was comforting her. Beside her, his grandparents held hands, lips narrowed.

"No one is *born* a homosexual, Tommy," Pastor Cunningham interjected, stepping forward. "We are all created in God's image, and he has some pretty specific things to say on this subject." He held aloft a Bible.

"No offense, Pastor Cunningham," Tommy said politely, "but if you're about to quote from Leviticus, about a man not lyin' with a man as with a woman, then I'll be forced to quote a little Scripture of my own." He pointed toward his Uncle Ned. "Or are *you* gonna be the one to tell my uncle here that the Bible says you can't have tattoos? Or maybe tell my momma that accordin' to the Bible, her sister, my aunt Jeanie, should be stoned to death 'cause she's divorced?" All the things he'd heard in those meetings came back to him in a rush.

That buzz grew louder, the sound almost painful. Momma's mouth fell open, and her hand flew to her chest. Daddy's nostrils flared, and his eyes bulged.

The pastor shook his head, his expression sad. "Oh, Tommy, now I understand better. They've brainwashed you, son, so you think that what you're doing is all right. But it isn't, I'm afraid. Doesn't it warn us somewhere about the Devil citing Scripture for his purpose?"

Tommy stared at him with wide eyes. "So if I quote Scripture to show you the Bible isn't infallible, I'm the Devil, right? But if you do it, suddenly that makes it okay?"

There were low gasps from his relatives, but Tommy was beyond caring. This was fast turning into a nightmare.

The pastor approached him. "Your parents called me and asked me to be here because they know I can help you."

"Help me?" Tommy blinked. His thoughts seemed to freeze.

Pastor Cunningham nodded, holding out his left hand, which contained some pamphlets. "There are places for people like you, Tommy. Places where you can be helped back onto the right path."

Murmurs of approval accompanied his words.

Tommy saw the light. Cold spread from his core to all his extremities. "You're talkin' 'bout reparative therapy. Camps where you 'deprogram' gays?" He shook his head. "I've heard about such places an' what goes on in 'em. An' *you* wanna talk about *brainwashin'*?" He turned to his parents. "Tell me you're not listenin' to this, Daddy, Momma?" He couldn't believe this.

His daddy rose to his feet. "We're offerin' you a choice, son, 'cause we love you. Either you do what the pastor says an' undergo some treatment, or...." He glanced down at Momma on the couch, who nodded. Daddy looked him in the eye and swallowed. "Or we can't have you under our roof." He straightened. "You will no longer be a part of this family. Not if you've chosen to follow the path of deviancy."

Tommy's blood turned to ice in his veins. "You... you can't mean that." *This isn't happening.* "You say you love me, an' yet you'd disown me because I'm gay?" Of all the times he'd heard horror stories about parents doing this to their kids, he'd never once imagined his parents being capable of perpetrating such a cruel act.

"Tommy, d'you think I'd ever be able to hold my head up in this town once word got out?" Momma looked stricken. "Why, people might think I condone your... behavior. They'd look at me an' wonder what I did wrong when I was raisin' you, for you to turn out this way."

Oh, this was too much. "You're prepared to kick me out because of how people might view your skills as a parent? Or what they might say 'bout you? Momma, can you hear yourself?" He drew in several deep breaths in an effort to calm down. "Momma, Daddy, this is how God made me." He gestured to his body.

"You blasphemin' little sack o' shit!"

Before Tommy knew what was happening, his uncle had launched himself from his armchair and aimed a punch at Tommy's face. His fist connected with Tommy's cheek and eye socket. Pain shot through him, exploding in his head, and he dropped to the floor like a sack of potatoes. His uncle stood over him, fists clenched.

"God didn't make you no homo, you little bastard!" Uncle Ned's face was bright red, his teeth bared, spittle flying from his lips. "Your fag friends did that!"

Daddy and the pastor were at his side in an instant, pulling him back.

"No violence, please!" the pastor pleaded.

His grandma and Mary were crying, his cousins standing by his uncle, looking daggers at Tommy. There was so much hate in the room it was clawing at him.

Tommy stared up at them, his cheek on fire. Daddy stood over him, face grave.

"Either you choose to come back to the path of righteousness, or you choose to carry on along the road to damnation," he intoned. "An' if *that's* your choice…." Daddy's eyes locked on his. "Then don't come back to this house until you're prepared to change your ways."

The room fell silent once more.

Tommy slowly got to his feet. "Then if that's all you have to say on the subject, I guess I'll go upstairs an' pack." He faced his parents, the bile rising in his throat.

Momma gazed at him, her face pale. "You sure you wanna do that, Tommy? There's still time to change your mind." He swallowed hard, and she pressed on. "C'mon, son, you're a good, God-fearin' Christian boy, always have been. I know if you look into your heart, you'll see the path the Lord wants you to follow."

Aw crap. "But that's just it, Momma. When I look inside myself, I see who I really am." He held his head high. "An' that person is gay."

She regarded him for a moment and then nodded. "Then you do what you have to, Tommy." Her face was ashen.

That was it, then.

Tommy stared at his parents for a moment, searching for the words, *any* words, that would make sense of it all, but he had nothing. He pulled himself up to his full height, turned around slowly, and walked out of the living room, pulling the door shut behind him.

Once he was standing in the airy hallway, he grasped the newel post and held on to it, bent over, shaking, fighting the urge to throw up. The whole situation had a surreal feel to it, like it was part of some nightmare. Any second now he was going to wake up in his bed, damp with sweat but out of this horrible dream, back in the comfortable, cozy world he'd inhabited since he'd arrived home.

Except, of course, he knew this was no dream.

Could *I do it? Could I go through their therapy, live my life as a straight guy?*

After all, the only place where he lived as an out gay guy was between his ears. Sure, he had fantasies, dreams, but none of it was real. Would it be so hard to give up something that didn't really exist?

Then it hit him, with all the force of a sledgehammer to his ribs.

I told them in the first place because I wanted to be true to myself, because I didn't want to hide. How could I live with myself if I deny what I am?

And if they didn't want a gay son, then that was their loss, painful though that thought was. He knew the pain would ease with time. Never mind that right then, it felt like someone had ripped his heart out of his chest with their bare hands.

Tommy went back upstairs and entered the room that had been his for all of his life. He gazed around it in a daze, unsure of where to begin. It was only just beginning to sink in that he wouldn't be coming back there.

What the hell do I take with me?

There was other issues, far more pressing ones. The dorms were closed for the winter break. Where was he going to stay until the semester started? And what about his studies?

A wave of sorrow and nausea rolled over him, and he was seized with the urge to get out of there.

He grabbed a suitcase from his closet and another couple of bags and proceeded to stuff as many clothes into them as he could. He scanned the bedroom for anything else to take, those items that really meant something to him. When he'd finished, he dragged the case and bags down the stairs, bumping each step as he struggled with his burden. The door to the living room was still closed.

Guess this really is it.

Tommy went out the front door to where his truck sat on the driveway. He slung his suitcase into the back of the truck, followed by the rest of his bags, and then he returned to the house to close the door. As he walked over to the truck, he glanced at the front window to see if anyone was observing his exit, but there was no one there.

His heart like a stone in his chest, Tommy got into the truck and pulled his phone from his pocket. He scrolled through his contacts until he found Ben. It took a few rings until the call connected.

"Whassa time? Hell, Tommy, why you callin' me before noon two days after Christmas?" Ben's voice was heavy with sleep.

"Ben, would it be okay if I stayed with you awhile?"

He heard the rustle of sheets. "Oh fuck. Something's happened." Ben sounded more alert. "Okay, you don't have to tell me now. An' of course you can stay. I'll tell the 'rents you're coming." There was a pause. "You all right, Tommy?"

The kindness in Ben's voice, his genuine concern, was the arrow that found its way through Tommy's defenses. His breathing hitched, and then the tears came, hot and plentiful, coursing down his cheeks until he was blinded by them, unable to hold back his sobs. He sat there, phone in hand, and wept for the life he'd just lost until he was all cried out.

He heard Ben clear his throat. "Come on home, Tommy, okay? We can talk when you get here."

Tommy wiped his face on his sleeve and sniffed. "I'll see you in about four, five hours, all right? Maybe a bit longer if I make some stops."

"That's fine. Just get your ass here, right?" Ben's chuckle tickled his ear. "Maybe tonight's the night I finally get you drunk."

The way Tommy was feeling right then? That was sounding more and more like a damn good idea. He disconnected the call and started up the engine. One final glance over his shoulder to the house where he was no longer welcome, and then Tommy pulled out into the street, leaving the dust of Americus behind him.

CHAPTER SEVEN

THE AROMA of fresh coffee tickled his nostrils, and Tommy opened his eyes to find Ben kneeling beside the sofa bed, mug in hand. "Morning, sleepyhead." Ben's eyes were kind.

"G'mornin'." Tommy propped himself up on his elbow and took the proffered mug. "What time is it?" He took a sip and sighed with pleasure as the flavor burst upon his tongue, rich and strong. "Damn, this is good. Thank you."

"Mom made it for you." Ben rose to his feet and crossed the room to open the blinds that covered the high windows. There wasn't much natural light that found its way into the basement apartment, but the halogen downlights more than made up for it. Ben came back to the sofa and sat on the edge of the mattress, dressed in only his boxers. "As for what time it is, it's nine thirty. I let you sleep in, you were so exhausted last night. How'd you sleep, anyway?"

"Off an' on," Tommy replied, drinking some more of the delicious, restorative brew. He vaguely remembered unfolding the sofa bed the night before and collapsing onto it. Ben's words filtered through. "What d'you tell your parents 'bout why I was stayin'?" He hadn't seen any of the family. Ben had let him in through the outer door to the basement.

"I told them it was for a couple days. They don't need to know more than that right now." Ben grimaced. "Not that they'd have taken in a word I was saying anyhow." He pointed toward the ceiling. "It's chaos up there."

Tommy sat up, the sheet pooled around his waist. "What's goin' on?"

Ben chuckled. "The 'rents are throwing a post-Christmas, pre-New Year party tonight. We're talking caterers, setting up a bar, bartenders, music…. I recommend staying out of it all. In fact, once you've had some breakfast, we might wanna think about escaping down here for a while and letting Mom get on with it. Her hairdresser-cum-makeup guy will be arriving after lunch." He pulled a face.

"What's wrong with that?" Tommy asked.

Ben shook his head. "Danny's good at what he does—don't get me wrong—but he's such a flamer." He scowled. "I'm just not that big on guys who make it real obvious they're gay."

Having seen Ben at the Jungle when he was pretty much full-on, Tommy found this more than a little ironic, but he bit his lip and kept quiet.

Ben studied him for a moment. "So, you gonna tell me what happened? 'Cause you didn't say a right lot last night."

Tommy sighed. "That's prob'ly 'cause there ain't that much to tell." It still hurt to think about the whole hateful episode. Now and again during the journey back to Atlanta, he'd had to pull over when the tears came. He'd sat by the side of the road, shaking, wiping his eyes, and feeling like a total loser.

Guess it was still sinkin' in. I mean, it's not every day your family kicks the shit out of you, psychologically speakin'.

"Well, you might wanna start with how you managed to get that black eye, for one."

Ben stretched out his hand and touched it tentatively with his fingertips. Tommy winced, and Ben withdrew instantly. Tommy drank a few mouthfuls of coffee, inhaled deeply, and then told Ben everything. His roommate's eyes grew wide with incredulity, and he shook his head, his fingers curling in the sheets. When Tommy was finished, Ben stared at him openmouthed.

"Well, shit."

"That about sums it up, all right," Tommy said morosely. He shook his head. "What I can't get over is them tellin' me they love me and then comin' out with all that…." He huffed. "What ever happened to 'God is love'?"

"I guess God is love unless you're gay," Ben said quietly. "Shit, Tommy, that sounds like it was awful. So what you gonna do now?"

"Well, I s'pose I need to think about my studies. I mean, I was studyin' organic agriculture so's I could take over the runnin' of the farm, for when Daddy wanted to call it a day, but now?" He stared into his half-empty mug. "I need to think about what *I* want to do. Payin' for my schoolin' won't be a problem, not with my college fund and the scholarships. But maybe it's time to think carefully 'bout what I want my major to be."

Ben regarded him steadily. "Sounds like you've got some decisions to make. Don't rush that. We've got just over a week before the new semester begins. I'm sure Mom and Dad won't mind you staying here 'til then." He grinned. "But that's something to be discussed after this damn party, okay?"

Tommy smiled. "Sure thing." Just then his stomach growled.

Ben snickered. "Looks like the first order of business is to feed you. When did you eat last?"

Tommy shrugged. He recalled snacking on a couple of bars of chocolate during the journey back to Atlanta, but food had been the last thing on his mind. He was still too churned up to eat when he'd arrived.

"Go grab a shower," Ben suggested, "and then we'll get some breakfast into you. We can decide what we're doing after that."

Tommy nodded in agreement. Ben got up from the sofa bed, and Tommy caught hold of his arm.

"Thank you," he said simply.

Ben's cheeks grew rosy. "What are friends for?" He patted Tommy's hand and walked into his bedroom. Tommy threw off the sheets and got out of bed. He then straightened them, tucking them in before he folded the bed back into its usual state. A shower would feel really good right then. And maybe things would look a little better with some food inside him.

'Cause Lord knew, they couldn't look much worse.

"MERCY, WHAT happened to you, Tommy?" Caroline's eyes grew wide when she caught sight of his face.

"I had a fight with a door in the middle of the night," Tommy explained weakly. He'd managed to avoid being seen by the family all day, keeping out of sight in the basement, but when Ben's parents had asked where his guest was hiding, it had been time to show his face.

She arched her finely sculpted eyebrows and pursed her lips, but that was all. Tommy had the distinct feeling that she wasn't buying it, however. Ben's momma was a smart one.

"Now you boys need to keep out of the way while everyone gets set up for this evening. Danny will be here any minute to do my hair and makeup, and then it won't be long before the first guests start arriving."

Every available surface in the kitchen was taken up with platters of party food, along with boxes of wineglasses and cases of wine.

"We still okay to stay downstairs?" Ben asked, helping himself to a large shrimp from a nearby platter on the counter and earning himself a smack on the hand for his efforts. "Ow!"

"Then keep your paws off," Caroline said with a firm stare. "And what makes you think I don't expect you to attend, Benson Cardiff Wellington?"

"Mom," Ben groused.

"It's your name, so quit complaining. And yes, you *will* be attending the party. Tommy, you can join us if you want."

"If you don't mind, ma'am, I'd rather not." Tommy gestured to his eye. "Not really feelin' presentable right now."

She nodded sympathetically. "I understand. You can stay downstairs." When Ben let out a plaintive whine, she glared at him. "Tommy has an excuse, whereas you do not. As you are so fond of telling your sister, 'suck it up.'" There was a mischievous gleam in her eyes. "Tommy, I'll have a plate of food made up for you a little later, okay?"

He nodded.

"Mom, Danny's here." Bethany called from the doorway, the hairdresser behind her.

Bethany promptly retreated. Tommy tried not to stare at the flamboyant Danny, who wore tight black leather pants, boots, and a bright blue shirt that fit his slim curves like a glove. His hair was black, short at the sides and longer, fashionably unruly on top. Danny breezed into the kitchen and air kissed in the general direction of Caroline's cheeks. He regarded her hair with pursed lips and then nodded.

"By the time I'm finished, you're going to look absolutely *fabulous*, honey," he said emphatically. He nodded politely in Ben's direction, and then his eyes lit up when he saw Tommy. His gaze traveled up and down Tommy's body with frank appreciation. "Well, hel-*lo* there."

Tommy froze to the spot, pulse racing.

"Danny, this is Tommy, Ben's roommate from college."

Danny grinned, revealing a set of perfect white teeth. "Hi, Tommy. Delighted to meet you." His eyes glittered as he moved closer. "Well, aren't you just *scrumptious* looking?"

He flung out his arm, hand extended toward Tommy, who was at a loss whether to kiss it or shake it. He was suddenly hyperaware of Caroline's presence. He grasped Danny's hand firmly, but shaking it was akin to holding a cold, dead fish. He released it quickly.

"Oh my, how butch."

Danny pursed his lips once more, letting his gaze move slowly up and down Tommy's body again. Tommy got the definite feeling Danny was picturing him naked. That tongue darting out to lick his lips only made him more certain of it.

"Why, honey, whatever did you do to your poor eye? Oh, that must've *hurt*." He stretched out his fingers toward Tommy's cheek.

"Excuse me, but you're here to do my hair, not ogle my son's roommate." Caroline tapped her foot, nails drumming on the counter. Danny retracted his hand quickly.

"And we've got things to do," Ben said hurriedly, tugging at Tommy's arm and dragging him toward the kitchen door. Tommy was only too happy to go with him. "Later, Mom."

Caroline waved her hand in acknowledgment and then launched into a discussion with Danny about how she wanted her hair done. Danny listened, nodding, but his gaze kept drifting over to where Tommy and Ben stood by the fridge, Ben reaching into its vast interior to grab bottles of water. Tommy was able to pick up the whispered conversation, which sent his heart plummeting.

"Yes, dear, your hair will be simply stunning." Danny was staring at him pointedly. "Maybe Mr. Big-n-Handsome would like to join me later for a drink."

Caroline smirked. "I doubt you're his type, Danny—i.e., you're male."

Danny arched his eyebrows. "Honey, that man is gay—I can feel it. My gaydar is banging all the way into the red zone."

Caroline gaped at Danny. "That boy is *not* gay. Now can we just get on with getting *me* ready for this party, please?"

Danny opened his eyes wide, hands held high. "Whatever you say." His eyes flicked in Tommy's direction, and those full lips pursed up yet again.

Ben chose that moment to pull him through one door and then another. He shook his head as they went downstairs into the basement. "Sorry 'bout that."

Tommy shuddered. "Really freaked me out, him lookin' at me so obviously and talkin' to me like that in front of your mom." Hearing the bartenders at Woofs say stuff like that was one thing—they were in a gay bar, after all—but standing in Ben's family kitchen was something else entirely.

Ben scowled. "Oh, he was looking at you, all right. He was staring at you like you were the last ice cream on the Fourth of July." He met Tommy's gaze. "Sorry, but I was really uncomfortable. I just felt you didn't need that, not right now. You've got enough on your plate without having to deal with Danny."

It was sweet seeing Ben being so protective of him. "Thanks," Tommy said with a smile. "Think I'm gonna stay down here and let the food come to me, though." Right then he didn't want to see anyone.

"Sure thing." Ben handed him a bottle of water. "Wanna hang out and watch a movie or something 'til I have to go join the fun?" He rolled his eyes.

"That sounds like a great idea." *Anything* so he didn't have to think. There was way too much going on his head.

"YOUR EYE'S looking a little better, Tommy," Ben's daddy commented over lunch a couple of days after the party.

"Thank you, sir." Tommy helped himself to more mashed potatoes and gravy. "I'll know to be more careful in future when I go to the bathroom in the middle of the night." The lie felt wrong on his lips, but it was better than telling the truth. It had been four days since he'd arrived to stay at Ben's house, and he was trying his best to stop thinking about his family interaction. He could still see their faces, though. Some things were too difficult to dismiss so easily.

"What you boys planning to do for New Year's Eve?" Caroline asked. "Because you can always join us at the aquarium. We're attending a fund-raising event, and I'm sure we can still get tickets if you want. I know it's tomorrow night, but we could manage it."

Ben grinned. "Mom, that sounds delightful, but I have a date."

Tommy stared at him in surprise.

"Anyone we know?" his mom inquired.

"Just a girl from my class, Della," he replied. "Her folks are throwing a party, and she invited me." He grinned at Tommy. "And Tommy here is going out too."

"Oh, just to a party at a bar in the city," Tommy added hastily, glaring at Ben. His roommate had been doing his best to get Tommy to tell him exactly where he was going, but Tommy wasn't about to do that. There were some secrets he wasn't prepared to share.

"Don't drink too much, now," Benson Wellington admonished. He lifted a forkful of roast beef to his lips and then picked up his newspaper, ignoring his wife's tut-tut of disapproval.

Tommy didn't plan on letting anything alcoholic pass his lips, New Year's Eve or no. His momma's lectures on the evils of drink still rang in his head. Another one of those things that was proving difficult to ignore.

Caroline appeared surprised. "I thought you might have been planning to go spend New Year's Eve with your parents, Tommy."

He winced, the reaction so instinctive he couldn't control it. *So much for puttin' it behind me.* Everything was still too raw. Across the table from him, Ben's expression was one of sympathy.

Caroline's brow furrowed. "Did I say something wrong?"

Before Tommy could say something to reassure her, Ben let out a heavy sigh and stared at Tommy.

"You know what? They deserve to know what's going on."

Tommy's heartbeat sped up. *Oh no, he wouldn't....*

Ben turned to his parents. "Tommy's staying here 'cause his parents kicked him out." He gave Tommy an apologetic glance.

Benson lowered his newspaper. "Why? What happened?" He seemed appalled by the revelation.

Caroline's mouth fell open, and she let out a gasp.

Ben bit his lip. "Let's just say they had a difference of opinion."

Tommy put down his fork and sighed. "Well, you've told 'em *that* much. They may as well know the whole story." He regarded Benson and Caroline, his heart racing. "I… I came out to my parents the day after Christmas, and they were none too happy about it." He paused, unsure of what else to tell them. It had been enough of an effort to share *that*.

"What about the rest of it?" Ben said hotly. "Tell them about the camp your parents and that pastor wanted to send you to, where they were gonna cure you of being gay." His face glowed.

Silence fell. Ben's parents stared at him, openmouthed. Finally Caroline spoke. "Oh, you poor thing. You should've told us, dear." She sighed. "Tommy, there is nothing wrong with being gay, y'hear? And you are welcome to stay here as long as you want. Isn't that right, Benny?"

Ben's dad nodded. "You're always welcome here, son. You're good for Ben. He needs someone like you around." Then he smiled. "You can even take one of the bedrooms upstairs if my sloth of a son gets to be too much for you," he added before picking up his newspaper once more.

"Thank you," Tommy said warmly. Ben was so lucky to have such supportive, understanding parents. He couldn't believe how unruffled they were by his announcement.

Then Caroline grinned. "Well, I'll be damned. It just burns me up that Danny was right after all." Her comment was met with chuckles from her family. Caroline rolled her eyes. Then she glanced at Bethany, who was sitting next to Tommy, a smug expression on her face. Caroline narrowed her gaze. "You already knew Tommy was gay, didn't you?"

Bethany's expression became innocent. "I may have."

Tommy squeezed her knee, and she smiled at him. There was a wicked gleam in her eyes as she glanced over at her brother.

"At least Tommy has taste. He'd never consider dating Ben."

Ben glared at her. "You little witch!"

Bethany shrugged. "I figured as long as Tommy was being honest, maybe it was time you were too." Her lips twitched.

Caroline regarded her son in silence, and Tommy watched as Ben swallowed. Then she gave him a wide smile.

"Oh, baby, like I didn't already know about you."

Tommy had to fight hard to hold back his laughter at the sight of Ben's dazed look.

"You know?" It came out as a squeak.

Caroline's expression was full of love. "Of course, sugar. Do you think a mother doesn't know these things? Though I admit, you had me fooled for a while, until I figured out you like boys *and* girls."

Benson's newspaper flapped. "Wait—what?" He frowned. "What was that about Ben liking boys?"

"Go back to your paper, dear," Caroline said with a wave of her hand. "Everything's fine. Our son is bisexual, that's all." She smiled sweetly in his direction.

"Oh, okay," he said absently. Then his paper flapped again. "Wait— Ben is bisexual? Why am I the last to know these things?"

"Benny." Caroline waited until he was focusing on her. "Do you have a problem with Ben being bi? Because *I* surely don't."

Benny's brow cleared. "Of course I don't. All I want is for our children to be happy." He smiled at Ben. "That's fine, son." Then he went back to his paper, still murmuring about always being the last to know.

Caroline turned to Ben. "See, honey? That wasn't so bad, was it?" She beamed at him and then swept a glance around the table. "Now, is there anything else we need to be told? No? Fine, then I for one am going to finish my lunch." And with that she picked up her knife and fork and calmly proceeded to eat her meal.

Ben just sat there, looking stunned. Then his face creased into a smile and he burst out laughing. His eyes met Tommy's. "You gotta love my family, right?"

Tommy looked around the dining table, his heartbeat back to normal. For the first time since he'd walked into his parents' living room, he felt a glimmer of hope.

Maybe all those people on YouTube were right. Maybe it does *get better after all.*

CHAPTER EIGHT

"I ALWAYS hated this part of the holidays," Mike said as he handed his mom the last of the Christmas tree ornaments for her to pack away in their box, ready to go up into the attic. He glanced around the living room. Everything always looked so bare when the trappings of Christmas were taken down. Mom insisted that this was done the last day of the year, ready to start the New Year with a clean slate.

Penelope Scott laughed. "Oh my, yes. I have vivid memories of you when you were five or six years old, asking me why we couldn't leave the tree up until next Christmas."

"Oh God, really?" Mike smiled. "I don't remember that." He handed her the last gold-colored garland. "There, that's the last of it."

His mom pointed to the top of the tree. "Uh-uh, you missed something." He glanced at the star, and she laughed. "You can get that for me. I can't reach that high without a ladder."

He chuckled. Mom was five feet nothing, yet he knew plenty of people who were scared of the tiny lady who'd started out as a millinery buyer for Rich's Department Store before ending up as a manager there. Mike stretched up and plucked the star from its lofty position. He laid it in its box and then stepped behind her, stooped to wrap his arms around her waist, and brought his chin to rest on her shoulder.

"Love you, lady."

She reached up to stroke his face. "Love you too, baby." She turned and stared at him, eyes alight with love, and then she stroked his beard. "Aw, my baby got gray." Her words were soft.

Mike laughed. "You'd be this gray too, if you only quit covering it up." He dodged her quick blow to his arm with a chuckle and then regarded her intently. "Maybe you should be thinking about retiring soon."

Mom snorted. "I could say the same thing about you, dear." He stared at her, and she shrugged. "I see how hard you work, at the bar, the shoots. You're always off somewhere or other, always busy...."

Mike sighed. "It is what it is, okay? I'm just trying to keep up most of the time. But it won't be forever. I've planned for the future, just like you taught me."

"Glad to hear it," she said simply. "You were always such a sensible young man."

Mike walked over to her front window and stared out at the quiet street beyond. "The industry is changing, Mom. Maybe I need to make some changes too."

"Might these changes include a man in your life?"

Mike groaned. "Mom." It was an old refrain. He walked over to her and led her to the couch, where they sat down. "We both know it would take a very special kind of man to put up with my career." God knew, he hadn't found him yet, and it wasn't for want of trying. But Dirk's departure had knocked it out of him, and he'd stopped looking.

"I could understand that being the case in the past, sure," his mom said quietly, "but if you retire, that wouldn't be a problem, right?" She leaned back against the comfortable cushions. "Something else you may want to think about too. You've always gone for the same type of man, son. If you keep fishing in the same pond, you're gonna keep reeling in the same kind of fish."

He stiffened. "I don't know what you mean."

Mom barked out a laugh. "Oh, come on, Mike. How long have I been working with gay men? We're talking the seventies, eighties, nineties… I see what goes on, I see the circuit groups, I hear about the white parties."

Mike stared at her. He couldn't believe he was hearing this. "Mom?"

She patted his knee. "Don't pretend with me, Mike. You hang out with a certain type of man. Your age or maybe older. Muscled. All gay clones of each other." She smiled. "Time to break the mold, son."

He couldn't help smiling. "You got someone in mind?"

Mom opened her mouth, but whatever she'd been about to say was interrupted by the sound of someone knocking at her front door. Mom's eyes flew open, and her cheeks were flushed.

Something rolled over in his belly. "Oh God. What have you done?"

She rose to her feet and went into the hall, Mike following. "I… I invited a guest for lunch," she whispered.

Suddenly everything became clear. Mike groaned. "Oh, Mom, tell me you didn't." He hung back, eyeing the shape beyond the frosted glass with distrust.

She laid a finger on her lips in warning and then opened the front door, a smile fixed on her face. "Darren! Come on in." She stepped aside to allow her guest to enter. Darren turned out to be in his early thirties, neatly groomed, dressed in slacks, shirt and tie, and a sports coat. He glanced at Mike briefly before kissing Mom on both cheeks. Mike was suddenly aware of his faded jeans and T-shirt.

Damn her for not mentioning this.

Mom introduced him. "Darren is a supervisor in the men's department."

Cool blue eyes appraised Mike, and his hand was taken in a firm shake. "And I've heard all about you. Penny talks about you all the time, not that I'm unfamiliar with some of your work, 'Scott.'"

"I see." Mike wasn't ashamed of what he did, but there was something about Darren's mouth that spoke of disapproval. *Well, fuck him.*

Lunch was not off to a good start. Mike was not happy about his mom's interference, and as the afternoon wore on, he grew unhappier still with Darren's attitude. There was nothing blatant to point to, but that faint curl of his lip when he mentioned "your industry" was starting to piss Mike off. Mom was looking none too comfortable either. Now and again she sent an apologetic glance Mike's way when Darren wasn't looking.

"So do you have plans for New Year's Eve, Darren?" she asked as they finished eating chicken salad.

Darren dabbed his mouth with his napkin. "I'll be spending the evening with a few close friends who are throwing a low-key party. We'll toast in the New Year, and that will probably be that." He gazed across the table. "Mike, I'm sure your evening will be completely different."

Mike chuckled. "Oh, there's no doubt about that."

"Mike will be working at the bar tonight," his mom explained.

"Oh really? What bar?"

"Woofs, a gay sports bar on Piedmont." Mike smiled politely. "In case you haven't heard of it." He thought it very unlikely that Darren had even seen it. He had "snob" written all over him.

Sure enough, Darren wrinkled his nose just the tiniest bit, but Mike caught it.

"How about you help me with the coffee in the kitchen?" Mom said, her hand on his.

Mike threw down his napkin, got up from the table, and followed her out of the room. Once in the kitchen, she quietly closed the door behind them and then turned to face him, her cheeks red.

"Oh, baby, I'm so sorry. I had no idea he was such a snob."

Mike hugged her and then pulled back to look her in the eye. "Now let this be a lesson to you. I know you meant well, Mom, but…."

"But nothing," she said, mouth pulled down at the corners. "Why, the way he talks to you is downright rude. Well, I won't be chatting with him anymore during our lunch breaks, that's for sure." Suddenly her eyes gleamed. "Makes me so mad, I just want to say something to… *ruffle* that smooth little bastard's feathers."

Mike gaped. Darren really had gotten on her nerves. "Remind me not to piss you off."

She chuckled, and he helped her put together the tray. When they were back at the dining room table, she poured out coffee into the delicate porcelain cups that had been her grandma's.

"Penny, what are your plans for tonight?" Darren asked before taking a mouthful of coffee.

She grinned at Mike, her eyes bright, and then smiled at Darren. "Oh, I'm gonna go hang out with the boys at Cockpit."

Darren almost choked, and Mike had to swallow his coffee rapidly.

"Do *what*? You're kidding me."

She regarded him with an innocent expression. "Why not? It's close to home. And besides, it'll be fun."

She bit her lip. Mike flashed a glance in Darren's direction.

He was staring at her, mouth open. "You?"

Mike was trying really hard not to laugh. He glanced at the clock over the fireplace and got to his feet. "Lovely though this is, I have things to do before I go to work, and I have a long evening ahead of me." He gave Darren a brief nod. "Darren, it was nice meeting you. Mom, I'll talk to you tomorrow." He walked over to kiss her on the cheek and brought his lips to her ear. "Don't have too much fun tonight." He felt rather than saw her restrained chuckle. Mike picked up his leather jacket from the hook on the wall in the hallway and left the house. He'd have to be at the bar by three thirty, four o'clock at the latest, and that left just enough time for a nice power nap.

Before all the New Year's Eve madness *really* began.

MIKE LOVED New Year's: the atmosphere in the bar; the expectant air as everyone waited for that ball to drop; the sight of guys kissing at midnight….

But what he loved most? The way the bartenders got to dress. S-E-X-Y. It all added to the fun, and there'd been some *really* interesting costumes over the years. He glanced at the guys working the bar and smiled to himself. This year was no exception. Kevin was wearing the skimpiest pair of shorts Mike had ever seen, together with an open-sided black T-shirt that showed off that big body with its gorgeous tats. Patrick was gonna be the cause of a lot of drooling that night. He'd turned up in full harness, leather shorts, and boots, that furry chest on display. All those guys who were into daddy bears were gonna lap it up. Don was wearing tight jeans and a T-shirt that showed off those body builder muscles to perfection.

There were only a few customers in the bar, so Mike took advantage of the quiet before the storm to put up a few more decorations. He was up a ladder, hanging the Happy New Year signs, when he got the distinct feeling of being watched. He twisted around to catch Kevin ogling him from behind the bar.

Mike snorted. "You'd get more done if you kept your eyes off my furry little ass." Not that Kevin could miss it. Mike was wearing nothing but a leather jock strap, a half harness, and boots. He figured it wouldn't harm his tips.

Kevin chuckled. "If you're gonna put it on display, you gotta expect people to look." He palmed his erect dick, which his shorts did nothing to hide. "Looking good there, Mikey. And by the way? There ain't nothing little about your ass."

"Bitch." Mike went back to his task, grinning when he caught Kevin's mock gasp. "Have you fetched down all the boxes of plastic champagne glasses yet?" The silence that greeted his words was answer enough. Mike shook his head. "Get your ass into gear, Kev. Time's a-wastin'."

He listened to Kevin's good-natured grumbling as he went off in search of the glasses. The bar was looking good, and it wouldn't be long before the customers started piling in through the doors.

It was gonna be a good night.

TOMMY GAZED at the plastic garbage bags and boxes full of clothes and heaved a sigh. He didn't have a clue what he was going to wear. He'd gone through everything at least twice already, and he was no nearer to making up his mind.

I just want him to notice *me.* Not that Mike wasn't gonna do that anyway, for all the wrong reasons. Tommy's black eye would take care of that.

"Okay, I've been listening to you sighing all evening, and it's driving me crazy." Ben emerged from his bedroom, looking smart in black jeans, dark blue shirt, and a matching tie.

Tommy smiled. "You look nice. I know it's not how you'd normally dress for a date, but I'm sure Della's parents will 'preciate it."

"Yeah." Ben shrugged. "It's gonna be a party full of relatives, so I thought I'd better look the part." He peered at the bags strewn around Tommy. "I gather you've not decided what you're wearing yet." He folded his arms across his chest. "What do you *want* to look like?"

Tommy considered his question for all of two seconds. He grinned. "Not like Danny."

Ben smirked. "Ya don't say." He pursed his lips, apparently deep in thought. A moment later, he smiled. "I think we need some help here."

Before Tommy could say a word, he disappeared out of the door that led up to the main house.

Tommy went back to pulling open the bags and perusing their contents. He looked up when he heard Caroline grumbling, getting louder.

"Can this wait? I'm right in the middle of getting ready myself." She followed Ben into the apartment.

Ben pointed to Tommy. "Look at all this, Mom. Tommy needs help. We're talking fashion disaster here."

She walked over to where Tommy stood and regarded him with a keen glance. "Okay, I'm thinking jeans, *nice* jeans that fit you, and *not* ones that make you look like you're wearing diapers."

Tommy's cheeks grew hot.

"And I may have an idea of what shirt would work. Perfect, in fact." She went back into the house.

Ben came over and burrowed through the pile of clothes until he pounced on something with a little cry of triumph. "Perfect." He slung a pair of jeans at Tommy. "How 'bout those?"

Tommy stared doubtfully at the jeans. "I haven't worn those in a while now, 'cause they're a little on the small side for me."

"Humor me," Ben said with a grin.

Shrugging, Tommy took off his sweatpants and squirmed into the jeans. "Hell," he said as he struggled to pull them up, "these are gonna be awful tight, Ben." He tried his best to stuff all the extra material of his boxers inside the jeans.

"Oh, Lord, you can't wear those!"

Tommy looked up to find Ben rolling his eyes. "Well, what else would I wear?"

"Nothing!" Ben said with wide eyes. "Which would be *my* recommendation."

Tommy swallowed. "I am *not* going commando."

Ben chuckled. "We can work up to that. Hang on a sec." He disappeared back into his bedroom and returned with a little plastic bag. He opened it up and took out a pair of white briefs with a tag hanging off them and a wide waistband bearing the name Trophy Boy. "Here. These are brand new."

He threw them at Tommy, who caught them deftly.

He stared at the garment with its generous pouch. "Think these'll fit me?"

Ben's eyes flicked downward. He grinned. "Oh yeah. Trust me, Trophy Boy was invented for guys like you. Now put them on before Mom comes back."

Tommy felt like his whole face was on fire. He shucked off the jeans, removed his boxers, and stepped into the tight briefs. His dick fit perfectly, and the briefs were comfortable, unexpectedly so. It didn't feel like he was wearing anything. He put the jeans back on and then assessed the situation. "God, they fit where they touch, that's for sure." He pulled a face. "I don't know 'bout this. I don't usually wear jeans this tight." And they weren't just tight, they were *Oh My God* tight.

"But they make you look good," Ben said with a gleam in his eye. "And what do you wanna bet that they make someone else look at you too?" He tilted his head. "There *is* someone whose eye you're trying to catch, right? Wherever it is that you're going tonight, which you haven't seen fit to share with me."

"If Tommy doesn't want to tell you where he's going, that's his choice," Caroline said as she came into the apartment carrying a white shirt. She smiled when she saw Tommy. "Oh, *very* nice." Caroline handed over what looked like a high-end tuxedo shirt. "This is one of Benny's old shirts. He thinks he'll get back into it, but that'll never happen. It will fit you, though. Go ahead. Put it on."

Tommy pulled off his sweatshirt and grabbed a white T-shirt to put on under the shirt, but Ben stopped him.

"No, nothing under it."

Tommy stared at him but shrugged and then slipped his arms into the cool cotton shirt. When he'd nearly finished fastening all the buttons, Ben stopped him once more.

"Leave the two top ones," he ordered. "And then roll up the sleeves. You got a black belt?"

Tommy nodded. "In that case over there."

He went over to where Tommy had indicated and sorted through the case's contents until he found what he was looking for. Then he crossed the room to where Tommy had lined up his footwear against the wall. "Wear these." Ben held up a pair of black cowboy boots.

Tommy finished dressing and then stood there, arms by his sides, feeling awfully self-conscious. "Well?" He glanced down at the crisp, pristine shirt. "Now all I have to do is manage not to spill anything on it."

"Oooh *my*."

Tommy jerked his head up, cheeks burning, at the sound of Bethany's drawn-out vowels. She stood in the doorway, grinning. "Well, aren't you the handsome one? You're gonna break someone's heart tonight."

Some of the tautness in his stomach eased at her words, and breathing became that little bit easier too. He smiled. "Really?" He wasn't aiming to break anyone's heart, but Bethany's compliment made him feel a lot more confident about walking into Woofs.

Bethany nodded, Ben nodding with her. Caroline looked him up and down him in silence for a moment, and then she grinned.

"Maybe it's a good thing Danny isn't here right now." She winked at him.

Damn. Didn't *that* make him feel good?

THE BAR was filling steadily, and by nine it was already looking pretty full. Kevin wasn't all that busy yet. He knew once it got past ten o'clock, however, they'd all be busting their asses. There were five guys working the bar, and things would get hectic the closer it got to midnight. Then everything would cool down rapidly.

Patrick was flexing for a customer and getting some very appreciative glances when the door opened and Tommy walked in. Kevin stared at him, mouth open. Damn but the kid looked good. Then he got a closer look at that firm butt encased in those tight-as-sin jeans that hugged Tommy's muscled thighs like a second skin. Scrap that—Tommy was looking fucking *hot*.

"Will you get a load of that?" he said quietly to Patrick, nudging him with his elbow.

Patrick glanced up briefly and then did a double take. He let rip with a loud wolf whistle. "Damn, looking *fine* there, Tommy."

Just like always, Tommy reddened instantly. He nodded at them both and proceeded to walk around the bar to his customary spot.

"He been in a fight or something?" Patrick said with a slight frown.

Kevin had seen the black eye too. Tommy didn't strike him as the sort to get into a fight. "Where's Mike?" Kevin asked, not seeing him anywhere.

"Just gone to get another box of glasses."

Kevin chuckled. "This is gonna be interesting." He peered around the bar to where Tommy was standing. Sure enough, the kid was already glancing up and down the bar. "Oh, I gotta see Mikey's face when he sees Tommy."

"Well, looks like you're about to get your wish," Patrick said under his breath, "'cause Mike's just come back."

Kevin jerked his head around to watch. Tommy looked toward the end of the bar just as Mike came around it, box in hand. It was like a moment out of a movie. Mike stopped and stared at Tommy, his eyes wide with shock. Tommy looked Mike up and down and then swallowed.

Kevin couldn't help grinning.

Mike nodded at Tommy. "Hey."

Kevin watched those blue eyes flicker downward before they focused on Tommy's face.

Tommy became real still, hand gripping the edge of the bar. "Uhhh...." His face was flushed, lips parted.

Kevin chuckled to himself. Mike had obviously scrambled the circuits in Tommy's brain. Mike cleared his throat and went over to the table where they'd been setting up the glasses for the midnight toast, like nothing was out of the ordinary. Except he was holding that box a bit lower, hiding his groin.

Damn, this was fun.

As the evening wore on, Kevin kept taking a peek at what was going on 'round that side of the bar. Not that he got much of a chance, as more and more guys poured in through the doors. Patrick was doing his fair share of observing the situation too. Kevin could tell from the looks he was getting from Don and Mitch that they wanted to know what the hell was going on. Kevin wasn't about to share. This was fucking *delicious*.

It was past eleven forty-five and Mike was setting up the plastic champagne flutes on trays, smiling and joking with the customers, not to mention getting the occasional pinch on that furry butt when he ventured out from behind the bar.

Patrick sidled up to Kevin. "Has Tommy taken his eyes off Mike yet?" He chuckled.

"Uh-uh," Kevin said, unable to tear his eyes away from the floor show. "And every chance Mike gets, he's doing some looking of his own." The two men were like satellites orbiting an unseen planet, never getting any nearer, as if closer contact would have them burning up.

Mike walked across to the bar. "Wanna give me the champagne and I'll start pouring?"

Kevin handed over a case of champagne with a smirk. "Want me to wipe up that drool from your chin, Mike?" He flicked his head in Tommy's direction.

"Fuck off," Mike said with a grin and went back to his task. Kevin couldn't help noticing, however, that Mike kept glancing at Tommy while he was pouring out the champagne. And when Mike was focused on his task, Tommy was checking out Mike's ass and legs. Not that Kevin could blame him for that. Mike was one prime piece of meat, especially for his age.

Of course Tommy looking that fine had been bound to attract attention. Kevin and Patrick had managed to fend off a few of the more persistent admirers, and at one point Kevin had growled at one of them.

Yeah, that had worked. Mike had just resorted to telling guys to back off. It was kinda sweet.

It was nearly midnight when Mike got back behind the bar. The TV was turned up loud, the screen showing the revelers in Times Square.

There was a buzz of energy throughout the bar as customers made sure they had a drink ready. There were quite a few guys who were already drunk and getting raucous. Thank God they wouldn't stay long once midnight had come and gone. Tommy stood up to stretch his legs, his gaze flickering between the TV screen and Mike, who was standing next to Kevin, handing out glasses of champagne.

Kevin placed a glass in front of Tommy. "Here you go, kid."

"But… I don't…."

Kevin grinned. "Don't you know it's bad luck not to drink champagne on New Year's Eve? And besides, you've been on Cherry Coke all night. You only have to drink a mouthful. It won't kill ya."

Tommy eyed the glass doubtfully and then nodded.

The countdown to midnight had begun. Everyone in the bar joined in, their voices getting louder as the seconds ticked by, and when the ball dropped, the bar rang to the cries of "Happy New Year!" Kevin looked at Tommy, who was taking a cautious sip of his champagne, and then at Mike, who was watching him do it.

"Oh, to hell with this," Kevin muttered. He leaned over the bar, grabbed Tommy firmly by the arms, and heaved him upward to plant a loud, smacking kiss on Tommy's mouth. Then he released him and grinned. "Happy New Year, kid!"

Tommy's mouth fell open, and he staggered back slightly. When he'd recovered, he gaped at Kevin, eyes wide. "Why'd you kiss me?"

Around him guys were drinking champagne, hugging and kissing, the mood jubilant.

Kevin snorted and gestured to Mike, who was staring incredulously at Kevin. "'Cause he was too chickenshit to do it!"

Mike spluttered. "Kevin!"

Kevin shook his head, laughing. "You know I'm telling the truth, Mike."

In front of him, Tommy sat back on his stool and took a drink of his champagne, looking anywhere but at them. He focused on the guys who were drunk, stumbling on their way out of the bar. He kept sneaking glances at Mike, especially when Mike came out from behind the bar or when he bent over to reach something low down.

Not that he was the only one. Mike couldn't tear his eyes away from Tommy for more than a couple of minutes at a time. Fuck, it was so sweet.

At twelve thirty, Don signaled to Kevin and Mike. "Okay, you guys were first in, so you're first out. Patrick, Mitch, and I got this." The bar was nearly deserted.

Mike disappeared for a few minutes, returning dressed in jeans, a T-shirt, and his leather jacket, a bag over his shoulder. "Well, that's me outta here."

Kevin grabbed Mike by the arm and flicked his head in Tommy's direction. "You gonna make a move on that?" Mike arched his eyebrows, and Kevin snorted. "Oh, c'mon, you've been staring at each other for long enough, that's for damn sure." He peered at Mike. "Do you even know his name?" Beside him, Patrick snickered.

"I'd be a poor bartender if I hadn't already picked up on *that*." Mike grinned. "His name's Tommy. Satisfied?"

"I will be if you get your act together," Kevin retorted.

Tommy put down his empty glass and nodded to them. "I… I guess I'll be goin' now. G'night… an' Happy New Year." His gaze lingered that bit longer on Mike, and then he slid off his stool and walked around the bar, out of their sight.

Kevin gave Mike a shove. "Go after him, you dumbass. *Now!*"

Mike hesitated for about five seconds, and then he sighed. "Fine. See you later. Night." He walked out of the bar with a wave to Scott and Mitch.

Kevin grinned at Patrick. "Well, go on, then. Get me a beer and a shot." He wasn't about to go out into the parking lot and interrupt whatever was going on.

Wonder what they're gonna say to each other?

CHAPTER NINE

MIKE SPOTTED Tommy walking toward a truck parked outside the bar. He watched him approach the vehicle and reach into his jeans pocket for his keys. The action pulled the fabric tight across that glorious ass. *Day-um.*

Mike was still unsure what the fuck he was doing out there. Hell, this was all Kevin's idea. Tommy had barely exchanged more than a couple of words with him the whole night. *What does Kev expect us to talk about?* Then he recalled that black eye. *Yeah, what was* that *about?* It was enough to make him decide that maybe a chat was a good idea.

"Going already?" he called out to Tommy.

The young man turned around to face him, his eyes open wide. For a moment Mike wasn't sure if Tommy was going to reply. Then he relaxed visibly, but only slightly.

"Well, a guy can only drink so much Cherry Coke." He stood still, keys in his hand, gaze focused on Mike.

Grinning, Mike walked slowly over to him. "Well, there is that." He stopped in front of Tommy. "Wasn't sure if you'd be here tonight. I'd thought you might've been at a party somewhere." The first sight of Tommy perched on that stool had been a pleasant surprise. Part of his anatomy had certainly thought so. It had only been after he'd watched Tommy for a while that Mike had gotten the impression all was not as it should have been. Tommy had made it to the ranks of the regulars, and Mike had grown accustomed to his shy smile and flushed cheeks, to say nothing of that gorgeous, muscled body. Tonight had been… different, notwithstanding the black eye.

He took a good look at Tommy. "Are you okay? You didn't seem yourself tonight."

Mike swore the kid's breathing hitched. Then Tommy took a long, slow breath. "I'm fine. There's just been a few things goin' on, that's all."

"Mmm-hmm." Mike was torn. He could walk away now, go home to his warm bed, or…. Something was tugging at him insistently, and it wouldn't let up. He'd been around long enough to trust his instincts. *Just go with it.*

Mike cocked his head. "You wanna go grab some breakfast?"

Tommy blinked. "At this hour?"

Mike shrugged. "Sure. The American Diner on Cheshire Bridge is open 24/7, serving breakfast around the clock." He gave Tommy an easy smile. "How about it?"

Tommy regarded him thoughtfully for a moment. Then those wide shoulders eased down a touch. "Okay. Breakfast sounds good." That shy smile was back, the one that did strange things to Mike's innards. "You wanna go in my truck?"

"Nah, I'll take mine and you can follow me. That way we can both get where we need to after we've eaten." Mike reached into his jacket pocket and pulled out his keys. "Let's go."

Tommy gave him a nod and then got into his truck. Mike climbed into his own truck and drove the couple of short miles to the diner, Tommy following him. The diner was fairly packed, and they had to wait awhile to be seated. It wasn't too long, however, before they were sitting in a booth, facing each other. Mike grabbed a menu and handed one to Tommy, and they scanned them in silence. There was plenty of noise around them, everyone talking animatedly.

"Seems like lots of folks had the same idea," Mike said once he'd decided on his breakfast.

Tommy looked around and shook his head. "I didn't think there'd be this many people havin' breakfast at this time o' the mornin'."

"Hey there, what you boys havin'?" Their waitress—Lola, according to her name badge—appeared at their table, pad in hand, pen poised.

"I'll have the country fried steak, hash browns, two eggs over easy, and biscuits and gravy," Tommy announced.

Mike had to smile at that. *Gotta love a guy with a good appetite.*

"Coffee with that?" Lola asked. Tommy gave a polite nod. She turned to Mike and gave him an appreciative smile. "What 'bout you, honey?"

"I'll have two bacon, two link sausage, two eggs over easy, grits, and whole-wheat toast. Coffee for me too." Much as Mike would've loved the biscuits and gravy, he had to watch his waistline. The camera always added ten pounds, or that was how it felt when he saw himself in the finished product. Mike wasn't a vain man, but he did have an image to keep up.

Lola nodded. "I'll be right back with your coffee." She walked off, her ass wiggling under her tight skirt. Mike leaned back and clasped his hands together on the table, regarding Tommy. The young man fingered the collar on his shirt and then rubbed the back of his neck. Mike's gaze was drawn to his blackened eye.

He pointed to it. "That's quite a shiner you got yourself there. What happened?"

Tommy glanced at the table. "I was clumsy, is all. I walked into a door in the middle of the night." He sat very still, not meeting Mike's gaze but keeping his eyes focused on the shiny metal tabletop.

Yeah, right....

"Mmm-hmm. Wanna try that again?" Mike kept his voice low. When Tommy jerked his head up to stare at him, Mike gave a half smile. "Working in a bar, I get to observe a lot of people. You learn a thing or two about body language." When Tommy swallowed, Mike softened his expression. "What really happened?"

Tommy's shoulders hunched over. "I finally came out to my folks, and it didn't go so well." He clammed up when Lola returned with the coffee, waiting until she'd walked away before he continued, his voice ragged. Mike listened in silence, relieved to notice Tommy becoming more relaxed as he got into his story. When Tommy finished, Mike let out a sigh.

Some people don't deserve to have kids.

He picked up his coffee cup and drank some of the aromatic brew before speaking. "Kid, I wish I could say that's the first time I've heard a story like yours, but unfortunately it's not. I know that's no consolation for you. I *will* tell you that it does get better."

"I keep hearin' that," Tommy said quietly, "but you know what? I don't see how." He stared gloomily into his coffee. "My own family doesn't want anythin' to do with me."

"Now come on." Mike leaned forward, elbows on the table. "You got a lot going for you. From the sound of it, this roommate of yours—Ben, is it?—has a nice family, and they've clearly taken to you. And you're gonna end up with more family than you ever thought you'd have."

"What do you mean?"

Mike smiled. "We don't get to choose our blood relatives, more's the pity. But you're gonna find there are lots of people out there who you will *call* family—gay guys, their friends and allies, *their* families...."

With all the shit that gets flung our way, we tend to stick together and support each other."

"I s'pose." Tommy sighed. "Can't be worse than the family I got now, *that's* for sure."

"And not to take anything away from what you've gone through, but you're one of the lucky ones," Mike told him.

"How'd you figure that?"

Mike pointed to the counter where a clear plastic box sat, stuffed with dollar bills and coins. "See that? It's a collection box for Lost-n-Found. They're a charity based here in Atlanta. They take care of LGBT kids that get kicked out by their families, just like you. Only, they have nowhere to go. We're talking kids that are homeless, living on the street, with no way of fending for themselves. And they're minors, for God's sake."

Tommy's eyes glistened. "Geez, when you put it like that, I *am* lucky."

Mike nodded. "See? At least you have a roof over your head." He knew Tommy was hurting, but he was a damn sight better off than a lot of kids in Atlanta. It would be all too easy to join him in a pity party, but negativity never had sat well with Mike. He'd always been a "glass half full" kinda guy.

"An' they said I'd always be welcome there." Tommy's face glowed. Mike nodded in approval, pleased that the young man was starting to see the positive side of things. It was a likable trait in a person.

Just then the food arrived. They both dug in, and conversation dried up for a while. When they slowed down and Lola had brought them more coffee, Mike noted Tommy's distant expression, the napkin he'd torn up into little pieces.

"What's wrong, Tommy?" he said softly.

Tommy pushed his plate away from him and sat back. "I was just thinkin' 'bout my schoolin'." He grew quiet for a moment, his lower lip caught in his teeth. "My major is in organic agriculture. The whole point of me doin' this is so's I can take over the farm." He looked Mike in the eye. "But if I'm not part of the family, why am I doin' it? What is the damn point of this degree?"

Mike thought for a moment. "Who pays for your schooling?"

"I'm on a full scholarship, plus there's my college fund that Momma set up."

"Okay, that's good." A scholarship pointed to Tommy being a bright student. That made things easier. "Then maybe you need to have a think about where you go from here. That might mean changing your major. Maybe there's something else you'd rather study." When Tommy's brow furrowed, Mike instinctively reached across the table and took hold of his hand. "And you don't have to start thinking right this minute, all right?"

Tommy glanced at Mike's hand covering his own and nodded, his cheeks pink.

Mike released him and sat back. "Now let's change the subject. How are you finding Atlanta?" He drank some more of the strong coffee.

Tommy chuckled. "I don't rightly know how to answer that. I've not really seen much of Atlanta."

Mike gave a theatrical gasp. "Well, if that ain't a shame. Kid, you're living in the gayest city in the South! How can you be a student here and not have sampled the gay delights of Hotlanta?"

Tommy's chuckle was music to his ears. Mike studied him for a moment, taking in his body language. Tommy had to be in his early twenties, but there was a vulnerable air about him, something that made him appear younger. Then it struck him.

Hell, this kid needed looking after. And Mike was just the man to do it.

"Tell you what. I'm working tonight and Sunday, but Monday is my day off. Why don't you spend the afternoon with me? I'll show you 'round the Ansley Mall, for one thing. We can visit some of the stores, like Brushstrokes, Boy Next Door, a few other places. Then we can have an early dinner at Cowtippers. Ever been there?"

Tommy shook his head.

"Thought that might be the case. Well, Tommy, I'm gonna show you the gay side of Atlanta." Mike was going to take Tommy under his wing and have some fun in the process. He couldn't wait to see Tommy's face when he took him into Capulets. He'd bet next month's paycheck that the kid had never seen the inside of an adult store before.

"That sounds great," Tommy said. He let out a sigh of satisfaction. "An' breakfast was great too."

"Wanna swap phone numbers?" Mike got out his phone and opened Contacts. "That way I can text you about where to meet on Monday."

"Sure." Tommy reeled off his number, and Mike programmed it in. Then he sent a text.

"There. Now you got mine too."

Tommy shifted on his bench seat, reached into his back pocket, and took out his wallet.

"Uh-uh," Mike said firmly. "This is on me."

"You sure?" Tommy paused in midaction.

"Yep." Mike pulled his wallet from his jacket pocket and counted out the correct money, plus tip, which he stuffed under his coffee cup. "And now I'm gonna go home and get some sleep. You should too."

He smiled and rose to his feet, Tommy joining him. They walked out after thanking Lola when they passed her. Outside there was still the odd noise carried on the air, as revelers went on partying. The road was busy as usual; the bars and clubs all along the street saw to that.

Tommy stopped by Mike's truck, hand outstretched. "Thank you, Mike," he said.

Mike was relieved to see he looked more relaxed than when they'd arrived. He ignored the hand and pulled Tommy into a brief but firm hug.

When he released him, he stepped back and nodded. "I'll see you on Monday, okay?"

"Yeah." Tommy gave him a warm smile before walking over to his truck. The street was humming with traffic as Mike climbed into his own truck and switched on the engine. He watched Tommy pull out of the parking lot, raising his hand to wave at Mike as he passed. Then he was gone.

Poor kid. Mike shook his head as he thought back on the way Tommy's family had treated him. The more he thought about it, the more convinced he became—Tommy needed someone to look out for him, like a big brother. Then it hit him that this was a little weird, considering how he'd undressed the young man in his head on more than one occasion. And the idea of spending an afternoon with the tall, muscled student was very pleasant indeed. It was only when he did the math in his head that he realized he had to be around the same age as Tommy's daddy.

Damn. That was *so* not a good thought.

TOMMY LOOKED around the interior of Cowtippers with interest. Most of the tables in the center of the floor were occupied, but the host led them to a booth and told them someone would be over to take their order shortly.

Tommy sat down and perused the menu. "What's good?"

"Everything. They do great burgers here." Mike grinned. "And I know how much you love a good burger."

Tommy had to laugh, seeing as that was all he ever ate at Woofs.

"Would you like something a little stronger than Cherry Coke?" Mike asked. "Say, a peach margarita?"

"Thanks for the offer, but no. I'll stick with a Coke." That glass of champagne on New Year's Eve had been the first alcohol ever to touch his lips, and it had been okay, but Tommy had yet to see what the attraction was regarding alcohol. He could still hear his granddaddy intoning something about not putting a thief in his mouth to steal his brains. And of course, Tommy was driving.

Their server appeared, and Mike ordered their drinks and two burgers with fries and fried pickles. When that was done, he leaned against the padded back of the seat and smiled. "You had a good afternoon?" His eyes twinkled.

That was all it took for Tommy's face to go from cool to scorching. He knew damn well what Mike was thinking about. "You shoulda warned me 'bout that place," he said in a low voice.

"I don't know what you mean," Mike said, eyebrows lifted. That smirk was still in evidence, however. Mike had taken him to Capulets and let him walk in first—to be confronted with a wall of sex toys. And that didn't include all the stands in the middle of the floor, containing even more sex toys. Then there were all the different kinds of lube, for God's sake. The other half of the store had been filled with DVDs, only Mike had steered him clear of those. Tommy had no argument with that. One glance at some of the covers had been enough—he hadn't known *where* to look.

And when Mike had suggested buying something for him, that had been enough for Tommy. Mike had ushered him out of there fairly quickly when Tommy hadn't been able to hide how uncomfortable the experience had made him.

Tommy had to admit, it had been a great afternoon, in spite of his embarrassment. Mike had taken him around lots of the stores at the Ansley Mall. They'd looked at underwear in Boy Next Door, Mike holding up the skimpy briefs on their little hangers and looking inquiringly at him.

More blushes.

Then they'd visited Brushstrokes, a gay bookstore, and *that* had been interesting. Mike had left him to wander through all the books. It had been fascinating. Tommy had no idea there was so much gay fiction out there. In the end Mike had had to drag him away. At least Tommy knew of its existence, and he could definitely see a return visit in the future.

Come to think of it, he now knew just how many gay businesses existed in and around Atlanta, and that had staggered him. Then there had been the sight of muscle-bound guys walking into the gym, holding hands. That was a first.

The server brought their drinks, and Tommy took a long slurp of his Coke. "Were *all* those businesses that we saw today gay businesses?"

Mike smiled. "Didn't you notice the rainbow flags on almost every door? The gay dollar contributes a helluva lot to Atlanta."

Tommy's concentration was broken by the sight of two guys who'd sat in the booth behind them, Mike's back to them. Not that seeing guys together was anything new after the afternoon he'd just spent. No, what made him stare was the way they sat with their arms around each other, kissing—and no one paid them the slightest attention. Like what they were doing was totally natural.

Then he smiled. *You dumbass—it* is *totally natural.* The thought warmed him.

"You listening to me?"

Tommy jerked his head up and stared at Mike, his face heating up. "'Scuse me?"

Mike chuckled. "Okay, where is your head at?" He shook his head. "In case you haven't noticed, our dinner has arrived." He pointed at the plate that had miraculously appeared in front of Tommy.

Shit. Tommy hastily began to dig in to his burger, trying to ignore the couple who were digging into each other. Damn, it was nice, though. They looked so lost in each other, sharing slow kisses and stroking arms and shoulders. Eating was difficult; his eyes were continually drawn to them. Mike was talking about how much power the gay population of Atlanta wielded, and Tommy was trying to listen, 'cause it was fascinating, but *damn....*

MIKE PUT down his silverware and wiped his mouth. He was dying to turn around and see precisely what had snagged Tommy's attention throughout dinner, but he had a feeling that would only serve to embarrass the young man. It sure was intriguing, though.

He'd had a great afternoon. Tommy had been relaxed, smiling and joking with him, and they'd had a lot of fun. It had been a while since Mike had chilled out with a guy. He'd been doing a lot of shoots recently, and it was great to just take a *breath* for a change. So much so that he wanted to do this again. Judging from Tommy's reaction, he didn't think the young man would mind all that much.

He got out his wallet and withdrew enough to cover the check plus tip, then finished his beer. "Shall we get out of here?" The heaviness in his stomach had nothing to do with his meal. He really didn't want this delightful day to end.

Tommy nodded, his Adam's apple bobbing.

Maybe he doesn't want it to finish either.

Mike knew he had stuff to get ready for his trip the next day. It was an early flight to NYC, and based on past experience, the shoot wouldn't be an overly long one. Still, he was sad their time together had to end.

They got to their feet, and as he edged out of the booth, Mike finally got a look at what had captured Tommy's attention. He smiled at the sight of the couple who were drinking cocktails and talking quietly with each other. *Always nice to see guys in love.* He led the way out of the restaurant and around to the parking lot, where their trucks were parked next to each other.

"So what do you—?"

The rest of his words died in his throat when Tommy grabbed him by the upper arms, pulled him close, and planted a kiss on his mouth. For a second or two, Mike was too stunned to react. Tommy's lips were soft and warm, his breath sweet. The kiss was all fire and no expertise, but it got his heart pumping all the same. Tommy let go of his tight hold and stepped back, lips parted, eyes shining.

Wow. I must still have it.

Mike pushed aside that initial thought and stared at him. "Okay," he began slowly. "Wanna tell me what brought *that* on?" For a moment his chest tightened. *Fuck—has he seen me in one of my films? Does he know what I do?* Mike was not ashamed of his career, far from it, but the thought that Tommy might know of it made his heart sink. And he didn't have a clue why.

Tommy swallowed hard. "That was my second kiss."

For a moment Mike was floored. *Second* kiss? Then Kevin was.... He stared at Tommy, his heartbeat racing as realization sank in. *Oh my God. He's a virgin.* The thought had him hot and cold, all at the same time.

Tommy gaped at him, and it suddenly occurred to Mike that he hadn't said a word in reaction. Like he knew what to say. When was the last time he'd been kissed by a twentysomething gorgeous six-foot muscled virgin?

"Okay...."

Tommy paled. "I... I'll see you, okay?"

He spun around and almost ran to his truck. Mike launched after him, but Tommy put the truck into gear and pulled out of the parking lot in an awful hurry. Mike stared after him, his head in a whirl.

Well, crap.

Chapter Ten

TOMMY SAT at the kitchen table, eating toast and drinking coffee. Ben was still asleep, making the most of the last Friday of the winter break before school started again on Monday. His parents were up and active, his daddy getting ready for work. Bethany was sitting next to Tommy, eating a bowl of cereal, a textbook propped open in front of her.

"Not at the table," Caroline admonished, arching her eyebrows when she spotted Bethany. She poured out another cup of coffee and handed it to her husband before sitting down next to him with her own.

Bethany sighed and closed the book, not without a sideways glance at her dad, who was reading his newspaper. Tommy nudged her knee with his. "You're on a break, remember? Plenty of time to hit the books next week when you're back at school."

She gave him a half smile. "You looking forward to getting back to school?"

It was Tommy's turn to sigh. "When I work out what I'm doin', sure."

Caroline paused, her coffee cup midway to her mouth. "What do you mean?"

Benson peered at Tommy over the edge of his newspaper.

"I just have some thinkin' to do, is all," Tommy said with a shrug. "'Cause I'm not sure I want to go on studyin' agriculture."

Caroline's smile was sympathetic. "Well, I can certainly understand that. Have you given any thought as to what you'd like to study? What is it that you love to do? That might be a good place to start."

"Can I butt in here?" Benson folded up his paper. "I would also add, what is gonna make you some money for a secure future? Because you have to be practical these days."

"You sure about giving up on the farming idea?" Bethany asked him.

Tommy considered the question. "To be fair, I liked workin' on the farm, but…." He smiled at them. "I liked workin' with my animals more. Lookin' after the pigs, takin' care of my horse, Titan, stuff like that."

Bethany beamed at him. "Then why not work with animals? Ben says you're a smart one. You could become a veterinarian!"

Benson was nodding. "If your grades are good enough, then maybe you should consider it. And from what you've told us already, you're on a Hope scholarship, so it's not like you're tied to a particular major. Sure, you might need some further funding, but there are other scholarships you can apply for."

"I think this sounds wonderful." Caroline rubbed her hands together. "You need to look into it, Tommy."

"But sooner rather than later," Benson added, picking up his paper once more.

Tommy nodded absently. Like he didn't have enough on his mind already.

Such as a certain bartender.

"YOU GOING out tonight?" Ben asked. "Or do you wanna stay in and have a Friday night movie? I could rustle up some popcorn, and we could veg out on the couch."

Tommy was in no mood to go out. Even though Mike had shown him lots of bars and clubs he might like to visit, Tommy wasn't sure about going to any of them. And as for going to Woofs? He could still picture that stunned expression on Mike's face.

Guess I messed that one up, huh?

"Think I'll stay in tonight."

Ben sat down next to him on the couch. "I did think you might be going to… wherever it is you go to." His eyes gleamed. "Still not gonna tell me?"

"Nope." Tommy picked up a cushion and threw it at Ben, who dodged it. "Besides, I don't think it matters anymore, 'cause I messed up." One whole week of thinking about how Mike's mouth had felt against his and Tommy'd had enough.

"Oh God, what have you done?" Ben stared at him.

"I kissed a guy, all right?" Tommy replied defensively.

Ben beamed at him. "But that's great! Isn't it?"

"Woulda been great if he'd liked it, I s'pose, but—" Tommy sighed heavily. "—I don't think that was the case."

Ben frowned. "Okay, change of plan." He got up and disappeared through the door that led to the main part of the house. Tommy grabbed the cushion he'd flung and hugged it close. He'd had such a good time on Monday, right up to the point where he'd thrown his good sense to the wind and kissed Mike. It had seemed like such a good idea at the time....

Ben crouched down next to him and held out a bottle. "Surprise!"

Tommy peered at it. "Peach schnapps? Where'd you get that?" Ben sat on the floor next to the couch and put the bottle on the little coffee table in front of it, along with a couple of shot glasses. "An' have you forgotten I don't drink?"

"It was left over from the 'rents' party," Ben explained, "and there's so much liquor upstairs, they'll never miss it."

"They will if I tell them."

Tommy gave a start at the sound of Bethany's voice. She stood at the foot of the couch, grinning and holding a third shot glass.

"I saw you take something from Dad's liquor cabinet, and I figured you were up to something."

Ben scowled. "Get lost."

Bethany's face fell, and Tommy's heart went out to her. He got on well with Bethany.

"Aw, don't be like that, Ben. She can stay, can't she?" Bethany was doing an awful good impression of a puppy dog, gazing pleadingly at her brother.

Ben rolled his eyes. "Oh, for God's sake." He speared her with an intense glance. "As long as you promise not to tell Mom or Dad."

She grinned. "If you're willing to share, my lips are sealed." She plonked herself down on the couch next to Tommy and held out her glass. "Fill 'er up."

Ben muttered under his breath but unscrewed the cap and poured her a glassful before filling his and Tommy's.

He handed Tommy the shot glass. "Here you go. And yeah, I know you don't drink, but there's a first time for everything." He winked. "And *this* is that time."

Tommy huffed in resignation and took the proffered glass, sniffing at its contents.

Ben laughed. "Oh, drink it. You're not a churchgoing choir boy anymore."

That made him chuckle. "Trust me. I was never in the choir. My singin' sounds like a cat bein' strangled." He watched Ben and Bethany toss theirs back in one gulp. *Oh, what the hell.* Tommy drank the shot in one go and then coughed when it hit the back of his throat. When he'd recovered, he licked his lips. "Hey, that's not bad." It made his belly warm.

"Kinda sweet, huh?" Ben refilled his glass and then the remaining two. "It tastes great over ice too." He leaned back against the couch, glass in hand. "So, you gonna tell me about this guy of yours?"

"You've got a guy?" Bethany bounced on her seat cushion. "Way to go, Tommy!"

"He's *not* my guy," Tommy insisted.

Ben waggled his eyebrows. "But you'd like him to be, right?" He peered at Tommy's glass and gave him a stern glance. "You're not drinking enough."

"Pushy, pushy." Tommy drank the second shot, only this time he didn't knock it back so fast. "That really is nice, y'know." Right then he was feeling warm and muzzy, and it felt good, like he was somehow disconnected from himself.

"Tell me about this guy," Bethany demanded, her eyes shining. "What's he like?"

"Well," Tommy began slowly, "he's older 'n me."

"How much older?" Ben twisted around to stare at him.

"I'm not rightly sure." Without thinking, Tommy stroked his chin. "He has a beard, an' there's some gray in it, if that helps."

"Oh my God, he's *old*!" Ben exclaimed, gaping at him. Bethany smacked him on the back of the head. "Ow!"

"You're not the one dating him, so shut up!" she said, eyes blazing.

Tommy chuckled, his head swimming just a bit. "I'm not datin' him either." He gave his head a little shake. Woo, this stuff was stronger than he'd thought.

"You may not be dating him, but you *have* kissed him," Ben said smugly.

Bethany let out a squeal. "You kissed him?"

Ben put his hands over his ears. "Geez, Beth, I think you just went ultrasonic." He grabbed the bottle and held it out to Tommy. "And *you* need some more of *this*."

"No," Tommy protested weakly, but Ben ignored him and filled his glass to the brim. Tommy stared accusingly at him. "You're tryin' t'get me drunk."

"Yeah, and by the look of things, I'm succeeding too." Ben gave a wicked chuckle. "Now drink it up."

Tommy brought the glass to his lips and drank its contents in one mouthful. Peach schnapps was definitely growing on him. He liked the way it made him feel, warm on the inside and so comfortable it was like he'd melted into the couch. He lay on his back, a cushion stuffed under his head and his socked feet on Bethany's lap. She didn't seem to mind, judging by the way she was rubbing them. *Damn, that feels good.*

He lay there enjoying the foot rub, letting the pleasurable sensations roll over and through him. "So what you wanna know about Mike?"

"Oh, his name's Mike." Ben was still sitting on the floor near his head. "Where d'you meet him?"

"At Woofs. 'S a gay sports bar. Mike works there."

"Is that where you were New Year's Eve?" Bethany asked.

Tommy nodded. "Lord, you shoulda seen 'im. He was wearin' this *teeny tiny* little leather jock strap that just about covered his dick." He was dimly aware of Bethany's muffled gasp. "An' he has these *really wide* shoulders, an' his chest is *furry*"—he grinned—"but not as furry as his butt. Oh, an' his *legs*? Oh *my*, the muscles in those thighs...." This time Tommy definitely caught Bethany's strangled giggle. "Whass'up?" He craned his neck to peer at her, but the room swam a little and he dropped back onto his cushion.

"Nothing," she insisted after clearing her throat. "So where'd this kiss happen?"

"Oh, after he took me 'round Atlanta las' Monday. We had a great time, an' then we had burgers at Cowtippers." He told them about the guys kissing behind them. "I kept thinkin', if they can kiss, why couldn't I? All I wanted was to feel those strong arms 'round me." He closed his eyes, recalling the feel of that wide chest pressed against his. "Damn, he felt good." That kiss had felt good—right up until the moment Mike had looked at him, that stunned expression so clear on his face.

"You got it bad, haven't you?" He could hear the sympathy in Bethany's voice. "What are you going to do now?"

"*Do*?" He snorted. "Girl, there ain't nothin' *to* do. Think I scared him off."

"Pffft. There'll be another one along, trust me," Ben said with a smirk.

"Ignore my brother. If you want this guy, go after him."

"An' how'd you propose I do that?" Tommy propped himself up on his elbows, trying to focus his eyes on Bethany, but they weren't cooperating. He blinked a couple of times, but she still looked a little blurry around the edges.

Bethany grinned. "Do like the girls do when they see a man they want—dress to kill. Make him notice you. Oh, and take him flowers."

Ben guffawed. "You don't take guys flowers."

Bethany gave him a superior look. "Sure you do. *Everyone* likes flowers." She turned her attention to Tommy. "When d'you plan on seeing him again?"

Tommy still wasn't sure about this, but Bethany seemed in earnest. "I *could* see him at the bar t'morrow night, I s'pose." His stomach did a little flip-flop.

"Excellent!" She glanced at Tommy's clothes. "Then I have an idea. How about Mom and I take you clothes shopping tomorrow?" Her eyes sparkled. "We'll have you looking like a million dollars. By the time you strut into that bar, Mike'll be eating out of your hand." She hugged herself, chuckling.

Tommy couldn't quite see that, but the way his head was feeling, he wasn't about to argue.

He wasn't sure about the strutting, though.

CAROLINE BEAMED at them. "Oh, I think that's a great idea! It would have to be this morning, because I'm meeting with my ladies at the club at three o'clock."

"Mom belongs to this group of ladies who do lots of charity work in Atlanta," Bethany explained to Tommy. She turned back to her mom. "We're not taking Ben with us, Mom. It's just you, me, and Tommy."

Tommy was sitting at the kitchen table, just trying to keep up. He had only the vaguest recollection of their conversation the previous night, so when Bethany had appeared next to him that morning in her pj's, as bouncy as Tigger, he figured the easiest thing was to go along with it. Still… clothes shopping? Not on his list of fun things to do on a Saturday, but Bethany was pretty determined. He wasn't quite sure what she hoped to achieve with their shopping trip. Clothes were clothes, right? They surely couldn't have the effect Bethany was anticipating… could they?

"There's just one thing," Caroline said slowly.

Both Bethany and Tommy turned to look at her. Caroline gave a little shrug.

"What do *I* know about how a young gay man should dress?"

Tommy smiled. "We dress like everyone else, ma'am." He was beginning to have a bad feeling about this.

Beside him, Bethany snorted. "Oh, puh-*lease*! Have you *seen* my brother when he goes out on the weekend?"

Caroline gave a gleeful smile. "Well, I may not have much experience in this field, but I know someone who does." She reached into her purse and pulled out her phone, her thumb sliding over the screen. Tommy nudged Bethany and gave her an inquiring look. Bethany's shrug and blank expression were no help.

"Danny? You got a minute?" Caroline listened with a grin. "Okay, I'm putting you on loudspeaker, so behave." She set the phone on the countertop.

Tommy stared at her. *Danny?*

"Honey, I *always* behave—badly!" Danny's voice echoed around the kitchen. "Now what can I do for ya?"

"Where would I take a little gay boy shopping?"

Tommy gaped and Bethany giggled. Caroline fired her a warning look.

"Well, that depends. Which little gay boy are we talking about?"

There was a pause while Caroline bit her lip. "That would be Tommy," she confessed reluctantly.

Danny's squeal was very loud. "I knew it, I *knew* it! Didn't I tell you, woman?"

Tommy listened to Danny cackling, his face hotter than hell.

"When you've quite finished gloating," Caroline enunciated patiently, "perhaps you can offer us some suggestions."

"Details, honey, I need details! Now, what are you shopping for?"

"We're going to help Tommy buy an outfit to snag his man," Bethany called out across the kitchen.

"Damn. Well, there go *my* chances." Danny sighed theatrically. "So who is this person? Tell me something about him. Where will Tommy be meeting him?"

"*Tommy* will be meetin' him at Woofs," Tommy called out. His face, neck, and ears felt impossibly hot. "An' he works behind the bar there."

"Ooh, we're talking butch crowd!" There was a pause. "Tommy? By the time I'm done with you, you'll have the *perfect* ensemble, right down to the cock ring."

Oh my God. Breathe, just breathe….

"TMI, dear, TMI," Caroline interjected when she caught sight of Tommy's open mouth. "We're talking baby steps, okay?"

"Gotcha. How about I meet y'all at Boy Next Door at Ansley Mall? That'd be a good starting place."

"You're coming too?" Caroline queried.

There was a gleeful cackle. "Honey, I wouldn't miss *this* for the world. How does eleven o'clock sound?"

"That's fine," Caroline assured him. "We'll see you there." She disconnected the call and then met Bethany and Tommy's gazes. "This could be… interesting." Her lips twitched.

That's one way of puttin' it.

CHAPTER ELEVEN

"ARE YOU sure 'bout this, Danny?" Tommy gazed at his reflection in the long mirror. "This T-shirt seems awful tight." *It damn well clings everywhere it touches.*

From behind him, Danny snickered. "Sweetcheeks, a T-shirt should be tight enough to show off *everything*—including your pulse." He peered over Tommy's shoulder, his gaze drifting lower. Danny grinned. "And those jeans—per-fection!"

Caroline paused in her perusal of shirts to nod her agreement. Bethany gave him the thumbs-up.

Tommy wasn't convinced. "I don't know 'bout that. They're so tight, I don't know how people are meant to walk in 'em."

Danny waved his hand. "Pfft. Honey, I have jeans that are so tight, when I wear them? You can tell I'm not Jewish." He winked and patted Tommy on the ass before wandering over to a display of briefs and jockstraps.

At least he looks a little less flamboyant today. Danny was dressed in jeans and a sweater—a fuchsia sweater.

Tommy groaned. "An' no more underwear! You've already picked out four pairs of briefs." Not to mention a jockstrap or two. *Why is it gay men all seem to like underwear that leaves little to the imagination?*

Danny stood still, one manicured hand resting on his hip. "You can *never* have enough underwear." He pouted. "And I can't believe you said no when I asked you to model them for me." There was a wicked gleam in his eyes. "There *is* a fitting room, after all."

"Danny." The warning tone in Caroline's voice was unmistakable. "Down, boy."

He huffed. "Spoilsport."

Caroline smiled sweetly. "Bite me, dear."

She went back to searching through the rack of shirts. Bethany stood next to her, and Tommy could tell from the shaking of her shoulders that she was laughing quietly.

Danny folded his arms, studying Tommy through narrowed eyes. "Now what you *really* need to set off the whole ensemble is a black leather jacket."

"Ooh yeah!" Bethany nodded enthusiastically.

"But I don't *have* a black leather jacket," Tommy explained patiently. "I have a jean jacket, an' that'll do." He was beginning to wonder what this shopping trip was gonna cost him. He had money from Christmas, given to him by various relatives who'd figured he'd have more need of cash as a student, but still….

Danny rolled his eyes and sighed. "We are talking Gay 101 here. *Every* gay boy needs a black leather jacket. Maybe a pair of tight leather pants too." His eyes sparkled. "And there's really only one place to go—Atlanta Leather."

"Say what?" This was getting out of control. *Leather pants?*

"Danny's right," Caroline announced emphatically. "So give me that basket, I'll go pay for these things, and then we can go find you a leather jacket." She stretched out her hand for the basket.

Tommy shook his head. "Sorry, ma'am, but I can't let you do that."

Caroline arched her eyebrows for a moment. "Last time I checked, I was over twenty-one, an adult, and could do whatever I wanted." Then her expression softened. "Tommy, let me do this, please? Think of it as a belated Christmas present." She winked. "Besides, I'm good for it."

He had no doubt about that. Their house, Benson's career, never mind membership for all the family at the Piedmont Driving Club….

"And before you get any ideas, that Christmas present? Also includes a leather jacket."

Damn, but the woman was stubborn.

"Yes, ma'am," he said resignedly as he handed over his basket of items. He knew better than to fight a losing battle.

TOMMY FINISHED dressing and stared at his reflection. He was so nervous, his knees were shaking.

Can I do this?

"I think you look great," Bethany said from behind him, standing in the doorway to Ben's bedroom. "Mike's gonna be knocked out."

"Mmm, still not sure 'bout this." His stomach was in knots.

Bethany came into the room and sat on the edge of the bed. "Tommy, if you really want this guy, then you need to make up your mind to go get him." She smiled. "Women have to do this all the time." Those brown eyes, so like her brother's, sparkled. "If you intend going fishing, then you need the right bait."

But what exactly am I fishing for?

The memory of that warm mouth, that firm chest, was enough to get his heart pumping. Yeah, he had a good idea what he was after, even if the very thought sent shivers running through him.

"Let Mom and Ben get a look at you, 'cause you know they're just dying out there, waiting to see what you look like in all your finery," she said with a grin. "'Cause you are surely gonna break hearts tonight." Her admiring glances and words were doing a lot for his morale.

Tommy followed her out of the bedroom to where Caroline and Ben were talking, leaning back against the couch. Caroline's eyes widened, and she gave him a huge smile.

"My, look at you. Why, I'd hardly believe it's the same young man I was talking to this morning in my kitchen. Tommy—" She let out a contented sigh. "—you look great," she said simply. Then she glanced at her watch. "And now that I've seen you, I'll go spend some time with my husband. Apparently he's feeling neglected, poor thing." With one last grin, she left them standing in the small apartment.

Ben gave a long whistle. "The way you look, you could ask for anything you wanted, and *anyone* would give it to you." He stepped closer, walking around Tommy slowly and then coming to stand in front of him. "You worked out what you're gonna say to Mike yet?"

Tommy shook his head. "I'm kinda playin' this by ear."

Ben tilted his head. "Well, what is it you want?"

His mouth was suddenly moist, and his breathing quickened. "Him."

Ben's eyes glittered. "Then make sure he knows that."

Bethany nodded. "If you don't ask, you don't get." She flashed him a wide grin. "So go get 'im, Tommy."

Ben chuckled.

Tommy took a deep breath and nodded.

Time to lay my cards on the table.

SATURDAY NIGHT was looking to be as busy as usual. It was ten fifteen and the bar was full.

Except there was no sign of Tommy. The sight of that empty stool made Mike's chest tighten.

"And I'm *still* not talking to you, bitch," Kevin grumbled, collecting glasses from the bar and handing them to Mitch, who was working as barback.

In spite of his apprehension, Mike had to laugh. "What's your problem?"

Patrick chuckled. "Oh, what you gone and done now, Mike?" He handed his customer his change and then turned to watch the two of them.

"It's not so much what he's *done*, as what he didn't do." Kevin looked for all the world like a sulky teenager. He'd been ignoring Mike all evening, which was fine by Mike. He was used to Kevin's moods after working with him for so long. Now that Mike thought about it, Kevin had been in a similar mood the last three nights they'd worked together. Mike had thought nothing of it at the time. There'd been a couple of days in New York in between, and he'd had other stuff on his mind.

Like a tall hunk with reddish-brown hair and beautiful green eyes.

Mike threw down the cloth he'd been using to wipe down the bar and beckoned to Kevin. "Okay, Princess, I'll bite. What haven't I done?"

Kevin huffed. "Not one word. Not a fucking word has passed your lips about New Year's Eve." He glanced at Patrick. "Has he told *you* what happened with Tommy? No?" Kevin smiled smugly. "So it's not just me."

"What are you talking about?" Patrick looked plain puzzled.

Shit. Mike should've remembered what a nosy bunch of queens he worked with. "What makes you think anything happened?"

Kevin grinned. "'Cause you've been too damn quiet all week, that's what." He folded his arms across that wide chest. "So?" That grin widened. "C'mon, Mike, give."

Oh, for fuck's sake.... "I took him for breakfast, okay? Then we met on Monday afternoon and I took him around Ansley Mall. And then we had dinner." He smiled. "Happy now?"

Kevin stared at him. "That was it?"

Mike sighed. "Except for the part where he kissed me, yeah, that was it." He groaned inwardly when Kevin's face lit up. "But it was one kiss, and then he left." *Ran away* might have been a more accurate description, but Mike wasn't about to share that much. He still felt he could've handled the situation better.

"You didn't try to tap that sweet ass? You're slipping, Mike. Now if he'd shown an interest in me...." Kevin leered and rubbed his crotch.

"He's just a kid," Mike protested.

Patrick laughed. "Yeah, like we're buying that. He's twenty-one, Mike. You've fucked twinks younger 'n him."

"For fuck's sake, I got *shoes* older than him!" Mike didn't want to get into this. Yeah, he had the hots for Tommy, but that didn't mean he was going to act on it.

"Oh. My. Fucking. God." Patrick's voice was hushed. "Would you look at that."

"What're you...." Kevin's voice trailed off. "Oh *my*." He stared at the far end of the bar.

Mike shook his head. "What the hell are you two going on about?" He caught sight of Tommy's head above some of the customers, and relief flooded through him. "I'd wondered if he was go—" The words died in his throat as Tommy came around the bar. "Dear Lord," he said weakly. Tommy was dressed in a pair of black leather pants that fitted him like a second skin, a white athletic shirt that clung to that stunning torso—and it *was* stunning; Mike could see every inch of it—and a black leather jacket that finished off the whole look beautifully.

Mike could have sworn that every head in the place turned in Tommy's direction. Not that he blamed them one little bit. The kid was sex on a stick. It was like everything was happening in slow motion: the way Tommy moved, slow and graceful; the slow roll of his hips as he walked; his arms swinging at his sides, hand holding a bunch of flowers....

Wait—*flowers*?

Tommy perched on his stool and looked Mike in the eye. "Hey."

There was that gorgeous shy smile.

Kevin gave Mike a hard shove and propelled him forward. Mike glared at him and then walked slowly across to where Tommy sat.

"Hey." *Fuck, he looks amazing.* Mike was trying not to stare, but *dear God*, Tommy was just stunning.

Tommy placed the flowers on the bar. "The usual, please, Mike."

He nodded and picked up a glass. "You eating?"

Tommy shook his head. "That's kinda why I'm here." He inclined his head toward the flowers. He swallowed and then lifted his chin to meet Mike's eyes. "Those are for you."

"Me?"

TOMMY LIKED that dazed look on Mike. Damned if Bethany hadn't been right; the flowers had been a good idea. Mike picked up the bunch of mixed flowers, gazing at the red roses, pink carnations, white chrysanthemums, huckleberry, and lemon leaf.

"I can't recall the last time someone gave me flowers," Mike admitted, smiling. He glanced once more at the bouquet, fingering the silky rose petals. "These are beautiful. Thank you." He lifted his chin and regarded Tommy. "To what do I owe the pleasure?" He grinned, his eyes traveling up and down Tommy's body. "'Cause I have to say here, looking at you surely is a pleasure." His lips parted, and those blue eyes locked on to Tommy's.

Oh hell. That sent a tingle down his spine.

Tommy breathed deeply. "I wanted to ask if you'd like to have breakfast with me when you're done here."

Mike's smile sent warmth spreading throughout his body.

"I'd like that. I'll be through here about one, one thirty. That all right?"

Tommy nodded, trying not to let his relief show. "That's fine. I'll just be right here, drinkin' my Cherry Coke." He grinned. Now that part was over with, he could relax a little.

Until breakfast time at least.

"Well, if that's all, I'd better get on with my work before Kevin starts bitching." Mike winked. He picked up the flowers. "I'll stick these somewhere safe 'til I'm finished." Mike gave Tommy one last lingering glance and then went to serve some customers.

Tommy spent the rest of the night sipping Coke and watching Mike, who in turn was watching him. Tommy'd have that prickly feeling at the back of his neck, and when he looked up, sure enough, there was Mike, serving customers, chatting with Kevin or doing whatever, his eyes fixed on Tommy or sneaking a glance in his direction.

And he wasn't the only one. Guys all over the bar kept staring at him, some smiling, others leering. It was downright creepy. He tried to ignore them and kept his focus on Mike. He loved watching those muscles in Mike's arms bulge when he strained them. He loved listening to him chat with the customers, laughing and joking around with them. But most of all? He loved it when Mike would turn and look at him, that measured gaze taking Tommy in from head to foot.

Part of him was relieved his change of clothes had had the desired effect, but that careful scrutiny was having another effect entirely.

It made his heart race faster and his breathing more rapid.

It made Tommy's dick hard as nails.

By two fifteen they were sitting in the American Diner, having just finished eating. Mike had been very complimentary about Tommy's clothes, and Tommy had shared the whole shopping experience with him.

"Danny sounds like he's a hoot," Mike said, chuckling. "He didn't really ask to watch you try on underwear, did he?"

Tommy nodded slowly. "An' I swear, he'd have gone into that changin' room with me at Atlanta Leather if Bethany hadn't said somethin' to her mom." He snickered. "You shoulda seen the look she gave him." He pushed his empty plate to one side and finished his coffee.

"You about done?" Mike asked him.

Tommy dipped his chin. Now that the meal was over, it was crunch time. Just the thought of what he was about to lay on Mike had his belly flip-flopping again. He'd rehearsed the words in his head over and over, but now that the moment had actually arrived, damn it, he had butterflies.

He watched Mike pull out his wallet and stopped him. "This was *my* idea, remember? You're my guest."

"You sure?"

"Uh-huh." Tommy took out enough bills to cover everything and then rose to his feet. He couldn't do it in the diner. There were far too many people around, for one thing, and for another, heads kept turning in his direction—male *and* female. It was driving him crazy. "Let's get outta here, okay?" He led the way out onto Cheshire Bridge, the customary persistent hum of traffic still in evidence. Mike followed him, putting on his own leather jacket over his black wifebeater and jeans.

Tommy got as far as his truck and then turned around to face Mike, almost stumbling into him, he was walking so close behind.

"That was nice," Mike said in a low voice. "But I've been wondering if maybe you had an ulterior motive for asking me to breakfast." He grinned. "Not that I'm complaining. I had a great view while I ate." His eyes shone, the streetlights catching in them.

Tommy's heart was pounding in his ears, loud and strong. "Actually, there was. I… I had somethin' I wanted to ask you."

"Oh?" Mike arched his eyebrows. "Now you got me all curious."

He fell silent, clearly waiting for Tommy to speak, except Tommy's throat had seized up. All the muscles in his belly were twitching, and his mouth was dry as a bone. Mike's expression grew sympathetic.

"Hey," he said softly. "Whatever it is, it can't be all that bad. Just spit it out."

Tell him. Just… tell him.

"I…." Tommy swallowed. "I want you to…."

Mike stared at him, head cocked slightly.

"I want you to…."

Mike placed his hand on Tommy's shoulder, the weight of it both comforting and yet not, all at the same time. "Tommy, it's okay. Just say it."

His voice had a gentle quality to it that soothed Tommy's nerves.

Tommy drew in a deep breath and met Mike's gaze head on.

"I want you to be my first."

CHAPTER TWELVE

I SURE didn't see that *coming.*

Mike stared at Tommy's earnest expression, those green eyes focused on him. He did his best not to let his own feelings of surprise show through. This was obviously important to Tommy.

"Wow," he said at last. "I don't know what to say. I mean, I'm flattered, but…."

Tommy's face fell. "You don't want me." His chin trembled.

Fuck.

"Wait," Mike said quickly, "let me finish, okay?" *Christ, I'm fucking this up again.*

Tommy stilled, his chest rising and falling rapidly, his gaze unfaltering.

Mike took a second or two to collect his thoughts. Sure, he was flattered, but at the back of his mind was this niggling little voice that wouldn't be silenced. He hoped to God it was wrong.

"Are you sure you shouldn't be looking for someone who's nearer to your age?"

Tommy's eyes widened. "No, that's not what I want." He swallowed. "I want you."

There was nothing for it but to ask. "Why me, Tommy?" Mike awaited his response, his stomach roiling. He had a sinking feeling he knew what lay behind the unusual request. *He's seen me. He knows I do porn. Why else would he be asking me?* The number of times he'd seen comments on his Facebook posts: *I want u to fuck me*; *Want that cock*; *Want you*; *Can we fuck?* It was all part and parcel of the industry, of course, but for some reason he hadn't expected something like that from Tommy. There was an innocent air about him, that vulnerability Mike had noted before.

Tommy seemed genuinely surprised. "Have you looked in a mirror lately, Mike? You're sexier 'n hell."

"Well, when you put it like that," Mike joked. He was relieved when Tommy laughed.

"Yeah, but that's not the only reason."

That earnest expression was back. Tommy's blush did little to alleviate Mike's fears.

"If I'm bein' honest? I trust you... I trust you to make it good for me."

Mike was stunned into silence.

Tommy plunged forward. "See, I feel safe with you. I know you'd take care of me, that you'd...." The blush deepened. "Hell, I'm sayin' this all wrong."

"No." Mike squeezed his shoulder. "Those are good reasons." Probably the best reasons Tommy could've given. And now that his panic had subsided, Mike let himself think about the situation. A gorgeous young man was offering Mike his virginity. A gorgeous young man that Mike had fantasized about, for God's sake.

A gorgeous young man who had to be at least twenty years his junior.

That made him stop in his tracks. This was no model on a shoot. This was a beautiful young guy who wanted his first sexual experience to be with someone who wouldn't rush him, wouldn't hurt him.... For all his years in the industry, Mike had never had a virgin before, and he wasn't sure how he felt about that. Apprehension and excitement warred within him.

Tommy was still standing there, watching him... waiting.

"Can I think about it?" When Tommy drew in a deep breath, Mike moved that little bit closer. "I'm not saying no, Tommy, okay? I really want to think about this."

Tommy nodded slowly. "That's okay, I guess." A hesitant smile curved his lips, and he breathed more easily. "Sure. Take your time. It's not like I'm goin' anywhere."

Mike smiled and impulsively drew him into a hug. Tommy stiffened for a second and then relaxed into it, his arms coming up around Mike's back. Mike moved his head, and suddenly Tommy's sweet face was *right there*. He could feel Tommy's breath fanning his cheek.

And Mike couldn't resist. Slowly he brought his mouth to Tommy's and kissed him, just the lightest brush of lips, before he brought his hands up to cup Tommy's head and deepened the kiss, keeping it chaste. Two mouths met fully, lips pressed together. Tommy's eyes were closed, and from behind those soft lips came the faintest whimper.

Then Mike released him and stepped back, his heartbeat racing. Tommy slowly opened his eyes and stared at Mike.

Mike grinned. "*Now* you've been kissed."

Tommy looked plain dazed. "Wow." He touched his lips with his fingertips and smiled. "I sure have."

"Now go home and get some sleep. You have school this week, right?"

Tommy nodded.

"Okay, then I'll talk to you in a few days. Don't be thinking about this all the time, y'hear? You need to concentrate on your studies."

"Okay, Mike." Tommy straightened, pushing his shoulders back. "An' thank you."

"For what?"

Tommy smiled once more. "For not givin' me the brush-off right away. For takin' me seriously."

Mike couldn't help himself. He leaned forward and kissed Tommy's cheek. "I meant every word. I *will* think about it." Then he grinned, grabbed Tommy by the arms, and spun him around to face his truck. "Now git." He swatted Tommy on that firm ass.

Tommy's laughter rang out as he got into his truck. He started the engine and pulled out of the lot, giving Mike a wave of his hand when he passed him. For the second time in a week, Mike watched him disappear from view. He got into his own truck and sat there for a moment, hands resting on the steering wheel.

I need some advice here.

MIKE WAITED until it was just the three of them. Don and Mitch had already gone, as they'd arrived first that Sunday afternoon, leaving him, Kevin, and Patrick to clear up once the last customers had departed. Patrick shut and bolted the door while Kevin did a last minute wipe down of the bar and tables.

"Can we talk?" he asked them. He'd spent all day thinking about Tommy's request, and yet he was no nearer to knowing what to do about it.

Kevin threw the cloth into the sink. "Sure. I was gonna talk to you anyway. You've been a bit distracted tonight." He came around the bar and sat on a stool. Mike joined him, Patrick not far behind.

Mike came straight to the point and told them about the conversation at the diner. They listened in silence until he was finished. Before he could ask their opinion, Kevin grinned. "You lucky dog. Talk about being handed it on a plate."

"This doesn't make you uncomfortable?" Mike frowned. *Is it just me?*

"No, but clearly something about it makes *you* feel that way," Patrick said, folding his arms across his broad chest. "Wanna share?"

Mike sighed. "I must be the same age or near enough to Tommy's dad. Don't you think it's odd him asking an older guy to fuck him for the first time?"

Patrick shook his head, smiling. "Mikey, this has been happening since ancient Greece. Y'know, older guys showing the younger ones the ropes? Tommy is probably just thinking that you're experienced. From what you've said, he has no idea you do porn, so he has no way of knowing you're the perfect person for this." He arched his eyebrows. "After all, if anyone knows what he's doing, it's you."

Kevin nodded in agreement. "Patrick's right. I wish I'd had an older guy for my first time." He grimaced. "It was painful, messy, and a helluva disappointment. Not to mention rushed." There was a distant look in his eyes.

"You can make it really good for Tommy. Just make sure you take your time," Patrick advised.

Mike considered their words. He couldn't deny they made a lot of sense, but as for taking his time, the situation wasn't ideal. Tommy was at school during the week, and he worked the three weekend nights.

Kevin gave him a wide smile. "How about next Saturday, we get someone in to cover for you? We do it when you're filming somewhere, so it's not like it's an unheard-of occurrence."

"Yeah, I like it." Patrick was nodding enthusiastically. "That way, you can plan something nice. Y'know, get Tommy 'round to your place, make him some dinner…." His eyes gleamed mischievously. "Of course we'd want to hear all the gory details on Sunday."

Kevin licked his lips. "What he said."

Mike snorted. "I thought there'd have to be a catch somewhere." He shook his head, chuckling. "Well, you can both fuck off. Whatever happens, it's staying between me and Tommy."

Kevin stared at Patrick, eyes wide in mock horror. "And after we offer to give him a day off too." He sighed heavily but then nodded at Mike. "Seriously, though, I think it's a great idea. Think of it like you're planning one of your scenes."

Mike liked that idea, liked it a lot. He thought back to his first sexual experiences. Yeah, there was a lot to be said for being with someone who knew what they were doing. And now he'd had a chance to think about it, the idea of being Tommy's first was turning him on.

"Thanks, guys," he said sincerely. "Think I'll do just that."

He was going to make Tommy's first time with a guy as pleasurable as he could.

TOMMY READ through the information on his laptop screen and made some notes. The notion of studying veterinary science was looking more and more promising. He wouldn't have to change the subjects he was already studying for his bachelor's. The only one he might need to take on was physics. But so far, the list of things in his favor was looking good. His GPA was more than adequate. The College of Veterinary Medicine required letters of recommendation, but that was doable. His farm experience would certainly help him get through the selection process. The only thing that made him stop for a moment was the need to have 250 hours of veterinary experience. His work on the farm only counted as animal experience. For it to count, he'd have needed to be working under a veterinarian. Then he thought about it some more.

How many years have I been workin' the farm and helped out Doc Lewis when he's attended foalings, problems with the cattle, pigs, dogs…? That sure would add up to a helluva lot of hours. And Doc Lewis might be prepared to write him a letter too.

He couldn't help the rush of excitement that coursed through him. It would mean more years of studying, but he was prepared for that, especially if it meant he got to do something he really wanted.

"You look happier." Ben came into his room and handed him a mug of coffee. "I figured you needed a break. You've been working since you got back from your last class."

Tommy took the coffee with a grateful smile. "Yeah, well, workin' keeps my mind off stuff." He'd spent the last three evenings with his nose buried in his books.

Ben's expression was sympathetic. "I s'pose. You've not had a great time of it lately, what with your parents being such assholes."

A hot flush of guilt crept up his neck and stole over his cheeks. While it was true he still couldn't believe his family could act like that, it wasn't what was at the forefront of his mind. That position was reserved for Mike. He tried not to keep looking at his phone, willing it to ring, but it was tough. He wanted to know what Mike was thinking. *If* he was thinking.

"I take it Mike hasn't called yet." Ben was watching him, leaning against the wall, coffee mug in hand.

"Not yet, no." He hadn't wanted to tell Ben what he'd asked of Mike, but it seemed mean considering all the trouble Caroline, Bethany, and Ben had gone to. And besides, he might need Ben's help if Mike....

His phone rang. Tommy peered at the screen and caught his breath. Mike.

"Well, answer it," Ben said with a smirk.

Tommy glanced up at him. "Can... can I have some privacy, please?"

Ben's eyes widened. "It's him, isn't it?" When Tommy nodded, Ben grinned. "I'll be in my room. Come find me when you're done. I wanna hear all about it." And with that he hurriedly left the room, closing the door behind him.

Tommy clicked on Answer. "Hey."

"I was beginning to think you didn't want to talk to me." Mike sounded amused.

"No, no, I was talkin' to Ben," Tommy explained rapidly. "How're you?" He groaned inwardly at his attempts at conversation, but his nerves had got the better of him.

"I'm fine, thank you for asking." Mike sounded pleased. "Okay, I'm sure you want to know what my decision is."

Oh shit. "Okay," he said slowly, drawing out the syllables.

"Saturday evening. My house. Dinner."

There was a husky quality to Mike's voice that went straight to Tommy's dick.

"I'll text you the address. Arrive sixish. That sound good?"

"Yeah." The word came out as a croak.

"Good. Then I'll see you Saturday." There was a pause. "Oh, and, Tommy? Plan on staying the night." Then the call disconnected.

Tommy's room was suddenly very quiet.

He stared at the phone. *Did he just say what I* think *he said?* Okay, so Mike hadn't come right out and said it, but Tommy'd have to be an idiot to not get the message.

Oh. My. Lord. Butterflies had invaded his stomach and were tramping all over it with little tiny boots. His heart was clearly trying to see just how hard it could pound before it burst inside his chest. His skin tingled everywhere, and as for his dick? No wonder he felt light-headed.

Tommy got up from his seat at the desk, exited his room, and went next door into Ben's. His roommate was lying on his bed, eyes closed, earphones plugged into his iPhone. Judging from the way his hips were moving, the music had a good rhythm to it. Not that Tommy had expected to find Ben studying. He'd heard Ben's daddy talking about Ben's grades.

Tommy touched Ben lightly on the arm. Ben gave a start and opened his eyes. He pulled the earphones free and sat up in a hurry.

"Well?"

Tommy sat down on the bed next to him, hands clasped together between his knees, leaning forward. "I'm invited to dinner on Saturday. An' he wants me to stay the night."

Ben let out a loud whoop. "Hoo boy! Tommy's gonna finally lose his cherry!" His face was contorted with glee.

Tommy whacked him on the arm. "Will you just hush?" There were two other bedrooms in their suite in the dorm, and he didn't really want their occupants knowing his private business.

Ben calmed pretty quick. "Okay, we need to talk." He pulled open a drawer beside his bed, rummaged around in it, and then threw something at Tommy, which landed at his feet with a thump.

Tommy glanced down, and immediately his face grew hot. "Just how many condoms do you think I'm gonna need?" Six or seven foil packets lay on the rug in front of him, along with a bottle of…. He picked it up and examined it, his ears hotter than ever.

"That hasn't been opened," Ben said. "And believe me, you're gonna need it. My advice to anyone having sex for the first time is always, 'Lube, lube, and more lube.'" He cackled. "A gay boy's best friend. And as for how many condoms you'll need, I'm just telling you to be prepared, is all."

Tommy stuffed the condoms into his jeans pocket. The lube was another story.

"And there's something else we need to talk about," Ben added, his expression more serious. "You need to go to the drugstore and buy yourself an enema kit."

"Say what?"

He became very still. Ben nodded, and Tommy swallowed.

"I really need one?"

"What if Mike wants to stick his tongue up your ass?"

Tommy gaped. "Why in *hell* would he wanna do that?"

Ben sighed. "I keep forgetting, you don't watch porn."

Tommy snorted. "Well, if *that's* what happens in porn, I don't *wanna* watch, no, sir!"

There was suddenly a knowing look on Ben's face. "Give it time," he said with a smile.

This was getting a little too real. "Seriously, Ben?"

Ben gave him a sympathetic glance. "Yeah, seriously." He hesitated. "You want me to come with you to the drugstore?"

Tommy thought about it. "No," he said after a moment. "If I'm old enough to have sex, then I guess I'm old enough to suck it up an' go get it myself."

Ben nodded in approval. "The important thing is to make sure you're squeaky clean—inside *and* out."

Tommy swallowed again, hard, and Ben patted his knee.

"It's gonna be fine. There's always a first time. Besides, you may not even need the condoms, but like I said, it pays to be prepared. Never assume your date is gonna have them—you have to take responsibility for *your* body. And if he does want to fuck, you make sure one—or both—of you is wearing one. You got that?"

Tommy had to smile at that. "It's okay. I had the 'putting the condom on the banana' class in high school too." Human Development classes had *really* gotten interesting at that point.

"One final piece of advice?" Ben smiled. "Enjoy it. Remember, it's supposed to be fun."

"Was your first time fun?" Tommy wanted to know.

Ben chuckled. "We were both virgins, we didn't have a clue, and yeah, it was fucking hilarious. At least Mike knows what he's doing. Well, he should, given his age." He winked. "You might like to find that out, once and for all, this weekend. Consider it homework."

Tommy had the impression he'd have far more important things on his mind.

CHAPTER THIRTEEN

MIKE TOOK a last walk through the house, checking everywhere was clean and tidy. The meal was in the slow cooker, and the potatoes au gratin were ready to shove into the oven. All that was left was to steam the broccoli and warm the bread through. The round glass table in his dining room was set, silverware and wineglasses gleaming, and the chairs had clean cotton covers over them. In the bedroom, he'd put fresh white sheets on the bed, and a white throw was on top of the ottoman. The house positively sparkled.

He glanced at his watch. Tommy should be arriving any minute. Mike was amazed to find he was nervous. He thought back. When was the last time he'd had someone to the house? Not since Dirk, that was for sure.

He felt the usual twist in his gut; Dirk had been pretty special. No, more than that—Mike had really thought he'd found a life partner. When he'd discovered how Dirk had been keeping his feelings quiet about Mike's career, it had been a real blow.

Sunday night, Kevin had asked, quite casually, if Mike intended to let Tommy know about the porn. His first reaction had been that Tommy didn't need to know. They were only gonna have sex, for Christ's sake. It wasn't as if Mike was proposing. Kevin had pursed his lips, making it clear he thought Mike was making a mistake. Mike shook his head at the recollection. Kevin could be such a queen.

The doorbell rang, and Mike almost jumped out of his skin.

Fuck. I need to calm down.

He walked into the hallway and opened the front door. Tommy stood on the step, dressed in the same jeans he'd worn on New Year's, a white shirt, and the black leather jacket. Mike was pleased he hadn't gotten rid of the scruff on his jawline. It made Tommy look *so* sexy.

"Come on in."

He stepped to one side to let Tommy enter. Tommy glanced around him, one hand rubbing against his jeans-clad thigh, the other clasping an overnight bag. Mike held out a hand.

"Give me your jacket and I'll hang it up for you in the hall closet." When Tommy dropped the bag to the floor to remove his jacket, Mike gestured to it. "Shall I take this from you and put it in my room?"

Tommy blinked. "Uh… sure." He nibbled at his lower lip, handing Mike both his jacket and the bag.

Mike pointed to the living room. "Have a seat, and when I come back, I'll get you a drink, okay?"

Tommy nodded and entered the room. Mike put the jacket on a hanger in the small closet and then hurried into the bedroom, where he placed the bag on the chair at the foot of the bed. When he returned to the living room, Tommy was gazing at the fireplace from his seat on the couch.

"D'you use it?"

Mike nodded. "The house was built in the forties, and it stays pretty warm throughout winter. But I do love a good fire on a cold night."

Tommy smiled. "Always did love a fire." He sniffed the air. "Something sure smells good."

"We're having coq au vin for dinner, so I hope you like chicken."

Tommy's eyes lit up, which Mike took for a yes.

"I have some red wine opened in the kitchen. Would you like a glass before dinner? Or do you still not drink?"

Tommy chuckled. "I kinda fell off that bandwagon the Friday before I asked you to have breakfast with me."

Mike widened his eyes, and Tommy flushed.

"Ben—my roommate—and his sister got me drinkin' peach schnapps."

That flush crept higher, to the tips of his ears, and Mike thought it adorable.

"Let's just say my tongue gets loose when I drink an' leave it at that."

Mike laughed. "I bet you were cute when you were drunk."

Tommy stared at him.

"What?"

Tommy smiled. "Hell, only my momma's ever called me cute. Oh, an' Kevin at Woofs."

Then that shy smile faltered, and Mike didn't need to guess why. The memory of what had taken place over the winter break must've still been pretty raw.

He clapped his hands together. "So is that a yes on the wine?"

"Sure." Tommy shrugged. "I don't know a lot about wine."

"You'll like this." Mike walked out of the living room into the kitchen, where the bottle of merlot stood on the countertop. He poured out two glasses and carried them through into the living room.

Tommy took a glass and sipped from it. He gave an appreciative nod. "Tastes good." He put the glass down on the tiny square table in from of him and drew in a deep breath.

Mike sat next to him. "You okay?" He set down his own glass and relaxed against the cushions, hoping Tommy would follow suit.

Tommy scraped his hand through his short hair and then rested his elbows on his knees, leaning forward. "This is harder than I thought it'd be," he said quietly. He laced his fingers together, eyes focused on the woven rug beneath the table.

Shit. Mike leaned over and stroked Tommy's back, keeping the movement slow. "You change your mind?" Not that Mike gave a flying fuck if he had. What was more important was that Tommy was okay.

Tommy inclined his head, his eyes large and round. "This... this is a huge deal for me, Mike." A tremor rippled through him.

Mike kept up the slow rubbing. "Listen, we don't have to do anything. You're here to have dinner, right?" He let his fingers travel up and down Tommy's spine, trying to ease the tension.

Tommy shook his head. "I... I want this, okay? Really, I do. It's just that—" He inhaled deeply. "—all my life my parents taught me that sex only had one place, and that was in marriage. That sex outside of marriage was plain wrong. I listened in church when they preached against immorality an' the 'pleasures of the flesh.'"

Mike listened in silence. He'd already worked out what it must've been like, growing up in Tommy's family.

"Then I get to college, an' everything changes." Tommy looked him in the eye. "I don't know if I can make you understand, but I'll try. It's like...." He closed his eyes. "Everything my life was based upon— the rules, the teachin's, how people are s'posed to behave—it all got stripped away, little by little." Tommy opened his eyes and looked at Mike. "I've spent more 'n a year an' a half in the real world, an' it's *so* different, Mike. I watch television, for one thing."

Mike stared at him. "You didn't watch TV at home?"

Tommy smiled. "Sure, we had one, but my parents got to choose what we watched. An' there was no cable. But the stuff I see on TV is...."

He shook his head once more, his expression bewildered. Then his eyes widened. "An' then there's sex. Mike, people're havin' sex *everywhere!*"

Mike laughed. "Well, yeah." He was beginning to see Tommy clearly for the first time, a young man who was slowly but surely breaking down all the barriers that had surrounded him all his life. All the structure he'd known had been torn away from him. Being away from his parents for the first time had to have been a real culture shock.

"Asking you to…." Tommy blushed furiously. "I've never been so forward in my life. I just knew I wanted you, wanted you so bad that you were all I could think about." He glanced at Mike through long dark brown lashes. "When you said you wanted to think about it, I was sure you were gonna say no."

Mike sighed. "Look at it from my point of view. Suddenly there's this gorgeous young man taking an interest in me."

When Tommy gaped at him, Mike had to smile.

"You know how you laughed when I asked why you'd picked me and you said, 'Have you seen yourself in a mirror?' Well, I could say the same thing to you." When Tommy tilted his head, Mike continued. "You have no idea how beautiful you were, standing there in that parking lot, offering me what amounted to a very appealing gift." He reached out and stroked Tommy's cheek. "One that I'd be a fool to turn down." There was a look of wide-eyed innocence about him that really got to Mike.

Before Tommy could say another word, Mike cupped his face and drew him closer, until their mouths were almost touching. Tommy shivered, but he said nothing. Mike inhaled, taking Tommy's warm, clean scent into his nostrils.

"Too much talking," he whispered, and then his lips met Tommy's, soft and pliant. Mike slid his tongue between Tommy's lips and explored his mouth as Tommy remained still. There was a fluttery feeling in his belly at that first taste of Tommy.

Then Tommy relaxed, hands tentatively coming to rest on Mike's biceps, while those soft lips were feeding him the sweetest little noises, ones that spoke of need and desire. Mike stroked his tongue in and out of that hot mouth, his fingertips caressing Tommy's cheek and chin. Tommy closed his eyes, and Mike eased him down onto his back on the couch, his own body coming to rest on top of that firm, muscled flesh. Tommy spread, one foot on the floor, his arms slipping around Mike, hands splayed across his back. Mike forced himself to lie still, concentrating on the mouth that pushed low moans into his. Tommy cupped the back of Mike's head and deepened the kiss, his tongue flicking over Mike's, hesitant at first but growing more confident. He opened his eyes to gaze up at Mike, and their lips parted. Tommy's breathing was shallow, his chest rising and falling. Mike could feel how hard the young man was, and he had to fight the urge to grind against him. He didn't want to rush this.

"I like how you kiss," Tommy said at last, his breath warm against Mike's mouth.

Mike gave him a slow smile. "Well, that's good, 'cause I like your mouth." He rubbed a thumb over Tommy's bottom lip and caught his breath when Tommy opened for him and sucked it into his mouth, his eyes never leaving Mike's face. *Fuck.* Tommy had good instincts. "That is very sexy." Tommy sucked harder, and Mike's already stiff dick jerked in his jeans. Tommy stared at him. Mike couldn't help himself. He rotated his hips, letting his erection rub against Tommy's hip. "You feel that? You feel how hard you're making me?"

Tommy freed his thumb. "Yes," he whispered, pupils growing larger.

All Mike could think about was that firm flesh, bare, against his. "You hungry?"

Tommy bit his lip, his eyes shining. "For you, yes."

There was only so much a man could take.

Mike sat up and held out his hand to Tommy. "Then let's move this to bed. Dinner's not gonna spoil."

Tommy gazed at his outstretched hand and then nodded. "Okay."

He clasped it, and Mike pulled him to his feet. Standing so close only served to remind Mike of Tommy's size. The young man was at least three inches taller than him and equally as wide as Mike across the chest.

He held that sweet face between his hands and looked Tommy in the eye. "Still time to change your mind, y'know." Mike wasn't about to push it if Tommy wasn't totally into the idea.

Tommy smiled. "You're a good man, Mike." He dipped his chin and kissed Mike softly on the lips. When he broke the kiss, his breathing quickened. "Where's this bedroom of yours?"

Mike laughed. "Eager, much?" He loved seeing the flush on Tommy's cheeks. Maybe not eager; Tommy was clearly nervous as hell. "Then come with me." He led him out of the living room, across the hall, and into his bedroom.

Tommy glanced at the room. The light was starting to fade as the sun had just set, so Mike switched on the two lamps on either side of the bed. Their light bathed the room in a warm glow. Tommy stood at the foot of the bed, staring at the white comforter, pillows, and cushions, his Adam's apple bobbing.

Mike crossed the room to stand beside him. "It's just a bed," he said quietly.

Then with a grin, he pushed Tommy backward onto it. Tommy laughed, a nervous edge to his voice, and shuffled back until he was fully on the bed. Mike followed, leaning over Tommy, straddling one thigh.

"I'm not done with that mouth of yours just yet." His voice sounded hoarse to his ears.

Tommy grabbed hold of Mike around the waist and lifted his head to meet Mike's mouth. They shared a soft, lingering kiss before Mike moved to lie beside him, his arm under Tommy's neck, his hand on his chest. Mike began with soft, slow kisses, keeping it chaste until Tommy finally stopped trembling and relaxed into the mattress. Mike smiled against his mouth.

"That's it."

He resumed kissing, only now he slid his tongue between Tommy's lips, deepening the kiss. Tommy fed a low moan into his mouth and cupped Mike's head, stroking his nape as he returned the kiss. Mike rubbed his hand slowly over Tommy's wide chest while he worked Tommy's mouth, licking and sucking. He caught Tommy's tongue between his lips and sucked, pulling at it gently and drawing soft groans from Tommy. Mike could feel Tommy's hips beginning to move, could hear those almost constant noises, whimpers and sighs that told him just how much Tommy was getting into this.

When he figured he'd just about melted Tommy into the mattress, Mike knelt up, legs straddling that firm thigh once more, and began to unbutton Tommy's white shirt. "Wanna see what I get to play with," he said, smiling.

Tommy gave him the first genuinely relaxed smile since he'd arrived. "We're playin'?"

"Oh yeah. This is supposed to be fun." Mike slowly pulled the shirt open to reveal Tommy's creamy torso, his abs well developed. Fuck, the boy was ripped. He bent over to kiss the warm skin, and Tommy giggled. Mike chuckled. "Ah, you're ticklish."

"Always have been." Tommy's hands were on his upper arms, his neck craned to watch Mike's slow progress as he kissed up toward those pecs, covered with reddish-brown hair. Tommy moved his hands to press against Mike's chest. "Do... do I get to undress you too?" His lips parted, eyes gleaming in the lamplight.

Mike grinned. "I'd be disappointed if you didn't." He liked that Tommy wasn't passive. While Tommy's fingers fumbled with the buttons, Mike pressed soft kisses to Tommy's forehead and cheeks, moving down to his neck. Those fingers stuttered in their task when Mike latched onto the silky skin and sucked, and a moan rumbled through Tommy. "You like that." It wasn't a question.

"Uh-huh." It seemed to be as much as Tommy could manage.

Mike sat up and pulled off the shirt, following it with the white T-shirt he wore underneath. Then he dropped back down to where Tommy lay and eased the shirt off his shoulder, kissing the flesh beneath and then moving back to the fragrant skin of Tommy's neck. He lowered his body to meet Tommy's chest and slipped his arms under him, then rolled until Tommy was sitting astride him, face flushed, mouth open. Mike stretched up and took off Tommy's shirt, and then unbuckled the belt around his jeans. He reached up and pulled Tommy gently down until their lips met once more. They kissed, Mike slowly moving his tongue in and out of Tommy's mouth. He could feel Tommy's cock, rigid against his.

"Undo my jeans," Mike whispered against his lips.

Tommy sat upright, hands shaking slightly as they first unbuckled Mike's belt, then unfastened his jeans. He moved to the side before grabbing the jeans and pulling them over Mike's hips, Mike lifting them to make things easier. His erection strained against the fabric of his dark blue briefs, and Tommy stared at it, eyes so wide.

Mike took hold of Tommy's hand and placed it over his crotch, moving it slowly while he gently rolled his hips. Tommy caught on and began to stroke Mike's dick through the soft cotton, his breathing growing more rapid as Mike's cock lengthened and thickened.

"Oh my," Tommy uttered breathlessly.

Mike laughed softly. "We're still wearing too many clothes here."

Tommy chuckled, his cheeks glowing, and proceeded to pull off Mike's shoes and jeans. He laughed out loud when he saw Mike's socks. "Oh my—Animal? Bethany watches this on TV sometimes."

Mike shrugged. "So I happen to like the Muppets. Bite me." He'd worn them on purpose, figuring they'd help lighten the mood. Tommy was still giggling when he tugged them off. "Hey, it could be worse— you could've caught me wearing my Animal boxers."

"They make those in men's sizes?" Tommy's eyes opened wide as he came to straddle Mike's hips once more, his briefs still in place.

Mike chuckled. "You'd be amazed what's out there." *Time to change the mood around here.* He slipped his hands around Tommy's waist. "My turn," he said huskily. He rolled Tommy onto his back once more and kissed him while he undid the button on his waistband. Tommy breathed heavily into his mouth when Mike eased his hand into Tommy's jeans and stroked his hard cock through his briefs. Tommy stared up at him, pupils big and black.

Mike had a harder time pulling off Tommy's jeans, they were so fucking *tight*, but Tommy wasn't laughing at his efforts. He was watching Mike, eyes shining, as Mike removed his boots, socks, and jeans and dropped them to the floor. Mike crawled up Tommy's body until his face was above Tommy's crotch. He caught Tommy's gasp when he pressed his lips to his bulge before moving back to take Tommy's mouth in a hard kiss.

Mike straddled Tommy's hips and pulled him upright, Tommy's arms going around him to hold him as they kissed. Mike stroked the back of his head, Tommy's hands moving gently all the time. He paused and looked Tommy in the eye. Tommy met his gaze, face flushed but calm. Mike gave a nod and then slowly pushed Tommy to lie down. He pushed at Tommy's arms until he was kissing one bulging bicep, licking it and feeling Tommy shudder beneath him. Mike kissed his way down to Tommy's chest, licking and sucking at the nipple that grew taut between his lips.

"Ohh." Tommy was moving now, hips rolling gently, pushing up against Mike's crotch.

Mike smiled around the firm little nub and then moved lower, kissing down the furry little trail of hair that disappeared under the waistband of his briefs. Tommy's breathing hitched when Mike paused, fingers gripping the elastic, before pulling it downward to reveal the base of Tommy's thick cock, surrounded by reddish hair. He looked back at Tommy and then kissed the silken skin of his dick.

He tugged at the briefs until Tommy's shaft was freed, wet at the tip.

"Oh shit."

Tommy's eyes had never been so wide. He held his breath while Mike held his dick steady around the base and slowly, so slowly, drew the firm column of flesh into his mouth.

CHAPTER FOURTEEN

TOMMY GASPED as his dick was surrounded by tight heat. He couldn't tear his eyes away from the sight of Mike, taking all of him into his mouth, as smooth as silk. And the way it *felt*, Mike's lips around his cock, the friction incredible. Then Mike was licking the head gently, running his tongue along the shaft before taking just the head into his mouth and tonguing it. And when Mike stroked and pumped the shaft at the same time, Tommy wanted more than anything to thrust his hips and push deeper.

Mike pulled free, his lips shiny, and grinned. "You *can* move, okay?" He grabbed Tommy's hands and drew them to his head. "Let me know how good it feels, Tommy." He lowered his head and slowly licked over Tommy's balls, his tongue dragging against the soft sac before tracing a line up the contours of his cock, back to the head. He took Tommy deep once more, only this time Tommy held Mike's head in position while he gently thrust up into his mouth, sliding over his tongue.

Mike moaned around his dick, and Tommy thrust that little bit harder. He didn't want to go too far—his cock wasn't exactly small—but he figured Mike would let him know if he did. Tommy closed his eyes and let himself *feel*. Damn, it was wonderful, sliding again and again into Mike's hot mouth. The way Mike was sucking that dick with so much enjoyment lit a fire in him.

"Can I taste *you* too?"

Mike slowly pulled off him and grinned. "I have no problem with that."

He lay down on his back and spread his legs wide, arms folded under his head. Tommy sat up and took a moment to take in the view. Mike's chest was wide, his pecs covered in hair that thinned out to a narrow trail from his breastbone down to his navel, where it widened once more. His upper arms and thighs were thick with muscle, giving Tommy an impression of controlled power. Hell, there was muscle *everywhere*. His belly was taut, hardly an ounce of fat on him.

Tommy ached to touch him, to run his fingers through that body hair, to feel the firm flesh beneath his fingertips. But right then he had something else he desperately wanted to do....

He crawled over the bed to kneel between Mike's spread thighs, his gaze riveted on those dark blue briefs and the cock that was swelling visibly inside them, its head poking above the waistband. Tommy leaned forward and slowly pulled off Mike's underwear. His dick curved upward, thick and long, the head wide, skin shiny and taut. A neat patch of hair sat above the base of his cock. Tommy tossed the briefs to one side and bent over to lick the tip tentatively. Mike let out a sigh of pleasure, and Tommy did it again, this time licking down the stony length as he'd seen Mike do. He wasn't sure how he'd expected a cock to taste, but Mike's didn't taste of anything much. There was the faintest smell of citrus, maybe whatever he used when he showered, but beneath that was a warm scent that Tommy *really* liked. Instinctively he kissed Mike's balls, earning a happy noise in return.

"Why don't you get more comfortable?" Mike suggested. "Lie down on your side next to me."

Tommy complied and lay down, his leg bent, head low over Mike's groin. His hand around the root, he held Mike's cock still while he sucked the head into his mouth and tried to take him deeper. His eyes watered, and his throat closed up in an effort not to gag. Tommy coughed and wiped his eyes.

Mike patted his leg. "Stick with taking as much into your mouth as you can. You'll be able to go deeper with practice, but no one takes a whole dick their first time." He chuckled. "And besides, I like how your tongue feels on the head. Do that again."

Eagerly, Tommy licked over the head, and Mike groaned.

"Yeah, just like that."

Tommy bobbed his head up and down on Mike's cock, working the shaft as Mike had done.

"Yeah, Tommy. That feels really good."

Tommy thought his heart would burst, he felt so proud. But then he dropped his head back onto the bed with a loud moan when Mike lifted himself up onto his elbow and sucked Tommy's dick deep. "Shit, Mike." He couldn't concentrate, not while Mike was sucking him like that.

Mike started stroking his hip, leg, back, all the while licking and sucking his cock, sending little tingles all along his spine. Mike paused and ran his hand slowly over Tommy's ass, squeezing it lightly, caressing it. Then he went back to working Tommy's dick with his mouth, that hand never losing contact with Tommy's ass.

Tommy lay there, trying to take in everything that was happening. He was naked, his hand wrapped around an erect cock, while a naked man stroked him and sucked his dick. *This is real. This is happening.* He was aware of everything: the feel of the comforter, soft against his skin; Mike's hands, big and strong yet touching him so gently; the feel of Mike's cock, hard as steel but silk to the touch. Things didn't get any more real than this.

And then Mike slid his hand into the crease of his ass, fingers rubbing over his hole.

Tommy's breathing quickened. His pulse raced. Something in his chest was fluttering wildly, and he clenched his ass.

"Hey." Mike's voice was soft. Those fingers stilled, and once more Mike stroked his ass, slow and gentle.

Tommy pulled in a couple of deep breaths. "Sorry. Don't rightly know what happened there."

Mike smiled. "You probably had an 'Oh my God, he's really gonna fuck me' moment."

Tommy laughed. That was one way of putting it. He was nervous, distracted, and turned on, all at the same time.

Mike moved until they were lying side by side on the bed, facing each other. He cupped Tommy's face. "Would it make you feel better if I made a little confession?"

Tommy stared at him, and Mike chuckled.

"Nothing bad, I promise. It's just—" He leaned forward and kissed Tommy on the mouth. "—I'm not gonna tell you how long I've been fucking guys. Just take it from me that it's a long time, so yeah, I know what I'm doing."

Some of Tommy's tension eased at Mike's words, and he exhaled slowly.

Mike nodded. "But for all that experience?" He stroked Tommy's cheek. "You're my first virgin. And that brings with it a bit of pressure, because I want to make this really good for you."

Tommy stared at him, his stomach roiling. "But you have! I mean… you are… that is…." He sighed. "Mike, so far it's been really, really good. Honest. It's just me. I want this, I really do, but I guess my nerves just got the better of me. I—"

Mike stopped his words with a kiss. When he broke it, he smiled. "Tommy? Hush."

Tommy flushed, aware of Mike staring at his mouth. Mike rubbed his thumb over Tommy's lower lip. Moving forward, he brought his mouth to Tommy's and slowly trailed his tongue over that lip before joining them in an intimate, sensual kiss. Tommy lost himself in it. Mike's mouth was warm, the hand on his cheek gentle. He eased Tommy onto his back once more, their mouths still joined. When he broke the kiss, he looked Tommy in the eye.

"It's okay. *Everyone's* nervous their first time. Everyone's afraid they're gonna do something wrong." He smiled. "And I agree. So far, it's been really good. But, Tommy?" The smile became a grin. "It's about to get even better."

Before Tommy could react, Mike moved swiftly to grab his legs and push them up toward his chest. Tommy caught his breath at the suddenness of Mike's actions—and then lost the ability to think when Mike bent over and licked across Tommy's hole.

"Holy *shit*." A shudder ran through him when Mike repeated it, slower this time, licking up a line to his balls and then back again. He alternated between licking his ass and sucking little kisses, making all the nerves down there zing into life.

Tommy clutched at the sheets, gripping them tightly. He didn't swear—had never sworn—but *fuck*....

Mike circled Tommy's hole with his tongue before pushing it into a point and pressing it inside him. *Oh my goodness....* Tommy trembled, hands fisting the sheets, as Mike pushed his face deep into Tommy's crease, his beard prickly against his cheeks, and fucked him with his tongue again... and again... and again. A bolt of lightning shot up Tommy's spine, and he was coming, spunk erupting from his dick all over his chest, leaving him helpless to do anything but lie there and shudder through it all. His chest tightened, and his face grew hot.

Holy crap, I came so freakin' fast.

Mike lowered his legs and sat up, chest heaving, a big grin all over his face. "Well, I don't have to ask if you liked that." He pushed out a long breath. "I need to catch my breath for a sec." He got off the bed and went into what had to be the bathroom. Tommy lay on the bed, his cheeks burning. He had a good idea what lay behind Mike's sudden departure.

He must be so disappointed in me.

He heard the sound of running water, and a moment later Mike was back with a warm cloth. "I think a washup is in order before round two, don't you?" He wiped slowly over Tommy's belly and chest, removing all traces of come. Then he grinned. "I already washed my face. Figured you might want to kiss a clean face after that." His eyes sparkled.

Tommy turned away. He couldn't look at him. Just… *couldn't.*

Mike became still. "Hey, what's wrong?" He cupped Tommy's chin, turning his head to face him.

Tommy let out a heartfelt sigh. "I'm sorry," he whispered.

"What on earth for?" Mike looked genuinely perplexed.

Tommy stared at him. "I came so fast!"

For a moment Mike frowned. Then a smile creased his face. "Oh, Tommy." He shook his head. "That was the whole idea." He leaned over him and slowly brought their lips together in a soft kiss. When he finished, he said quietly, "You feel more relaxed, right?" When Tommy nodded, Mike grinned. "And at your age, you'll be hard again in no time. Now I get to make you come all over again." He rolled his body on top of Tommy, his face inches away, and rotated his hips, letting Tommy feel his hot, hard cock. "And you still want this, don't you?"

"Lord, yes," Tommy moaned softly, pushing up with his hips, his dick already starting to fill. "I want this."

Mike chuckled. "I guess you do at that." He pushed a knee between Tommy's thighs and spread him wide, then dropped his head to Tommy's shoulder. "But not half as much as I want to be inside you," he whispered.

"Oh my." Tommy shuddered. Mike's words made him light-headed and tingly all over. When he'd fantasized about this, he hadn't given much thought to who did what. The sheer illicitness of it all had been uppermost in his mind. Now that he was here, Mike's weight bearing down on him and that hard dick rubbing against his hip, Mike's words painted a picture in his head that set him on fire. "I-I want that too."

Mike pushed up onto his hands and stretched over toward the bedside cabinet. He opened the drawer and took out a bottle and several foil packets. Tommy watched, heat racing through him. Mike dropped the condoms onto the bed and then opened the bottle and squeezed some of the viscous liquid onto his fingers. Then he lay down next to Tommy and leaned over him to kiss him once more, his arm moving under Tommy's neck to pull him close, on his side.

"Hook your leg over mine," he whispered.

Tommy obeyed, the movement bringing his body into contact with Mike's. He could feel the heat that radiated from him. He wrapped his arms around Mike and held on while Mike kissed him. He closed his eyes and concentrated on the feel of Mike's lips on his, Mike's tongue sliding into his mouth. Mike's hand stroking his ass while he slipped a couple of slick fingers between Tommy's asscheeks. Tommy swallowed and opened his eyes.

Mike stared into them, nodding. "Have to get you ready for my cock." He rubbed over Tommy's hole, pressing one fingertip lightly against the puckered skin. "Oh, you're hot there."

Tommy was hot *everywhere*.

Mike kissed him, sliding his tongue deep into Tommy's mouth while he gently, *so* gently sank a single finger into his hole. Tommy let out a low moan into Mike's mouth. It felt so strange and yet so good at the same time. Mike's finger stilled inside him, and Tommy breathed deeply, hyperaware of every sensation. After a moment Mike started to move inside him, taking it slowly. He deepened the kiss, stroking his tongue in and out of Tommy, keeping pace with the finger that now stroked slowly in and out of his body.

"Does that feel good?" Mike murmured against his lips as he pushed in a bit deeper. Tommy groaned, the sound swallowed up in Mike's fervent kiss. Mike moved his lips to Tommy's neck, nuzzling the skin below his ear and chuckling. "Gonna take that as a yes."

Tommy couldn't make up his mind. It burned, but the sensation was so good. And when it got to the point where it stopped burning and started to feel really, *really* good, Mike added another finger, taking Tommy's breath away. He tensed up, and Mike kissed him again, lips warm and silky, tongue exploring him, tasting him. And then two fingers were moving inside him, making him hot, making him *need*….

Mike pulled free of Tommy's body and rolled him onto his belly. He straddled Tommy, that heavy, thick cock hot against his ass. Mike kissed across Tommy's shoulders and down his spine, his dick rubbing between Tommy's cheeks. He edged lower until he was spreading Tommy's ass with his thumbs. Tommy grabbed a pillow and hugged it as Mike's tongue renewed its acquaintance with his hole, circling it, licking, sucking, pushing inside him once more. *Oh God, the sounds Mike was making*…. Tommy panted, pushing back to get *more*, wanting more of that tongue that was fucking him, driving him out of his mind.

His cock rubbed against the comforter, already hard as nails, the skin sensitized. When Mike spread him wider, stretching his hole and pushing farther into him, Tommy cried out, the sound loud and harsh.

Mike crawled up his body, kissing his way up Tommy's spine, his cock hot against his hole, sliding through his crease as Mike rolled his hips. He reached Tommy's shoulder and kissed it before nuzzling into his neck.

Tommy didn't care anymore where Mike's mouth had just been. He only knew he wanted Mike's kiss. He turned his head and moaned softly. Mike was there instantly, kissing him, pushing his tongue deep, and Tommy took it, body writhing beneath Mike. He arched his back, leaning up on his elbows, and Mike wrapped one arm around him, hand splayed over his chest, the other over his shoulders against his collarbones, body tight up against his.

"You want this?" he murmured in a low, urgent voice next to Tommy's ear as he rocked his hips, pushing his dick faster and faster over Tommy's hole. "You want my cock inside you?"

Tommy pushed back, groaning. "Please... please, Mike." He clutched the pillow tightly, hips bucking, dick so damn hard against his belly. Mike's shaft was searing his ass with its heat, every slide over his hole bringing the promise of what was to come.

"You're gonna feel so good, Tommy, your body hot and tight around my cock."

Oh ho-ly shit. Mike's words set him on fire, his body crying out for more. And then it was *Tommy* that was crying out, Tommy's voice cracking. "Oh, now, please, Mike—*now!*"

"Okay, then."

Mike's warmth disappeared, and then Tommy heard foil tearing, latex snapping. He felt Mike's thumbs pulling his cheeks apart once again—only this time, cool, slick, blunt flesh pressed slowly into him, *so* slowly, opening him up.

Except Tommy's body had other ideas. He tensed, fighting the intrusion, his ass on fire. He couldn't help the whimper that rolled from his lips.

Mike stilled instantly and dropped his head to Tommy's shoulder, his breath warm against his ear. "It's okay, Tommy. I know—it burns, right? You just need to relax, is all, 'cause right now I'm about halfway in and your hole is gripping me like a vise." He rubbed Tommy's back, the touch soothing. "I want you to push out with your muscles, like you're trying to force my cock out of you."

Tommy froze. "Yeah, but…." He couldn't say it, but the thought was there in his head, much as he didn't want it to be.

"Trust me." Mike's voice was soft. "Nothing's gonna come out, okay? But it'll relax the muscles, and I'll slide in all the easier." That hand on his shoulder was so gentle. "Go on, Tommy, let me in."

Tommy shivered and then nodded. He closed his eyes and held his breath.

Mike kissed his shoulder. "Breathe, okay? Deep breaths. That'll help too." Another kiss. "Tommy, I swear, by the time we're done, it'll feel a whole lot better, all right? But you gotta trust me."

Tommy inhaled slowly and let his body relax. He bore down and almost cried with relief when Mike slid into him, spreading him, filling him, until his whole world had shrunk and all it contained was that hard dick, all the way inside him.

Then Mike started to pull out and *oh my Lord*, it burned. His whole body tensed, his ass clamping down tight on Mike's cock. "Oh Lord, oh *Lord.*"

Mike buried his face in Tommy's neck and groaned. "Fuck, you're tight." He held himself still, his arms rigid on either side of Tommy. "Breathe, Tommy, remember? Push me out again."

Tommy obeyed, and there it was again, that almost blissful feeling when Mike moved more easily inside him, the motion slow and controlled. His breathing became less ragged, and he focused on relaxing his muscles.

Oh wow, yeah. The burn began to fade, Mike still moving so slowly that Tommy was hardly aware of it. "That… that feels better," he gasped out.

"Good." Mike cupped his face and turned it toward him, kissing Tommy on the mouth, his tongue parting his lips, the movement as slow as that of Mike's dick. "That's it," Mike praised when Tommy finally let himself relax as the burn melted into nothingness. "Yeah, oh yeah." He rocked his hips, keeping the motion slow, blanketing Tommy's body with his own, Mike's arms once more around him, holding him close.

Tommy closed his eyes and lost himself in the slow push and pull of Mike's dick, in, out, in, out…. Mike was kissing him, gently moving inside him, soft noises escaping his lips as he buried his shaft to the hilt in Tommy's channel and then withdrew, only to repeat the sensual movement all over again.

Except now it was starting to feel good. Really good.

"It feel okay?" Mike whispered close to his ear before kissing down his neck.

"Lord, yes," Tommy gasped out, finally starting to push back, slowly at first but then picking up speed as the sensations built steadily. He dropped his head and shoulders to the bed and reached under his body to touch his aching dick. Mike kissed his shoulder blades, then between them, whisper-soft kisses. He grasped Tommy's shoulders and squeezed, thrusting a little harder, using long strokes that made Tommy want to shout out how *freakin' amazin'* it felt inside him. He tugged at his cock, hand moving quicker as something within him came to the boil, bubbling up, permeating every fiber, every cell with what could only be described as joy. His balls tingled, high and tight, and—

Tommy didn't want to come like this.

"Wanna see you," he moaned.

Mike withdrew, and the sensation of having lost something was so acute that Tommy wanted to weep. Then Mike was flipping him onto his back, pulling his legs up until Tommy's ankles rested on Mike's shoulders. Mike aimed and pushed, that hot, solid cock filling him once more, thrusting hard into him, his hands tight around Tommy's hips, pulling him onto his dick.

It wasn't enough.

"Kiss me?" Tommy pleaded, his breathing ragged.

Mike nodded, moving swiftly to lie between Tommy's thighs, as Tommy grabbed his shoulders and pulled him down. His mouth met Mike's in a hot, all-consuming kiss, Mike plunging his tongue deep into Tommy's mouth, mimicking his cock. Tommy groaned and locked his arms around Mike's neck, desperate to deepen the kiss, deepen the contact.

Mike broke free of the kiss and arched, gasping, filling him all the way. "Oh *fuck*, Tommy."

And suddenly Tommy was *there*, coming, coming so hard, the feeling white hot as it raced through his body, through every vein and artery, bursting out of him in a thick arc that hit Mike squarely on the chest. Tommy howled, a wordless cry that rebounded off the walls and ceiling, while his body trembled and shook. He gulped in air, conscious of the heat from Mike's body, the muted heat within him. Their bodies lay pressed together, their skin damp, tiny shocks jolting through them. His heart pounded, his pulse raced, and his skin tingled all over.

Mike kissed him slowly, moving up his neck and along his jaw until their mouths met in a soft fusion of warm lips and tongues. Mike lay on him, letting Tommy's body support him, stroking over the damp skin of his chest. He raised his chin and looked Tommy in the eye, his breathing ragged.

"That was… amazing." His eyes shone. His arms bracketed Tommy's head as he kissed him, over and over, the kisses robbed of all their previous urgency. Mike's weight felt good, comforting.

Tommy sighed, feeling languid and relaxed, his body glowing. Mike was still inside him, and the thought sent warmth pulsing through him. To be so intimately connected to another was a heady sensation. Tommy wasn't ready to lose that just yet.

He stroked the back of Mike's neck, keeping it slow. When Mike looked him in the eye, Tommy smiled. "Can we do that again sometime?"

Feeling Mike laugh while his cock was still inside him was definitely surreal.

CHAPTER FIFTEEN

MIKE OPENED his eyes and stretched. Damn, that felt good. He *loved* Sunday mornings in bed. Nowhere to be but under the covers, soft sheets surrounding him, sunlight already creeping in at the window. He could hear birds singing outside and the faint hum of traffic now and again. That was what he loved about living in Morningside—not that much traffic and the streets were peaceful.

He rolled onto his side and smiled at the sight that met his eyes. A broad, creamy back, muscled and firm, leading down to an equally firm, tight ass. A head of reddish-brown hair, mussed up. And the *cutest* little snores coming from Tommy's mouth. It was the snoring that made him smile, that and the memory of the previous night.

It had certainly been a night of firsts for Tommy, and Mike had loved it all. Popping Tommy's cherry had been the highlight, of course. Mike hadn't been sure what to expect, but seeing Tommy grow in confidence as the night wore on had been a real turn-on. He hadn't been prepared for how fucking fantastic it had felt to see Tommy come with Mike's cock deep inside him, feel his body tightening around him. For a man who'd lost count of how many times he'd made a guy come, there had been something so new about the whole experience. For the first time, Mike had seen the act through someone else's eyes, and it had been almost… humbling.

The shower afterward had been pretty damn good too. Mike had to smile. Tommy had seemed amazed to be having his third orgasm of the night. He'd gripped Mike's shoulders so tightly, Mike would not be surprised to find bruises there. As for him, kneeling before Tommy and sucking him off until he pumped come down Mike's throat had been such a rush. The sight of Tommy leaning against the tiles, that red flush across his chest, rising up his neck and cheeks. But what stuck in his memory was the way Tommy had leaned into him while he washed Tommy slowly, stroking his fingers through Tommy's short hair, working up a rich lather. The way Tommy hadn't hesitated when Mike had kissed him under the jets, his eyes closed, soft noises escaping his lips while Mike took his time, unwilling to let the moment end.

"Mornin'."

Mike eased back into his tranquil Sunday morning. "Good morning. Did you sleep well?"

Tommy gave a shy, not quite awake smile. "I'm not sure about 'well.' It sure was different, sleepin' with someone else in the bed." His cheeks pinked up. "It was nice, though, 'specially when…." He bit his lip.

"When what?" Mike asked, intrigued by the way Tommy's face glowed.

Tommy chuckled. "When you kinda spooned an' put your arms around me. Never snuggled with someone before."

Mike's morning had just gotten better. He held out an arm. "Morning snuggles are the best kind. Scoot that ass on over here." He grinned. "And there's nothing wrong with a little snuggling."

Tommy edged his way across the mattress. There was the tiniest wince as he moved, before he pressed his warm body against Mike's side, his arm across Mike's chest, head resting on his shoulder. Mike wrapped an arm around him.

"So," he began, "you had a good time last night?"

Tommy chuckled against his skin, and Mike smiled.

"Oh, it was *that* good, huh?" When Tommy said nothing, Mike got the message. The shy young man in his bed did not want to talk about sex. Now that Mike knew a little more about him, this wasn't surprising. In fact, it was downright adorable. There was no way he was going to mention Tommy wincing just then. The poor guy might die from embarrassment.

He stroked down Tommy's back. "Okay, okay. Let's change the subject."

Tommy craned his neck to look at Mike, blinking. "There is one thing."

"Oh?" Mike waited for what was coming, noting how Tommy wasn't meeting his gaze. *Interesting….*

"Last night, I… I asked if we could do this again sometime." Tommy's cheeks blended perfectly with the reddish tinge of his hair.

Mike didn't have to guess what "this" referred to. "I remember." It had been amusing last night, coming so hot on the heels of Tommy's orgasm. Except now? Tommy was obviously serious. Mike considered the prospect. It wasn't like he was short of guys wanting to have sex with him. Hell, he could walk into any number of bars in Atlanta and be inundated with offers. But that wasn't what he wanted.

Spending more time with Tommy, however? That was another matter. Mike genuinely liked him. What was more, he liked the idea of doing this on a regular basis. Tommy wasn't just another pretty boy, all looks and no substance. Mike could have his pick of that type, but damn, it got boring after a while. Some of them were such dumbasses. Tommy had brains, that was for sure. And Mike liked seeing this new world through Tommy's eyes. He imagined watching Tommy blossom and grow into a strong, confident gay man would be something pretty special.

Mike found himself wanting to be around to see that.

Tommy was regarding him, eyes wide, lips slightly parted.

Time to put Tommy out of his misery. "I like that idea," Mike said quietly. "We could meet up at Woofs on Saturdays as usual, but you could come home with me after. Does that sound okay?"

"Yeah, it does," Tommy admitted, a half smile on his lips.

Mike rolled onto his side to face him. "Hey, we could do other stuff too, y'know. We could go out for lunch on Sundays, or maybe brunch if we're not too tired." He grinned, and Tommy blushed furiously. "And there's other places I could show you around Atlanta too, if you'd like."

Tommy's face lit up. "I'd really like that."

His enthusiasm, so genuine and earnest, was like a welcome breath of fresh air in Mike's life. It was plain Tommy wasn't all about the sex, and that was just fine in Mike's book.

Mike sat up and stretched, arms high above his head. He liked the way Tommy looked at him, his gaze traveling over Mike's body. Just feeling those green eyes on him had Mike's cock filling.

And Tommy noticed. He gave a strangled cough and lowered his gaze.

Mike bit back a smile. *This is just too cute.* "How about we get some breakfast? We could have some here or go out, depending on how hungry you're feeling."

Just then Tommy's belly growled, and Tommy looked like he wanted the ground to open up and swallow him whole.

Mike chuckled. "Guess that answers *that* question." Unable to resist poking just a little, he waggled his eyebrows. "Well, we did expend a lot of energy last night. Looks like my coq au vin didn't fill you up enough."

"Oh no, it was plenty!" Tommy protested. "It's just that, well... I have a big appetite." His cheeks glowed, becoming a brighter shade of red when his stomach grew more vociferous.

Mike laughed. "Okay, okay, I get the message! How about we go to the diner and get some chicken fried steak into you?"

"That sounds good," Tommy admitted. "I can't stay too late. I gotta get back to Ben's and pack up my stuff to drive to Athens later. Is that okay?"

"'Course it is," Mike said with a nod. "We can go eat, then come back here for a while before you have to leave. I'll just grab a shower first."

"Another one?"

Lord, the boy was adorable. Mike chuckled. "I like my showers, okay?" Not that he needed one, but his morning wood required some attention. He threw back the sheets, climbed out of bed, and walked into the bathroom. He wasn't about to cover up. Tommy had already seen everything he'd got, up close and personal. Speaking of which....

Mike peered around the bathroom door to find Tommy lying in bed, looking like he was lost in his own thoughts. "Hey there," Mike said softly. Tommy rolled onto his side to gaze at him. "I'm standing here in the bathroom, trying to remember how your mouth felt around my dick last night, but I'm having a little trouble. Seems like I can't quite get the details clear in my mind. Wanna help me out in the shower?" He grinned. "Only if you want to, of course."

Tommy's lips parted, and his breathing got faster. His eyes shone. "Okay," he said in a quiet voice. Mike could've believed it was reticence on his part, except for the fact that Tommy's cock jerked under the sheet, plain as day. *Oh, he likes that idea....*

"Well, get your beautiful ass in here, then!"

Tommy got out of the bed, that lovely shy smile in evidence, and walked over to Mike, his dick pointing straight at him. Mike stretched out his hand and led his young lover into the bathroom. His morning shower was suddenly looking *much* better.

TOMMY GLANCED around the apartment, scanning the living room in case he'd missed anything. His bag was packed and ready to be thrown into the truck for the journey back to Athens. He hadn't seen Ben since his return from Mike's, which was fine by Tommy. He had a feeling Ben would be asking questions, not that Tommy was about to give him any answers.

There are just some things you don't talk about. Tommy couldn't believe sometimes the way his classmates talked about sex so openly, like it was nothing. Not in Tommy's book. Sex was something... private, something intimate. It had been a relief when Mike hadn't pushed it that morning. Lord knew, he was only checking that Tommy'd enjoyed the experience.

Tommy paused in his survey of the bathroom when he caught sight of his reflection in the mirror. Enjoyed? They'd need to invent a new word to describe how Tommy had felt about Mike f—

There was that word again, the one he never uttered, but nevertheless the word that best fit what they'd done. Tommy stared at his pink cheeks and breathed deeply. *Just suck it up and say it.*

"Mike fucked me."

Even whispering the words to himself in the quiet little bathroom brought heat to his face—and his groin. For the seventh or eighth time that day, once again his mind took him back to that shower, on his knees, his mouth around Mike's cock, Mike's groans of pleasure rebounding off the tiled walls. It had been so... good? Amazing? Hotter 'n' hell? All of the above? And then, once he'd come, to have Mike hold him under the jets, his hand working Tommy's dick until he orgasmed, shuddering in Mike's arms while Mike kissed him through his climax, had been just... bliss. After all that, there was no way he could've left without saying something. Tommy had been raised right, and that meant showing appreciation, even for getting laid. It had been as much as he could manage to whisper into Mike's ear, while the last of his come was washed away by the swirling water, that he'd really, *really* liked it.

Mike's slow smile had been comment enough.

Just thinking about that shower made his hole clench tight, and he winced. Yeah, everything was still a little... tender. He'd been relieved when Mike hadn't wanted them to do... "it" again. Much as he'd loved how he felt when they finished, even the thought of taking Mike's cock inside him again made him tense up.

Then he'd thought about it. Maybe Mike had stuck to oral for a reason. Maybe Mike had done it because he knew exactly how Tommy was feeling, and he didn't want to cause him any more discomfort.

The more time Tommy spent around Mike, the more he liked him.

The outer door to the apartment banged shut, snapping Tommy to attention.

"Tommy? You here?"

"In the bathroom," Tommy shouted out to Ben, hurriedly collecting himself. He gave the room a quick scan, and satisfied he'd gotten everything, Tommy exited the bathroom and went into the living room, where Ben had flopped down onto the couch and was staring at him with an expectant air. "What?" Tommy kept his features schooled. Like he didn't know what Ben was after....

Ben grinned. "So? How was it?"

Tommy snorted. "As if I'd tell you."

Ben pouted, making Tommy snort all the more.

"An' you can forget tryin' to get 'round me with them big puppy dog eyes. I mean it, Ben. I'm not gonna talk 'bout this."

"But you did fuck, right? Mike did pop your cherry?"

"Ben!" Tommy stared back at him, his face and neck hot.

Ben screwed up his face. "You're no fun." Then he gave Tommy a smug glance. "I'm gonna take that as a yes." He smiled gleefully. "Okay, now we have to find you a nice, hot guy."

Everything just... stopped.

"What d'you mean?" Tommy stood at the end of the couch, hands by his sides, curling into fists.

Ben frowned. "What do *you* mean, what do I mean? Now's the time to find yourself another guy." He waggled his eyebrows. "You need to get out there an' sample what's available."

"But why would I do that?" Tommy persisted. "I'm with Mike."

Ben stilled. "You're not '*with* Mike,'" he said, hooking his fingers in the air. "Don't make it out to be more than it was, okay? It was just sex."

Icy fingers picked their way down Tommy's spine. "An' what if I want to be with Mike?" he said softly.

The look of genuine puzzlement on Ben's face made his heart sink.

"Why would you wanna do that?" Then he peered intently at Tommy. "An' never mind what *you* want—what does Mike want?"

Tommy couldn't continue the conversation. "I'm just about done here. I'm gonna go find Bethany an' say good-bye to her an' your folks." Anything rather than try to figure Ben out.

"Fine," Ben said with a wave of his hand. "I'll get my stuff together."

"You do that." Tommy left the living room and went up the stairs into the main house, heading straight for the kitchen. He found Bethany alone in the kitchen, making herself a sandwich, headphones on and be-bopping away to whatever music was playing on her iPhone. He stopped for a second and watched her from the doorway. For all her mature remarks and insights, sometimes he forgot that she was only seventeen.

Bethany whirled around, arms outstretched, and came to an abrupt halt when she caught sight of Tommy. An involuntary "Eek" escaped her, and she turned off the music. "Warn a person, why don'tcha?" She blushed.

"Sorry, Bethany." Tommy came fully into the kitchen. "There any coffee left?"

Bethany shook her head. "I was about to make some tea. Want some?"

He nodded, and she filled the kettle and set it on the stove to boil. Tommy sat at the table, his mind still reeling from his talk with Ben.

"You want half my sandwich?"

He looked up. "Nah, I'm good."

Bethany stood with the counter to her back and leaned, tilting her head to one side. "You okay, Tommy?"

He opened his mouth to tell her he was fine, but that wasn't what came out. "I just don't get your brother," he blurted out.

Bethany gave him a sympathetic look. "What's he done now?"

Tommy hesitated, and Bethany held up her hands.

"You know what? If you don't wanna tell me, that's fine. But I do know what he's like."

Tommy made up his mind and relayed their conversation. Bethany listened, her hands busy making the tea. When he'd finished, she brought over the two mugs and sat down next to him. Bethany regarded him with a speculative glance.

"Tommy, Ben is a slut. Surely you must know that by now?"

He stared at her, mouth open, and she laughed. "Go on, then, tell me I'm wrong."

Tommy said nothing, although there was plenty he *could* say. He knew there were nights during the week when Ben didn't come home. He knew where Ben spent his Saturday nights. He was just too polite to say so.

"Tommy, just ignore him, okay? Let him live his life the way he wants to. You don't have to do likewise." She studied him intently. "If you want to be with Mike, then you go get him, y'hear?"

He smiled, the tightness in his chest easing. "Thanks, Beth." Her support meant a lot. Tommy found it difficult to put into words what he was feeling. Ben's words had disquieted him, making him doubt himself. That last question about what Mike wanted still rang in his ears. And if his classmates knew what he was thinking in that moment, doubtless they'd laugh at him.

Is it so wrong to think that last night meant something? That it was important?

Tommy couldn't help it. His upbringing, his parents' teachings, all of it led him to one conclusion: he and Mike had shared something that you didn't just walk away from. He had no way of knowing if Mike wanted this to go any further, but Tommy wanted to see where it led next.

It was the least he owed Mike.

MIKE WALKED into Woofs that Sunday afternoon to be greeted by a round of applause from Kevin and Patrick.

"We were wondering if you were gonna show up for work tonight, or if you'd be too busy with your boy toy," Kevin said with a leer.

"Fuck. Off," Mike said shortly, taking off his leather jacket and stashing it behind the bar. He'd known it was coming, of course. There was no way Kevin would've been able to resist.

Kevin joined him. "Aw, come on. I've been dying for you to get here and spill the beans. Did it all go according to plan? Is Tommy a good fuck?" His voice took on a wheedling tone. "Aw, Mikey, play fair. After all, we helped ya get together with Mr. Farm Boy, didn't we?"

Mike sighed. "I am gonna say this just once. Tommy is a good kid, and I am not gonna talk about him behind his back. So I will not be sharing details, ya got that?" He didn't understand why Kevin's question put his back up. Mike often shared what went on during his scenes.

This felt… different.

Kevin folded his arms across his wide chest and stared at Mike. "Fair enough. Just tell me one thing. Does he know about the porn?"

Mike shook his head. "No," he said emphatically. When Kevin pursed his lips, Mike huffed. "Look, if he knew, there's no way he'd be able to hide that. Trust me." Mike imagined Tommy would no sooner watch porn than he would swear in church.

Kevin nodded. "Then you need to tell him."

Mike gaped. "Why the fuck would I do that?"

There was a moment's silence before Kevin replied. "Ask yourself why you don't want him to know."

That made him stop and think. He'd been in a few relationships that had crashed and burned once his partners had found out about his other career.

Except I'm not in a relationship with Tommy, am I?

Damn, that boy just scrambled his circuits.

Kevin was looking awfully smug. "Now I got ya thinking. So while you're doing some reflecting, reflect on this. You've been doing porn for a long while now, Mike. Someday, maybe sooner than you think, that boy is gonna *see* something, *hear* something, and then that cat is out of its bag. It's gonna be better if he hears it from you first."

Fuck. Much as he didn't want to think about that, Kevin had a point.

"Okay," he said, nodding. "You're right. I will tell him." *Just not yet.*

Mike liked the way Tommy had looked at him. He had a feeling that just might change once Tommy knew how Mike earned some of his dollars.

And damn if that thought didn't make Mike feel sad.

CHAPTER SIXTEEN

MIKE SWITCHED off the car engine and grabbed his bag from the passenger seat. Instead of getting out of the car, he sat there for a moment, staring up at ManFactory's exterior. He was still fuming over that little shit's review of his last scene.

Not many sites reviewed porn, but there were a few. Most of them just published the stills and the abstract, but a few sites—one in particular—went further. It didn't matter that most of the industry hated the PornWatch blog. That didn't stop its one—and only—reviewer from coming out with the most incendiary reviews out there. Oh, they brought in the readers, and they certainly helped bring up his ratings, but the whole blog was kind of the supermarket checkout line tabloid of the gay porn world. That last review had been almost rabid. He'd sounded off about how poor the acting was. The most entertaining thing about it all had been the comments. One guy had actually written, *"Er, excuse me? We* are *talking about porn, right? I don't know about most of you guys out there, but* I'm *not watching it for the quality of the acting, and the performers certainly aren't aiming for Academy awards."*

Sitting there fuming about it wasn't going to improve his mood.

Mike got out of the car, locked it, shouldered his bag, and walked across the parking lot to the main door. It was midday. He'd been ready to leave the house at eight thirty, and Paul's phone call had caught him halfway out the door. Apparently there'd been a delay and they wanted him later.

What now? Something else to piss him off, no doubt.

He pushed open the glass door and walked up to the main desk. Paul glanced up and gave him a nervous smile, blinking rapidly. "Hey, Scott." He handed over the clipboard. "Tony's waiting for you in the prep room."

That stopped him in his tracks. Tony normally gave him a while to get the paperwork done and talk through the scene before wanting to see him. "Is Troy there too?" Mike knew Troy Rosen of old. Working with him was always a lot of fun, and Mike had been pleased when

ManFactory had sent him the e-mail a couple of weeks ago, informing him of their scene together. Troy was a real power bottom and something of a rarity in the industry—his husband was also a porn actor. The couple were often interviewed about their life in the spotlight. Lately they'd been the focus of an online hate campaign, conducted in the full glare of social media. Troy's husband, Carl, had reached out to their thousands of fans, and they'd received an overwhelming amount of support. They were quickly becoming the most well-known gay couple on the Internet.

Mike often wondered what their secret was. Both of them working in the industry might've had something to do with it, he supposed, but they'd clearly found a way that worked for them. Whatever it was, Mike sure envied them. You only had to look at photos of the couple to see they were in love.

What I'd give to find someone who looks at me the way they look at each other.

Paul rubbed the back of his neck. "Sorry, Scott, there's been a change. It's all on the documentation." The phone rang, cutting short the conversation. Paul took the call, giving Mike an apologetic glance.

A change? Mike walked through the main area of the studio, skirting the sets where scenes were already being filmed, and into the prep room. Tony was nowhere to be seen. Mike shrugged off his jacket and sat down at the table to read through his notes. One look at the name on the sheet was enough to make him groan out loud.

"Aww, crap."

The sound of someone clearing their throat behind him made him straighten and turn around. Tony Ford stood in the doorway.

"I take it you've read the notes." His expression was decidedly unhappy. "Look, I know this is short notice, but—"

Mike didn't bother trying to hide his disappointment. "Chad Bone? Really?" It was bad enough that in the—almost—four months since he'd arrived at ManFactory, Chad had managed to prove all Mike's predictions true. Despite his relatively short time at the studio, he'd quickly become one of their most popular actors. It seemed like he was performing in two out of every five scenes that ManFactory put out.

No, what made matters worse was the reputation Chad was already gaining in the community. He'd bottomed—twice—and made such a song and dance about it that the company now paid him twice the going rate every time he did it. There was no denying the boy was the proverbial goose, but Mike was certain one of these days it was gonna backfire on ManFactory, and *that* egg sure wouldn't be made of gold. That one was gonna stink to high heaven.

Quickly, Mike scanned the scene notes. "Shit." Chad was topping.

"I know you're not happy about working with Chad," Tony began, "but—"

"Not happy?" Mike growled. "I hear the stories, okay? You think you're doing a good job of keeping a lid on it, Tony, but word gets around. The kid's a homophobic little asshole and a nightmare to work with." He fixed Tony with a steely gaze. "Go on, tell me I'm wrong."

Tony came into the room and pushed the door shut behind him. "I'm sorry, okay? This wasn't my decision." He pulled out a chair and sat down, head in his hands.

"Huh? But you're the director."

Tony let out a sigh that was so heavy, Mike almost felt sorry for him. Almost.

"Well, that's as may be, but it seems the management wants to give Chad a lot of exposure. They've been giving him scenes with all the more experienced guys." He shrugged. "It's their company. What am I supposed to say?"

Mike knew he had a point. He dropped the clipboard onto the table and shook his head. "Is he here yet?"

Tony nodded. "He's in the shower. Make sure you're good 'n' prepared, Scott. Kid's got a helluva dick on him. We're talking nine inches. And thick."

Mike snorted. "Yeah, I read that in his profile. Wasn't sure if I believed it or not, but…." He gave a halfhearted smile. "After all, they got me down as six feet tall."

Tony barked out a laugh. "Oh, they got it right. Chad's equipment is very… impressive." He got up from the table. "I'll let you get ready, okay? And Scott… play nice, all right?"

Mike opened his eyes wide. "Why, whatever can you mean?" He attempted a look of pure innocence.

Tony bit his lip. "Yeah, that's funny. No, I mean it. You've got a reputation around here too, y'know. You're a shoot-from-the-hip kinda guy. It wouldn't do to ruffle anyone's feathers, if you catch my drift." He went to the door and paused. "You hearing me?"

Mike nodded. "I hear ya." He picked up the clipboard. "Just give me a few minutes to read this thoroughly, and then I'll be in the shower too." He arched his eyebrows. "Mustn't keep His Highness waiting."

Tony shook his head. "You're playing with fire, Scott. Just be careful you don't get burned." He exited the room, leaving Mike staring at the door.

This was *not* going to be fun.

"OKAY, LET'S take a break before the penetration scene," Tony called out.

Chad was off the bed and onto his iPhone in seconds. Mike watched him walk aimlessly around the studio, eyes down, focused on the screen, thumbs flying as he messaged... whoever. His cock pointed the way, bobbing gently. Not that anyone could miss it.

Damn, he's big. Tony hadn't been kidding. Mike had bitten back a smirk when he'd laid eyes for the first time on a naked Chad. That skinny butt was furless after all, as was the rest of him.

"I think that's our next evolutionary step," Seb, the cameraman, said with a grin.

"Huh?" Mike got up from the bed and walked to the small couch, where he'd left his bag containing the dildo. A last minute bit of stretching wouldn't go amiss. Mike lubed up the dildo, the biggest one he had with him, and then lay on his back, knees to his chest, and slid it home. He breathed out, letting his muscles relax. It didn't help that he'd been tense throughout the scene so far. Okay, so his initial mood had been lousy, but Chad had certainly played his part too.

Mike closed his eyes, trying to inject a calm he didn't feel.

"I said, I think that's our next evolutionary step," Seb repeated, crouching next to him. "We're all gonna have this bend in our necks, just for looking at our phones." He chuckled. "I think Chad is surgically attached to his."

Mike fought hard not to growl at the mention of his name. "Can we talk about something else?" he said through gritted teeth.

Seb peered at him. "Yeah, I can understand why you're pissed. I would be too, if I had someone speak to me the way he did to you." He shook his head. "But it's not you, you know that, right? He's like that with everyone he does a scene with." Seb scowled. "Little bastard's just plain rude, if you ask me."

Mike groaned. "Seb, I'm trying to get into the right mind-set for this, and sorry, dude, but you're not helping."

Seb flushed. "Aw, sorry, Scott. I'll leave you alone, okay? See you in a few." He rose to his feet quickly and left Mike on the couch. Mike closed his eyes.

Just think of something else. Anything.

It was always frustrating as hell when Mike had to film a scene with a guy with whom there was no chemistry. He really had to work hard at the pretense, and that was fine when he was going through the mechanics of fucking. Mike could light up his eyes, kiss, smile, like there really *was* passion between them. The one thing that was impossible to fake, however, was the cum shot. He had to get it right, and it had to be good. And when the chemistry wasn't there, it became so much harder to do it well. Mike had his rituals for when this happened, that inner room in the back of his head where he kept a catalog of his happy places—moments with exes, moments where the sex had been damn good—and he simply rolled his head back into them and relived them. It was a repertoire that worked for him. The funny thing was, he could watch the scene later and recall instantly what had been on his mind when he'd come.

His fingers touched the wide base of the dildo, and he pulled it out a ways before pushing it firmly into him. The thought rose, unbidden. *I wonder how Tommy would feel about some toys.*

And *there* was his good mood. Mike kept his eyes closed, preferring the view in his head. Tommy, a nice fat dildo plugging him while Mike fed him his dick, slick with Tommy's spit, dripping with it.

Except the picture didn't stay that way.

Suddenly in his head was Tommy sitting next to him on his couch at home, head resting against the cushions while Mike kissed him, slowly and thoroughly. Tommy in Mike's bed, all warm and sleepy, hands soft on Mike's back, his nape, his ass. Tommy in the shower, staring down at Mike as he sucked Tommy off, hot water hitting Tommy's shoulders and falling over Mike in fine droplets, Tommy's dick hard and hot in his mouth….

"Scott, we're ready to continue."

The voice of reality intruded, dispelling Mike's pleasant recollections. He opened his eyes with a sigh and pulled the dildo free of his body. Once he'd wiped it on his towel, Mike dropped it into his bag and heaved himself up off the couch and back over to the set. Chad was already there kneeling on the bed, that arrogant cock pointing straight up. Chad tapped his fingers against his thigh, his lips pursed.

"C'mon, let's do this, okay? I got plans for later."

Mike gave Chad his politest smile. "Well, this *is* what they pay you for, isn't it?" Not that he wanted to spend more time on the scene than was necessary. He climbed onto the bed and got on his hands and knees, ready for Chad's dick. Seb was back, camera poised.

He felt the mattress dip as Chad positioned himself at Mike's ass. "You ready for my cock?" Chad said in a low voice, his hands on Mike's cheeks, pulling them apart to reveal his hole.

"Any time you're ready." Mike kept his tone even.

"When you two are done," Tony said dryly. They started with Chad rocking his hips and rubbing his dick over Mike's hole, Mike making low moans for the camera.

Chad curved his slim body over Mike's, cock pressed firmly between his cheeks. "Gonna open up that boy pussy for me?" Chad rocked faster, his slick, bare dick sliding through Mike's crack. "You like havin' a dick up your ass, don'tcha?" He straightened and slapped Mike's ass, the sound as loud as a crack in the quiet studio. Mike gasped, and Chad laughed. "Yeah, you like it rough, don'tcha?" He did it again, only harder this time.

Mike snorted. Chad had *no* idea. Mike doubted the little turd had even so much as *peeked* at a website like Bound Gods. He might've had a shock. Mike had lost count of how many times he'd filmed for them. He wanted to laugh out loud at the notion that a mere slap was rough. *Fucking little know-it-all kid....*

There was a lull in the proceedings while Chad gloved up, and then he was demanding entrance, pushing insistently at Mike's pucker until he was all the way inside. "Big enough for ya?" he said with a cackle.

Mike bit back his moan. He wasn't about to give Chad the satisfaction. Then he caught Tony's signal. *Shit....* He had a job to do. Chad might be an unprofessional little shit, but Mike most definitely was not. On cue, Mike dropped his chest to the mattress and let out a groan. "Fuck, your dick is huge."

"You know it," Chad crowed, withdrawing until just the head of his cock was inside him, then powerfully shoving back into him. He sped up his thrusts, hips starting to piston. "You gonna be my bitch? Huh?" Chad cackled once more, thrusting into him with long, deep strokes. "Yeah, you *like* being my bitch." He slapped Mike on the ass, and it stung. "C'mon, then, bitch. Back up onto my cock like you want it."

Mike pushed back, fucking himself on that thick shaft. Then he was shoving back, impaling himself on it, his breathing rapid while he worked his cock.

"Yeah, look at this big ol' bear." Chad's voice was gleeful. "Bet you thought you'd be fucking *my* tight little ass, huh?" He snorted. "That right? You think about fucking me? Yeah, right, like I'd let some big ol' queer put his dick up *my* ass."

"Break!" Mike yelled. Without waiting for confirmation from Tony, he moved forward, feeling Chad slide out of him, hot and slick. Mike was off the bed and striding away from it, breathing heavily, fists clenched tight. By the time Tony reached him, he had his rage down to a simmering point.

"Scott, what are you playing at?"

Mike gaped at his director. "What am *I* playing at? Did you not hear that little bastard? Who the fuck does he think he is, Jeff Stryker or something?"

"Aw, come on," Tony said softly, moving closer.

"Come on, nothing." Mike stared at him. "It was bad enough before we started filming. I got the feeling we were all taking up his precious time, he was so disinterested. There was me, coming up with suggestions for the scene, and there was him, not giving a fuck." He scrubbed his hand across his beard. "But all that crap? Why the fuck should I have to put up with that?"

"Just bear with it, okay?" Tony pleaded. "You know that once the sound editor gets finished with it, not one word of it will end up in the final version. Please, Scott." He laid a hand on Mike's arm. "Let's just get it done, all right?"

Mike took several deep, cleansing breaths, pushing out all the tension with long exhales. "Okay," he said at last. He and Tony walked back to the set, where Chad was once again on his phone, looking bored out of his skull, hand idly stroking his dick.

Chad glanced up at their approach. "Y'all done now? Hissy fit over?" He grinned.

Mike felt Tony's hand on his shoulder and bit back his retort. He flashed Chad that polite smile again. "Let's just finish this, okay?"

Chad shrugged. "Wasn't me callin' for a break, but there ya go." He put his phone down where it was still within reach and climbed back onto the bed. Mike resumed his last position and readied himself. Chad quickly pushed back into him and was soon grabbing his hips and yanking him back onto that big cock. "I looked you up, y'know," he said between thrusts.

What the fuck? "Huh?" Mike did his best to ignore the distraction and concentrated on getting erect again. Heaven knew it was proving more difficult than usual.

Chad bent over him, hips rocking as he fucked him faster, harder. He brought his lips to Mike's ear. "Yeah, you got quite a history, don'tcha? Just how many dicks has this big ol' hairy butt of yours taken?" His hips slammed into Mike's ass, the sharp slap of flesh against flesh.

"I don't actually keep score," Mike ground out, fighting the urge to stop the scene right then. "How about you shut up and let me do my job?" Talk about unprofessional…. Out of the corner of his eye, Mike caught a signal from Tony, and Chad suddenly clammed up. Mike sent Tony a silent vote of thanks and did his best to give the scene his full attention.

Things went better from then on, and after a couple of position changes, it was clear Chad was about to come. He whipped off the condom, and after a few tugs he shot his load over Mike's chest with a low cry. The camera moved in for a close-up of his creamy come, pooling between Mike's pecs, caught on the mat of hair.

With a satisfied sigh, Chad grabbed his towel and wiped himself down before giving Mike a smug smile. "Well, that's me done. Your turn." He sat back on his haunches, hands resting on his thighs.

Mike knew it was going to take a while. He closed his eyes and withdrew into his happy places. He replayed Saturday night, every look, every caress, the sounds that had poured out of Tommy' sweet mouth….

"Didn't know it was gonna take *this* long." Chad's bored tone drilled its way into his thoughts, and he tensed, doing his best to shut out the arrogant little prick. He brought his mind back to Tommy, hands gripping Mike's shoulders in the shower, the water pouring off him in a torrent, lips parted in a breathless *O* while Mike brought him to climax with his mouth. Little sounds intruded: Chad's fingers, tapping the bed frame; Chad's sighs, soft yet oh so fucking annoying; his tongue clicking, noises that spoke of impatience….

It took Mike several minutes to reach that point where his orgasm was finally in sight. He flicked his hand in a signal to Seb and then focused on pumping his cock, body tingling as his climax approached….

And then everything went to hell as he reached the point of no return and had to reel it back from the edge when Chad got up from the bed and walked away to send a message on his *fucking phone*.

Mike squeezed hard around the base of his dick, groaning in frustration. "Tony, for fuck's sake!"

He was gonna kill the little fucker.

"Chad, you need to keep your position, okay?" Mike caught the brief flicker of anger in the director's voice. Mike was in pain, his dick was so hard, his balls throbbing. The second that Chad was back where he should have been, Mike let it rip, his come erupting from his cock in an arc, hitting Chad square in the chest. Mike growled, body shaking, balls tingling. He waited until the shocks had died away, and then he lurched up from the bed toward Chad, who was wiping Mike's come off his body with a towel.

"Well, you got there eventually," Chad said with a smirk, arms folded across his chest.

That was fucking *it*.

Mike pulled back his fist to wipe that smug smile off Chad's face and knock him into the middle of next week, when Seb grabbed his upper arm. "Scott, no!" Wayne, the photographer, was at Mike's side in an instant, his hand on Mike's shoulder. Chad backed away from him, arms by his sides, his muscles tensed.

Something in Seb's voice broke through the red mist of Mike's rage, and he froze, his fist slowly unclenching. Chad was staring at him, quiet for once, the faintest flicker of fear across his face.

Mike shrugged himself free of Seb and Wayne, picked up his towel from beside the bed, and strode off the set to the showers. He was still trembling when the first rush of hot water hit his body. Mike braced himself against the tiles, elbows locked, head down, letting the shower wash it all away, all the anger, the frustration, that scary feeling that he'd just been about to make a very grave mistake. He had no idea how long he stood under the jets, but at last he regained his composure and reached for the shower gel to wash himself properly. By the time he was dried off and dressed, Mike was calm enough to think clearly. There'd been no sign of Chad, thank God. Mike wasn't *that* calm.

He walked out of the showers and across the now empty set to the little room that served as the office. Tony was seated at his desk, staring at his computer monitor. When Mike entered the room and softly closed the door behind him, Tony glanced up. He swallowed.

"You okay?"

Mike dropped onto the worn chair facing the desk. "Not really, no." He ran his fingers through the short layer of hair on top of his head. "I've been around this business long enough to realize nothing will be done about Chad. He brings in a lot of subscribers, I know. So while they got their little cash cow, they're gonna let him get away with a lotta crap."

"Hey, come on—"

"It is what is it, all right? It's business. I get that. But I'm not here to talk about Chad, okay?" Mike inhaled deeply. "Tony, I need you to do something for me."

"Okay," Tony said slowly, a hint of nervousness apparent in his voice.

"I want you to give Rod a message. I'd tell him myself, but this way I get to keep my temper, which I'm sure would be preferable for all concerned."

Tony's tight expression eased a little. "Yeah, that sounds like a good idea."

Mike paused. He knew Rod Bingham, ManFactory's owner, was a decent man, but right then Mike really didn't trust himself to stay calm. "Can you tell him to bear in mind when he plans future scenes for me—if he still wants to use me, after today—that I will *not* do any more scenes with gay-for-pay actors. You got that, Tony? Only gay or bi guys from now on."

Tony stared at him. "You sure about this, Scott? 'Cause this could seriously affect your career with ManFactory, and maybe other companies too, once it gets out. And you know it will."

"Well, that's a chance I'll have to take." Mike couldn't deny it was a big step, but his mind was made up. There was no way he could go through this again. It was undoubtedly the easiest solution, but he knew Tony was right—there *would* be repercussions.

Guess I'll just have to deal with them if—when—*they arise.* Maybe the writing was on the wall for Scott Masters, after twenty years in the business.

And maybe Scott Masters was just about ready for it.

CHAPTER SEVENTEEN

SOMETHING WAS up with Mike.

He'd seemed pleased to see Tommy when he arrived at just past ten o'clock, even gave him a little peck on the cheek, which had set Tommy off blushing like crazy, not that anyone seemed to notice. However, Tommy had been studying Mike since then, and yeah, all was definitely not well. He couldn't put his finger on it at first. Mike seemed tired, his eyes lacking their usual sparkle. Then he realized it was more than that.

The man was clearly feeling down.

When it got to midnight and nothing had changed, Tommy decided a little investigating was in order. He waited until Mike had disappeared around the other side of the bar and then caught Patrick's attention.

Patrick beamed at him. "Hey, sugar, whassup?" He puffed out his chest and flexed his arms, showing off those big guns of his. "You tired of ol' Mikey yet? Wanna try a *real* man for size?" Tommy stared at him, speechless, until Patrick cackled. "It's okay, hon, I know you're Mike's, all right? Now what's up?"

It took Tommy a second or two to get over the rush of warmth that Patrick's words released in him—*I'm Mike's?*—but then he recovered. "Is Mike okay? He doesn't seem like himself."

A little crease appeared between Patrick's eyebrows. "You don't miss much, do ya?" He regarded Tommy steadily for a moment, until Tommy was squirming under such scrutiny. Then he gave a satisfied nod, and Tommy had the distinct impression that he'd been given some sort of approval. "He's been like this for a couple days now. Whatever's buggin' him, he ain't talkin' about it. See if you can get him to open up, okay? He might talk to you."

"Sure, I can try." Privately Tommy thought Mike's coworkers had more of a chance than he did, but he was willing to try.

"Good boy." Patrick smiled at him and then glanced at his empty glass. "You want another Cherry Coke, or are you finally ready for something stronger?" His eyes twinkled.

Tommy chuckled. "I think I'll stick with the Cherry Coke, if that's all right. I still gotta drive later."

His face heated up when Patrick leaned across the bar and kissed him on the cheek. "Sugar, you are just so adorable." He walked away, chuckling to himself, only to return a minute later with a refill. Tommy thanked him and took a drink of the cold liquid, gazing around the bar. It was a relatively quiet night. As always some game or other was playing on the TV screen, and most of the guys in the bar were watching. Others were sitting around, chatting, laughing, and drinking. He caught sight of Mike out of the corner of his eye and watched him surreptitiously. Mike wasn't doing much talking, that was for sure. He flashed the odd smile at a customer, but there was none of the playful banter that Tommy loved to hear. It was starting to worry him.

By the time Mike was ready to leave, Tommy was in a real mess. He knew Mike had said he was okay meeting like this, but Tommy wasn't about to hold him to it if he wasn't in the mood. It wasn't like Tommy was desperate to repeat last Saturday's experience. He'd loved the sex, sure, but what concerned him most right then was that something was wrong, and he wanted to help, even if that meant letting Mike go home alone, if that was what he wanted.

Mike came from behind the bar, leather jacket in his hand. "You ready to go?"

Tommy nodded, unwilling to say anything in earshot of the other staff. Once they were outside, Mike got out his keys.

"You gonna follow me to my place?" He spoke quietly.

Tommy laid a hand on his arm. "It's okay if you wanna go home without me, all right? I mean, I get it that you might wanna be alone." Just looking at Mike made his heart ache. Whatever was weighing the man down sure was heavy.

Mike stood very still, eyes fixed on Tommy's. For a moment he said nothing, but Tommy got the impression that there was a lot going on behind those blue eyes. Then his careful expression melted into the first genuine smile Tommy had seen all night.

"You know what? Right now, being with you is all I want."

That smile and those words lifted Tommy's spirit. "I'll follow you, then."

Mike leaned closer and kissed him, nothing like the peck he'd received earlier. This was slower, more thorough, like Mike was relearning how Tommy tasted. He broke the kiss and stepped back. "Let's go."

Tommy got into his truck and followed Mike's car to the house. The neighborhood was peaceful, only a few lights showing in the windows of the houses nearby. He parked in Mike's driveway and climbed the steps to Mike's front door, where Mike awaited him. Once inside the hallway, Mike took Tommy's jacket and hung it up, along with his own.

"I'm gonna pour myself a drink," Mike said, heading into the kitchen. "You want something?"

Tommy followed him. "You got somethin' soft?"

Mike poured out a couple of fingers of bourbon and then reached into the fridge to pull out some cans. "I got pink lemonade, Coke, and cider."

Tommy accepted the can of pink lemonade. He emptied its contents into a glass and watched Mike take a long drink from his tumbler. Tommy couldn't keep silent anymore. "You wanna tell me what's botherin' you?"

Mike paused, the glass midway to his lips. He sighed and put down his bourbon. "It's a long story, and talking about it wouldn't help, but thank you for asking. Let's just say I have a few things on my mind, and I have to work through them, okay?"

"Okay. I just wanted to help, is all." Tommy watched as Mike drained the glass and then ran it under the faucet. He turned to face Tommy, such an air of fatigue about him that Tommy's heart went out to him. He put down his glass of lemonade and grabbed Mike's hand. "How 'bout we get you into bed, huh?" When Mike arched his eyebrows, the ghost of a smile on his lips, Tommy felt the red flush of heat that crept up his neck and cheeks. "To sleep, okay? Maybe some cuddlin'?" He could still recall how damn good it had felt to have Mike's strong arms encircling him the previous weekend.

That smile widened. "Cuddling, huh?" It was so good to see that sparkle in Mike's eyes. "Y'know, that sounds damn near perfect." He tightened his fingers around Tommy's. "Let's go to bed. I'll have a shower in the morning." He led Tommy out of the kitchen, flicking off the light as he passed the switch, and across the hall into his bedroom.

Tommy thought a night of snuggling with Mike sounded perfect too.

MIKE YAWNED and stretched, warm and relaxed. That had been the best night's sleep he'd had in a while. Of course falling asleep with his arms wrapped around Tommy's lean, warm body might've had something to do with it. He'd lain there under the soft cotton sheet, his face buried in Tommy's neck, inhaling his scent until he'd drifted off into a peaceful, dreamless sleep.

Wait a moment.... It was only now that he realized something was missing, namely Tommy. Mike raised his head from the pillow and caught the sound of running water, followed by the faintest whiff of freshly brewed coffee. *He's made coffee.* The thought brought a smile, and he fell back onto the pillows, feeling absurdly happy.

Tommy's arrival at Woofs the previous night had brought with it a certain amount of internal conflict. Mike was pleased to see him, that much was certain, but he was in no mood to even contemplate taking the young man home for a night of hot sex, which was undoubtedly what Tommy was expecting.

Mike smiled inwardly. *Boy, did I get* that *wrong.* It had become apparent after a while that Tommy wasn't there for the sex. Not only that, Patrick had made some comment about Mike being a lucky son of a bitch. Tommy must've said or done something pretty impressive to gain that reaction. Patrick was a tough customer, fiercely loyal and supportive.

He bit back a groan. *Patrick and Kevin.* He owed them big time. Mike knew he'd been a bitch ever since he'd gotten back from the shoot. He'd been unable to shake the incident, and the memory had clung to him like a bad smell. He figured he'd better treat the boys to breakfast soon to make up for being an asshole.

The aroma of coffee grew stronger.

Mike looked up from the bed to see Tommy standing in the doorway, hair damp, wearing nothing but his briefs and carrying two mugs of coffee. "Good mornin'."

Mike beamed. "Any morning where I wake up to coffee and the sight of a gorgeous young man is a good one." He sat up and held out his hands for a mug.

"Was it okay for me to take a shower?" Tommy worked his bottom lip. "I tried not to wake you."

"Of course it was okay." Mike sipped the coffee and sighed. "Damn, you make good coffee too. Boy, I think you're a keeper." He loved the way Tommy blushed. "I don't know about you, but I'm in a snuggling kinda mood."

Tommy's face lit up. "That sounds like my kinda mornin'."

Mike pulled back the sheets. "Then get back in here." Tommy moved around to the other side of the bed, and Mike cleared his throat. "I should warn you, there's an unwritten rule in this house."

"There is?" Tommy seemed startled, his gaze fixed on Mike.

He nodded, keeping his face straight. "Nudity at all times." He inclined his head toward Tommy's briefs. "Lose 'em." Then he grinned. "Now."

Tommy's breathing hitched, but he placed his mug on the nightstand. He eased his briefs down over his hips and firm, muscled thighs, and stepped out of them. Mike gazed up at Tommy's wide chest and taut belly with appreciation. The young man was beautiful. He lowered his gaze to take in that long, thick cock. Tommy noticed his observation and quickly climbed under the sheets, pulling them up around him. Mike hid his smile. Tommy's modesty was delightful, a refreshing change from the guys he usually mixed with.

Then it struck him. How many of those guys, when faced with the prospect of sharing Mike's bed, would be happy to cuddle?

In that instant, Mike's plans for Sunday morning changed. He wanted nothing more than to spend an hour or so in bed, holding Tommy, kissing him, caressing him, maybe having him touch Mike. And judging from Tommy's reaction, that was fine by him too.

It was exactly the balm Mike needed.

"MIKE, THIS place is amazing!"

Mike loved hearing the note of genuine awe in Tommy's voice. He smiled to see Tommy craning his neck to stare up at the curved acrylic tunnel, eyes wide as a manta ray floated serenely above their heads.

"How big is he, d'you reckon?"

Tommy shook his head, difficult as that was to do when he was staring up. "Eight feet across, maybe nine? Lord, just *look* at him. Isn't he beautiful?"

Coming to the aquarium had been a great idea. It had been an idle comment during breakfast when Mike had mentioned the glass tunnel. Tommy's reaction had been instantaneous. From that point, Mike couldn't wait to watch Tommy's face as they walked around the exhibits. All around them were visitors wearing the same expression, small children tugging at their parents' hands to pull them toward the acrylic wall.

Mike couldn't remember the last time he'd felt this relaxed. There was no pressure, just the simple enjoyment of spending time with Tommy. And after the rage and frustration of that last shoot, this trip to the aquarium was exactly what Mike needed. Space and time to be himself, to leave Scott Masters behind, even for a little while.

When did I last feel so comfortable with a guy? It certainly didn't feel like it was only their second weekend together. Tommy was easy to be around, made no demands, and seemed free of artifice. What was there not to like about a guy like that?

The most refreshing thing about Tommy was his innocence. This wasn't some twink playing at being coy; Tommy was the real deal.

He took a moment to study the young man from a distance. Tommy seemed relaxed, dressed in a pair of jeans, boots, a sweater, and a jacket. Even the way he looked was refreshingly different. Mike could easily picture Tommy working on the farm. Those calloused hands spoke of a young man who wasn't afraid of hard work.

"Y'know, this is the second largest tunnel of its kind in the world? How much water do you suppose is behind that acrylic?"

Tommy whirled around to look at him. "Hell, I don't have a clue." He squinted at Mike. "Bet you already know, don'tcha?"

Mike nodded. "Would you believe, over six million gallons of it?"

"Lord," Tommy exclaimed softly, eyes wide with wonder.

"You know this was built by the Homo Depot, right?"

"The what?" Tommy's mouth dropped open.

Mike chuckled. "And you call yourself gay? That's how every gay man refers to the Home Depot." An embarrassed Tommy was truly a thing of beauty. Mike smiled and then jerked his head up, frowning. "Did you feel that?"

"Feel what?"

Mike stretched out his hand, palm facing upward. "I swear I just felt…." He shook his head. "Nah, I must be mistaken."

Tommy gaped at him. "No, what did you feel?"

Mike bit his lip. "Well, for a moment there, it felt like a drop of water landed on me." He stared up at the curved surface of the tunnel. "Do you suppose… I mean, it *could* happen, couldn't it? All that pressure, all that water… must put a real strain on the tunnel…." He snuck a peek at Tommy's face and tried to hold back his laughter. Tommy was staring up at the tunnel, mouth still open.

Then suddenly he jerked his head back to glare at Mike. "You... you..."—his gaze narrowed—"you're just yankin' my chain, ain'tcha?"

Mike was really fighting the urge to grin. "Maybe."

From the expression on Tommy's face, he was trying not to grin too. "Damn, you almost had me believin' you." He shook his head. "Not gonna believe nothin' you say after this." He walked off, head held high, but Mike didn't miss Tommy's shoulders shaking.

They walked on together, marveling at the fish, the sharks, the rays. It really was impressive. Tommy caught sight of a giant grouper and burst out laughing.

Mike peered at it, but for the life of him, he couldn't see what was so amusing. "I give up. What's tickled you?"

Tommy pointed at the huge fish. "I swear, Mike. That fish is the spittin' image of my aunt Jeanie."

Mike gazed at the huge, downward curving mouth of the gray fish. "I'm just guessing, mind, but... your aunt Jeanie, she's not a very cheerful person, is she?" He tried not to smirk.

Tommy stared at him and promptly dissolved into giggles. When he recovered, he wiped his eyes. "Shit, no. She's an ornery ol' lady who doesn't have a pleasant word for anyone."

It was the first time Mike had heard Tommy talk about anyone in his family since that awful day when he'd told him about their intervention. He left it there, unwilling to risk spoiling Tommy's good mood. "Let's go to the touch tank next."

Tommy nodded eagerly. "I'd like that." As they walked along to the tank, Tommy was humming to himself, a happy little tune.

"You enjoying this?"

Tommy smiled. "Oh yeah, this is just great. Thanks for suggestin' it." He gave Mike a sideways glance. "How much longer do we have 'til you have to go to work?"

"Another hour or so." Just thinking about it brought him down. It took a moment or two for him to realize it wasn't the idea of going into Woofs that depressed him—it was the thought of calling an end to their time together.

Enough of this. Mike gave himself a mental shaking. *Day's not over yet.* "C'mon, let's go stroke a baby shark and some rays," he said with a grin.

The way Tommy's face lit up did wonderful things to his insides.

Damn, he's good for me.

CHAPTER EIGHTEEN

FIRST WEEKEND in February and it was pouring rain, so Mike's idea of going to the arboretum on Sunday afternoon was a no go. Still, Tommy had to admit his backup plan was original—playing Scrabble.

He was feeling mellow, warm and content, not surprising after a morning spent in bed. But what a morning. Hours of languid touching, kissing, and listening to the sound of the rain as it hit the windows. Lying in Mike's arms, just talking, more kissing, everything slow and sensual. And that was just fine by Tommy; the night before had been plenty hot enough. Just thinking about some of it sent the blood rushing south.

"Where's your head at?" Mike demanded, tapping the table with a Scrabble tile, the sharp sound snapping Tommy back into the present.

Tommy gave a start. "Sorry." He cleared his throat and shifted on his chair.

Mike's grin widened. "Do I need to guess what you were thinking about?"

Damn the man. "Whose turn is it?" He peered at his tile holder and realized it only had three letters sitting on it. "Oh." Apparently it was his. Tommy ignored Mike's rich chuckle and rummaged blind in the green fabric bag that contained the remaining tiles, drawing out four. He placed them on the holder and gazed intently at them. *Another shit selection.* Tommy glanced at the piece of paper by Mike's right hand and pursed his lips. Mike was winning. Again. Not surprising when his last word had been seven letters on a triple word score.

"How about I make us some hot chocolate while you're working it out?" Mike suggested. "It's just the sort of day that's perfect for hot chocolate."

"That sounds real nice," Tommy admitted. "Thank you." Mike rose to his feet and left the room. Tommy listened to the sounds emanating from the kitchen before it sank in that he had the perfect opportunity to sneak a look at the letters on Mike's holder. Then he reconsidered. He couldn't bring himself to cheat. That just wasn't him, even if his own letters were worth shit. *Damn it.*

Tommy hadn't realized until then just how competitive he was. By the time Mike returned with two steaming mugs, he was no closer to coming up with a decent word. *What's the point of havin' two decent scorin' letters and nowhere to use 'em?*

Mike said nothing but sat facing him, sipping his drink, peering at his tiles and smiling smugly. "It's a good thing we're not timing this," he said with a smirk.

"Not helpin'," Tommy said under his breath.

"You could always change all your letters and forfeit your go," Mike said with an innocent air

Tommy snorted. "You'd like that, wouldn't you? I'll just *bet* you've already got another seven letter word lined up, haven't ya?"

Mike feigned a suspicious gaze. "Did you peek while I was out of the room?" He chuckled. "Aww, c'mon, it's just a game."

"Yeah, an' you've already won once."

"I have, haven't I?" There was that smug smile again.

That. Was. It.

Tommy stroked his chin thoughtfully. "We-ell," he began, "there *is* one word I could put down." He strove to keep his face straight.

"Go for it." Mike peered at the board. There were a few open areas left, but so far Tommy hadn't come up with anything worth putting there.

Tommy tapped his index finger against his lips. "Okay, then." He chose six tiles and placed them carefully on the board. "There." He started adding up the score. It wasn't great, not in the same league as Mike's last effort, but it was better than nothing. "That gets me fifteen."

Mike's brow furrowed. "What's 'reborum'? I've never heard of that."

"Oh?" Tommy arched his eyebrows. "It's a natural fertilizer. It's been used in cotton fields since forever."

Mike shrugged. "You learn something new every day." He added the score to the sheet and then gazed at his holder. "You did better than me. I've got mostly consonants." He chose four tiles and added them to another word. "That gets me five, plus another eight for making a plural, so a total of thirteen. Still, not bad."

The game progressed for another thirty minutes, with Tommy coming up with more words to do with farming and agriculture. With each new addition, Mike noted the score, but Tommy had a feeling he might have pushed his luck with the last one.

Mike sat back in his chair and gazed levelly at Tommy, arms folded across that broad chest. "If I was to look up that word in an online dictionary, would I find it?" His eyes bored into Tommy.

Well, shit—busted. Tommy went for a bluff. "Sure, why wouldn't it be?" Mike stared harder, and Tommy fingered the collar of his shirt. "Of course, maybe my spellin' might be wrong, but yeah, I'm pretty sure it'd be in there."

Mike's mouth fell open. "Oh my God. Tommy Newsome, did you just lie to me?"

"No-oo," Tommy protested, but he could tell from Mike's face that the jig was up.

Mike shook his head, tut-tutting. "Wow. What can I say? An' there was I thinking what a nice, good, wholesome young man you were." He gave Tommy a sad smile.

Tommy stared at him, aghast. *Aw crap.* His heart sank—until Mike's smile suddenly morphed into a shit-eating grin, and Tommy didn't know whether to weep with relief or hit Mike for putting him through all that. Then he caught sight of a wicked glint in Mike's eyes. *Uh-oh....*

"Gonna put you over my knee and paddle your ass for that," Mike said, rising to his feet and making a show of rolling back his shirtsleeves. That grin of his hadn't budged an inch.

In spite of his racing heartbeat, Tommy chuckled. "You gotta catch me first." He stood up slowly, trying to work out what Mike would do next. Tommy edged around the table, his gaze trained on Mike. "An' who says I'm gonna let you whup my ass, even if you do catch me, *papaw?*" He grinned. "I'm bigger 'n' you." He started to back away carefully from the table, unsure of his footing but not daring to take his eyes off Mike.

Mike laughed. "Yeah, but I'm faster." Suddenly he lunged toward Tommy, hands ready to grab him. Tommy squealed, turned—and went flying over the arm of the couch, to land on the seat cushions with a *whump.* Mike yelled out a triumphant, gleeful shout and dived on top of him, those fingers going to work immediately, pulling up Tommy's sweater and T-shirt and tickling his ribs.

"Arrgh, Mike, no!" Tommy yelled, squirming, but there was no way to escape the torture when Mike's weight was pinning him to the couch. He tried to heave Mike off, but damn, he was stronger than Tommy had reckoned on.

"Ha! You thought I'd forgotten you were ticklish? Fat chance." Mike let his fingers dance over Tommy's abs until Tommy was crying and laughing, all at the same time. Mike's eyes sparkled. "You had enough yet? Huh?" All the while he kept up the remorseless assault. "Ready to say 'uncle'?"

Tommy could hardly see for the tears streaming down his face. "Uh-uh!" He didn't know how much more he could take. Mike paused, and for one blessed moment Tommy thought it was over—until Mike yanked up his T-shirt and started blowing raspberries on his belly. "Aw... shit, Mike... no!" He could barely scream out the words, his voice hoarse, his breathing ragged.

Mike let out a maniacal laugh. "Hell, I can do this all day if I have to."

There was only so much torture a boy could take.

"*Uncle!*"

Mike froze. "I win?" His face was inches from Tommy's, eyes bright, cheeks flushed.

"You win, you win," Tommy gasped out, heart pounding, face unbelievably hot. And then his pulse raced for an entirely different reason when Mike moved slowly, so slowly, and took his mouth in a soft kiss. "Oh." Tommy relaxed, melted into the couch, and let his body go limp beneath Mike's. He brought his hands up to cup Mike's head, wanting more, *needing* more.

Mike shifted to sit on the couch and pulled Tommy into his arms before sinking back into that kiss. Tommy looped one arm around Mike's neck and stroked his face with the other, eyes closed, breathing Mike in. His chest was still rising and falling from the exertion, heart beating strongly, but all he knew was Mike's lips, Mike's tongue that gently demanded entrance, Mike's strong hand rubbing his belly.

Mike broke the kiss to murmur against his mouth. "Mmm, making out on the couch on a rainy Sunday. Now, *this* is perfect."

Tommy was inclined to agree. "Yeah," he whispered, his fingertips seeking out the warm flesh of Mike's chest through the gaps between the buttons of his shirt.

He opened his eyes to see Mike smile and slowly undo the buttons, pulling the shirt to reveal the firm pecs with their soft covering of hair. "You wanna touch?" He grasped Tommy's hand and guided it to his nipple. "Play with it," he whispered. "I like that."

Tommy inclined his head to look directly at Mike. "Can... can I lick it?"

The rich chuckle that rumbled through Mike's chest was answer enough. "Lick it, suck it, bite it even." Mike grinned. "But I get to touch too." Before Tommy could say a word, Mike moved his hand down Tommy's belly to the waistband of his jeans and popped the button free. He lowered the zipper and slipped his hand inside, stroking over Tommy's briefs, where his dick was starting to harden.

Tommy's breathing stuttered, and Mike laughed quietly. "Hey, weren't you and my nipple getting acquainted?" His eyes gleamed.

Tommy brought his mouth to the firm little nub and licked over it, loving the shudder that coursed through Mike's body, the way his hips pushed up just that little bit. A lightness spread through Tommy's chest when realization dawned. *I did that. I made him feel good.* Damn, that felt amazing. A sense of power surged through him, and he took the nipple between his teeth and tugged it. There was no mistaking Mike's reaction. He rolled out a groan and pushed his hand into Tommy's briefs to wrap it around his shaft, pulling it free and working it gently.

It was Tommy's turn to shudder.

The pair of them sat there on the couch, Tommy teasing and biting Mike's nipple, his hand stroking that firm, taut belly, while Mike put his head back against the cushions and made low noises that went straight to Tommy's dick. Mike spat into his hand and then curled his fingers around Tommy's cock, sliding on the silken skin, moving slowly, gently building up speed.

Mike grabbed the back of Tommy's head, his fingers through his hair, and pulled him free to bring their mouths together in a not too gentle collision that left Tommy gasping for breath. Mike plundered his mouth, sucking on Tommy's tongue, that hand job not stopping for an instant. Tommy's hips bucked, body trembling, and then there he was, creaming over Mike's hand and moaning into that kiss. Mike held him steady throughout, until the jolts of orgasm had faded away. Tommy laid his head on Mike's shoulder and watched as Mike lifted his come-covered hand to his lips and lapped it all up, his gaze fixed on Tommy.

Oh my dear Lord, that is so hot. Then he got to taste himself when Mike kissed him, slowly, thoroughly, tongue sliding between Tommy's lips. Tommy closed his eyes and leaned into Mike's touch, enjoying the feel of that warm, hard body against his. He didn't want to think about leaving, about the coming week that was going to drag until he got to see Mike again. All that mattered was this, the two of them, curled up together, Mike's kiss, Mike's touch.

Who was he kidding? The way he was feeling right then, all that mattered was Mike.

MIKE WAVED Tommy off, watching until the truck was out of sight. He closed the front door and then walked into the kitchen to make himself a cup of coffee. Within the next half hour he needed to be showered and changed, ready for Woofs. Only, he didn't want to go.

He hadn't wanted Tommy to go either.

His phone's shrill tone broke through the quiet. He picked it up from the coffee table and groaned aloud. *Aw crap*. When the call connected, he braced himself for the onslaught. "Hi, Mom."

Her huff was clearly audible. "Oh, so you *are* alive, then. I was beginnin' to wonder."

"Don't give me that," he retorted, his chest tightening. "I know why you're calling."

"Have I done somethin'? Said somethin'?" she demanded. "Because it's been a few weeks now that I haven't had the pleasure of your comp'ny for Sunday lunch, and it's startin' to worry me."

Fuck. Mike felt like such a heel. "Look, I'm sorry, okay? It's just that I've been a little… busy these last weeks."

There was a moment of silence. "What's his name?"

"Excuse me?" Damn his mom's intuition.

"You heard me, Mike Scott. What's the name of the guy that's keepin' you away from your momma?" She chuckled. "I'm right, aren't I?"

"I will neither confirm nor deny your suspicions," Mike said with a grin. *Let her chew on that.*

"I knew it." She sounded insufferably pleased with herself. "Okay, you're forgiven. Only, mind you bring him along to meet me if it gets serious, y'hear?"

"Bring who? Did I say there was someone? Well, did I?" Mike was trying hard not to laugh.

His mom breezed on like she hadn't heard a single word he'd said. "Now I've got the yellin' out of the way, s'pose you tell me what's goin' on in your life? That's if you have the *time*, of course."

Mike sighed. Mom always knew how to twist the knife.

"HOW'S THE schedule looking for the next month or so?" Kevin asked Mike as they cleaned up, the last of the customers having just left. "You gonna be away filming at all? We're drawing up the new roster."

Mike got out his phone and pulled up his calendar. "Far as I can tell, unless anything changes, I got a shoot in Palm Springs at the end of February that'll be three days, going over a weekend." He wasn't looking forward to that one. The last shoot for TopMen had not gone well. There had been five or six guys staying in a house out in Palm Springs, and tempers had gotten a little frayed, to say the least. Two of the actors had complained that the company hadn't provided enough food for the shoot, and shopping for more hadn't been an option, given that the location was a tad remote. It had been bad enough that Ryan Prentice had already told Mike privately he wouldn't be filming for TopMen anymore, unless they got their act together and put on the shoots in more hospitable locations.

Mike couldn't blame him. What he couldn't get over, however, was Alex Travis. Unlike Ryan's low-key reaction, Alex had gone onto Twitter and very publicly lambasted their director. It had been downright ugly. Pete Harden, the director, had retaliated, declaring that if that was how Alex felt, then Pete wouldn't be happy about working with him in the future. It all left a sour taste in Mike's mouth. He could only hope that the situation had improved by the next shoot. He didn't have a clue who his costars would be, but then he hadn't known the last time either.

He put his phone away and got on with wiping down the bar. The hairs on the back of his neck prickled, and he glanced up to find Kevin staring at him. "What's up with you?" Mike asked, not slowing in his task. He was tired, and he wanted to get home to his bed. If he was real lucky, it would still smell of Tommy.

The thought was both comforting and torturous.

Kevin studied him for a moment. "Yep, he's good for ya." He gave a smug little smile and carried on putting away the cleaned glasses behind the bar.

Mike waited, but when nothing else was forthcoming, he growled. "That's it? That's all I get?"

Kevin chuckled. "Don't give me that. You know exactly what I'm talking about. Tommy. Patrick and me, we've noticed, okay? You've been different since he showed up."

"Is that so?" Mike threw down his cleaning rag and folded his arms across his chest. "You're full of shit, y'know that?"

Kevin shook his head and laughed. Mike couldn't let it go. "Different how?"

Kevin straightened and faced him. "You're more relaxed. You smile more. Laugh more. Stuff like that." He winked. "'Course, if it was me banging that gorgeous ass, I'd be smiling too." Kevin grinned.

"Ah, so you think it's just the sex." Mike shook his head and went back to his wiping.

"You mean it's not?" That brought Kevin to a standstill. "Mike?"

Mike sighed and gave up on his cleaning. He leaned against the bar. "I like him, okay? I like talking with him. He's… he's smart, Kev, like really smart. We laugh. And yeah, the sex is good, but it's not like we're tearing each other's clothes off the minute we get through my front door. Some weekends we don't even fuck, we just… cuddle." Mike laughed when Kevin's eyes widened. "Yeah, really."

A slow smile crept across Kevin's face. "Well, day-um." He lunged at Mike and hugged him, those thick tattooed arms squeezing him tight. "Hallelujah 'n' praise Jesus, Mikey's got himself a guy." He released him and stepped back, eyes shining.

Mike snorted. "Don't go getting ahead of yourself, now. We're not a couple, okay?"

Kevin gave him a knowing look. "Give it time, Mike. Just give it time."

Mike gazed at him intently. "You are *not* to go making out there's more to this than there is, especially when Tommy's here. You've seen what he's like. Kid'll probably die of sheer embarrassment." He glared. "I mean it, Kev."

Kevin held up his hands. "Okay, okay, I hear ya." His eyes gleamed. "But you can't blame a guy for thinkin'." He tilted his head to one side. "So when you're off filming in a few weeks' time, you're telling me you're not gonna miss him?" He waggled his eyebrows and walked off around the bar, whistling.

Mike stared after him. His protestations sounded hollow, even to his ears. And Kevin had made a valid point, damn him. Never mind missing Tommy when he'd be away filming—it was getting so that he missed him from one weekend to the next.

The "we're not a couple" argument was looking flimsier by the minute.

CHAPTER NINETEEN

TOMMY WAS trying to do justice to the delicious dinner Caroline had prepared, but his belly was all knotted up. Every mouthful felt like he was trying to swallow a bowling ball, not that he was hungry anyway. His appetite was all shot to shit. Beside him, Ben was wolfing down chicken like he didn't know when his next meal was coming. That was Ben, though. It took a lot to distract him from food, bless his heart.

Tommy gave up pushing his dinner around his plate and set down his silverware. He took a drink from his water glass and deliberately steered his thoughts away from their present course and onto the conversations that flowed around him. Caroline was listening to Bethany, who was regaling her with an animated account of what had happened that week at school. It seemed there'd been a major bust-up between Bethany's friends, and some of the more popular girls had taken the issue onto Facebook. Caroline nodded and made noises in all the right areas, but being the lady she was, she didn't talk much while she was eating. Benson was eating his dinner and giving long glances toward the financial papers that Caroline had taken away from him and placed out of reach. Every now and then he asked Ben a question about school, but Ben was too busy inhaling his dinner to provide any coherent answers.

Tommy loved these Friday nights. All the family gathered around the table for a meal, movies and popcorn later, a real sense of belonging….

And there he was, right back where he'd started, Momma's letter gnawing at him.

"Tommy? Tommy?"

It took a second or two to register Caroline's voice. Tommy jerked his head up and met her inquiring gaze. "Yes, ma'am?"

She studied him for a moment. "You all right, honey?" Her eyes were kind. "You were looking kinda lost there for a minute."

Tommy swallowed. "I'm fine," he lied. He wasn't about to talk about this at the dinner table, if at all. Caroline peered intently at him and then gave a nod of acceptance. Tommy made a last-ditch attempt to eat a little more, but his stomach was having none of it. He wanted to leave the table, but he knew that would only raise questions afterward, so he sat there, his mind turning over and over Momma's words.

With a shock he realized that dinner was over.

"Why don't y'all go set up the movie?" Caroline suggested to her husband and children. "I don't think we've chosen one yet that we all agree on. I'll clean up in here." She glanced at Tommy. "And you can help me fill the dishwasher, okay?"

"Yes, ma'am." Tommy began collecting the dirty plates and rinsing them before loading them and the silverware into the dishwasher. Benson, Ben, and his sister disappeared, but he caught laughter and exclamations coming from the media room where they usually watched movies. Choosing a DVD was half the fun of Friday nights. Finding one that everyone wanted to watch was usually an exercise in compromise.

"So, you gonna tell me what's on your mind?" Caroline paused in her task of setting up the coffee machine and regarded Tommy steadily. "And don't lie to me, Tommy, because I know there's something."

Tommy sat down at the table, hands clasped in front of him. "I… I got a letter today. From my momma."

"Oh?" Caroline left what she was doing and came to sit beside him, her hand reaching out to cover his, warm and soft. "This the first you've heard from her since Christmas, right?" He nodded. Caroline pursed her lips. "I'm assuming it wasn't good."

He let out a heavy sigh. "To be honest? After how my family was, I didn't expect to hear from anyone. So this was kind of a shock. She said my daddy didn't know she was writin' to me." Tommy's mind went back to that awful day. It had been Momma who'd tried at the last minute to get him to change his mind.

"What did she say in the letter?" Caroline asked quietly.

He breathed in deeply before replying. "She wanted me to know that if I came home an' agreed to have the therapy, all would be forgiven. That she loved me. An' she believed in her heart that I would see 'the error of my ways.'" Tommy closed his eyes. "She's not gonna change her mind any more than I am, is she?"

A gentle hand stroked his hair, and the touch was so tender that he had to fight hard not to weep.

"Sweetheart, I don't think so. Maybe it's best if you see that now. Don't hold on to a false hope." He felt her lips press softly against his forehead. "Tommy, look at me." He opened his eyes slowly and gazed at

Caroline's face. She smiled. "Any time you need someone to talk to, I'm here for you, y'hear? I can only imagine how hard it must be, not having the support and love of your parents. So if you ever need a substitute momma? I'm it." Her eyes sparkled as tears welled there, catching on her thick lashes, and she quickly wiped them away with her hand. "Look at me, getting all misty-eyed."

Impulsively, Tommy threw his arms around her and hugged her, his face buried at her neck where he could smell her perfume, the subtle scent of jasmine. She held him, stroking his hair, his back, and then they parted. Caroline kissed his forehead once more. "You are precious, you hear me?"

Tommy smiled. "Yes, ma'am."

She rose up from the table and went over to the coffee machine. "Can I ask you somethin'?"

"Sure." He joined her, collecting mugs from the cabinet for the coffee.

"How are things working out with... Mike, isn't it?" She tilted her head to one side. "Or am I not supposed to ask that?"

Hell, there went his cheeks, burning up again. "Things are just fine. Thank you for askin'." *An' please don't ask me again*, he begged silently.

"You haven't said much about him, is all." She got the cream jug from the refrigerator and set it on a tray. "So what does he do? Besides work in a gay bar."

Tommy shrugged. "I don't rightly know. We never talk about that." He'd tried a few times to find out a little more about his—*what do I call him? My boyfriend? Lover?*—about Mike, but somehow the conversation had always gone off on a tangent, leaving Tommy none the wiser. But now he was thinking about it once again, that was for sure. *How much do I know about Mike, beyond his taste in music an' movies?* He wasn't even certain of Mike's age.

Caroline arched her eyebrows. "'Course, that assumes you two actually *do* talk." There was a glint in her eyes, and right then Tommy wanted the ground to open up and swallow him whole.

Yeah, sex takes up a lot of our time. How would Mike feel if I said "More talk, less sex"?

Then he reconsidered. The sex was fantastic, not that he'd ever have said so.

"Dad wants to know what's keeping the coffee," Ben said from the doorway, grinning.

Caroline put her hands on her hips. "You can tell your father if he's in that much of a hurry for his coffee, he has my permission to come make it himself."

She met Tommy's gaze and shook her head. He bit back a smile. Ben disappeared. Caroline turned to Tommy.

"I meant it, Tommy. Any time you want to talk, you know where I am." And with that, she carried the tray containing the mugs, coffeepot, cream, and sugar out of the kitchen.

Tommy reached into the cabinet and brought out the bag of popcorn, his smile emerging. Caroline was something special, even if she *did* make him blush fire engine red.

MIKE STOOD in the doorway of his bathroom, watching Tommy under the shower. Except Tommy wasn't washing himself. He was standing there, head bowed, one hand on the tiles, the water hitting his head and shoulders. Mike had known minutes after Tommy had walked into Woofs that something was going on with him. They'd gone for breakfast, and Tommy had still been far too quiet for Mike's liking. Mike had waited to see if Tommy would share whatever was bugging him, but it had soon become clear that he wasn't ready to talk about it.

Well, no time like the present.

Mike walked slowly over to the shower and slid back the door. Tommy straightened and turned to face him. "Hey."

Mike stepped into the steamy enclosed space.

"I figured you might like someone to wash your back." He poured himself a handful of body wash and commenced soaping up Tommy's broad shoulders. Tommy relaxed into his touch and dipped his chin, sighing as Mike massaged the firm flesh. He could feel knots of tension in the muscles and started to knead them with his thumbs, keeping the pressure firm.

"Damn, that feels good."

Tommy braced himself against the tiles, and Mike went to town, working over that wide expanse of flesh. Mike pushed his thumbs into the hollows above Tommy's ass, and Tommy groaned.

"Oh God, there."

"You are all kinds of tensed up," Mike said after a few minutes of rubbing. He eased up on the pressure and concentrated on making

Tommy feel good. "You wanna tell me what's on your mind that's made you so tense?"

There was that sigh again. "Had… had some things on my mind, is all." Tommy turned slowly to face Mike, but when those green eyes didn't meet Mike's, he knew there was more to come. "I'm sorry." The words came out as a whisper.

Mike lifted Tommy's chin, his hand curved around that pink cheek. "What are you sorry for?"

That flush deepened. "I didn't want to…." He fell silent, his gaze lowering once more.

Ahhh. Mike brought their lips together in a soft kiss, keeping it chaste. When they parted, he smiled. "Tommy, I don't mind, really. No one said we have to have sex every time you come over."

"You don't mind?" Tommy looked him in the eye. "I know there've been a few times when all I wanted to do was just fall asleep with you, but I didn't know how to tell you."

"Yeah, about that." Just then the water ran cooler, and Mike shivered. "Let's get out of here and into bed. We'll be warmer in there, and we can talk, okay?"

Tommy nodded, and they quickly rinsed off.

When they were dry and once again under the sheets, Mike lay on his side, facing his young lover. "Okay, this is important." Tommy nodded, his gaze focused on Mike's face. "Tonight I sort of got the message that you didn't wanna fuck. Now, I'm no mind reader. It would've been a damn sight easier if you'd actually come right out and said, 'Mike, can we not have sex tonight?'" When Tommy opened his eyes wide, Mike smiled. "I know why you didn't, though. You do *not* like talking about such things, do you?"

Tommy bit his lip. "It's the way I was brought up, y'know? Sex is… dirty."

Mike stopped dead at that. "That what your parents brought you up to believe?"

He nodded. "An' that it was sorta… private. You just don't talk about it."

Mike regarded him in silence for a moment. "Baby, sex isn't dirty." He hesitated. "Well, it *can* be, but not in the way you're thinking. Sex is beautiful. It can be many things: loving, hotter 'n' hell, passionate…. And as for not talking about it, I'm the one you're having sex with!

You're supposed to tell me stuff!" He cupped Tommy's cheek. "Look, when you're in a relationship…."

Lord, but Tommy's eyes grew large and round at that. "Relationship?" His lips formed the word like he was tasting it, savoring it.

Mike nodded. "Well, what else do you call it when you've been coming over to my house for the last six weeks and spending the night in my bed? Going to the aquarium, the botanical gardens, playing Scrabble…."

Tommy's eyes sparkled at that one.

"My point is, when two adults are in a relationship, they talk about things, and that includes sex." He trailed his hand down over Tommy's chest and flicked his nipple with his thumb. Tommy shivered, and Mike grinned. "See, I know you like that. Not 'cause you *told* me, mind you, but because I watch you and I pay attention." He did it again. "Now tell me, does that make you feel dirty?"

Tommy's eyes were wide again. "No," he whispered. "Feels… feels good."

Mike leaned forward and kissed Tommy lightly on the mouth. "I'm glad. You should always feel comfortable enough to tell me when you like something that we do, when you *don't* like something, to ask me to do something, even beg me if need be…." He chuckled when Tommy coughed suddenly. "So, do you think you can do that?"

Tommy nodded. "Yeah…. Well, I can try."

He smiled, and seeing the light in his eyes sent warmth spreading through Mike.

"Good, I'm glad we got *that* straightened out." Mike grinned and leaned forward. "Does this mean you're gonna tell me what turns you on?" *God, this is fun.*

Tommy swallowed hard. "You mean, what I like you doing to me?"

Mike nodded, and Tommy flushed a deep red.

"Okay, maybe this might take a while 'til I feel more comfortable doin' that."

Mike couldn't hold back his laugh, and the bed shook with its force. Tommy's ears were bright red, but then he started laughing too. When they'd regained their composure, Mike rolled onto his back and held out his arm. Tommy knew what that meant. He edged closer across the mattress until he was lying next to Mike, his head on Mike's chest.

"Okay, *now* can you tell me what's been on your mind?" Mike stroked his hair absentmindedly.

Tommy's sigh was warm against his chest. "I got a letter from Momma, but I talked about that with Caroline, Ben's mom. She helped me calm down a little, but then she asked me somethin' that got me thinkin'."

"What was that?"

Tommy lay so still for a moment that Mike could almost have believed he'd fallen asleep.

"She asked me what you did, apart from workin' at Woofs, an' it made me realize how little I know 'bout you."

Fuck. Mike knew the fear was irrational, but that didn't stop his heartbeat from racing. It was only when he realized that Tommy would be able to feel it that he managed to calm himself. He inhaled slowly. "Okay," he began, "I suppose it's a fair point."

Now's the perfect opportunity to tell him about the porn. He could almost hear Kevin yelling at him, *"What are you waiting for? Tell him!"* But he couldn't. Just… couldn't. He'd been here too many times, had felt the same swell of hope that this time it would work out: *this* time his revelation wouldn't get the same reaction. He thought he'd found that hope with Dirk, thought he'd finally found what he'd been searching for—only to have that hope battered to a bloody pulp three years down the line when Dirk confessed how he really felt.

Not this time. Not with Tommy. The thought of seeing all the light die in those gorgeous eyes, watching that dawning horror….

Mike wasn't prepared to run the risk. Not yet, anyway. It was still early in their relationship for all that. He'd told Kevin that he would reveal the truth, but now he came to think about it….

"I'm an only child. When I was eight years old, my dad divorced my mom. He lives in Texas, and we're not close." He kissed Tommy's forehead. "Remember what I said about not getting to choose our blood relatives?" Tommy nodded. "Well, my dad still thinks being gay is a choice."

"Aw, I'm sorry, Mike." Tommy placed his hand on Mike's chest, rubbing him there.

That felt really good. "It is what it is. Anyhoo, Mom brought me up on her own. She was a working class girl from Atlanta, and she's worked hard all her life in department stores downtown. And she has no problem with having a gay son."

"That's good." Tommy stirred, snuggling closer. Mike heard the first note of fatigue creeping into his voice. He stretched out his arm and switched off the lamp, plunging the room into semidarkness.

"I finished high school and went off to college, where I majored in business. I graduated after four years from Georgia Tech. All through college I worked in bars. Back then I was earning $300 a night as a barback. I worked my way up to bartender at the Armory in midtown Atlanta, working nights, including weeknights. It wasn't long before I realized I was making more money working in gay bars than I would be in a job related to my degree. So I stuck with that."

"It really pays that much?" Tommy said with a yawn.

Mike chuckled. "I was working full time at Backstreet bar." He sighed. "Happy days. That was a great club." That was about as far as he could go with his history.

Tommy rolled away from him and onto his other side, grabbing Mike's arm and pulling it over his waist. "No wonder you're so good at your job," he said drowsily. Not surprising, since it was past three in the morning.

"Go to sleep, Tommy." Mike curved his body around Tommy's, relishing the feel of muscle and firm flesh. Tommy was slightly longer in the body than Mike and wider. "We can talk more tomorrow." Mike had something wrapped up and ready to leave with him, to be opened the following weekend. That was gonna be *all* kinds of fun. Mike had been planning this for a week.

"'Kay."

Tommy was already making those cute little noises that told Mike he was half asleep. Mike splayed his hand across Tommy's chest, feeling the reassuring beat of his heart beneath Mike's fingertips. He nuzzled Tommy's hair, breathing him in, letting the scent of freshly washed hair and clean skin fill his senses.

Mike's last thought before sleep took him was that this felt perfect.

Too perfect to run the risk of losing it. If the day ever came when he thought Tommy could deal, then he'd consider it. Not yet.

CHAPTER TWENTY

MIKE WALKED out onto the concourse of Palm Springs's tiny airport and spotted Don immediately. He'd been the driver the last time Mike had come out there to shoot for TopMen. Don waved at him and grabbed his bag.

"How was the trip?"

They walked toward the parking lot. Mike really liked the airport. It was small but cool due to the concourse being completely open air. Not having a roof was a nice touch. There were only a couple of little restaurants and shops, and they were enclosed and air conditioned, but otherwise passengers were basically outside.

Mike shrugged. "As good as any trip can be when you have connecting flights." At least Phoenix hadn't been too crowded, and he'd only had a ninety-minute layover. "Everyone arrived yet?" He yawned and covered his mouth. "Sorry. I didn't sleep too good last night." Thankfully the filming wasn't due to start until Saturday morning.

"You're the last," Don informed him. They arrived at the car, and Don dropped the bag into the trunk. "You wanna ride up front with me again?"

Mike smiled. "That'd be cool."

As they drove out of the airport's environs and through Palm Springs, Mike reflected on the choice of location. TopMen was a relatively new company, just emerging on the porn landscape. The decision to locate in Palm Springs looked ostensibly like a good one on paper. The town was very gay, but it was a sleepy little place and a touch remote. The residents seemed to have no problem with the appearance of a porn company filming in their drowsy borough, but it was just becoming clear that there'd been a huge problem in the community with drugs. So much so that the authorities were particularly sensitive to the issue.

Mike wasn't concerned. There'd been no evidence of drug use the last time he'd come out there to film, so it wasn't as if they'd have the local police breathing down their necks.

About half an hour later they pulled into the driveway of a large ranch-style house set back from the main road. A couple of cars were parked outside. Mike grabbed his bag, his laptop bag already slung over his shoulder, and strode along the cute little path that led to the front door, Don behind him. It opened before he could knock, and Pete, the director, stood in the open doorway, smiling.

"Hey, you made it! These guys have already got the party started." He stepped to one side to let the two men enter.

The instant Mike crossed the kitchen threshold, he was tackle-hugged by a huge bear of a man, dressed in only a pair of jeans. "Scott! It's been ages. How are you? Who you doing these days?"

Mike snorted. He wrestled himself free and dropped his bag to the floor. "Good to see you too, Nico. You've gotten bigger since the last time I saw you."

Nico grinned and flexed for him. "Thanks for noticing. I've been working on my upper body for the last few months."

It showed. Nico's abs were well defined, his pecs a firm handful. He posed, tightening his biceps.

Mike smiled and patted them appreciatively. "Yeah, very nice." He glanced around the roomy kitchen with its green cabinets. The breakfast bar was loaded with bags of food and bottles. Mike winked at Peter. "I see we're learning from past mistakes?"

Pete let out a groan. "God, don't remind me. At least Ryan's not here to eat us out of house and home this time." He indicated the two young men seated at the bar. "This is Jesse Bell and Kyler Foster, two of our newest recruits. You'll be doing a scene with Kyler. Guys, this is Scott Masters."

Jesse gave a polite nod and a smile in Mike's direction, but Kyler stared at him with wide eyes. "Oh my God," he said softly. He whipped his head to one side to look at Pete. "You didn't tell me I'd be filming with Scott Masters." He regarded Mike once more, cheeks flushed and licking his lips.

"Well, now you know," Pete said dryly. "I thought I'd surprise you." He winked at Mike as he took in Kyler's large eyes and rapt attention. "Obviously I thought correctly." Pete shook his head. "C'mon, Scott, I'll show you to your room."

Mike nodded to the two young men and followed Pete from the kitchen, with a last pat to Nico's broad back. As they went along the hallway, Pete let out a low chuckle.

"Young Kyler there has a real case of hero worship going on, in case you hadn't noticed."

Mike laughed quietly. "Yeah, I might've caught that." He placed his bag and laptop on the floor and looked around. The accommodation was basic. There was a mattress on the floor, a lamp beside it, and a clothes rail with hangers. One plastic chair stood by the window. "We gonna be shooting in different rooms?"

Pete nodded. "This room, the basement, the living room, and one of the rooms set up like a bedroom." He pointed to a sheaf of papers on the mattress. "That's your script. You can go through it tonight, ready for an early start tomorrow. We're gonna have us a full day of filming, so try *not* to go to bed at four in the morning, huh?" He grinned. "I've heard stories of what you and Armando get up to on shoots, so I *have* been forewarned."

"Armando?" Mike became still. "He's filming here?" There was a sudden fluttery feeling in his belly.

"Yeah, you two are playing the dads who are best friends. You're not filming a scene together, though." Peter gave him a speculative glance. "You okay with that?"

"Sure." Mike gave him what he hoped was a reassuring smile. "I've not seen him for a while, that's all."

Pete nodded. "Well, you'll be able to catch up tonight. Nico's cooking, God help us." He genuflected, and Mike snorted. "Dinner will be at six, so you've got a few hours to read through the script. If there's anything you want to know, I'll be in the garage with Tony, discussing final details. We can talk about lines, lighting, whatever." Pete smiled. "Glad to have you back with us, Scott. Especially after last time." His smile faltered.

Mike bit back his growl. "Yeah, I'm sorry Alex was such a little shit. I saw the tweets, the posts. He had no goddamn right." Having a big name like Alex Travis publicly vilify a fledgling company and its director couldn't have been good for business.

Pete shrugged. "Yeah, yeah. The damage is done. Let's hope we can salvage something with this shoot, right?" He patted Mike on the back. "But hey, we got Scott Masters!" His eyes sparkled. "And there's one young man in this house who can't wait to get fucked by you. Your stellar reputation goes before you." Pete grinned and exited the bedroom.

Mike smiled to himself. Stellar reputation. *That's what you get after twenty years in the industry*. His smile faded. *Jeez, twenty years*. All of a sudden Mike felt *old*.

Then it hit him. *Jack* was here. Not only that, Jack was filming with them. He figured Pete had to know Jack's status, and things must have been okay for him to have the go-ahead for the shoot. Some studios could be funny about using positive performers.

And then all such reflections were driven from his mind by one single thought.

We're gonna have to talk, him and me. What the fuck do I say to him?

Mike didn't have a fucking clue.

He gazed at his laptop bag, and suddenly there at the forefront of his mind was the reason for its presence, that conversation with Tommy from the previous Sunday. He clung to it as a welcome diversion. He couldn't think about Jack, not yet.

"So, will Ben be going out Saturday night?"

Tommy paused in the middle of packing his overnight bag and tilted his head. "Why'd you wanna know? You're gonna be God knows where." There was the teensiest pout that was just adorable.

"Because I have something planned for Saturday, and it would be best if you had the apartment to yourself. Locked door, no Ben likely to show up...." Mike grinned. "Think you can arrange that?"

Tommy's eyes glinted. "Yeah, that's doable. Wanna tell me what you got in mind?"

"Nope." Mike chuckled to see Tommy's expression of consternation. "You'll just have to wait 'n' see. But there is one thing I need to know. You've got a laptop, right?" Tommy nodded. "Does it have Skype?"

"No, but I can always download it. Why?" Tommy's eyes lit up. "We gonna chat via Skype while you're away?" He grinned. "I'd really like that."

Mike opened the drawer in his bedside cabinet and withdrew the gift-wrapped item. "Take this with you. You can't open it, mind. Not until we're Skyping next Saturday, okay?" He speared Tommy with a keen glance. "You promise? No peeking?"

Tommy laughed. "How old am I, six? Yeah, I promise." He packed the gift carefully into his bag and then moved to stand in front of Mike. "Just so's you know? In the spirit of sharin' how I'm feelin', like you asked?" He placed his hands on Mike's shoulders and looked him square in the face. "I'm gonna miss you next weekend." The words were uttered softly. He leaned forward and kissed Mike on the mouth, his hands looping around Mike's neck and drawing him closer.

Mike wrapped his arms around Tommy's firm torso and held him while they kissed, slowly, just a brushing of lips at first, but soon they were feeding soft moans into each other's mouths, hands moving restlessly over backs, arms, shoulders.

"Think we got time to make out a little before you have to go?" Mike murmured against his mouth, stroking down his back to cup that round ass. Tommy didn't reply, but Mike took his groan and slow nod to be answer enough.

The gentle tapping at his door dispelled the pleasant memory. Mike walked across and opened it to find Jack standing there, dressed in jeans and a dark blue T-shirt that showed off his ripped body and tattooed arms. The tattoo that curled around his collarbones was just visible above the neckline of his T-shirt.

"Hey." Jack gave him a half smile. He ran his hand through the short layers of hair on top of his head. "I was waiting for you to arrive." He glanced to his right down the hallway toward the kitchen. Mike could hear Nico laughing and chuckles from the two younger men. "Can I come in?" There was a jumpiness to him that was new.

"Sure." Mike stepped aside and let Jack into the room, closing the door behind him. He watched his former lover walk across the room to the window, shoulders hunched forward, his gait lacking his usual fluid grace. Mike frowned. "What have you done to yourself?"

Jack turned, eyebrows lifted. "Damn, that was quick." His smile widened. "I forgot how much you see."

Mike was having none of it. He took a deep breath, as if that would help to quell the anger and hurt welling up inside him. Fat chance.

"What the fuck, Jack?" He clenched his hands at his sides, staring at his old friend, suddenly finding it difficult to breathe.

Jack paled. "Mike?" He swallowed hard.

"Fucking *bareback*? What the fuck are you thinking of?" Mike's heart hammered so strongly, it caused him pain.

"Oh God. You know." Jack reached out for the plastic chair by the window and crumpled into it. "I shoulda known you'd get to hear about it." He gripped the arms of the chair, his knuckles white.

"Oh yeah, good news sure travels fast in this industry," Mike said with a snarl. "Far more important to me, however, is why I got to hear about it from William fucking Marks and not from you!" He couldn't keep a lid on all the emotion that bubbled up to the surface. "I can't believe you didn't tell me. After everything we talked about, our agreements…."

"Mike, please, hear me out," Jack pleaded, his face now white. "I can explain."

"We always talked about this, damn it!" Mike yelled. "Have you given a thought to the ramifications for your costars? 'Cause I'm thinking about *them* right now, not *you*, you selfish bastard. Damn it, you're supposed to care about people! The Jack *I* knew cared. He wouldn't risk the people he filmed with, curled up with, loved…." Mike struggled to draw a breath, his pulse speeding, heartbeat pounding.

Jack rose slowly to his feet, his breathing rapid, his expression pinched. "I don't have to listen to this." He walked stiffly to the door without a backward glance at Mike and shut the door after him.

Mike stared at the wooden door, the bile rising in his throat. He swallowed, fighting to compose himself.

Well, that *could've been handled better.*

He dropped down onto the mattress and lay on his back, gazing at the ceiling. He'd had no idea just how much Jack's decision had affected him. Little by little his anger dissipated, leaving him with an ache in his chest and a heaviness in his limbs.

I overreacted, plain and simple. Jack didn't deserve that much venom, not after all their years together. *What the fuck came over me?* Maybe it was a good thing he and Jack weren't shooting a scene together. Then it occurred to him that he hadn't exactly been quiet. The others would've heard everything. *Talk about awkward.*

He sat up and picked up the script from beside him. Not that he was in any mood to read it, but it was something to focus on. *Anything* to stop seeing Jack's ashen face in his head. He stared at the script, trying to take it all in, but the words just danced on the page, making no sense at all. When the call came for dinner, he abandoned the sheaf of papers with a sigh and got up from the bed. In the bathroom, he splashed cold water on his face and then dried it. He gazed at his reflection in the cool light above the washbasin, not in the least bit hungry.

With a sigh he straightened, flicked off the light, and headed down the hall into the brightly lit kitchen.

Dinner was… uncomfortable. Jack was silent, picking at the lasagna Nico had prepared. The two young men kept glancing at each other, their foreheads furrowed, faces unsmiling. Pete tried to make conversation but gave up after his jokes and funny stories fell on stony ground. It was a relief when the meal ended and everyone disappeared into their rooms for the rest of the evening, with the exception of Jesse and Kyler, who went outside to shoot some hoops, the yard lit by an outdoor light. Nico collected the plates and the leftover lasagna, clearly unhappy.

Mike retreated to his room and spent an hour or so rereading the script. He knew from the last shoot with this studio that the emphasis would be on the reactions of the actors to each other, their emotions and expressions, rather than focusing the camera on what went where. He hardly noticed the passage of time. When he was ready to call it a day, he waited his turn for the bathroom he shared with Nico to be empty, and then Mike slipped in for a wash before bed. His shower would wait until the morning, when he would go through his preshoot routines. Once back in the bedroom, he slid under the blankets and switched off the light. Little noise intruded from the outside world. Mike closed his eyes and worked on switching off his brain, but Jack was there, that white-faced stare, the pain in those brown eyes.

Let it go, he told himself. *Just… let it go.*

He turned his thoughts to Tommy. Damn, but it felt like he was a million miles away right then. Mike comforted himself with the anticipation of seeing his young lover the following night, even if it would only be via Skype. It was better than nothing. He'd hear that lovely Georgian drawl, see that sweet face. It wasn't long before Mike was drifting off to sleep, warm and cozy….

Only to awaken when the blankets lifted and a smooth, naked male form pressed up against him—an unmistakably horny male.

CHAPTER TWENTY-ONE

"WHAT THE fuck?" Mike shifted across the mattress and had the lamp switched on within seconds. He blinked in the bright light at Kyler, who lay beside him, frozen and wide-eyed. Mike expelled his tension in a long push of air. "Kyler, what are you doing?"

The young man gave a nervous laugh. "I-I'd have thought that was obvious."

Mike sighed. "I get to fuck you tomorrow." He glanced at his watch and shook his head. "Today," he corrected. "Is that not enough?" He gave Kyler a hard stare.

Kyler bit his lip. "I just wanted... it'll be different on set... I thought...."

Mike snorted. "I doubt you were thinking at all, except with your dick." One look at Kyler's ashen face reined in his frustration. God, the kid had to be barely legal. Mike let out another patient sigh. "Can I ask you something?"

"Sure." Kyler was watching him so carefully, his teeth working that full lower lip.

"How many scenes have you filmed so far? Not just with TopMen—what's your all time total?"

There was a moment's silence while Kyler stared at him, those eyes still wide. Mike could see the teeth marks in his lip. "This... this is my first," he admitted at last.

Mike nodded, his suspicions confirmed. He sat up cross-legged under the blankets, forearms resting on his thighs. "Then you need to listen to what I'm about to say, okay? And remember it."

Kyler gave a quick, nervous nod. Mike indicated Kyler in the bed.

"*This* is unprofessional. I don't know if you've gotten the impression that in the porn industry, everybody sleeps with everybody else, but it's not true. This is the start of what you probably hope will be a successful career. You're gonna be filming with the same costars for a lot of the time, and no, it is not professional to be sleeping around."

Kyler swallowed. "Really?"

Mike nodded. "These are guys who take intimacy *off* camera as seriously as they take it *on* camera. And these guys are only human. Here's a for instance. Say you got your wish and spent the night with me. Next morning, Jesse gets to hear about it. Jesse wonders why you wanted to sleep with me and not him. Jesse wants to know why he wasn't good enough to get to share your bed. You understanding this, kid? Feelings. Get. Hurt." He speared Kyler with an intense gaze.

Kyler squirmed. "I got it," he said quietly.

"Good." Mike pulled back the blankets to reveal Kyler's naked form. "Go back to your own bed, Kyler, 'cause nothing's gonna happen here, okay?"

He watched as the young man climbed off the mattress and padded out of the room without a backward glance. *Great, now there'll be an atmosphere on set.* He shuffled down under the blankets and switched off the lamp. He supposed he could have found Kyler's attentions flattering, but all he could think of was yet *another* twink who wanted to be fucked by Scott Masters. They didn't want Mike, they wanted his alter ego.

It took him a while to find that warm, fuzzy state again, but once he'd found it, Mike slipped into it like putting on a comfortable sweater and let it cling to him, distancing him from the tension and frustrations of the day. He was dimly aware of his bedroom door opening and closing, the soft footfall across the floor, the dip of the mattress as someone climbed into his bed again….

"Oh, for fuck's sake, Kyler," he began wearily, reaching for the lamp switch. "I thought we'd—" The words died in his throat when he saw Jack lying beside him.

"I couldn't sleep," Jack said simply. He met Mike's gaze, his face grave. "We need to talk."

Mike stared at him, his gut clenching. He'd known it was coming, knew it couldn't be avoided, but there in the quiet of his room, the prospect tightened his chest and quickened his breathing. "Okay," he said with a nod.

"Only…." Jack indicated the lamp with a flick of his head. "Can we turn the light off?" He swallowed. "I'd rather we talked in the dark, if you don't mind."

His request sent Mike's heart sinking. He could only guess at the pain Jack was experiencing—pain for which he had to take some of the blame. "Sure thing." He flicked off the lamp and lay down, keeping a little distance between them. For a moment the silence was overwhelming. This was his friend, his former lover, and yet Mike had never felt so far apart from Jack.

How the hell do I start this? The last thing he wanted to do was to jump down Jack's throat—again.

"I'm sorry I didn't call you." Jack's whisper crept out of the darkness. "I wanted to—God, how I wanted to—but the time never seemed right. I meant to call you six months ago when I got injured."

Mike's stomach churned. "What? What happened?" His breathing quickened. "Christ, Jack, you *should've* called me." The awkwardness he'd felt vanished in a rush of concern for his ex. He shifted closer, feeling for him. His hand found Jack's shoulder, and he gave it a light squeeze. "Hey. It's okay. You're here now, and we're talking, right?" He realized Jack had the right idea; the darkness was a comfort. "Talk to me, Jack." A moment's silence and then firm fingers found his, their hands intertwined. The contact felt good, reassuring.

Jack sighed. "About a year ago, I got to thinking that I was done with the industry. Don't get me wrong, I've had a good run, a pretty long career, but yeah, my star is definitely on the wane. More than once I've considered retiring."

Mike could deal with that. "Yeah, I know that feeling."

"You should—you've been in this game longer than me."

Mike pushed out a low growl, no real menace in it, but something he knew would bring an unseen smile to Jack's lips. He waited for his friend to continue.

"But then something happened. About six months ago, I got injured in a wrestling porn scene, and after that, getting regular work proved more and more difficult."

Mike's stomach clenched at the idea of Jack injured. "Was it bad?"

He felt rather than saw Jack's shrug. "I saw the physical therapists, the chiropractors, and that was made easier with the settlement from the company. They were really awesome about it. Little by little, things improved, and although it was harder to pay the bills, I scraped by. Then... I met someone." His voice brimmed with feeling. "Luca is... pretty special."

Mike heard the unspoken words. "I can tell," he said softly. Part of him was glad. Jack had spent so much time alone in recent years. It had hurt Mike just to see him every time he made the trek across the country to San Francisco where Jack lived. The nights he'd lain in bed with Jack in his arms, cradling him, telling him there was someone out there who was perfect for him—someone who would love everything about him. And then there were the long nights when Jack had wept in his arms, when another relationship failed because the newest love interest could not deal with Jack being HIV positive.

Kevin knew about Jack. Each time Mike told the bar staff that he was off to San Francisco, he'd joke that Mike was going to see his "West Coast hubby." Mike would smile to himself at that. Throughout his whole career, all his relationships, there had always been Jack in the background. It had been rare for Mike to find a partner who'd understood that he wasn't about to give up his relationship with Jack. There were a few friends that he curled up with on a regular basis, but that didn't mean he wouldn't commit to one guy, like he did with Dirk. When the right guy came along—even when he thought it was the right guy—he was committed.

A thought struck him. When was the last time he'd curled up with one of his close friends? There'd been no one since Dino, back at the end of September.

Jack let out another soft sigh, bringing Mike back into the moment. "Luca lives in Seattle, and we'd been together barely two months when we started talking about moving in together—me moving there. Thing was, I did the math and realized how much the move would cost me. So when Rock Hard Men got in contact, wanting to run this bareback company idea past me, I jumped at the chance." He fell silent for a moment. "God, the number of times I had the phone in my hand, about to call you to ask your opinion."

"You could've called me, y'know." Mike still couldn't believe Jack had taken such a leap without speaking to him. Abandoning his principles like that....

"Yeah?" Jack removed his hand from Mike's and shifted, until Mike could feel the heat radiating from Jack's body. "And what would you have said, Mike?" He could feel Jack's breath on his face.

Mike considered the question carefully. He'd really let it rip earlier, and he didn't want to hurt Jack again. "I would have told you that it wasn't something I could ever do, but that if you felt like it was what *you* needed to do, and if you wanted to do it, then—" He swallowed. "—I'd have said do it, and do it well. And that I'd still love you."

Silence. "Oh, Mike."

A large yet gentle hand found Mike's face. Jack's breath was warm as he moved closer to take Mike's mouth in a lingering kiss. Mike closed his eyes and lost himself in the memories evoked by that sweet embrace.

But that's just it—memories. That was the past, not now. It doesn't belong here in the present, not when I have Tommy.

The realization sent a flush of adrenaline tingling throughout his body. Tommy. He had Tommy, who was back in Atlanta, waiting for Mike to call him later that day, and here was Mike, kissing Jack....

When there were things that still needed to be said. Important things.

Mike took hold of Jack's hand and gently pulled it away from his face, breaking their kiss. "Enough about you. Enough about me. There's stuff we have to discuss." He took a deep breath. "Tell me you're looking out for your scene partners, Jack. Tell me you take goddamn Truvada every single fucking day. Tell me you're at least looking for some sign that *they're* on PrEP, and that you're being careful."

There was that overwhelming silence, and suddenly Mike had to see Jack's face. He switched on the lamp and stared at his ex, blinking in the light. "We made promises to each other, babe," Mike said at last. "Remember? We promised that wherever we were, whomever we were filming with, *we* would be the person on set who was taking care of everyone, making sure everyone was safe. 'Cause we knew we couldn't rely on the studios to do it for us."

Jack nodded. "Yes, I remember," he whispered.

Mike studied him. "But we both know there are days when you've got an infection, and your viral load soars. What then, Jack, when you're putting those around you at risk? Are you being careful then? Taking care of those you curl up with?"

Silence. Jack looked for all the world like he'd just taken a blow to the stomach. "You're really asking me that?"

Mike's heart sank to see Jack's pallor. "Babe, I have to. I never thought you'd do bareback, and yet here you are. I never believed you could do this. I... I thought you had more integrity than this." *Oh fuck. I said it.* The words were out, no taking them back. And with them, Mike found himself facing a prospect he'd never contemplated—losing Jack.

Jack winced, and the light died in his eyes. "Shit, Mike."

He grasped Jack's hand. "There are guys in this industry who do bareback because it's work and because, let's face it, there's no such thing as a full-time job in porn, is there? That also means there are guys out there who can't afford Truvada, which we both know costs an arm and a leg, so you can forget about health insurance. So yeah, you bet your ass I'm asking if you're taking care of them. 'Cause I don't think for one goddamn minute that Rock Hard Men is making sure every guy you film with is positive." He stared intently at Jack. "Tell me I'm wrong."

Jack bowed his head, but Mike still caught the words.

"You're not wrong."

Mike gazed at Jack's head, his heart pounding as he awaited Jack's next words. Jack lifted his chin and met Mike's gaze head on.

"Yes, babe. I swear. I'm being careful. I take my meds every single morning. I talk to guys on set, make sure they know the facts about Truvada. And you can bet I'm fucking careful on set too."

Mike looked into those expressive brown eyes. Jack seemed to be holding his breath. Finally Mike nodded. "Thank you." He was shaking.

Jack sagged onto the pillow, his relief evident. "Fuck, Mike. If you only knew how much I'd been dreading this conversation. I knew it was gonna be bad, but babe, you…." A shudder coursed through him.

Mike shifted on the mattress and pulled Jack to him, enfolding him in his arms. "Shhh, it's over now." They lay there in the silence, Mike's heartbeat returning to its normal pattern. He felt Jack's tension ease little by little, until he lay quietly, his head tucked against Mike's chest. For the first time since he'd laid eyes on Jack a few hours ago, Mike relaxed. "It *is* good to see you." It was the best signal he could give to let Jack know normal conversation could resume.

Jack picked up on it and eased himself out of Mike's arms. "You too. I'm just sorry we're not doing a scene together. Mine's with Jesse, who seems like a nice guy. Young, but aren't they all these days?" He smiled. "Anyway, enough about me. What's happening in the world of Scott Masters?" The color had returned to his cheeks.

"Not much." Mike chuckled. "I say that, and yet I have news similar to yours." He smiled. "I've met someone."

Jack's eyes widened. "But that's great news! Tell me all about him."

They lay on their sides, facing each other, heads propped up on pillows, while Mike told Jack all about how he'd met Tommy, their weekends together, Tommy's history. Jack made unhappy noises when he heard about Tommy's family and their ultimatum but snorted when Mike regaled him with the Scrabble story.

"He sounds like he's really good for you," Jack said with a smile. "Well, he's obviously good for you, 'cause you've never looked better."

"Flatterer."

"No, really. You look great, Mike." Jack's face glowed in the lamplight. "So, does he know about the porn?" Mike let out a heavy sigh, and Jack sat up in bed, eyes wide. "Oh fuck. You haven't told him, have you?"

"Not yet."

Jack studied him. "That sounds like you've thought about it, at least. Wanna tell me why you've put it off so far?"

"Does Luca know about you?" Mike demanded.

"Luca knows everything." Jack's face was soft. "*All* of it—the porn, my status, even those friends I curl up with when I'm away from him. And he's fine with it all."

"Then he's an exceptional man." Mike scraped a hand across his scalp. "Jack, the number of times I've thought 'This is it. This is the one.' Then he finds out about Scott Masters and bingo—adios." The thought of Tommy's face, lined in disappointment—or even worse, horror—was too much to contemplate.

"Mike, you have to tell him," Jack stressed. "You're hiding a huge part of yourself by not telling him."

"And what if I don't want to run the risk of losing him?"

"Mike." Jack's voice was gentle.

"Look, I'll tell him. I've already said I would, haven't I? It's just a question of finding the right moment."

"Then *make* the right moment," Jack suggested. "It's nearly spring break, isn't it? Why don't you take Tommy away somewhere, just the two of you? I'll bet with all your traveling, you've amassed enough frequent flier miles to be able to take him wherever you might wanna go."

Mike had to admit it was a good idea. In fact, now he thought about it, the idea really appealed to him. "I'm going to call him tonight. I'll put it to him then."

"Great." Jack stretched out his hand and stroked Mike's cheek. "So… can I sleep here with you tonight?" His voice softened.

Mike became still beneath that hand. "Since when have you and I ever shared a bed and just slept?" He knew what Jack was asking, and for some unknown reason his stomach clenched.

"True." Jack chuckled. "So I guess what I'm asking is, do you want to?"

Mike drew in a couple of deep, even breaths. "Would you be really hurt if I said no?"

Jack stared at him. Just... stared. Then his face creased in a slow, radiant smile. "Well, whaddaya know?" he exclaimed softly. "Mike Scott is in love."

The world seemed to spin just that little bit slower. "What?"

Jack tilted his head to one side. "Tommy's not just some guy, is he? You're in love with him. Or falling in love with him. Whatever." His lips parted, his breathing hitched. "Oh my God. Talk about blind." He grinned. "You really can't see it, can you? Oh, this is just... delicious." He leaned forward and kissed Mike on the lips. "I am so happy for you, Mike, really. I wish you every happiness."

Jack's words were more than a blessing. They were his way of letting Mike go, and Mike knew it. What was more astonishing was that Mike was ready for it. He'd expected a wrench that left him heart sore and hurting, but what he got instead was a slow release of... peace.

Mike curved his hand around Jack's face and kissed him on the mouth, a gentle brushing of lips. He smiled at him. "Thank you," he said softly. *Message received and understood.*

Jack's eyes sparkled. "Sleep well, babe." He threw back the blankets and got up from the mattress to stand next to it, gazing down at Mike, still wearing that same smile and shaking his head. "Who'd have thought it, huh? Mike Scott in love." He left the room, chuckling to himself.

Mike turned off the light and pulled the blanket up over his shoulders. He lay there, the words still ringing in his head. *In love with Tommy?* His first thought was that Jack was seeing something that simply wasn't there. Except the more he thought about it, the more sense it made. He pictured Tommy's face, that sweet smile, the way Tommy looked up at him when they were in bed together, that light in his eyes, the way Tommy made him feel....

Well, fuck. Maybe Jack wasn't so wrong after all.

BREAKFAST WAS over, the dishes cleared away, and everywhere was clean, ready for work to begin. The five actors sat around the breakfast bar with Pete and Tony, talking through the script, while the production crew got set up in the living room.

"We're going to film the five scenes in chronological order," Pete told them. "So that means Scott and Kyler first, the night of Kyler's eighteenth birthday. Then it's Jesse's scene with Armando, after he's seen Kyler and Scott asleep naked on the couch. The scene ends with Armando's wife coming home early to find him in bed with Jesse. Scene three is Armando's friend Nico coming 'round, and Jesse spying on him and Armando fucking in the basement. The next scene will be Jesse getting into bed with Kyler, and then it's the scene with Scott and Nico."

There were nods from everyone. Kyler was a little sullen and kept sneaking glances at Mike but said nothing. Jesse was calm and collected, although this would only be his second scene. And Nico was, well... Nico. Mike had to smile. The large man had an even larger personality, effervescent and full of enthusiasm.

Jack looked relaxed and content. He winked at Mike. "How ironic that you and I don't get to do a scene, given our history."

"I'd have thought you'd gotten your fill last night," Kyler blurted out. He glared at Mike. "You send *me* packing, but then you fuck *him*. I saw him sneaking into your room."

Jesse jerked his head up. "What were *you* doing in Scott's room in the first place?" He seemed upset by the revelation.

Mike sighed and shook his head. "And this is *exactly* what I was talking about last night." He stared at Kyler. "For your information—not that it's any of your business—I didn't fuck anyone last night. Correct?" He looked to Jack for confirmation, who nodded, his face tight. Jack hated confrontation. Mike gazed at Kyler. "Except now we have the situation where you and I are about to do a scene together. Bravo, Kyler. I'd say not only is the chemistry virtually nonexistent, it's going to be extremely difficult to make a convincing show that I've always wanted you. So you need to take on board what I said last night and *grow the fuck up*." He got up from the table and glanced at Pete. "I'll be upstairs getting ready. Call me when you're ready to shoot." He gave Kyler one last look and then exited the kitchen.

Jack caught up with him outside the bathroom. "Hey, don't let him get you down." He leaned close to whisper. "And if you have any difficulties, I'm sure you have some happy place you can go, right?" He chuckled, and the vibration tickled Mike's ear. Jack kissed his cheek and then stepped back.

Mike smiled. Jack really did know him. "Thanks for that." He returned Jack's kiss and then smacked him on the ass. "And now fuck off and let me go do my thing." He grinned. "And tell my scene partner to use the other bathroom, okay? He's done enough damage this morning. Don't let him add to it by disturbing my routine."

Jack smiled and disappeared down the hallway. Mike entered the bathroom and leaned against the door.

He really wasn't sure he could do this for much longer.

MIKE PULLED off the condom and shuddered, spraying Kyler's belly with come. He gripped the back of the couch and held on until his cock had stopped pulsing and the last drop had been squeezed from his slit. Breathing heavily, he leaned over Kyler and kissed him, stroking his hair and chest. Kyler moved as Pete had directed, until he was lying on top of Mike, eyes closed, apparently sated. Tony pulled back on the camera, capturing the view of the pair of them, lying peacefully in each other's arms. He cut to Jesse, standing in the doorway, staring at them and then walking away.

"Perfect." Pete applauded loudly, and Mike raised his head to see his director beaming. "Nice work, guys. And, Kyler? Congratulations on your first scene."

Kyler grinned. "Thanks, Pete." He propped himself up on his arms and gazed at Mike, his cheeks flushing. "Thanks, Scott."

Mike ruffled his hair. "You did good, okay? Just keep in mind my advice."

"I will. I promise." Kyler climbed off him, grabbed his towel from a nearby chair, and proceeded to wipe himself down.

"Okay, a ten-minute break for the crew, and then we'll do scene two an hour from now in the main bedroom. Jesse, Armando, be ready," Peter called out before going to talk with Tony, the two men peering at the screen on Tony's camera.

Mike got off the couch and wiped off his and Kyler's come with a towel.

"Nice to see you in action again," Jack said with a smile, stepping out of the way as the production crew picked up and moved cameras and studio lights, a buzz of activity around them. "I was trying to remember the last time we filmed together."

Mike scratched his beard. "Was it early last year? February, maybe?" He beamed. "We were filming for ManFactory, and that new director, oh, what's her name?"

"Alexa Stephens."

Mike nodded. "I haven't worked with her since. Pity. I like her stuff."

"Well, that's good to know," Pete said, looking up. "She's going to be directing with TopMen too."

Mike was pleased. It was yet another reason for considering working with the studio again in the future. Alexa's films had a lovely feel to them, and her scenes were in keeping with TopMen's aesthetic.

He glanced down at his sticky torso and now limp dick. "Okay, shower time." There was the low buzz of a phone vibrating. Mike shook his head and laughed when he saw it was Pete's. "Talk about good timing," he joked. He'd lost count of how many scenes had been ruined when a ring tone cut through the quiet, or worse still, the moans and groans of the actors.

Pete smiled and mouthed to him to fuck off as he pressed the phone to his ear. "Hey, hi, Michelle. What can I—" The smile died on his face, and his eyes widened while he listened intently. "Oh, for fuck's sake. Christ, I'm sorry that—" Mike was alarmed to see Pete's face whiten. "He did *what*?"

By now the living room had filled as everyone stood around, all eyes focused on Pete. The director's face was contorted, his brows knitted, nostrils flaring. "Okay, Michelle. Thanks for the heads-up. I'm on it." He disconnected the call and turned to face his cast. "You are not going to fucking believe this! Not content with lambasting me on Twitter, Alex Travis called Michelle, the lovely lady who owns this house, to inform her that porn was being filmed on the premises." Pete was shaking. "Fortunately she's a family friend, and she knows exactly what we're doing here, so no harm done. Except that little bastard went further. He told Michelle he's contacted the local newspaper and the police to inform them of the same thing, but has also implied heavily that drugs are being used here."

"That fucker!" Nico's face was crimson. "You don't *do* shit like this to colleagues—and *friends*, for fuck's sake!"

Jack snarled. "That is *it*. I want nothing more to do with that diva. As far as I'm concerned, he's just burned his bridges. I mean, what the fuck? Just because he was pissed about a bad experience, he goes and puts his friends in possible legal danger?"

"I think he's already burned a few bridges with the attacks on Pete on Twitter." Mike shook his head. "He wasn't exactly tactful about the last shoot. If word's gotten around, I wonder if it's lost him work and he's decided if *he* doesn't work, neither do we."

"Talk about selfish." Jesse stared unhappily at them. "This sucks. This *really* sucks."

"Look, standing around here discussing Alex is going to solve nothing," Pete growled out. "We have much more pressing concerns. For one thing, any minute now the police may be on our doorstep, wanting to search for drugs." He stared at them, chest heaving. "There's nothing for it, guys, but to shut this down, clean up, pack up, and get the fuck out of here. I for one want to be able to film here again." He stared at them all. "Well, what are you waiting for? Let's get moving!"

That last command proved the catalyst. Everyone began hurrying about the place, packing up and cleaning. Mike hurried to the bathroom to grab a quick shower before going to his room to pack his things and then get on with the general clear-up. As he bustled around the house, helping to pack away equipment, he worked hard to keep a lid on his anger. Alex's temper tantrum had not only cut into his income, which wasn't that great a worry, but it also meant that he had no idea where he would be that evening when he was supposed to be calling Tommy.

As far as he was concerned, Alex Travis was persona non grata. And God help him if Mike ever got his hands on him.

No one messed with Mike Scott's friends.

CHAPTER TWENTY-TWO

TOMMY'S PHONE pinged, announcing the arrival of a text, and he flew across the apartment to peer at the screen. When he read the words, he couldn't help smiling.

Lock your door—now. Skype on & present within reach. Waiting for you....

He put the phone down and scooted across the apartment to check he'd actually locked the door. Ben was out for the night—where, Tommy had no idea—and the rest of the Wellington family were upstairs, watching a movie. They'd asked Tommy if he wanted to join them, but he'd declined graciously. All he wanted was to see Mike.

He sank down onto the couch and opened the laptop, his mouth dry, his breathing quickening. He'd been unable to stop thinking about Mike all day, his thoughts a whirling, confusing muddle. There'd been very few Saturdays when he hadn't seen the sexy bartender, but unlike the previous occasion weeks ago, today had been the first time Tommy had been unhappy not to be seeing him. His hours with Mike had become important to him, and although he'd see him on the screen, it was definitely not the same thing.

The laptop was on his knee, Skype was loaded, and Tommy waited for the incoming call notes, his heart beating just that little bit faster. On the couch beside him sat the gift-wrapped box. The number of occasions that past week when he'd been dying of curiosity to know what was inside....

"There you are."

Damn, just hearing that voice made Tommy feel good. He grinned at the screen, where Mike's head, shoulders, and bare chest could be seen. "Hey. You in a hotel?"

Mike nodded, shoving a pillow behind his head and leaning against it. "And seeing you makes up for this crappy day." He smiled. "You have no idea how much I've been looking forward to seeing you."

Oh, I wouldn't be too sure 'bout that. Tommy couldn't give voice to the thought, however. He still found it difficult to share how he felt, in spite of Mike telling him that was what he wanted. "Why was it a crappy day? D'you get a lot of business done?" Mike had told him he'd gone away to California to do some consultation work.

Mike groaned. "This has been one fucked-up day. Nothing I'd planned came off." His expression softened. "The thought of seeing you was the only thing keeping me going."

"Oh." Inside, Tommy kind of... *melted* at Mike's words. He couldn't put his finger on it, but something was different about his lover. Maybe it was the unguarded way he was regarding Tommy. Whatever it was, it gave him a nudge to be bolder. "I... I missed you this week." It was the plain, unvarnished truth.

Mike stared at him in silence. Then he smiled, and it lit up his face, reaching his eyes and making them shine. "I missed you too," he said softly. "Listen, there's something I want to talk to you about. How'd you like to come away with me for a few days during spring break?"

"Really?" Tommy gaped, openmouthed. "Like, where?" His heart was pounding at the thought. This was different. This was... adult. Not that what they were doing wasn't adult. It just felt.... *Damn it, he messes with my head.*

"Wherever you want," Mike said simply. "I've got enough frequent flier miles for us to go anywhere you'd like. Panama City, or maybe even down to Fort Lauderdale or Key West." His eyes sparkled. "Maybe a gay resort?"

Tommy's heartbeat sped up. "Wow, that sounds... great." And terrifying. And illicit. And a whole bunch of other adjectives, all of which made his mouth dry and his body tingle. "Do I have to decide right now?"

Mike laughed. "No. We can talk about it when I see you next Saturday. You've only got this next week before spring break begins, that right?"

He nodded.

"Well, then, it can wait till next weekend. We can always try to book something last minute. The main thing is, you have a think about where you'd like to go." He lifted his eyebrows. "That's assuming, of course, that you *do* want to go away with me."

"Oh, I do!" Tommy hurried to assure him. He smiled. "I've never been on a plane before."

Mike chuckled. "This is turning out to be a year of firsts for you, isn't it?" He grinned. "So, did you manage to get through the week without peeking at my present?"

Tommy laughed. "You don't have much faith in me, do you?" He grabbed the gift and held it where Mike could see it. "There. Satisfied?"

"Well, that depends." Mike's voice suddenly had this husky quality that went straight to Tommy's dick. "Is the door locked like I said?"

"Uh-huh." Tommy swallowed.

"No chance we're gonna be disturbed?" Quieter.

"Uh-uh."

"Then open it."

Tommy tore at the paper, ripping it to shreds and tossing it onto the floor. He was holding a plain cardboard box, no indication of its contents. He lifted the lid and... stared.

"Well, take it out." There was an impatient edge to Mike's voice.

Tommy lifted out the dildo, which had lain on a cushion of tissue paper, and the small bottle of lube. "You bought me a dildo?" It was long and thick, a vibrator protruding from its base with a small dial that turned.

"Not exactly." Well, damn. Mike was blushing. "Look closely at it."

Tommy turned the dildo over in his hands and examined it. There was something familiar about it. With a rush of heat, he realized what he was looking at. "Mike... this is *your* cock."

Mike grinned. "Good boy. Nice to know you're paying attention when you're on your knees sucking me off." Tommy's cheeks were on fire. "I bought a kit that lets you make a cast of your dick. Then you clone your cock." He chuckled. "I figured if *I* couldn't be there in body, I could at least send part of me."

Tommy felt the heat flush over his whole face. He traced the contours of Mike's dick, captured in silicone. Damn, it even had that thick vein that ran along the top, the one Tommy liked licking, 'cause it always made Mike shudder.

"Tommy."

He jerked his head up, lost in his own little carnal world, and swallowed hard when he saw Mike on-screen. His lover had set the laptop at a distance from him at the foot of the bed, and now Tommy could see Mike was naked, his legs spread, knees bent, his hand gently stroking that rigid cock.

"Tommy, you're wearing far too many clothes." Mike grinned. "Take 'em off."

Oh… wow. He put down the dildo on the seat cushion beside him, then placed the laptop next to it. In a daze, Tommy rose to his feet and took off his T-shirt, his heartbeat pounding in his ears. He couldn't believe he was doing what Mike had asked, just because he'd asked it.

"It would be better if I could see you." Mike's voice sounded muffled coming from the speaker underneath the laptop. "So I'm just imagining you stripping for me." That husky quality again. It added to the whole… *wicked* feel of the situation. Tommy fumbled with his belt, all fingers and thumbs. "You gone shy on me, Tommy?"

Heart quaking, Tommy stepped into the camera's field of vision. Mike smiled.

"Oh, look at you."

The way he was staring at Tommy sent blood rushing to his dick and made him feel light-headed and dizzy. He lowered the zipper on his jeans and pushed them down, stepped out of them and then straightened, feeling so self-conscious.

"God, you have a gorgeous cock."

Fire rushed through him at Mike's words, the whole situation still with that illicit feel to it.

When he was naked, Tommy sat on the couch and turned the laptop to face him, seeing his chest and above in the small screen. Mike shook his head, laughing.

"Uh-uh, I want to see *all* of you. Stick the laptop at the end of the couch, and make sure you can see yourself on your screen."

Tommy did as directed, placing the laptop at the farthest end. He caught sight of himself in the bottom right-hand corner. Lord, he looked positively wanton sitting there, naked as a jaybird. He struggled to keep his breathing regular, but his gaze flitted between Mike's wicked smile and slow, slow hand, and the sight of his own shaft, lengthening and thickening.

"Fuck, you're beautiful." Mike stared at him, lips parted. "Shove some cushions behind you, so you're comfortable. And then spread for me. Let me see you, Tommy." His hand moved slowly over his dick, squeezing it, fingers stroking over his balls, his eyes never leaving Tommy.

Tommy bent one leg and pushed it against the back of the couch, and then placed his other foot on the floor. He shivered when he took in the view. Mike could see his ass, cock, balls…. "This feels…." Tommy shuddered, unable to finish the sentence.

"Show me how you jerk off," Mike whispered.

Shock rocketed through him. "That's… that's private."

Mike smiled. "Tommy, I've been inside you. It doesn't get any more private than that. But I wanna see how you make yourself come, when it's just you, alone in your room, your dick so hard it aches." He stroked the length of his cock. "Come on, baby. Show me. It's just you and me. Show me," he coaxed. "Show me how you play with yourself."

Tommy swallowed. "This… this is…."

"Scary?" Mike suggested, his expression warm. "I know. But I want to know you, everything about you." He fell silent, his gaze trained on Tommy. "So imagine I'm there with you. I'm sitting at the end of your couch, watching you." He laughed softly. "Like I can't keep my eyes off you, my *hands* off you."

The look he fired at Tommy was so intense, it made his knees weaken.

"God, I wanna be touching you right now."

"Yeah?" Tommy reveled in the feeling of power that coursed through him. He forgot about his fears, his inhibitions, and palmed his heavy, full cock, eyes focused on Mike. "Wish you were here too."

"What would you want me to do, if I was there?" Mike licked his lips. Tommy's new boldness faltered a little, and Mike smiled. "C'mon, we talked about this. Both of us telling the other how we felt, what we wanted…."

He was right, of course. Tommy drew in a deep breath. "I like it when… when you put your fingers inside me." He loved that, loved how it stretched him, loved the sensations when Mike stroked over his prostate. What he also loved was how Mike was making it good for him, getting him ready. He loved looking into those blue eyes while Mike fingerfucked him, his face showing just how much Mike loved doing this too.

"Oh yeah." Mike grinned. "Well, then, grab the lube." Tommy picked up the small bottle. Mike nodded. "Now get your finger nice 'n' slick."

Hands shaking, Tommy opened the cap and squeezed a few drops onto his index finger. He put the bottle aside and looked back to Mike, who was watching him closely.

"Stroke over your hole, nice 'n' slow. Pump your dick while you do it." Mike was playing with his balls, rolling those heavy orbs through his fingers. Tommy slid his finger over his hot pucker, shivering. "Now push it slowly inside you. Close your eyes if you want, pretend it's *my* finger, Tommy."

Tommy closed his eyes and slowly sank his finger into soft heat. It was easy to switch off his inhibitions and imagine Mike was stretched out on the couch in front of him, exploring him.

"How does it feel?"

"Feels... feels hot and tight. Burns a little," he panted. "But... feels good." He pulled his cock, trying to alleviate the aching sensation. The burn eased, and he moved his finger in and out a bit faster, starting to push down on it, hips rolling gently.

"Oh fuck, what you look like."

Tommy wanted to see.

He opened his eyes and gasped at the sight of him fucking himself, holding his dick rigid. He could feel precome, sticky and trickling down the shaft. It wasn't enough. "Want... want more," he confessed, his face hot.

Mike nodded. "Want to watch you fuck yourself with my cock." His voice was hoarse. "Slick it up, now."

Tommy's fingers were slippery, fumbling with the cap and dribbling the clear liquid onto the thick dildo. He tossed the bottle aside and lay back, holding the wide head against his hole. The silicone was cool to the touch, nothing like skin.

"That's it," Mike encouraged him. "Now push in the head, slowly. I'm there, Tommy, kneeling between your legs, my dick pressed against your hole, wanting in."

Tommy could hear the urgent need in his voice, and damn, it felt good. *He wants me.* He pushed, the muscle resisting him at first, until the head was inside him.

"Love how that feels." Mike's voice was soft. "You're always so hot, so tight, your body just taking me in like I belong inside you. You feel like you felt that first time I took you." His voice shook. "Fuck, Tommy, you felt so good." He laughed. "What am I saying? It *always* feels good with you, every single time."

Tommy's heart soared. "Love... love it when you're inside me," he gasped out. "When you're so deep, it's like you're a part of me." In spite of Mike wanting him to pretend, it was easier like this. Mike was thousands of miles away, and Tommy felt free to say the things he'd never voice in a million years. He slid the dildo into him, groaning as it stretched him. "Oh, man, that's thick." He stilled, letting his body adjust.

"Oh God, look at you." He heard the awe in Mike's voice. "God, I want to be there, want it to be me inside you."

Tommy wanted that too.

The burn melted away, and he began to fuck himself with the dildo, fingers reaching down to feel how it spread him wide, opened him up. He rode it hard, his mind seeing Mike there, hands on his hips as he thrust into Tommy. "Yes, oh yes." He trembled, the muscles in his thighs jumping.

"Push it all the way in," Mike whispered. "Now, turn it on."

Tommy complied and pushed out a low moan when the vibrations began. He could feel it *everywhere*. It pulsed through him, through his prostate, sending shivers radiating outward until his whole body was shaking. Tommy tugged faster on his cock, the dildo filling him to the hilt.

"Close, Mike." He could feel it.

"Gonna be coming with ya," Mike said with a groan. "Fuck, just watching you is bringing me to the edge." His breathing was loud and harsh through the speakers.

Tommy gripped his cock as it sent come shooting over his chest, his body tight around the dildo like a vise. He shuddered as wave after wave of pleasure rolled through him and over him, dimly aware of Mike groaning through his own orgasm. Tommy glanced at the screen to see Mike's body arching up off the bed, head thrown back, mouth open, hand covered with come as he held his dick. He looked… wonderful. Tommy flopped back onto the cushions and closed his eyes while his body lessened its grip on the dildo until he could push it out of him with a soft cry.

Little by little the shocks jolting his body died away, his breathing and heartbeat returning to normal. He could hear Mike's breathing, less rapid, more even. Tommy lifted his head and peered at his lover.

"Wow," he said, his voice quavering. "That was intense." Mike smiled, sitting upright and wiping himself with a towel. Now there was a thought. "You might've mentioned *before* we got started that I'd need one of those handy by the time we were done," Tommy said accusingly. He bit his lip to hold back his smile as he reached for his laptop to drag it closer.

Mike chuckled. "Oh, I don't know. Covered in come is a good look for you." He grinned and then put his hands behind his head. "Well, that was worth waiting for. It even made up for the crap I had to put up with today." He shook his head. "Anyway, gonna forget all about that. I'm flying home in the morning, early."

"You workin' tomorrow?"

Mike nodded. "It's over six hours' flying time, but I'll be back for my shift."

"Oh, okay." Tommy didn't want the call to be over. Despite Mike's insistence that he share his feelings, he didn't want to bother Mike if his lover had to go. "Well, if you need to get some sleep before—"

"Do you have to go?" Mike interjected. "I mean, right now?" He glanced at his watch. "It's six thirty here, which means it's nine thirty there. I need to eat something soon, but…." He moved and pulled the laptop closer, until his head and shoulders filled the screen. "I'd just like to spend some time talking with you, if that's okay."

Warmth surged through Tommy. "I'd like that too, only…." He paused and glanced downward. "Can I call you back after I've had a shower?"

Mike laughed. "That sounds like a good idea. Tell you what, I'll grab one too, and then I'll call room service. That way we can talk while I eat. Whaddaya say? Give me fifteen minutes?" He chuckled. "Or maybe not. Room service isn't known for being that speedy."

Tommy nodded, smiling. "Yeah, I can do that."

"Great." Mike beamed. "See you then." He disconnected, and the screen went black.

Tommy hurriedly put the laptop to one side and made a dash for the bathroom. The prospect of talking with Mike some more had him grinning like an idiot.

Like he cared.

CHAPTER TWENTY-THREE

TOMMY HELPED himself to more coffee, yawning widely.

"Looks like someone didn't get much sleep last night," Caroline said from behind him. She chuckled. "Did you stay up late or something?" The kitchen was quiet. Bethany had already left to play tennis at the club, and Ben was nowhere to be found. He hadn't come home the previous night, not that Tommy was about to share that with his mom. She didn't need to know.

He covered his mouth politely with his hand and turned around to face her. "Sorry. I was talkin' with Mike on Skype for a while." "A while" translated as four hours. One of the things they'd been discussing was Tommy's plans for the future. Mike had been impressed that if everything went according to plan, Tommy would have to study for a total of seven years to become a vet. What had impressed him most was that Tommy was prepared for that. Tommy knew it was going to be hard work, but it was what he wanted. It had felt really good talking through all his plans. They'd discussed summer school, his scholarship, *everything*.

It had been so nice, curled up in his sofa bed, the laptop on the mattress next to him where he could see it, Mike lying in his hotel room, the two of them talking. Tommy had been amazed at how quickly time had flown. He still couldn't get over the idea of Mike wanting to take him away.

"Okay, do I wanna know what just crossed your mind?" Caroline was grinning. "Because you have this little smile on your face right now."

Tommy knew he was blushing. "I guess I can tell you, seein' as you're sorta my substitute momma."

Caroline beamed at that. "Damn straight." He chuckled, and she laughed. "You know what I mean."

He couldn't help smiling. "Mike has asked me to go away with him for spring break. Just for a few days." His pulse raced at the thought.

Caroline arched her eyebrows. She poured herself more coffee. "And how do you feel about that?" She sat back in her chair, regarding him steadily.

Tommy shrugged. "Okay, I s'pose. Guess there's a first time for everything, right?" It did excite him, the idea of spending time in a hotel with Mike.

"Hmm." Caroline pursed her lips. "I'm gonna put on my substitute momma hat, in that case."

Tommy stared at her, chest tight. Caroline drummed her beautifully manicured nails on the tabletop.

"I want to meet him." She pressed her lips together.

"Meet Mike?" Tommy straightened, mouth open.

She nodded. "Bring him to lunch next Sunday." Caroline stared at him intently. "And I will *not* take no for an answer, y'hear? I'm the next best thing you've got to a momma right now, and I intend to take my responsibilities seriously. So if Mike wants to take you away, he has to meet *me* first." She smiled sweetly. "Sunday, midday. I will expect to see both of you." Her eyes glittered. "And now I'll take my husband some more coffee, while there's some left." She got up and crossed the floor to the coffee machine.

Tommy watched her, his mind in a whirl. He had no way of knowing how Mike would feel about Caroline's... invitation. All he knew was that it felt too much like introducing his lover to his prospective in-laws.

Talk about bein' taken home to meet the parents.... Damn, this was getting scary.

So why did he like the idea?

"MIKE? YOU still there?" The silence at the end of the phone was beginning to worry him.

"Sorry. You sorta caught me off guard for a minute. Let me get this straight. Caroline, your *roomie's* mom, wants me to come to Sunday lunch? *This* Sunday? So she can basically *vet* me?"

"Uh, yeah." Now that Tommy thought about it, he could understand how Mike might see it as kind of a weird setup. "You know how things are. She looks out for me. Hey, she was the one who took me shoppin' for that outfit I wore, the leather jacket 'n' pants? An' she 'n' her husband have been really good to me since...."

"Yeah, I know," Mike came back quickly. "And now that I've had time to think, it's not a bad thing. Like you said, she's looking out for you. Hell, for all *she* knows, I might be some old pervert who's about to kidnap you and sell you into sexual slavery."

The maniacal laughter that followed had Tommy giggling.

"Oh, man, you're gonna be trouble, aren't ya?"

Mike chuckled. "If it makes you feel any better, I'll be on my best behavior on Sunday, okay?"

It took a moment for his words to register. Then Tommy smiled. "So you're comin'?"

"Of course I'm coming. I'm gonna be charming, polite, funny, whatever it takes to show Caroline and the rest of her family that you'll be safe with me." He paused. "That I'll take care of you." His voice was soft.

It was Tommy's turn to be quiet. A warm glow spread throughout his body. "Thank you," he said quietly. He took a quick look at the clock. "Sorry, but I need to go. I'm working on a paper that's due Friday, an' I wanna make sure I've covered everything."

"Sure, you go get your studying done, Mr. Future Veterinarian."

Tommy chuckled. "I'll call you later, okay? Before I go to sleep?" It was a recent habit they'd gotten into and one that Tommy loved. Lying in his bed, listening to Mike's voice on the phone, feeling warm and cozy….

"Sounds good." Mike's voice grew husky. "Later, then."

"See ya." Tommy disconnected the call and placed the phone out of reach. He glanced at the pile of books to his left and sighed. Talking with Mike was a pleasant distraction, but there was work to be done. Time enough to chat with his lover when he'd finished his task.

Something Mike had said flashed through his mind, something about taking care of him, and just for a second the words got Tommy's dander up. *I don't need takin' care of.* For goodness' sake, he was nearly twenty. Then he got to thinking about it some more. *Does Mike see me as vulnerable? Innocent?*

The thought gave him pause.

Tommy liked how things were going with Mike. It was a good balance of sex and friendship, and he felt like it was moving in the right direction. He had no way of knowing if Mike felt the same way, but if his words were anything to go by, maybe they weren't on the same page—yet.

Then maybe I need to do something so he sees that I'm a man.

Tommy had been content to follow Mike's lead when it came to sex. Despite Mike's demand that he share his likes and dislikes, it still wasn't something he felt comfortable doing.

Then maybe it's time I did.

Ben might be into playing the field, but that wasn't Tommy. He guessed every bone in his body was monogamous, but he was just fine with that. Now all he had to do was make Mike see that he was *it*, pure 'n' simple, as far as Tommy was concerned.

Mike was the one.

THEY HADN'T stopped kissing once, not since they'd gotten through Mike's front door.

Boots kicked off, clothes off, followed by a collision of lips and tongues as Mike had steered Tommy backward into his bedroom, Tommy moaning into his mouth the whole time.

"Missed you… want you…." It was the first time his young lover had given voice to his need, and Mike hadn't hesitated.

Mike had seen it coming ever since Tommy had walked into Woofs. Christ, the looks he'd kept giving Mike, so fucking hot that Mike was hard as a rock by the time they'd left. It was a good thing there were no cops around, because he was damn sure he'd broken the speed limit, trying to get home in such a god-awful hurry. And Tommy had been right behind him the whole time.

Sex had *never* been this hot between them. Tommy was on fire, pulling him down to kiss him while Mike fucked him, arms around his neck and back, keeping them connected. Mike kept slowing down to kiss him. He wanted it to last a while, but there was little chance of that. He was drowning in sensation: the sound of their breathing, harsh in the quiet of his room; the feel of Tommy's thighs around his waist, ankles crossed on his back, his heels digging into the swell of Mike's ass; Tommy's kisses, hot, sloppy, and *so* fucking perfect.

Mike dropped his head to Tommy's neck, hips pistoning as he fucked him hard. "Close, baby," he panted. He rocked into Tommy, who met his thrusts with equal passion, the two of them gaining momentum as Mike punched his cock deep into Tommy, balls slapping against Tommy's ass. He stared down at Tommy and shoved his dick deep. "Whose ass is this?"

"Yours," Tommy cried out, eyes impossibly wide. Mike thrust hard again, and Tommy sobbed out, "Yours!"

His arms tightened around Mike, fingers digging into the flesh, until Mike could feel Tommy's nails scoring him, Tommy's mouth open in a breathless scream of pleasure.

That was it. "Oh, fuck, coming!"

"Yeah, oh, yeah!"

Tommy grabbed at the back of his head and kissed him, tongue going deep, moaning loudly while his ass gripped Mike's dick. Tommy's shaft was trapped between them, leaving sticky trails of precome over their abs.

"Oh shit!" Mike howled as he came, filling the condom, spilling into Tommy as deep as he could get. Heat spread between their bodies as Tommy came with a loud cry, arching up off the bed, body rigid as his orgasm hit. Mike held him, his dick pulsing inside him, unable to move as Tommy's muscles held him prisoner. Not that he wanted to.

They clung to each other, bodies racked with tremors, breathing erratic, until little by little, muscles relaxed, tension slipped away, and they lay in each other's arms, kissing, caressing, small noises escaping that made little or no sense. Mike nuzzled Tommy's neck, kissing the soft flesh, loving the way Tommy turned his head to meet Mike's lips with his own.

At last Mike eased out of him and shifted to lie beside him, stroking across his chest, both of them damp with perspiration. He gazed at Tommy and grinned. "Wow. Obviously I need to go away more often, if *this* is the reception I get when I come back." Tommy opened his mouth to speak, but Mike stopped his words with a gentle kiss. When they parted, he smiled. "I missed you too."

It was a while before either of them spoke, which was fine as far as Mike was concerned. Their beating hearts, exchanged looks, and tender caresses said more than words ever could. It had been a long time since Mike had felt this close to someone, this… connected, and there was a rightness to the relationship that Mike felt bone deep. He couldn't deny it.

He was in love with Tommy.

TOMMY GOT out of his truck, locked it, and waited for Mike to join him. He observed the way Mike kept straightening his tie and smoothing down his shirt. Tommy shook his head and chuckled.

"What?" Mike stared at him, brows knitted. He glanced down at himself and then back at Tommy. "Is there something wrong?"

Tommy walked across to where Mike stood next to his truck and kissed him on the cheek. "You're nervous. You're actually nervous." It was really sweet.

Mike made a gruff noise in the back of his throat. "Let's just say it's been a while since I've had to pass an inspection, okay?" Then he smiled. "So, will I do?"

"You look fine." Tommy ran his hand over Mike's chest, his fingertips brushing over his nipple. He loved how Mike shivered. "You like that?"

Mike pulled him closer and growled into his ear. "You *know* I like that. I liked it last night, and this morning, and every other goddamn time you do it. And if we didn't have to come *here*, we'd still be in my bed, where you could get your mouth around it. And then we'd be making love like we were last night."

It was Tommy's turn to shiver. "About last night," he began, but Mike cut him off with a kiss. When he'd finished, Tommy let out a slow exhale. "Wow."

"'Wow' is right. I haven't got a clue what got into you last night, but I gotta tell ya...." Mike broke off and wrapped his arms around Tommy's waist, looking him in the eye. "You were amazing, and I loved every second of it."

He kissed him again, slow and thorough, holding Tommy tight against him, for which Tommy was grateful. Mike's kiss was leaving him weak at the knees.

It had to come to an end, of course. Mike broke the kiss and stepped back. "And now it's time for me to make a good impression." His eyes gleamed as he held out his hand for Tommy to take it. The intimate gesture sent a thrill trickling down Tommy's spine. They walked hand in hand to the main door of the house. Mike glanced up at the house and shook his head. "They may live in the same neighborhood as me, but this place is worlds away from mine."

"It *is* a great house," Tommy admitted. "Wait 'til you see the inside." He lifted his hand to ring the bell, but the door swung open before he could connect with it. Caroline stood there, dressed in cream slacks, a cream cotton shirt, and a button-up sweater in pale green, open at the neckline to show her string of pearls. Her eyes widened the tiniest bit when she saw Mike, but she schooled her features quickly and gave him a warm smile.

"You must be Mike. Hi, I'm Caroline. Please, come on in." She stepped aside to let Mike enter and kissed Tommy on the cheek as he passed her. "Hi, honey." Once she'd closed the door, she led them through the airy hallway into the formal living room and gestured to the two-seater couch. "Take a seat. My husband will be here shortly. He's just taking a call in his den. Lunch is nearly ready, but I thought it would be nice to talk a little first."

Mike's eyes twinkled. "What you're really saying is you want to know what my intentions are." He sat down on the couch, flicking his head to Tommy to indicate that he should sit next to him. Caroline took the armchair facing them.

She beamed. "I like a man who's a straight shooter." She leaned against the seat cushions. "Tell me about yourself, Mike."

"Not that much to tell." He reached for Tommy's hand and placed it on his leg, Mike's hand covering his. There was a rightness to the gesture that sent a flood of warmth slowly spreading through Tommy. He sat there and listened as Mike talked about college and his life as a bartender, the sound of Mike's voice comfortable and familiar. Caroline listened intently, focused on Mike.

The living room door opened, and Ben and Bethany walked in. Bethany was all smiles when she caught sight of Mike, and when he wasn't looking, she gave Tommy the thumbs-up. Ben was a different story. He stared at Mike, mouth open. Caroline noticed instantly and frowned at him before turning her attention to Mike and smiling.

"Mike, these are my children, Ben and Bethany."

Mike rose to his feet and extended a hand to Bethany, who shook it vigorously. "A pleasure," he said. "Tommy's spoken about you a lot"—he winked—"and all of it good."

Bethany giggled. "I'll bet." She glanced at Caroline. "Anything I can do in the kitchen, Mom?"

"The rolls are warming in the oven. Could you get them out, please, and put them on the table along with the butter?"

Bethany nodded, and with one last smile at Mike, she left the room. Ben stood at the end of the couch, still staring. The tight knot of tension in Tommy's belly proved difficult to ignore. He wondered if their difference in ages was what caused Ben's reaction. Whatever it was, he didn't like it, and neither did Caroline, judging by the warning glances she kept sending in Ben's direction.

Benson made an appearance, and more introductions were made. Mike seemed at ease, chatting with him about his job as an international lawyer. Tommy was delighted to see how quickly Caroline and Benson warmed to Mike. The three of them talked at great length about what was going on in Atlanta, and Mike seemed sincerely interested in Caroline's work with her charities. He mentioned fund-raising events he'd undertaken or organized for several LGBT charities, and Caroline's face lit up. Tommy couldn't help smiling as he watched their conversation grow more animated. Bethany appeared from the kitchen with a tray of glasses full of sweet tea, and Mike accepted a glass with a smile. Ben, on the other hand, was a mystery. After about ten minutes or so, he'd quit staring, but he didn't say a whole lot. Mike appeared puzzled, and Tommy could understand that. He'd told Mike so much about his roomie, and this just wasn't like him. It was something of a relief when they all went into the dining room to have lunch.

Caroline had prepared roast beef with mashed potatoes, green beans, carrots, and gravy. Mike complimented her on the meal, and when he took a second helping of beef and mashed potatoes, she smiled widely. The atmosphere was relaxed for the most part, except for Ben talking very little. Tommy kept glancing at him, trying to work out what was bugging him, but Ben seemed to be avoiding meeting Tommy's gaze.

Throughout lunch Tommy was aware of Mike next to him. Now and again, Mike would stroke his thigh under the table, a light touch to connect them. His arm would brush against Tommy's, and he would catch a whiff of Mike's scent, a mixture of his cologne and, underneath it, the warm, earthy smell of pure Mike. The meal would have been perfect, if not for Ben.

Coffee followed, and Mike appeared genuinely sad to have to leave. A couple of hours had flown by, and Tommy was really pleased with how things had worked out. He guessed from Caroline's initial reaction that she might have something to say about Mike's age, but from the way lunch had gone, he wasn't so worried. Mike had obviously worked his magic.

"It was lovely meeting you," Caroline told Mike as she walked him to the front door. "You'll have to join us for dinner soon."

Tommy stood beside Mike, resisting the urge to take his hand.

Mike shook Benson's hand firmly and then leaned forward to kiss Caroline's cheek. "It would be a pleasure. I had a great time, and it was good to finally put faces to the names." He straightened, and his expression grew more serious. "I'm glad Tommy has you in his corner."

Caroline's cheeks flushed, and she smiled. "We love that boy like he's our own. And I feel a whole lot better about him going away with you, now that we've met." Her blush deepened.

Mike chuckled. "Caroline, I didn't mind in the least. You were looking out for Tommy, and that's a big deal in my book." He glanced at Tommy. "Gonna walk me to my truck?"

"Sure."

With one last nod to Caroline and Benson, Mike turned and walked down the driveway, reaching for Tommy's hand, their fingers entwined. When they got to the truck, Mike darted a glance toward the house before taking Tommy in his arms.

"I'm glad they invited me," he said quietly. "And I'm also glad I've put their minds at rest. So that means…." He cupped Tommy's cheek and kissed him slowly, taking his time, as though he was savoring the taste of him. Tommy closed his eyes and molded his body to Mike's as he leaned against his truck, thoroughly engaged in the kiss. He was aware of birdsong, the distant hum of traffic, the slight breeze that caught his hair where it was longer on top. But most of all, he sank willingly into Mike's embrace, his heartbeat quickening at the thought of his lover leaving.

Mike broke the kiss and leaned back. "I'll be calling you tonight when I finish, if you're still awake."

"I'll be awake," Tommy assured him. He wouldn't miss a chance to talk to Mike.

"And tomorrow we can discuss where we're going to go next week. Then I'll book us some flights, and we can be off for three or four days." He craned his neck and kissed the tip of Tommy's nose. "I can't wait."

There was that huskiness that made all Tommy's blood head south. "Me neither," he confessed.

Mike kissed him once more and then sighed. "It's no good. I gotta go, baby." He released Tommy and climbed into his truck. "I'll talk to you tonight."

"I'll be waitin'."

Mike rolled down his window and regarded Tommy in silence. Tommy's skin prickled. He had the strangest feeling that Mike wanted to say something, but the moment passed. Mike switched on the engine and, with a wave of his hand, pulled out of the driveway.

Tommy watched him until the truck was no longer in sight. He turned back toward the house and slowly walked up to the front door, which was ajar. When he got inside, he expected to find Caroline waiting for him, but instead it was Ben, who seemed agitated.

"Why didn't you tell me?" he demanded, eyes wide. "For God's sake, Tommy, how could you keep *that* quiet?"

"Tell you what? Keep what quiet?" Tommy shook his head. "You're not makin' sense."

Ben gaped at him. "Why didn't you tell me you're dating Scott Masters?"

CHAPTER TWENTY-FOUR

TOMMY WAS starting to think Ben had seriously lost it.

"What are you talkin' 'bout? You know his name's Mike."

Ben goggled. "You really don't know, do ya?" He grabbed Tommy's hand and tugged him through the hallway toward the door that led down to the basement apartment. "You need to come with me, *now*."

"But—" Tommy pulled back, but Ben held on tight.

"I mean it. This can't wait."

Tommy gave up fighting and just went along with whatever it was had Ben so fired up. He yanked his hand free of Ben's. "Okay, okay, I'm comin'." He followed Ben down the staircase and into his bedroom, sorely perplexed.

"Sit," Ben commanded, pointing to his bed, and then grabbed his laptop from where it sat on the floor next to the nightstand, charging. Tommy did as instructed. It was clear something was eating away at Ben, and the sooner he got it out, the better. Ben opened up the laptop and went online.

When Tommy saw the site, he groaned. "I do *not* wanna watch porn, okay? You know that stuff doesn't int'rest me." Having sex with Mike was one thing. He did *not* want to watch other guys having sex. His parents might have disowned him, but there were some things so deeply ingrained that he couldn't have gone against them if he tried.

Ben ignored him, peering at the screen, obviously searching for something. Suddenly he let out a "Yes!" and turned the laptop toward Tommy. On-screen, two guys were having sex on a couch, and even with the sound turned down low, he could hear their moans and cries.

Tommy was getting riled. "Okay, you're clearly not gonna listen to me, so I'm just gonna—" He choked on the words when the camera angle changed and he was staring at a guy who looked just like Mike on the screen. A younger Mike, no beard, fewer muscles maybe, but yeah, no question, it looked like Mike. Only it couldn't be—this guy had to be in his midtwenties.

"There," Ben said with a flourish of his hand toward the screen. "*That's* what I'm talking about. *That* is Scott Masters. He's a porn star.

Hell, he's one of the most famous porn stars around. He didn't tell you that, did he?"

Tommy blinked, then peered at the screen. He took a deep breath. "No," he said, stretching out the vowel, "that's not Mike. He just looks like him. That guy is way younger than Mike, for one thing."

Ben stared at him and then sighed. "Okay. We'll play it your way." He turned the laptop to face him, his finger moving over the pad.

"I think you need to stop this," Tommy started, but even as he said the words, Ben was turning the laptop once more and Tommy was confronted with a different view, a bed, two guys as before, but this time....

Oh dear Lord, it *was* Mike. *His* Mike, with the graying beard, even the glasses.

Mike, his dick deep in some guy's ass.

Mike, his face buried between the guy's asscheeks.

Mike, kissing this guy with passion, his hands all over him.

I think I'm gonna hurl. Bile rose in his throat.

It was like his insides had turned to ice. He dragged his gaze away from the screen and stared at Ben in absolute silence. No words would come. His throat was tight, his chest tighter.

"I'm sorry." Ben regarded him, his expression watchful. "I thought you knew. When I walked into the living room and saw him sitting there, I... I didn't know what to think. And when I watched the two of you.... Man, you were so comfortable with each other, I shoulda figured that you couldn't have known." He bit his lip. "Me tellin' you the way I did was harsh too."

"Tommy, can I talk with you for a minute?" Caroline walked into the bedroom, smiling. "I just wanted a word about Mike, that's all."

He hadn't heard her approach. Tommy shook his head. Numbness spread slowly through him, and he fought the nausea that threatened to overcome him. "Not... not right now." He rose slowly to his feet and teetered slightly. "Sorry, but I...." He couldn't fight it anymore.

Tommy ran past a startled-looking Caroline to the bathroom, slammed the door shut behind him, sank to his knees, and threw up his lunch. His throat burned, and the retching wouldn't quit. When it got to the dry heaves, he forced himself to draw in deep breaths. He closed his eyes and waited for the world to stop spinning and trying to throw him off. Behind him the door opened, and he felt Caroline's gentle hand on his shoulder.

"Sweetie, did something you ate for lunch disagree with you?" She rubbed across his back.

Tommy shook his head. He opened his eyes, reached for the toilet paper, and tore off a couple of sheets to wipe his mouth. His legs shook, and the muscles in his belly quivered.

Caroline crouched next to him and held her palm against his forehead. "You don't have a temperature."

Ben came to the doorway, his face miserable. "How you doing?"

Tommy looked up at him and raised his eyebrows. "How'd you think I'm doin'?"

Caroline turned to gaze at Ben. "Okay, what's going on here?"

After Tommy fired him a warning glare, Ben said quickly, "Tommy's not feeling so good."

"Well, that much I can see for myself." She stroked Tommy's back once again. "Can I get you anything, sugar?"

Tommy bit back the sob that was right there behind his lips to hear the kindness in Caroline's voice. "Just…. Just give me a minute, please." He leaned over the toilet bowl, his stomach tense, but there was nothing else in there. He caught Ben's whispered, "Come on, Mom," as he led her out of the bathroom. Tommy flushed and then sat with his back against the tub, his insides a swirling mass of tension.

Mike is a porn star. There was no getting away from it. The proof had been right there on the screen, not just once, but twice. Then it hit him, the difference in ages. Mike had obviously been doing this for a long time. Mike… having sex with guys on camera… *lots* of guys.

The thought was as physical as a blow to the solar plexus.

Tommy drew his knees up toward his chest and hugged them, his forehead pressed against them. He felt hollow, as fragile as the crystal that adorned the shelves of Caroline's china cabinet. One more shock and he'd shatter, splintered into thousands of tiny sparkling shards. In his head he kept seeing Mike on that screen, the expression on his face as he….

Tommy wanted to scream, as if that would force the images from his mind.

"Mom's gone back upstairs." Ben came into the bathroom and hunkered down next to Tommy. "I didn't say a word." He lightly stroked Tommy's arm. "How about we get you up off the bathroom floor and onto the couch? It's a damn sight more comfortable, for one thing."

Ben tried to help Tommy to his feet, but Tommy shrugged off his hand. "I can manage by myself." Pain pulsed through his temples as he stood up. One look at Ben's stricken expression was enough to set his stomach fluttering. He knew it wasn't Ben's fault. The resentment that filled him was nothing to do with Ben and everything to do with Mike having lied to him.

But did he? Lie to me? Or did he just keep his mouth shut?

Whichever way Tommy looked at it, Mike had chosen to keep silent about something that was huge.

Tommy walked into the living room, Ben hovering at his back. He went into the little kitchen area and poured himself a glass of water and drank the whole thing in a few gulps. All of a sudden he felt bone tired.

"Am I gonna be in your way if I lie down on the couch?" he asked Ben. "I just wanna close my eyes for a while." *And maybe sleep will help turn off my brain, 'cause right now, I can't take much more of this.*

Ben nodded. "Sure. I'll go upstairs and get out of your way." He hesitated, then pushed on. "I'm sorry, okay? I just didn't think—"

"No, you did not," Tommy said heavily. "But give me a while, an' I'll be fine." He locked gazes with Ben. "I know you felt you had to tell me, fair enough, but right now I'm havin' a hard time gettin' my head 'round that."

"I can understand that," Ben said quickly. "You take all the time you need." He stepped away from Tommy and headed for the stairs.

Tommy flopped onto the couch and put his arm across his eyes. It was no good. Mike was still there, still balls-deep in some other guy's ass, still whispering in his ear while he….

Hot tears pricked his eyelids and spilled out in a torrent that couldn't be held back another second. He turned his head to the back of the couch and sobbed into the seat cushions, letting it pour out of him. He cried his heart out until the back of his throat felt raw and his stomach muscles ached. When it had passed and he lay there, limp and exhausted, he curled up, arms tucked under his knees.

What do I do now?

What *could* he do? He was in love with a guy who he'd just discovered made his living from having sex with guys for thousands of other people to watch. And that was just the tip of the iceberg. There were the feelings of betrayal that twisted Tommy's guts into an ugly mess. Because Mike had just taken something that was *theirs* and stomped all over it.

OKAY, THIS was getting weird.

Tommy not answering his phone the previous night was kind of understandable. It was already past 1:30 a.m. when Mike had called. He figured Tommy had fallen asleep, and left him a message for when he woke up—a sexy message, seeing as there was no school for him and they were going to discuss plans for their little getaway. So when he woke up and reached for his phone to read Tommy's reply, he got….

Nothing. Not a word.

Mike sent another text. And another. And another.

When it got to midday and five texts had gone unanswered, the panic set in.

Something was really wrong. And Mike wasn't about to sit in his house when Tommy was only a few blocks away. He needed to make sure Tommy was okay, because this wasn't like him. He grabbed his jacket and his keys and hurried to his truck.

Tommy's truck was parked in the driveway when he got to the house. Mike went up to the front door and rang the bell. Bethany opened the door and smiled when she saw him.

"Hey, come on in."

Mike thanked her and stepped into the light hallway. Caroline came out of the living room to greet him. "Hey, Mike, what brings you here so soon?"

"Hi. Sorry to disturb you, but I wanted to see Tommy. I've been trying to reach him all morning, but so far there's been no word from him." He spoke calmly, despite the fact that his stomach was in knots and had been that way ever since his first few texts had gone unanswered.

Caroline's brow furrowed. "Really? He's around here somewhere." She walked along the hall a little ways and opened a door. "Tommy? You down there? Mike is here to see you." She turned back to Mike and smiled. "He shouldn't be long. He and Ben haven't been out of the house so far today." The smile became a grin. "You know what boys are like. Give them any excuse to stay in bed."

He returned her smile, hoping she was right and that was all it was. Only Tommy didn't strike him as the kind of young man who'd waste a morning in bed. Lord knew, he was always awake before Mike on

Sundays. Now Ben, yeah, he could believe that, based on what Tommy had shared about his roomie.

Ben appeared at the door, no trace of a smile. "Tommy doesn't want to see you." He stuck his hands in the pockets of his jeans.

What the fuck? "Is he all right?" Mike's heart pounded.

Caroline scowled at her son. "Ben, you're being rude. Apologize to Mike."

Ben gave him a sharp look. "No, I will not apologize to Mr. *Masters*." He stared at Mike unblinking.

Oh *fuck*.

Mike suddenly found it difficult to breathe as an invisible band tightened around his chest, cinching him in until it fucking hurt to draw breath.

Caroline became very still. "Okay, just what is going on here?" She faced Ben. "Tell me the truth, Benson."

Ben winced but then straightened. "Tommy found out yesterday that Mike Scott is none other than Scott Masters, a porn star." He glared at Mike. "You got any idea how much you've hurt him? You lied to him, for *months*."

Caroline turned slowly to regard Mike with wide eyes. "Is this true?"

Mike swallowed past the bowling ball in his throat. "Yes." It was all he could manage in the circumstances.

Caroline pulled herself up to her full height. "Then I'd like you to leave. Now." She seemed to be breathing more rapidly.

Mike was frozen to the spot. He wanted to argue that he hadn't lied, he'd just… omitted some details.

"Now, Mike—or whatever your name is." Caroline drew her mouth into a straight line and then bit her lip.

There was nothing for it but to leave.

Mike gave a slow nod and turned around to where Bethany was still standing by the front door, bright spots of color on her cheeks. She lowered her gaze when he passed her, and held open the door. Mike walked out of the house and along the driveway to his truck, resisting the urge to give a backward glance. When he climbed into the truck, he sat there clutching the steering wheel, his heart beating erratically.

What the fuck do I do now?

He couldn't leave things like this, that was for sure. It was way too late for that. Not when he was already lost, heart, body, and soul, in love with Tommy. Walking away wasn't an option.

Mike needed to go someplace quiet and think.

He switched on the engine and slowly pulled out of the driveway, the thoughts in his head colliding. He knew this whole fucked-up situation was his own doing. He could have been honest with Tommy from the start.

Except that probably would have been the shortest relationship in the history of short relationships.

Mike had been burned enough to know he'd wanted to put it off as long as possible. Christ, he'd planned to tell Tommy everything when they were away together. He'd told Kevin, told Jack….

Only someone had gotten there first. Probably Ben. That would account for the looks and the weird vibes Mike had been getting all through lunch. He wondered how long it had taken Ben to spill the beans once Mike had left. He had no way of knowing how Tommy felt; that was what was eating him up. Ben hadn't shown disgust. His attitude appeared to be one of concern for Tommy, and Mike couldn't fault him for that.

By the time Mike reached home, he was no nearer to coming up with a solution. There had to be one, because he loved Tommy and was not about to give up on the best thing that had ever happened to him.

Whatever it took, Mike was going to find a way. But at that moment? Fuck, he needed a drink.

CHAPTER TWENTY-FIVE

"ANOTHER, PLEASE." Mike rapped his empty glass on the bar. He was feeling comfortably numb, but not numb enough. The ache that filled him each time he tried to imagine what Tommy was feeling was proof enough of that. It was the not knowing that was killing him.

"I think you've had enough." Kevin folded his arms and did his best to glare at him, but that shit never worked on Mike anyhow. "What you really need to do is talk to me. What's wrong, Mikey? I've never seen you in here on a weeknight, for one thing. An' I thought you an' Tommy were going away for a few days."

Mike leaned forward, elbows on the bar, and counted off on his fingers. "One, I haven't had nearly enough. Trust me on that. Two, I'm in here 'cause I've spent the last two nights drinkin' alone an' I've had enough of my own sorry ass for comp'ny. And three, Tommy is the reason for my drinkin' in the first place." He held up the empty glass. "So don't make me climb over that bar and beat you, Kev. Pour me a drink."

Kevin contemplated him in silence for a moment and then nodded. He picked up the bottle and poured out a measure. "We're almost done for the night. You wanna hang around and talk when everyone's gone?"

Mike snorted. "Talkin' about this whole fucked-up mess is the last thing I wanna do. But I guess you deserve to know what's goin' on, after puttin' up with me whinin' all night."

Kevin's expression softened. "Dude, you haven't whined once, but you *have* worried the hell out of me. So drink that—slowly, mind—and we can talk later." He walked off to serve another customer, leaving Mike to gaze into the dark amber liquid.

Staring at his own four walls had grown too stultifying. It didn't help that he kept seeing Tommy in his bed, in the shower, at the dining table—hell, that boy was *everywhere*. When it all got too much, Mike grabbed his keys and left the house. Although he might have to take a cab home. He didn't dare risk driving in his state.

His head started to pound, and the bourbon lost its attractiveness. Mike leaned over until his forehead touched his crossed forearms on the bar, and closed his eyes. This wasn't him. Mike Scott did *not* let a guy get to him like this. Dirk had left him pretty messed up, and Mike had sworn that was the last time, but here he was, head over heels in love.

How'd Tommy get in so goddamn fast?

Mike knew how love could be. He'd seen guys meet one night at the bar, and the next weekend one of them was turning up at the other's place with a U-Haul. He knew couples who'd begun their relationship after a matter of days, that were still together decades later. Conversely, he'd watched many a relationship fall apart, even when everyone who knew the guys had felt sure this was it, love with a capital *L*.

Mike knew the truth. Love was a fickle bitch. Love was sneaky, devious, and had a mind of her own. The last thing he'd expected was to find himself ensnared in her tangled web again, hooked and pulled in by a fresh-faced, beautiful soul like Tommy. He just hadn't seen it coming.

It was something of a shock to realize the bar had gone quiet.

Mike looked up to find the place had emptied. Patrick was busy wiping down the bar and tables, and Kevin was collecting the last of the glasses. The pain in Mike's head had eased down a notch or two, and he slipped off his stool to stand on unsteady legs.

"I'm gonna go, guys."

Kevin was at his side in an instant. "Oh no, you're not. Patrick is gonna make us some coffee, and you are gonna sit there and tell us what's going on." Patrick nodded from behind the bar and headed back in search of coffee.

Mike sighed. Like he'd expected anything else.

One cup of coffee later and he'd told them everything. Kevin's face was a picture of misery, and Patrick looked glum.

"So what happens now?" Kevin asked him. "You're not just gonna walk away, right? I mean, you love him, don't ya?"

Mike stared at his empty coffee cup. "Yeah, I love him. I just need to figure out what my next move is."

Patrick grabbed his arm and gaped at him. "I'll tell you what your next move is. You quit feeling sorry for yourself and drinking like a fish, and you talk to him. You call him, and you *keep* calling him until he answers the fucking phone!"

Mike lifted his eyebrows at the outburst. "Hey, don't hold back, Patrick. Say what you feel." He gave his fellow bartender a wry smile.

Patrick shook his head, scowling. "I'm serious, Mike. That boy loves you. The age difference don't matter, your porn career don't matter, but he *does*. So you'd better fight for him, with everything you've got. An' you don't quit until you're certain you've done everything you possibly could. Is that clear?"

"Crystal." Mike rose to his feet, and Patrick copied him. He pulled Mike into a fierce hug and then released him with a huff. Mike patted his cheek. "Thank you."

Kevin eyed him keenly. "You're not thinking of driving that truck, are ya?"

Mike shook his head. "I'll call a cab and come by later to pick it up." He paused, regarding his two friends. "And I will call him. I promise. As soon as it's daylight and I know he's awake." It was Wednesday but only just, and enough time had passed to ease the severity of Tommy's emotions—he hoped.

It was Kevin's turn to give Mike a brief hug. "I hope it works for you two. I really do." He patted Mike on the butt. "Now go home and get some sleep." He grinned. "Us working dudes gotta finish up so we can grab some sleep too."

Mike picked up his jacket from the stool next to him and pulled his phone from his pocket. He scrolled through to find the cab firm he usually used and called to order a taxi. Outside the bar, the early morning air was cool enough to feel refreshing against his slightly aching head. He stood at the curb, watching the steady passage of cars and trucks past the bar, even at this early hour. Sleep had been elusive the last few nights, and Mike was hoping to crash for a while at least.

Then it would be time to call Tommy and see if they could sort out this mess.

TOMMY PEERED into the cabinets, but there was no sign of any hot chocolate. There wasn't much in them at all, actually. Ben tended to grab food from the family kitchen if he was hungry, but Tommy kept a supply of energy bars downstairs for between meals. He knew he was welcome in the family kitchen, but raiding those cabinets felt like too much of an intrusion. Except this was his third night of not sleeping so good, and he had the idea that hot chocolate might help. Nothing to do but to go upstairs. Ben was home for once. Tommy'd had the notion that his roomie might have made the most of spring break, but Ben had seemed reluctant to go out to his usual clubs.

He crept upstairs as quietly as he could, given that it was past one in the morning, and into the darkened kitchen. The light above the range hood was plenty enough for his purposes. Tommy reached into the cabinet to take out the container of hot chocolate. He figured heating milk on the stove was quieter than using the microwave. He leaned against the countertop, waiting for the milk to reach its temperature.

Is it too much to ask for a few hours of interrupted sleep? Apparently so. Tommy had stopped looking in the bathroom mirror when the dark smudges under his eyes grew darker still.

"Can't sleep, sweetheart?"

He gave a start when Caroline's quiet voice broke through his reflections. She stood in the doorway, dressed in her satin pajamas and robe pulled tight around her slim waist.

Tommy shook his head. "Thought this might help. Did I wake you? I'm sorry."

She walked over to him and put her arm around his waist. Caroline's head only reached his shoulder. "You didn't wake me, hon." She peered into the pan. "If I add some more milk, could you make me a cup too? Seems like we both had the same idea."

"Sure." Tommy crossed the room to the huge refrigerator and got out the milk while she spooned hot chocolate into another cup.

She came to stand at his side, leaning against him. "You haven't said a word to me since Sunday. In fact, I've hardly seen you." He could hear the quiet reproach in her voice.

"I'm sorry," he said at last. "But to tell the truth, I've hardly spoken with Ben either. Just wasn't in the mood, I guess." He switched off the stove and poured hot milk onto the brown powder, stirring as he did so. When he was done, he handed her a cup and then rinsed the saucepan under the faucet.

"Wanna talk about it now?" Caroline sat at the table, her eyes focused on him. "You never know. It might help sort out your thinking."

Tommy joined her and sagged into the chair. "That's just it. I don't know what to think. This business has me turned inside out." At least the numbness had passed, only to be replaced by brief flashes of rage when he thought about how Mike had kept hidden such a huge part of his life. When the rage had dissipated, all that remained was doubt.

Is it me? Did I bring this on myself? He'd thought of little else the last few days.

"I can understand that finding out Mike is a porn star might upset you," Caroline began.

"Ya think?" Tommy shook his head. "Ever since I was old enough to listen, my parents spoke of the evils of the world, an' porn was right up there at the top of the list. An' I listened but good. You prob'ly think it's strange to find a guy who's nearly twenty who's never watched a minute of porn in his entire life, up until Ben showed me… well, never mind what he showed me."

Caroline covered his larger hand with her more dainty one. "Not strange, sugar, refreshing. There's too little innocence out there these days. I'm just sorry you had to lose yours like that."

"Well, it's over now," Tommy said with a heavy heart. His tears had passed. It had taken until that morning for him to realize what he was feeling was grief. He was mourning the loss of Mike from his life, because he couldn't see a way back for them, not after this.

He sipped his hot chocolate, wincing when it burned his tongue. It took a moment or two to register that the quality of the silence had altered. He glanced across at Caroline, to find her staring at him with a mixture of sympathy and incredulity.

"What is it?" he asked her.

She gazed at him steadily and then sighed. "Sweetheart, you have to talk to Mike."

Tommy had never been so still. "Why?" he whispered. "Give me one good reason why I should ever speak to him again."

Her eyes were kind. "Because you need closure, honey."

The tears he'd sworn were finished caught on his lashes. "Uh-uh."

She nodded. "Trust me, darlin', it's better to hurt a little more at the beginning than to hurt a whole lot more at the end, with no answers." She stroked his cheek. "Baby, you need answers. You have to talk to him."

Tommy shivered. "Really?"

Caroline's eyes sparkled as tears welled up. "Oh, Tommy, I know right now it's the last thing you want to think of, but I know what I'm talking about. I've been around a lot longer than you. Has he tried calling you?"

Tommy nodded. "An' texts. It got to the point where I just switched off my phone."

Her fingers laced with his. "Then turn it back on and wait for him to call again. Only this time, answer it." Those fingers tightened. "Besides, you can't just switch off your feelings like that. And you do have feelings for Mike. That much is obvious." She tilted her head. "You wanna know something? Right up until the point where I found out he'd lied to you? I liked that man." She held up her hands. "Okay, I admit when I first saw him I was a tad worried about his age. But then I got to know him a little over lunch. More importantly, I watched the two of you."

Tommy swallowed. "And?"

Caroline's expression was warm. "I liked the way he was with you, the way he looked at you. This is why you need to talk to him. I don't care how this started out between you two, whether it was just sex, whatever…. That man cares deeply for you."

Pain surged through him, sharp and acute. "An' yet he wasn't truthful with me." He knew she was right, of course. He needed to hear what Mike had to say, but the thought of seeing him, being close to him…. Whichever way he looked at it, that conversation was going to hurt plenty.

"Go back to bed, Tommy, and try to get some sleep." Caroline stroked his hair. "Things always have a way of looking better in the light of day." She rose to her feet and held her arms wide. Tommy didn't hesitate. He stepped into them and was enveloped in a tight hug. "Lord, but you're big," she said with a chuckle. "I can barely get my arms around you."

Tommy smiled in spite of his sore heart. "Thank you for listening."

Caroline craned her neck to look him in the eye. "You're welcome, sugar. Anytime." She gently patted his cheek. "Now get." She grinned. "And thank you for the hot chocolate."

He nodded, and she released him. Tommy made his way through the quiet house to the staircase that led to the basement. Once he was on the couch, curled up under his blankets, the lamp extinguished and the apartment in darkness, he went over Caroline's words in his head.

Tommy didn't have a clue what he was going to say to Mike when they eventually got to talking. It would have been easier if his emotions weren't so tangled up. Betrayal, hurt, anguish…. He'd spent a couple of days at the mercy of one strong emotion or another, until he was exhausted. But what hurt most was the knowledge that he'd lost the man he loved, his first lover—the man he hoped would be his first *and* last.

CHAPTER TWENTY-SIX

MIKE PARKED the truck, switched off the engine, and took a long, deep breath as he stared at the Wellington family home. His stomach churned, and his hands were clammy.

Mike had never been this scared in his entire life.

He'd slept like the dead for about eight hours, which was probably the result of too much alcohol and not enough sleep for a few nights. After a hot shower, lots of coffee, and toast, he was feeling more human again. Nervous but human. And sick 'n' tired of doing nothing but wait. So there was only one thing left to do.

He got out of the truck and approached the front door, wiping his palms on his jeans. He'd parked behind Tommy's truck, so there was a good chance of finding him there. At least Mike hoped he was, now that he'd finally found the nerve to get up off his ass and do something. He took one last lung-filling breath and rang the doorbell.

A moment later the door opened and Caroline stood there, looking unsurprised to see him. "I thought you might be along at some point. Come on in." She stepped to one side to allow him entrance. "Tommy's in the kitchen. We've just finished lunch. Have you eaten?"

"I had some toast this morning. About all I could manage, but then I've not had much of an appetite lately."

Caroline turned to lead the way into the kitchen, but Mike stopped her with a hand to her arm.

"I know you probably don't want me to be here, but—"

"Tommy needs to talk to you, so it doesn't matter if I want you here or not," she said quickly, pulling away. "But I will say this. That boy is hurting, so don't you come here with any ideas about assuaging your own feelings of guilt. You have to do what you can to ease his pain. You got me?"

Fuck. "And what makes you think Tommy's the only one in pain right now?" he blurted out.

Caroline gazed at him, and Mike could've sworn he saw a flash of sympathy in her eyes.

"Yeah, I thought as much. So why don't you take Tommy downstairs where you can talk without being disturbed? Ben's gone into Atlanta."

Mike gave her a grateful nod. "Thank you."

She dipped her chin once and then went along the hall into the kitchen. He could hear the soft murmuring of voices, and for a few seconds panic raced through him. *Suppose Tommy doesn't want to see me after all? Suppose—*

"Hey."

Tommy was there, in the hallway, his face pale, eyes dull, hands shoved into his jeans pockets. The sight of him knifed into Mike, stealing his breath and making his heart quake.

"Hi." Now that he was standing there with Tommy, his resolve decided to take a hike. "Thanks for seeing me."

Tommy gestured with a flick of his head. "Let's go where we can talk, okay?" He opened a door. "After you."

Mike filed past him, conscious of the smell of freshly washed hair and Tommy's familiar scent. At the foot of the stairs he pushed open a door and found himself in an apartment. He could see a living room area, a little kitchen on one side, and a couple of doors leading off from the main floor. He recognized the couch instantly, and the memory of that night hit him forcibly. *Was that only just over a week ago?* He walked over there and waited for Tommy to join him.

"Do you want somethin' to drink?" Tommy inquired.

"Some water would be good." Mike was suddenly aware of his dry mouth. He sat down while Tommy fetched two glasses of water. He handed one to Mike and then sat at the other end of the couch, his back rigid. Mike found himself mimicking Tommy's posture. The silence that fell between them was almost tangible.

Well, one of us had better break the ice.

"Why didn't you tell me, Mike?"

Tommy stared at him, and fuck, the pain in those green eyes cut Mike to the bone.

Mike took a drink of cool water and placed his glass on the coffee table in front of him. "I was going to tell you this week," he began, keeping his voice low.

Tommy said nothing, but those eyes never left Mike.

"Look, I put off telling you because I've had relationships in the past where as soon as they found out about the porn, they were outta there."

Tommy's eyes widened. "An' right now, I don't blame 'em." He winced. "*Porn*? Mike, have you any idea how that makes me feel? You... you have sex with guys for a living?"

All Mike could do was nod.

Tommy pressed his lips together, his gaze locked on Mike. "How long? Just how long have you been doin' this? An' how in the world did you get into this in the first place? 'Cause it's not exactly a career choice that's discussed at high school, is it?" His chest heaved, and his breathing quickened.

"Remember I told you I worked at Backstreet?" Tommy nodded, and Mike pushed on. "I was twenty-three. Well, one night this guy starts hitting on me. He was gorgeous, cute, sexy, and I was flattered because I'd seen him in porn movies. I couldn't believe he was even talking to me. He sat in front of me all night, chatting away, flirting like crazy. Suddenly there's this guy next to him—turns out he was a director for a porn studio—and he's asking me if I wanna do porn. Just like that."

Tommy nodded. "Go on."

"I was saving up for a house, so the offer came at a really good time."

Tommy stared at him. "That was it? You just said yes?"

Mike sighed. "I was twenty-three. I enjoyed having sex. I figured, why not get paid for doing something I loved?" He gave a shrug. "Then I started getting popular. Before long I had an endless supply of shoots and was able to buy this house."

"I'm guessin' you still love doin' it, judgin' from what I saw on the Internet." Tommy shifted on the couch, gazing at the glass in his hand.

It took a moment for Tommy's words to register. "Wait—what?"

Tommy swallowed hard. "It was bad enough when I found out about the... the porn. But watchin' you on-screen, that was...." He shuddered.

"What? Tell me what you were thinking."

Tommy took a moment before responding. "I... I thought what we had was special. Somethin' that only we shared." He breathed deeply. "I close my eyes sometimes, an' I can picture you in my mind, the way you look at me when... when you're inside me. I can hear the sounds you make, the noises that tell me how much you're lovin' it...." Tommy closed his eyes for a moment and then opened them to look straight at Mike, his cheeks pink. "So imagine how I felt when I saw you... makin' love to someone else, that same look on your face, those same noises, the way you were touchin' him." He shook his head. "It was like a kick to my guts."

Oh Christ.

Mike felt the blood drain from his face. "Baby, what we have *is* special. Why'd you think I've waited so long before telling you? I couldn't bear the thought of you walking out of my life." He left his seat on the couch and knelt on the floor in front of Tommy. He wanted so badly to touch him, but it felt as if to do so might be a step too far for Tommy right then. "Tommy, why do you think I'm here? I don't want to lose you. I… I love you."

Tommy froze, his eyes locked on Mike. "You love me? A week ago, I'd have been dancin' on the ceilin' to hear those words, but now? Mike, you were makin' love with another guy. Hundreds of guys, for all I know."

"But that's not real." Mike leaned forward, itching to reach out and place his hand on Tommy's knee.

"I saw it!" Tommy yelled. "There, on the screen." He lunged to his feet, fists clenched, and began pacing around the couch. "So don't you tell me it wasn't real. I *saw* how you looked at him! Like bein' inside him felt so damn good. It could've been *me* lying underneath you, *me* whose ass you were slidin' into—*that's* how real it was!" His eyes flashed. "An' how do I know what you're doin' in the week when we don't see each other? For all I know, you spend every night in a diff'rent guy's bed." He stopped pacing and stood at the back of the couch, his fingers digging into the seat cushion, staring wide-eyed at Mike. "How do I know anything anymore? I just found out you've been lyin' to me ever since we've been—"

"Listen to me, baby."

"Don't you call me that! I heard you say that to him too." Tommy bowed his head, his shoulders hunched over. "I don't know what's real anymore," he said in a whisper.

Mike got up from the floor and walked around the couch to where Tommy stood, approaching him slowly, trying not to spook him. He came to a stop next to him, hands by his sides. "Tommy, look at me." When he got no reaction, he edged closer. "Please, Tommy."

Slowly, Tommy raised his chin and turned to face him.

Mike lowered his voice. "What we have is real. There is no one in my life but you. You hear me? No one. And it's been like that since September. You are all that I want. What you see on that screen is not reality, it's acting. Sex on set is *not real*. You see me acting, with porn actors." He held out his hand, palm up, and to his relief Tommy took it. Mike grasped his hand tightly. "Think about all the emotions an actor portrays on your TV screen or at the movies. You don't think it's real, do you?" Tommy shook his head. "Well, porn is no different. It's all an act for the camera, so that people watching think we're really in love, that I'm really lusting after my boss, that I have a thing for my straight best friend, et cetera, et cetera. I could go on and on, but I'm hoping you get it." He clasped his other hand around Tommy's. "*This* is real. *This* is love. And whatever else you believe, you can take this one to the bank. I fucking love you, Tommy Newsome, and I will do whatever it takes to convince you of that, because I cannot lose you."

Tommy looked down at their joined hands in silence. Mike waited, his pulse racing, breath hitching. Finally Tommy slowly raised his head to gaze at him. "How do I know what's real an' what isn't, Mike? I mean, how'd you expect me to tell the diff'rence? If I can watch you on-screen an' think it's real, then how do I know that what I see when we're makin' love is real?"

Mike was shocked into stillness. *How the fuck do I answer that?*

Tommy was watching him and nodding. "You don't have an answer for that one, huh?"

Mike stared at him, openmouthed, desperately searching for the right words. Tommy let out a sigh that seemed to come from someplace deep inside him.

"That's okay, 'cause I don't have an answer either. But it's somethin' I need answerin', if we're gonna go any further." He sat forward and touched Mike's face lightly. "For the record? I love you too, Mike. So you'd better figure it out, 'cause I don't wanna lose you either."

Tommy's words sank in. *He loves me.* In spite of the uncertain situation, the pain Mike had caused him and the potential for fucking up big time, Tommy loved him.

"You need to go now, y'hear?" Tommy laid his hand on Mike's arm. "I'll be here if you need to talk. I'm not goin' anywhere durin' spring break. But you got some thinkin' to do."

"Did you mean it?" Mike said softly. "That you love me?"

Tommy smiled, the first smile since Sunday lunch. "Yeah, I love you. That's why I'm not walkin' away, and that's not gonna change. But where we go from here is up to you." He leaned forward and kissed Mike's cheek.

Mike closed his eyes at the feel of those soft lips against his skin. *It's not over. Thank fuck for that.* He opened them and stepped back. "I'll be in touch soon."

Tommy walked him to the door that led out of the apartment. "You'd better," he said with a half smile as he opened the door. Mike moved to step past him and couldn't resist pulling Tommy into a hug.

"Thank you," he whispered, his arms wrapped around Tommy's firm body.

"For what?" Tommy was warm against him, his scent stronger than ever.

"Not walking away." Mike kissed him on the lips and released him. He left the apartment, his heart feeling lighter for the first time in days.

Tommy was right on the money. He had some thinking to do.

TOMMY CLOSED the back door and locked it, his legs trembling. Now that Mike had gone, he surrendered to the nerves that had plagued him throughout the entire conversation. The empty feeling in the pit of his stomach was still there, and his skin was sensitive to the merest touch.

"How'd it go, sugar?" Caroline came into the apartment from the main house.

Tommy dropped onto the couch. "Okay, I guess. Better than I thought it would."

"I suppose what I'm asking is if the two of you are still together." She came around the couch to sit next to him.

Tommy leaned back and closed his eyes. "For the moment." He tried not to think of the alternative. Mike had become such an important part of his life. The thought of losing him sent ice rushing through his veins.

"And is he gonna continue to be a porn star? That's the million-dollar question."

Tommy opened his eyes to find Caroline watching him, her eyes warm and sympathetic.

"And if the answer is yes, how'd you feel about that?"

Tommy sighed. "I don't know if he truly understands just how… wrong his career feels to me." He snorted. "That may well be because I didn't tell him."

Caroline stared at him. "Why not?"

"Mostly fear, I guess. What if he chooses porn instead of me? But to be honest, I wouldn't do that," Tommy explained earnestly. "I don't want him to do anything for me that he wouldn't do for himself. If he chooses to quit porn, it has to be his decision." He clasped his hands in his lap and gazed at them. "All I can do is wait… and hope."

"Sweetheart, just how long are you willing to do that for?"

He shrugged. "For as long as it takes. What choice do I have? I love him. He says he loves me, so I have to believe in that."

"Oh, honey, I hope you're not setting yourself up for more hurt." Caroline laid her hand over his. "I mean, does he really love you, or is he just saying that?"

Tommy smiled at her. "I believe him. An' no, I don't think I'm headin' for more hurt. You know why? 'Cause I have faith."

Caroline's eyes grew misty. "You know something, Tommy Newsome? You're a wonderful young man. You just blow me away with how much you've grown since I've known you. And Mike should think himself plain lucky to have you." She wiped at her eyes and sniffed. "I only want the best for you, and if what you want is Mike, then I'm behind you. I hope it all works out for you, because Lord knows, you deserve some happiness."

Tommy hoped the Lord was listening, 'cause Mike was all he wanted.

CHAPTER TWENTY-SEVEN

"HEY. DIDN'T think I'd hear from you so soon." A pause. "Uh, why aren't you asleep? It must be, what, 2:00 a.m.?" Another pause and then Jack's voice was laced with concern. "You okay?"

Mike put the phone on speaker and folded his arms under his head, the pillows piled high. "It's been a helluva few days, babe."

He heard another voice in the background. "Yeah, some tea would be nice, with honey. Thanks, baby." The soft rustle of sheets. "Okay, you have my attention. What's up?"

"Am I disturbing you?" Mike had visions of interrupting his ex in the middle of something intimate.

Jack chuckled.

"Nah, Luca and I were having an early night. We're sitting in bed, watching TV." He laughed. "I must be getting old. An early night used to mean something entirely different. So, wanna tell me what's wrong? Because I'm sure this isn't a social call."

Mike pushed out a sigh. "Tommy found out about the porn."

"What do you mean, found out? That implies you didn't tell him." Jack's tone was sharp. "I thought you were going—"

"Someone beat me to it, okay?" Mike let out a low growl. "And now everything's changed." He relayed the conversation, holding nothing back. Jack remained silent at the other end until he'd finished.

"Ouch."

"Yeah, tell me about it."

"So have you come up with anything?"

It had been over twelve hours since he'd spoken with Tommy, and so far Mike had come up with zilch. "How, Jack? How can I prove to him that what he sees isn't real?"

"Lemme think for a sec." Mike caught the rustle of sheets. "Oh, thanks, babe."

A pause when Mike heard the distinctive sound of kisses being exchanged. He smiled to himself, happy for Jack.

"No, you can stay, honey. This is Mike. Remember, I told you about him?" More soft murmurings. "Yeah, snuggle up and keep me company while we talk."

It made for a pleasant image in Mike's head. "D'you want me to call back another time?"

Jack laughed. "No, you're okay, honest. And I may have a suggestion."

"Oh?"

"Why don't you show him what reality looks like?"

For a moment Mike was stumped. "Huh?"

Jack chuckled. "I think you need some sleep. But what I meant was, show him the reality of porn. We both know what happens on a shoot is a completely different animal to what appears on-screen. So why not show him that? D'you think the guys at ManFactory would object if you turned up with Tommy and asked if he could watch while they shot a scene? If you asked them ahead of time, of course. You'd be there to watch it with him, explain what was going on, what he was seeing...."

Mike liked that idea. Liked it a lot. "You might just have something there."

"Can you picture Tommy's face if he got to see some gay for pay guys filming? Now there's a heavy dose of reality for ya right there." Jack snorted. "'Course, you don't tell him that often there's a spark between actors, 'cause he does *not* need to know *that* shit. But he can see what it's really like on set." He chuckled. "You'll probably blow his mind, from the sound of it."

"Jack, you're a genius."

Soft laughter came out of the phone. "Hey, guess what, hon? Mike says I'm a genius." A pause and the rustle of sheets. "Glad to have been of service. Let me know how things go." His voice lowered. "So I guess you're really serious about this guy?"

"As serious as it gets."

"Oh, Mike, that's great. Maybe one day you can bring him out west so I can meet him? Because he has to be pretty special, babe, to have *you* all in knots."

Mike wasn't sure how Tommy would feel about that. "We'll see. Right now I'm just flying by the seat of my pants." *And praying it all works out for the best.* "I'll call ManFactory in the morning, see if I can arrange a visit soon." A thought occurred to him. "Hell, I'm supposed to be filming there on Monday." The silence that fell at Jack's end was sudden. "Jack?"

"I was just wondering what Tommy would make of that. I mean, okay, so now he knows you do porn. Knowing is one thing, Mike. Accepting the situation is something entirely different."

In spite of his newfound optimism, a shiver of apprehension rippled down Mike's spine.

"Let's just see what happens at ManFactory, all right?" He couldn't think about that now. Especially when he had the sinking feeling that Jack might have a point. Tommy might not have said as much, but the chances were pretty high that he wouldn't want his boyfriend continuing in the porn industry.

Mike knew that from bitter experience.

TOMMY POURED out another mug of coffee and then sat down at the kitchen table, his breakfast finished. Spring break had flown by, and all he had to show for it was a pile of reading he'd gotten done. He hadn't been in the mood to go out, even when Ben had suggested going to see a movie the previous night. So there he was, Friday morning, the weekend upon him once more, and no idea if he was going to see Mike. He'd had no word from him since Wednesday, and he was trying not to let it worry him.

Caroline ruffled his hair. "I'm going shopping this morning in Atlanta. You wanna come with me, keep me company?"

He shook his head. "Would you mind if I said no? I don't feel like it." Not that he had anything better to do.

She sighed. "Oh, sweetie. I hate to see you like this." The door chime interrupted them. Caroline raised her voice. "Ben, be a dear and get that?" His roomie was in the media room, playing with his PS3. Tommy could hear him grumbling as he went through the hallway. She huffed. "That boy would spend all day being a couch potato if I let him."

Tommy had to laugh. Caroline had Ben pegged.

Ben appeared in the kitchen doorway. "Someone to see you, Tommy." His neck and cheeks were flushed.

Tommy straightened. It could only be one person. Sure enough, Mike walked into the kitchen behind Ben. Tommy couldn't help his body's reaction. His breathing quickened at the sight of Mike in his faded, worn jeans and white cotton shirt, open at the collar, the sleeves rolled up.

Damn, he looks good.

"G'morning," Mike said, addressing Caroline. His gaze met Tommy's. "Hey."

"I'm just going to check and see if the laundry's finished its cycle." Caroline got to her feet and left the kitchen after giving Tommy a quick smile.

"I'm in the middle of a game, so if you'll excuse me." Ben disappeared, leaving Mike standing in the middle of the floor, looking bemused.

Tommy shook his head. His adoptive family were wonderful. "Subtle, aren't they?"

Mike smiled. "It was nice of them to give us some space." He took a breath. "You need to come with me, now."

Tommy arched his eyebrows. "Oh? An' where are we goin'?" Mike's forthright approach made him smile.

"You're gonna have to trust me on that. All I'm gonna say is if you love me, come with me." Mike held out his hand, palm upward, and gazed at Tommy, unblinking.

Tommy swallowed. "You *know* I love ya."

Mike grinned. "Then come on." He beckoned.

Tommy hesitated for all of three seconds and then stretched out his hand to Mike, who grasped it firmly. "Do I need to bring anything?"

Mike shook his head. "Just you." He led Tommy out of the kitchen and through the hallway.

"I'm goin' out with Mike," Tommy called hastily in the direction of the living room.

"'Kay!" Ben shouted back.

He followed Mike out of the house and over to his truck. "We goin' far?"

"No, not really. I'll bring you back when we're done. I have work this afternoon."

Mike unlocked the truck, and Tommy got in. A thrill of anticipation coursed through him at this unexpected turn of events. Mike pulled out of the driveway and onto the road. Tommy glanced at him before giving his attention to the road, curious about their destination. They drove into the center of Atlanta and out toward Lakewood.

"I've missed you," Mike said quietly, his eyes focused on the road.

"Me too." Tommy had missed the evening calls and texts. The sound of Mike's voice always made him feel good. He watched the passing scenery, his mind going over endless possibilities, but for the life of him, he couldn't guess where Mike could be taking him.

About forty minutes later, Mike pulled into a parking lot, in which sat a low white building with a glass front. The sign above the door said ManFactory.

"What is this place?"

Mike switched off the engine and turned to face him, hands resting on the steering wheel. "This is one of the studios where I come to shoot scenes." He regarded Tommy steadily, his gaze focused on him.

Lord, no. Tommy didn't believe what he was hearing.

"You've gotta be kiddin'." Tommy shook his head. "I am *not* gonna watch you in a—"

Mike stilled instantly, his mouth open, eyes widened. "Oh, God, no! *No*, Tommy. That is not why we're here." He took a deep breath. "I've arranged for you—for us—to watch a shoot."

"Why?"

Mike stared at him. "I told you porn wasn't real. I wanted you to see that for yourself."

Tommy didn't know what to think. The very idea of watching porn sent alternating rushes of ice cold and heat racing through him. It was… wicked. Sinful. Just plain… wrong. But beneath the shock, aside from his pounding heart and shortness of breath, there was the lure of the illicit. The curiosity that tugged him, just to *see*.

"You okay with this?" Mike was gazing at him, sitting so still beside him.

Tommy gulped in air. "No, but I asked you how I was s'posed to tell the difference, an' I guess you're tryin' to show me that." He looked out at the innocuous building before them. "So maybe I should just trust you an' go see what you've been talkin' about."

Mike nodded. "And I'll be right there with you." He held out a hand, and Tommy took it gratefully, squeezing it tight. "Shall we?"

Tommy shrugged. "Now or never, I s'pose." He tried to smile, but damn, his stomach was in knots.

Mike released his hand, got out of the truck, and came around to Tommy's side to open his door. "Any time you wanna leave? You just say the word, and we're outta there."

"'Kay." Tommy clambered out and waited while Mike locked up. Then he sighed with relief when Mike took his hand and intertwined their fingers. Tommy glanced down at their joined hands.

Mike nodded. "I'll be introducing you as my boyfriend, just so you know." He smiled. "That okay with you?"

Tommy breathed easier. "Yeah." He really liked that. It made him feel… safe.

Mike led him to the main door and held it open for him to enter. Once inside the cool interior, they crossed the floor to the glass desks of reception, where a young man smiled broadly when he saw Mike.

"Hey, Scott. Tony said you were coming in today." He gazed inquiringly at Tommy. "This is your guest?"

Mike nodded. "Hey, Paul. This is Tommy, my boyfriend. You got a visitor's badge for him?"

"Sure." Paul reached into a drawer and handed over a white plastic badge on a red lanyard. He smiled at Tommy. "Can you sign in, please?"

Tommy gave a nod and stepped forward. His hand shook slightly when he signed his name, and he had to wipe the pen on his jacket before he passed it back to Paul. His palms were clammy with sweat. Mike passed the lanyard over his head and then kissed him on the cheek.

"Ready?"

"No, but we're here now, so let's do this thing." Tommy took several deep breaths. "Lead the way."

Mike stunned him by pulling him into his arms and kissing him on the mouth. He brought his lips to Tommy's ear. "Just remember that I love you."

Tommy was aware of the small noise of approval Paul made behind him. "Love you too," he whispered. Mike released him, grasped his hand, and led him through the wide doors beyond the reception area. Tommy held on tight as they passed through a long corridor and out into a wide space.

"This is the main floor of the studio," Mike told him. "There are different sets here, but they tend only to shoot one scene at a time, to cut down on noise interference."

Tommy just nodded, gazing around him, trying to take it all in. He could hear noise coming from off to the left. Mike steered them in that direction, and Tommy saw they were in what looked like a hotel bedroom. There were lights set up around the bed, and reflective panels at various angles. A man was walking around the set with a light meter in his hand, while two men in bathrobes were sitting on plastic chairs, chatting about....

"Football? They're talkin' about *football*?" he said incredulously.

Mike took one look at his face and laughed. "Why not? Hell, I've sat waiting to be filmed and discussed the elections, the previous night's TV, just about any topic you can think of." He grinned. "Why? What did you imagine they'd be doing?"

Tommy gave a nervous laugh. "I thought they'd be, you know… kissin'? Makin' out? Stuff like that?" He'd imagined the actors getting in the mood, certainly not participating in a boisterous argument about a recent game.

"Hey, Scott!" A young man with a camera walked over to them. "I thought I heard you were coming in." He gave a polite nod to Tommy. "Hi, I'm Wayne. I take the publicity shots. And you must be the boyfriend."

Mike guffawed. "Word sure gets around here fast. This is Tommy."

Wayne extended a hand to Tommy. "Delighted to meet you." He turned to Mike. "Oh, I meant to tell you. The wife has sent you that recipe you were after, the one for peanut butter pie?"

Mike let out a moan of pleasure. "Oh, great. She's been promising me that for months. Thank her for me, will you?"

"Sure." Wayne grinned and then gave Tommy another nod. "It was nice meeting the man who got our Scott. You must be pretty special." He walked off the set.

Tommy stared at Mike. "His wife?"

Mike nodded. "Wayne's straight. Having said that, a lot of the guys that work here are straight."

This was definitely not what Tommy had expected. Then he got a further shock when a short, pretty woman walked over to them.

"Scott! Nice to see you again. Did Tony tell you I was gonna be filming some of ManFactory's scenes?"

"Hey, Alexa!" Mike hugged her. "Yeah, he might have mentioned it. You're shooting this one?"

She nodded. "We're just about to get going. You guys wanna take a seat?" She turned to Tommy. "I hear you're Scott's boyfriend. It's a real pleasure to meet you. About time this guy settled down with someone. He's been on his own for far too long."

Her smile was infectious, and Tommy couldn't help but return it.

Mike pointed to a couple of chairs out of the cameras' viewpoint. "There," he whispered.

Tommy followed him and sat, his stomach roiling. He didn't have a clue what to expect next. He regarded the two actors who were disrobing. "Do you know them?" he asked in a hushed tone, his eyes focused on the lean bodies emerging from the white robes. Both men were tall and slim, with defined abs and well-toned arms and legs.

Mike nodded. "The dark-haired guy, that's Trey. He's been in the industry for a while now, about five years. And the blond, that's Nick. He's fairly new. He's a sweet guy, very professional, even if filming with him can be a pain."

"Why?" Tommy's throat tightened at the thought of Mike having sex with the gorgeous young man before him. *What could be a pain about making love to* him?

"Well," Mike began, leaning closer, "it's difficult to film with a guy who has to keep stopping 'cause he can't stay hard for too long."

Tommy stared at Nick, his gaze drifting lower to the actor's dick, which was soft. "Does… does he have a problem? I mean, with gettin' hard?" He couldn't imagine someone with a medical issue like that lasting long in porn, even with his inexperience.

Mike chuckled. "Let's just say, he'd find it a whole lot easier if Trey was a girl."

Tommy gaped at Mike, openmouthed, and then glanced over at Nick. "He's… straight?" Mike nodded. Tommy was bewildered. "But… he's doin' gay porn! Why would he do that? Why not just do porn with a girl?"

"Because this pays better." Mike's expression had lost some of its good humor. "That's why there are loads of guys in this industry who are straight. We call them gay for pay."

Tommy studied his face. "You don't like them."

Mike shrugged. "Some gay-for-pay guys are okay, like Nick over there, but there are others who are a nightmare to work with." He tapped Tommy's hand with his finger. "They're ready."

Tommy gave his attention to the scene on set. Alexa was instructing the two men, who were now lying under the white sheet. The lighting made it look like early morning, and it became clear they were just waking up together. Alexa stepped back, and the cameras started rolling. Nick was spooned around Trey and was kissing his neck and shoulder, his arm reaching over to stroke his dick under the sheet. Trey let out a soft moan and twisted around to face Nick, kissing him and pushing the sheet down past his groin to reveal his stiffening cock. He pushed up gently with his hips, and Nick kissed him while he worked Trey's hardening dick.

Tommy was mesmerized, not by the men's actions but by the emotion he was seeing on their faces. Nick was gazing at his costar, his soft moans so real that Tommy could believe they were lovers. Nick shifted and rolled on top of Trey, his hips rocking as he rubbed his cock against Trey's, getting faster, their moans increasing in intensity.

"Yeah, want you inside me," Trey whispered, gazing up at Nick before cupping his head and drawing him down into a passionate kiss that made Tommy's toes curl just watching it. And then abruptly everything came to a halt when Alexa called for a break. Nick and Trey broke apart. Trey lay there on the bed, resuming their previous conversation as Nick sat up and was handed a tablet.

"Why'd they stop?" Tommy demanded. "An' what's Nick doin'?"

Mike moved closer until his breath tickled Tommy's ear. "They stopped because Nick is about to top Trey, and it's a little difficult to fuck a guy when you don't have an erection." He indicated Nick with his finger. "Right now Nick is watching straight porn and working on getting his dick hard for the next bit."

Sure enough, Nick's gaze was focused on the tablet, his hand sliding up and down his dick, which lengthened and thickened as Tommy watched. Now and then he'd acknowledge something Trey had said with a smile or a nod.

Tommy turned to Mike. "When they were kissin' before, if you hadn't told me Nick was straight, I'd have believed they were both gay." More than that, he'd have believed they were lovers. The way Nick's eyes lit up when he looked at Trey, the way his hands caressed his costar's body, lovingly, tenderly.... Except looking at them now, the passion was gone. Tommy stared at Mike. "That's what you were tryin' to tell me, wasn't it? That it's just an act."

Mike nodded. Just then Alexa called out that they were about to film again, and all conversation ceased. Nick put aside his tablet, and he and Trey resumed their positions.

Tommy watched the entire shoot from beginning to end. As each part of the scene progressed, he was amazed by the number of breaks and the almost clinical feel to it. The sensuality and heat of the scene was only present when the cameras were rolling. Otherwise, it was a case of stop-start, stop-start, with precise instructions as to what the director wanted to see on the screen. It wasn't romantic, it wasn't hot, and Tommy finally understood that it was just a job.

When it was over, the cameras stopped rolling, the lights were moved off to another set, and the actors went to the showers. Alexa came over to speak to them.

"Was it what you'd imagined?" she asked Tommy.

"No, ma'am," he said gravely. Mike's hand tightened around his.

"I'll be seeing you on Monday, right?" she addressed Mike. "I'm filming your scene with Sean Devlin."

Mike nodded, and Tommy's gut rolled over. *Mike's doing a shoot?* The rest of their conversation went over his head. All he could think of was Mike, having sex where they were standing, surrounded by cameras and lights, him touching another guy....

"Hey."

Tommy gave himself a little mental shake. Mike was regarding him, eyes full of concern.

"You all right?"

"Can we go now?" Tommy just wanted to get out of there. Yeah, he'd had his question answered, but it still left him with an awful big dilemma, one he was reluctant to mention.

"Sure." Mike led through off the floor and back to reception, where Tommy handed over his badge. They walked out into the bright daylight, yet despite the warmth of the sun, Tommy felt cold.

This changes nothing. He understood clearly what Mike had tried to tell him, that it wasn't real, but it didn't alter the way Tommy felt about porn. Okay, so it was just a job to the likes of Trey, Nick, and Mike, but deep down inside him, Tommy couldn't overcome his feelings of revulsion. There was a... wrongness to it that he couldn't get past, no matter how hard he tried to see it from Mike's point of view.

He was quiet throughout the journey back to Morningside, lost in his own thoughts. Mike didn't attempt to engage him in conversation, for which Tommy was grateful. But it was a shock when the truck came to a stop and Tommy realized they were parked outside Mike's house.

"What... why are we here?"

Mike gave a sheepish smile. "I thought we might spend some time together before I have to go to work." He reached across the seat to take hold of Tommy's hand. "I've really missed you this week."

Lord, what do I say now?

He knew what Mike wanted. He knew where they'd end up—in Mike's bed. And right then? Tommy couldn't. Just… couldn't. There was too much turmoil in his head. He wanted to yell at Mike, to ask why he couldn't see what this was doing to Tommy. But he didn't trust himself to speak. The words would come tumbling out of his mouth, and then everything would change yet again. He could almost picture the look of hurt on Mike's face, a look that he would've put there.

Tommy knew there was only one thing he could do.

"Take me home, please?"

Mike stared at him. "What's wrong?" He tightened his grip on Tommy's hand, but Tommy pulled it away. "Tommy?"

"Please, Mike," he begged. "Just take me home? I… I can't talk about this right now."

Mike paled. "Talk to me. Maybe I can help."

Yeah, you could quit doing porn, Tommy wanted to scream at him. "Trust me, you… you don't wanna be 'round me right now. I'm… my head's not in a real good place."

Mike sat there so still. "You're unhappy."

Tommy kept silent. There was nothing to be said.

Mike sighed, the heavy sound rolling out of him like it came from his soul. "I'll take you home." Even his words had weight. He switched on the engine and backed out of the driveway.

"Thank you." It was about all Tommy could manage. The hope that had filled him when Mike appeared in Caroline's kitchen that morning had evaporated, leaving in its place a sick feeling of dread.

What if we can't get past this? What if this really is the end?

CHAPTER TWENTY-EIGHT

"SO ARE you gonna tell me what's wrong, or do I have to beat it out of ya? Who pissed in your Cheerios?"

Mike carried on wiping down the bar, his back to Kevin. "Just leave it, will you?"

"Like hell I will. You've hardly said a word all night." Kevin grabbed the cloth from Mike's hand. "Okay, *now* talk to me." He stood his ground,

"Back. Off," Mike growled. He'd had half a mind to call in sick. The thought of trying to be sociable with the customers just made him feel nauseated. The worst thing was, he couldn't figure out what he'd done wrong. All he knew was Tommy was hurting, and it seemed to be his fault. At least the shift was over and he could go home, lock the door, and have a really good stiff drink. It wouldn't alleviate the pain he was feeling, but it sure would dull the edges.

Kevin regarded him for a moment and then walked away. Mike's relief was short-lived. He returned a minute later and placed a glass in front of him, filled with about two fingers of bourbon. "I think you need this."

Mike gazed at the glass and then sighed. "You're not gonna give up, are you?"

Kevin heaved himself onto the stool next to Mike and gave him a sweet smile. "Not a chance. Now start talking." He leaned forward to where Patrick was crouched behind the bar, shifting stuff. "You okay for a minute, Patrick, while I talk with Mikey?"

"I got this," Patrick called back. "See if you can find out who stuck a burr up his ass while you're at it."

"I *am* here, y'know. I *can* hear ya." Sometimes working with these queens was like working with a bunch of women—scrap that, it was worse. Mike picked up the bourbon and took a long drink, relishing the burn as it hit his throat. He closed his eyes and let the fiery liquid warm him.

"What happened?" Kevin's voice was softer.

Mike rested his arms on the bar and sagged. "I thought I'd found the answer, Kev." He recounted how he'd taken Tommy to the shoot.

He'd had such a good feeling about that, only to have it all go to hell when Tommy had asked to be driven home. "He looked so goddamn miserable when I dropped him off this morning." He took another drink of bourbon.

The silence that followed was unnerving.

Mike glanced over at Kevin, who was staring at him, arms folded. "What?"

"You're kidding, right?" Kevin quirked his eyebrows. "You gotta know why Tommy's miserable, because it's as plain to me as the fuckin' nose on your face. I can totally see where he's coming from."

Mike stared at him. "You can?"

Kevin nodded. "He doesn't like you doing porn."

"Then why didn't he say so?" Mike demanded.

"Maybe 'cause he was hoping you'd work it out for yourself, you dumbass!" Kevin shook his head. "You haven't had a boyfriend *yet* who was happy about you doing porn. Why should Tommy be any different? And yeah, I can understand his attitude. If you were my guy? I would be on your case day and night, trying to get you to quit."

"You've never said a word about my career." Mike's head was spinning.

"Mikey, when you're on that screen, working that body? You're some guy's sexual fantasy. I just know that if you were my boyfriend, I wouldn't feel comfortable knowing there were all these men out there lusting after that gorgeous bod. Patrick's been there, so's Don. They've both dabbled in porn, nothing like you, of course. Yeah, so we know there are some guys who get off on the idea of dating a porn star, but when you're trying to find a partner, someone to go the distance…." He shook his head. "Yeah, good luck with that. You don't know how lucky you are."

"What do you mean?"

Kevin stared at him. "Tommy, that's why. He hasn't walked away from you. He's giving you a chance to make the right decision." He smiled. "Let's face it, Mike. You've been making 'I'm-thinking-of-quitting' noises for a while now. Maybe this is the push you need."

A heavy feeling settled in Mike's stomach. *Quit porn?* He'd always hated change, preferring to keep things as they were. *But is that sufficient reason to keep the status quo?* Especially if there was a chance that he'd lose Tommy in the process?

"Go home, Mike, and think about it." Kevin chuckled. "I just got déjà vu, 'cause I swear I've said this once already this week. But I remember something else I said too. I told you your porn career didn't matter, but that Tommy did. That ain't changed." Kevin got up off his stool. "So go home and think about that farm boy who loves ya." He grabbed Mike in a tight hug.

Mike patted Kevin on the back. "Okay, okay, I got the message."

Patrick came from behind the bar and handed him his jacket.

"Thanks, guys. I'll see you this afternoon." He walked slowly around the bar to the door.

"I mean it, Mike," Kevin called out to him as he crossed the threshold into the street. "Think about it."

Mike intended to think long and hard. Because right then he felt like a horse's ass for not seeing what was so clear to his friends and colleagues. *Talk about blinders.... How could I have missed this?* Kevin had Tommy pegged. His lover wouldn't be so selfish as to push his desires ahead of Mike's. Mike, on the other hand....

He got into the truck and sat there, staring through the windshield. *What a fucking selfish bastard I am.* All his life, he'd focused on what he wanted out of life, what he could get for himself: the house, the vacations.... Okay, so it was good to have that kind of focus, but now that he looked back? Damn, it felt like he'd made an art of it. *Did I ever consider how others felt?* For the first time he looked back on his previous disastrous relationships with new eyes. Maybe it wasn't just the porn that had driven them away. Maybe it was just... Mike.

And if that was the case, then it was Mike who needed to change. Because losing Tommy was not an option.

"WOW, TWO phone calls in as many days. I'm honored." Jack yawned. "Have you just finished work?"

Damn. Mike hadn't considered the time, knowing Jack was three hours behind. "I'm sorry. Are you in bed?" It had to be eleven at night in Seattle.

Jack chuckled. "Relax, babe, I was just getting ready to call it a night."

Mike caught the sound of a whistling kettle in the background. Ah, Jack's habit of drinking tea before bed. It was nice to know some things hadn't changed.

"What can I do for you? Have you had any more thoughts about my idea?"

"Jack, am I selfish?" Mike blurted out.

Silence. "You okay, Mike?"

Mike sighed. "No. No, I am *not* okay. It's been brought to my attention that I am a thoughtless, selfish prick. And you know what? It's true."

"Whoa there." Jack's voice was soft. "Okay, you'd better start at the beginning."

Mike took a deep breath and let it all pour out of him: the porn shoot, Tommy's unhappiness, Kevin's summations, Mike's own realizations.... "And he was right, Jack. Here I was, blaming all my exes for my own inadequacies."

"Hey, speaking as one of those exes, I think you're being a little hard on yourself."

"You think?"

Jack's wry chuckle lifted him. "Babe, you may be selfish at times, but that doesn't make you a bad guy, all right? Hell, we're all selfish at times. What matters in this instance is that now you can see where you went wrong in the past. But I'm digressing. Right now you have a much bigger question to ask yourself."

"Go on." Mike held the phone to his ear and rolled onto his side, the sheets cool against his bare skin.

"Do you love Tommy enough to quit porn for him?"

And there it was, the heart of the matter. Mike lay there, the question rolling around inside his head.

"You wanna know what I think?" Jack continued.

Mike laughed. "Since when has anything held you back from giving your opinion, *ever*?"

"Fuck you," Jack said good-naturedly. "Okay, for what it's worth, here's my take on it. Tommy hasn't told you what to do, has he? He hasn't come out and demanded that you quit porn. He hasn't laid a guilt trip on you, but he *has* let you know, without words, what he needs."

"All of that is true."

There was a pause. "That boy is a keeper, Mike."

Mike laughed. "Tell me something I don't know. I think I've already worked that one out for myself."

"Then there's your answer. If you don't want to lose him, then you do what you have to, to make sure you keep him in your life. And if that means giving up your porn career, then that's what you do." Jack laughed. "See? That was easy."

"The easy part is coming to that conclusion," Mike said quietly. "The hard part is actually doing it."

"Ah, that's not hard, not if you love him enough. And here we are, right back at my million-dollar question." He chuckled. "Besides, it's not like you'd starve, right? You've always been smart, saving money, investing it, for a day just like this. You still have your job at Woofs, don't you? With all your bartending experience, you're never gonna be short of work." Jack paused, and when he spoke again, his voice was lower. "You don't know how lucky you are, babe, having that to fall back on. And if you don't believe that, just look at me. Why d'you think I had to do a one-eighty on bareback, huh? Because I didn't have experience like yours."

Mike fell silent. Jack had a point.

"Apart from the more practical side of giving up porn, there's something else you need to think about. You've had a wonderful career as Scott Masters. You know that, right? I mean, we're talking the Golden Tale of porn careers here."

Mike laughed, but he knew Jack was right. To have survived—no, more than that, he'd *flourished*—in such a fickle industry for as long as he had was something of a miracle.

"But let's face it, Mike. You don't feel at home in porn like you once did, do ya? And I remember our conversations, back when we were really hot, where we agreed to retire before our laurels started to wilt?" Jack snickered, and Mike joined him. "Well, it seems to me this is as good a point as any to bid farewell to the world of porn. Go out while you're still popular, while guys are still checking out every scene you release." He fell silent for a moment, and Mike heard the sound of water pouring into a cup. "Well, was I any help?"

"Yeah, you were," Mike conceded. Talking with Jack always helped him to focus. "I guess all that's left is to make a decision."

"Babe, you've already made it. So take my advice, get some sleep, and think about how you're gonna word your resignation letter." He chuckled once more. "Just how many studios will you be sending it to, anyway? I lose track of what the great Scott Masters is up to these days." A pause. "Aw, who am I kidding? I still follow you, babe. I love you, always will."

"Love you too, Jack." Mike wished him good night and disconnected the call. He placed the phone on the nightstand, switched off the lamp, and lay there in the blackness, his mind going over Jack's words.

When you put it like that, it does all boil down to that one question. And Jack was right. He already knew the answer to that one.

There was only one more person to talk to before he made a move.

"I THOUGHT you'd be bringing someone else with you." Mom had been pouting ever since he'd turned up for Sunday lunch alone. She placed the dishes into the dishwasher while Mike made coffee. "Or had I not made myself clear on this?"

Mike sighed. "Sorry, Mom, but there have been a few issues this week. I promise I'll bring him next time." That was providing everything worked out.

She stopped in midaction and straightened. "Mike Scott, what have you done?"

"What makes you think whatever it is has anything to do with me?" he asked indignantly, mimicking her posture, hands on his hips.

His mom raised one eyebrow. "Because I know you, that's why." She peered intently at him. "Go on, prove me wrong."

"If I'd known you were gonna give me the third degree, I wouldn't have come for lunch," he grumbled as he poured coffee into the pot.

Mom waited until he'd finished pouring before speaking. "What's wrong, Mike?"

He picked up the tray with the coffee and walked through into the sunny living room. Once he'd set it down on the table, Mike sat on the couch, elbows on his knees, hands clasped between them. "I've been thinking about retiring."

His mom froze and stared at him. "Well, I never." Her smile lit up her face. "Really?"

Mike had to chuckle. "Don't have to be Einstein to figure out you like that idea."

She gave a roll of her shoulders. "Well, you're not getting any younger." She tilted her head. "'Thinking' implies you haven't made up your mind yet."

"That's because I wanted to talk to you first."

Her cheeks pinked up. "Aww, sweetheart, I'm flattered. But if you're considering retiring"—she gazed at him thoughtfully—"what's holding you back from making an outright decision?"

"I guess it's the whole 'stepping out of my comfort zone' thing. Doing porn feels safe." Then he thought about it. Lately it hadn't felt safe at all. In fact, the ground was starting to feel decidedly shaky.

"What about this man? Y'know, the one you're too scared to bring home to Momma? 'Cause you know that's what I'm gonna think when you show up without him. My mind goes into overdrive."

Mike laughed. "His name is Tommy, and I promise, I *will* bring him to meet you. But what about him?"

Mom pursed her lips. "Well, you talk about porn being comfortable, safe. Seems to me that if you have Tommy at your side, it makes stepping out of that world a little easier. Doesn't it? Wouldn't you feel safe with him?"

He let her words settle on him, allowed them to permeate his thoughts. He felt safer with Tommy than with any of the men he'd let in previously. Only, he hadn't let him in, had he? Tommy had slipped through Mike's defenses like he was meant to be there. Slipped right on in there and made his home in Mike's heart.

Mike was suddenly aware that all he could hear was the birds singing in the trees in the yard and the slow tick of the grandfather clock standing in the corner. Mom was gazing at him, smiling.

"You'll make the right decision," she said emphatically. "Now why don't you pour your momma some coffee, and then you can tell me all about Tommy." She grinned, and her eyes sparkled. "Can't wait to meet him."

He laughed as he poured out a cup. He couldn't wait to see her face when she laid eyes on Tommy. He imagined his lover's age might figure in the ensuing conversation. Not that it mattered to Mike.

When you know, you know….

TOMMY LAY in the darkness, listening to the sounds of the house in the early hours of the morning. Dawn was a long way off, and he wasn't remotely sleepy. His brain didn't have an off switch, apparently. All he could think about was Mike, the studio, Mike's upcoming shoot….

His phone had been quiet since Friday, but Tommy was hoping that was a good sign. He knew Mike had been working the last three nights as usual, and he hoped there'd been time for him to think about where they went from here. This last week, with little contact, had really brought home to Tommy just how much it meant to have Mike in his life. Not having him around made Tommy's heart ache.

Noise filtered through the blackness: the flush of the toilet, the *pad-pad* of bare feet, the sound of water running. Tommy waited for the sounds that told him his roomie was back in his bed. Ben had been quiet too. He hadn't been out to the clubs during spring break, and Tommy had to wonder about that. Ben had stuck close to home, playing his games and watching TV. Tommy had seen the glances Caroline had sent in her son's direction. Yeah, this wasn't like him.

"You awake?" Ben's whisper came from behind the couch.

"What gave me away?" Tommy asked, sitting up and switching on the lamp beside him. Ben stood at the end of the couch in his boxers, blinking in the sudden light.

"You sound different when you're asleep." Ben came around to perch on the mattress.

Tommy snickered. "Is that a polite way of sayin' I snore?"

Ben smiled. "Well, not snore exactly, but you do make some pretty cute noises." He tilted his head. "You couldn't sleep either?"

"Nah." Tommy grabbed a cushion and stuffed it behind his head. He tapped his temple. "Got too much goin' on in here."

Ben flushed. "That was sorta what was keeping me awake too." He drew his legs up onto the mattress and sat cross-legged. "Can we talk?"

Tommy snorted. "We're talkin', ain't we? And seein' as both of us are havin' trouble gettin' to sleep, seems like the perfect opportunity." He took in the way Ben rubbed his knee, his jumpiness, the lack of eye contact. "What's wrong?"

Ben blinked and then let out a sigh. "This business with Mike. This is all my fault."

Tommy stared at him. "How'd you work that out?"

"Well, if I hadn't said anything, you two would still be together." Ben hung his head. "I saw how upset you've been this last week, an' I guess I feel responsible."

The words were indistinct, but Tommy heard every one.

"Me and my big mouth. If I hadn't shown you that video, you'd be none the wiser."

"Whoa, now wait a minute." Tommy sat up straight. "First of all, far as I know, Mike 'n' me are still together. Leastways, neither of us have mentioned breakin' up, okay?" His heart pounded at the thought. "An' yeah, I *have* been upset, but not with you. Okay, so maybe at first I was a bit pissed, but I got past that. Mike should've told me. This is down to him, not you."

"You mean that?" Ben jerked his head up and looked Tommy in the eye.

Tommy nodded. "You were lookin' out for me. Can't fault you for that." He speared him with a look. "Your methods could've been better. That's for sure." When Ben flushed from his chest all the way up to his cheekbones, Tommy smiled. "But we're past that. You're still a good friend."

"I'm glad about that." Ben sighed once more. "D'you really think you an' Mike can get through this? 'Cause I gotta say, you've been so happy since he's been around. And the two of you really did fit. I suppose it all comes down to you being able to date a porn star."

Tommy fell silent. He'd had this wonderful dream—though it might have been more appropriate to call it a fantasy—where Mike came to him and told him he was gonna quit porn. Lord knew, it was what Tommy wanted to hear with all his heart.

But what if he doesn't? What do I do then? The thought left him cold. *Could I stay with him, even though he's doin' something that is totally against everything I believe?*

It was something that had crossed his mind countless times during the last couple of days.

What would stayin' with Mike in those circumstances do to my love for him? Would I love him any less?

Tommy had to be honest. He didn't know the answer to that one.

Chapter Twenty-Nine

MIKE PUSHED open the glass door and walked across the tiled floor to where Paul sat at the desk, engaged in a phone conversation. Mike took the opportunity to gaze up at the banners on the wall behind him. There were ManFactory's finest models, and there he was, still among them. He couldn't help frowning when he saw the newest addition. Chad stared down at him, wearing only a pair of scruffy jeans and that cocky grin.

Like I didn't see that one coming.

"You okay, Scott?" Paul covered the mouthpiece of the phone, regarding him with concern.

"Yeah, I wanted to—"

"Sorry, here's your paperwork. Can we talk later?" Paul thrust the clipboard into his hands and then spoke into the phone. "Yeah, sorry, you were saying?" He gave Mike an apologetic shrug and carried on talking.

Mike shook his head. One of these days, Paul needed to ask for another receptionist to work with him.

He passed through the wide doors that led to the studio and went straight into the admin room. From the sets came the clear sound of several guys fucking, at least three or four. Mike was in no mood to see. He flopped into one of the plastic chairs and stared at the paperwork attached to the clipboard. His last scene....

He glanced around at the room where he'd sat so many times, chatting with his scene partners. *Talk about the end of an era.* A weekend of introspection had brought him to the conclusion that his friends were right. It was time to call it a day. Once he'd made the decision, he was amazed at how he felt. Had it been that much of a weight on his shoulders, to account for the lightness in both body and spirit that felt so wonderful?

Maybe I should've done this years ago. It was a sobering thought. His life might have been so different. *Yeah, but would I have met Tommy?* The thought of life without him was even more sobering.

Through the open door, he heard Alexa calling an end to the scene and voices raised as the actors went off to shower, all laughing and chatting. He would miss the camaraderie, his colleagues. Then he recalled a few of his scene partners through the years.

Maybe he wouldn't miss *all* of them.

Mike sat quietly, recalling some of the great guys he'd filmed with, some of them still close friends.

"Hey, Scott, I'm glad you're early." Tony entered the room and pushed the door shut behind him before sitting at the table with Mike. He glanced at the sheets in front of him. "Oh, good, you got your paperwork," he said absently.

First the door, now the distracted air. "Are you okay?" Mike asked him. "Because you don't seem yourself today."

Tony took off his glasses and rubbed the bridge of his nose. "I wanted to catch you before the shoot to have a talk with you."

"Yeah, about that. I—"

"Sorry, but this is important." Tony leaned on the table, toying with the arm of his glasses. "The parent company who owns ManFactory made an announcement last night, which was then sent to their three studios in an e-mail. There'll be a press release later this week when they've had the chance to talk to all the models. Soon as I heard, I knew we needed to talk."

All the hair stood up on the back of Mike's neck. "Go on," he said slowly. He leaned back in his chair and folded his arms.

Tony fidgeted, now rubbing the back of his neck. "It's been decided that ManFactory will become a bareback only studio." He swallowed and then fell silent, his gaze flickering up to catch Mike's, his breathing quickening.

Mike stared at him, lost for words for a moment. Then he began to laugh, softly at first but growing louder and heartier, until he was wiping the tears from his eyes. Tony gaped at him, bewildered. When Mike finally regained his composure, he nodded, smiling.

"Thank you. Seriously, thank you."

"What... I don't...." Tony sat back, speechless.

"I walked in here this morning, ready to tell you this was it—I was retiring. I was gonna do this last shoot, because I didn't want to leave you in the lurch." Mike pushed the clipboard toward Tony. "But you know what? In the light of what you've just told me, I have no qualms about telling you to find someone else. After all, you just fired me."

Tony sat bolt upright. "What the fuck are you talking about? I didn't fire you!"

"No?" Mike folded his arms and regarded Tony steadily. "You know how I feel about bareback. Hell, *everyone* here knows that, because I'm not exactly quiet on the subject. So you knew damn well that if this studio goes down that route, there was no way in hell I would follow." He lifted his eyebrows. "Oh, come on, Tony, be honest. Look how nervous you were, telling me. You knew how I was gonna react. Well, you did me a favor. You just confirmed that I've made the right decision." He gave the director a sweet smile. "Okay, so maybe you didn't fire me exactly, but the end result is the same—I quit."

Tony sagged into the chair. "Honest, Scott, that wasn't my intention. It was the owner's decision. I—"

Mike straightened. "Yeah, and we both know why ManFactory has done this, don't we? It's good business. Bareback sells better than condom porn these days. Isn't that right?"

Tony nodded, his gaze locked on Mike's face.

Mike clenched his fists. "I can understand a company deciding to make a move that brings in more money. That's the nature of business. What I *can't* stand, frankly, is the hypocrisy."

"What do you mean?"

"Why do studios make condom porn in the first place? Most of them started out just taking care of their stars, which is fair enough. But that's not what ManFactory—and a few others I could name—said, was it? I *remember*, Tony. I remember the line about the studio 'setting a good example.' But now we have the situation where they're editing out the rubber, which does seem to negate everything they've been saying for more than a decade, doesn't it?" Mike rose to his feet. "I guess that's just the way this business is going. And you know what? I actually feel relieved to be out of it."

"You're quitting?"

Mike turned toward the door at the sound of a familiar voice. Four men stood in the open doorway, staring at him, Dino among them, looking shocked. Mike gave them a relaxed smile.

"Hey, fellas, good to see ya." He stepped away from the table to hug his friend. "You just missed my retirement speech."

"I caught enough of it," Dino said with a chuckle, and Mike could feel him smiling against his cheek. "You never were one to hold back, were ya, Scott?" He released Mike and moved aside as the others stepped forward, hands extended.

"Aw, sorry to hear that, buddy."

"Glad we got to film together."

"I can't believe it! Scott Masters, retiring!"

Mike accepted the handshakes and hugs from his now former colleagues, guys he'd filmed with on more than one occasion. Then he remembered Tony, who was still sitting at the table, looking like a train had run him over. Mike held out his hand. "It was good knowing you, Tony. You were always great to work with, y'know that? And I'll send my resignation in an e-mail once I get home." He had a few of those to compose.

Tony stood up and shook his hand firmly. "For the record, I'm sorry to see you go. Professionals like you are few and far between these days." He gave a brief nod. "You take care, Scott, and good luck for the future." He picked up the clipboard and sighed. "And now I need to find me a porn star. I've got a role that needs filling." With one last smile, he exited the room.

"Hey, you wanna go for a drink to celebrate your retirement?" Dino asked him with a grin. "I'm thinking champagne." The others murmured in agreement.

Mike laughed. "It's a bit early in the day, even for me. Thanks for the thought, but right now there's a young man I gotta see. I have some important news to share with him." He winked.

Dino broke into a huge smile. "Aw, Scott, that's terrific!" He seized Mike in a fierce hug. "So pleased for ya," he whispered.

Mike patted his friend on the back. "Thanks, Dino. I'll be in touch, okay?"

Dino stared at him as he stepped away. "You'd better." He grabbed Mike, spun him around, and then smacked him on the ass. "Now go find your man."

Mike laughed. He said his good-byes and hurried out of the studio, giving Paul a friendly wave as he went through reception. Right then, all he wanted was to see Tommy's face when he broke the news.

MIKE READ through the e-mail one last time and smiled to himself. It was polite but to the point. He picked up his phone and hit speed dial. A couple of rings and there was that familiar voice in his ear.

"Hey. I was just thinkin' 'bout you."

Tommy's words filled him with warmth. "I haven't stopped thinking about you since I saw you last. You doing anything right now?"

"Just lyin' on the couch, readin'."

"Come to my house? Please? I need to see you." Mike fought hard to keep his tone even. He wanted Tommy in his arms so badly, he ached for it. The last few days had brought home to Mike just how much he loved having Tommy in his life.

The line went quiet. Mike could only guess at what was running through Tommy's head. He awaited Tommy's decision, his heart beating that little bit faster.

"Sure. Gimme twenty minutes an' I'll be there."

The tension in his arms and back eased. Mike sagged into the chair. "Great. See you soon." He disconnected, put the phone down, and returned his attention to his laptop screen. "Only one thing left to do," he said out aloud. He slid his hand over to the mouse and clicked on Send. Mike pushed out a long breath. Done. He'd already written a post for his blog that announced his retirement. All he had to do was upload it. Aware of how quickly his fans usually responded, he knew it wouldn't be long before word got around. He logged in to the site, uploaded the personal message, and added a photo of himself, clothed and smiling. "Adieu, Scott Masters."

Damn, it felt good. Better than he'd imagined.

Mike shut down the laptop and put it into its bag, along with the mouse. He took one last look around the house to make sure everything was as it should be before Tommy's arrival. He'd come back from the studio and begun cleaning and tidying, not that the place had been a mess. It had been a spring cleaning, sweeping the dust bunnies of Scott Masters out of the house so that Mike Scott could have a clean start.

He had just enough time before Tommy arrived for one last call. Mike smiled as it connected. He just wished he could see her face. "Good morning."

"And good morning to you too, baby—what's left of it at any rate. It's almost lunchtime." She paused. "You sound happy. Any particular reason for that?"

He chuckled. "You know what I'm gonna say, don't ya?" He shook his head. Mothers and their intuition. "Well, it's done and it's official. I'm out of the porn industry."

"Thank heavens! We can celebrate this Sunday when you bring Tommy to lunch," she said pointedly.

Mike guffawed. "You just don't quit, do ya? Okay, I'll bring him to lunch. Happy now?"

"I'll be happier on Sunday when I lay eyes on him," she replied dryly. "What is it about him that you're not telling me?"

There was no way Mike was going to spoil the surprise, but he couldn't resist teasing her, just a little. "Put it this way, Mom. I didn't go fishing in the same pond as usual."

That got her quiet, at least for a moment. "Well, I'll be damned. Looks like you *do* listen to your momma sometimes, after all." A pause. "Lord, but you're an evil child. You tell me this on Monday, knowing full well it's gonna drive me crazy all week 'til I meet him!"

He laughed loudly. "You raised me, Mom. I must've learned it from you." He glanced at the clock on the wall. "Is it okay if I cut this short? I'm expecting someone any minute."

"Would that someone be Tommy, by any chance?"

"It might." And Mike had enough time to grab a shower beforehand. "Love you, Mom," he interjected before she could start asking more questions, "and I'll see you Sunday, all right?"

She said her good-byes, although her grudging tone told Mike there was more she wanted to say, but he was conscious of the time. He disconnected, put the phone down, and hurried into the bathroom. Within minutes he was under the jets, soaping away the tensions and worries of the day. He resisted the temptation to jerk off, even though he was hard as a rock. *Better to make this quick.* The thought of Tommy in his home once more wasn't helping matters. If anything, it was making him harder, if that were possible.

He put on his jeans and a clean dark blue shirt, leaving his feet bare. He always preferred to be barefoot around the house, even in the wintertime. It wasn't long before he heard Tommy's truck pulling up in the driveway. Mike opened the front door and watched his lover walk up the front steps, that familiar shy smile in evidence.

Mike didn't say a word but stepped to one side to let Tommy enter. Mike closed the door behind him, and Tommy stood there, rubbing his palms on his jeans like he always did when he was nervous. It only took a second for Mike to recall how Tommy had been on Friday, unhappy and uncomfortable. At least he seemed more relaxed, but there was an expectant air about him.

Mike had no intentions of torturing him.

He held open his arms. "So, do you have a hug for a retired porn star?"

Tommy stared at him, those green eyes widening. "You quit? Since when?"

It wasn't quite the reaction Mike had been expecting. Given that Mike hadn't shared his career with Tommy, Mike could understand his apparent disbelief. He lowered his arms slowly. "Since this morning."

"But… you had a shoot today. Didn't you?" Tommy's eyes never left him. "What happened? Did somethin' happen at the studio?" He bit his lip. "Sorry, but after we talked about this, I had no idea you were even thinkin' 'bout quittin'. 'Specially as you were gonna do a shoot." He blinked rapidly, hands falling to his sides.

Mike took his phone from his pocket and went online to his blog. Just as he'd thought, the comments were already coming in, thick and fast. He took a second or two to take in the best wishes of his fans, along with comments expressing disappointment in his decision, offering him congratulations on his amazing career, and still the odd request for Mike to fuck someone. He scrolled back to the top of the entry and handed the phone to Tommy.

"Take a look."

Tommy took it in silence and spent a few minutes reading. Mike studied his face, the concentrated expression. Tommy jerked his head up, lips parting as he began to smile. He placed the phone on the hall table.

And then he pounced.

There was no other word for it. Mike had the air pushed from his lungs when Tommy enfolded him in his strong arms and caught him up in a tight embrace, their mouths meeting in a kiss full of heat and need. Mike went with it, surrendering to the sensual onslaught, lifting his hands to grab Tommy's head and pull him deeper into the kiss.

Tommy gasped and broke the kiss, leaning back to gaze into Mike's eyes. "Why'd you do it? Why'd you quit?"

"For a lot of reasons, I guess, but there was one main motivation."

Tommy tilted his head. "Yeah?"

Mike leaned closer and kissed him, loving the way Tommy sighed into his mouth. He cupped Tommy's cheek. "You. I couldn't lose you, Tommy."

Tommy's mouth opened to speak, but Mike pressed two fingers to his lips. "Baby, I'll tell you everything, I swear. But right now? I wanna hold you, touch you, kiss you… make love to you." He watched the flush of red that rose up past the neckline of Tommy's white T-shirt, up his neck, and spread across his face.

Tommy kissed his fingers. "I love you," he said quietly. "You know that?"

Mike stroked his hair, caressed his cheek. "I do. I love you too, baby."

"I still can't believe you quit. I… am I talkin' too much?" Tommy asked, smiling. Mike nodded, and that smile grew shy. "Then—" Tommy swallowed. "—then maybe you need to put somethin' in my mouth to shut me up."

It was the boldest thing Mike had ever heard from Tommy's lips. And *day-um*, if it didn't go straight to Mike's dick. His skin tingled and his pulse raced. "Maybe I do at that." His voice sounded hoarse to his own ears. "Bedroom, now."

Tommy released him and stood there, tall and still. "Lord, yes," he whispered.

Mike grinned. "Then don't just stand there. Get that cute ass in my bedroom and let me see this gorgeous body I've been missing." He palmed his cock, heavy and thick behind his zipper. "'Cause I got something that will fit in your mouth *perfectly*."

Oh my God. The look of naked hunger on Tommy's face nearly had him coming in his jeans. He grasped Tommy's hand and tugged him across the hallway and into his bedroom. He backed Tommy up to the bed and pushed him until he fell, laughing. Mike was on top of him in seconds, sucking Tommy's top lip, pulling it with his teeth, sliding his tongue into hot wetness. Tommy gave as good as he got, writhing on the bed beneath Mike, noises pouring out of him that occasionally made sense: "*More, now, kiss me….*"

Mike never let up with the kissing while he slid his hand lower to fumble with Tommy's belt buckle, Tommy eagerly helping him. Then jeans were pulled down, almost savagely, Mike tugging at them as if they offended him before tossing them onto the floor. He crawled up Tommy's body, spreading him wide and thrusting his jeans-encased shaft against Tommy's briefs, which were already damp with precome. Mike rocked against him, Tommy's cock pushing against the fabric, and kissed his neck and face. Tommy nodded and shuddered, hips moving as he pushed up to meet Mike's thrusts.

Mike couldn't hold back on his desires, not now there was nothing hidden between them. He wanted Tommy to see just how much Mike wanted him, needed him. He sucked at Tommy's neck, feeling his lover shiver. Mike bit at his earlobe and then caressed it with his tongue.

"Want me inside you?"

"Yes, oh, yes." Tommy opened his eyes wide. "Want you deep inside me."

The words thrilled him. It seemed Tommy wasn't hiding anymore either.

Mike scrambled to his knees and undid his belt and jeans, then pushed them down to free his dick, which sprang up, the slit already wet with precome. Tommy groaned at the sight and flipped over until he was on all fours before Mike, hungrily taking that solid shaft between his lips, head bobbing as he took him deep. Mike moaned and placed his hands lightly on Tommy's head, letting him work at his own pace. Tommy licked and sucked, using lips and tongue to worship Mike's cock. Mike fought hard to hold back his orgasm at the sight of Tommy's muscled back stretching out before him, narrowing at the waist and then swelling into that perfect ass encased in tight briefs. He let Tommy know with noises and caresses that the blowjob was wonderful. Mike stroked along Tommy's spine, aching to dip his fingers into that cleft and find what he knew was waiting for just him. When Tommy reached into his briefs to pull at his own dick, Mike knew his lover was wanting too.

"My turn," he said and pulled free of Tommy's mouth, his dick dripping with saliva. He grabbed the hem of Tommy's T-shirt, then pulled it over his head and off. He moved to kneel behind Tommy, stroking slowly up and down his back before sliding a finger between his cheeks to rub over his hole through his briefs while he reached under to cup Tommy's cock, the fabric barely containing him.

"Please," Tommy begged, lowering his chest to the bed and pushing his ass into the air. "Please, Mike."

"Tell me," Mike demanded, his breathing rapid. "Tell me what you want."

"Your… your tongue in my ass." Tommy spoke into the sheets, but Mike heard every word. "Love it when you do that."

"That's it," Mike praised him. "Say what you want, what you need." He gripped the waistband of Tommy's briefs and pulled them slowly over that firm ass until they were around his knees. Then he leaned forward, spreading Tommy's cheeks and pushing his face into his crease, rubbing his beard over the soft skin.

"Oh yeah." Tommy's low moan rolled out of him and morphed into a full-blown groan of sheer pleasure when Mike flicked his tongue over his hole. "More," he gasped, pushing back, and Mike slowly licked from his tailbone down over his hole, over the perineum to his balls, rolling them in his fingers and then moving to stroke firmly down his shaft. Tommy moved faster, hips rocking as he reached back to push Mike's face more deeply into his crack. Mike chuckled.

"Fuck, you're hungry." And without waiting another second, he pushed his tongue at the tight pucker, again and again, until he could feel the muscle give a little. "That's it, push out, just like I told you."

He was rewarded with another low moan, and suddenly Tommy relaxed. Mike licked into that hot little hole, loving the cries that spilled from Tommy's lips until he was moaning constantly, begging for more.

And Mike wanted more too.

He rolled Tommy onto his back and kissed him before pulling off his briefs and dropping them to the floor. Tommy pulled Mike down on top of him, unable to lie still beneath him. Mike kept up the slow rubbing of his cock against Tommy's, rocking his hips, getting faster, until Tommy was pushing up hard. Mike grabbed on to him and rolled them so that Tommy was on top. He stared up at his lover, breathing more rapidly. "Condom… nightstand."

Tommy nodded. He knelt astride Mike and reached into the drawer to pull out a condom and the bottle of lube. Mike held his dick around the base, and Tommy rolled the latex down over it, fingers tight around the shaft. Mike shivered at his touch; this was gonna be quick. Tommy slicked up his hand and then coated Mike's cock before reaching behind him to slide his fingers over his hole and then slip them inside him. Tommy was almost vibrating with need as he stretched himself, preparing for Mike's cock.

Mike held his breath as Tommy moved into a position where he could guide Mike's dick into him, easing him in slowly, until finally every inch of Mike's shaft was buried in that tight ass. Tommy shuddered and rolled his hips, a slow, careful movement.

"Oh, you *are* deep. That's perfect." He leaned forward and kissed Mike on the mouth. "Love you."

Mike put one hand on Tommy's waist, the other around his cock, which pointed upward, hard as granite. "Love you, Tommy." He smiled. "You feel so good on my dick. You gonna ride me, or shall I do the work?"

Tommy's lips parted. "Oh, I love it when you push up into me." He brought his chest down to meet Mike's, their lips almost meeting so Mike could feel his warm breath on his face. "Please, Mike, do it. Do it hard." A shudder rippled through him. "I need you. Need to feel you inside me, fillin' me."

His words fulfilled a need deep inside Mike. To hear Tommy giving voice to his desires was sheer heaven.

Mike wrapped his arms around Tommy, holding him tight as he began to thrust up into him, slowly at first, hips rolling up off the mattress to slide his cock into that hole that pulled him in.

Tommy never lost eye contact. "Like that, yeah," he said breathlessly.

Mike kissed him. "You mine, Tommy?" He gave another roll of his hips, going deeper this time.

Tommy shivered. "Yours. Have been yours since you took me that first time." He smiled. "Been waitin' for you to catch on."

Fuck. Mike thrust faster, fucking up into that tight body that welcomed him, drew him in. Tommy groaned and joined their mouths in kisses that matched the intensity of his thrusts.

Mike pulled at Tommy's dick. "Getting close, baby." His fingers were slick with precome.

Tommy sat up and leaned back, his lower body rocking on Mike's cock. "Me too. C'mon, Mike. Make me come."

Fuck, yeah. Mike wanted to feel that splash of heat on his chest, feel that ass clenching around his shaft. The two of them moved together, bodies damp with perspiration, skin glistening in the afternoon light. His balls were tight, the feel of Tommy wrapped around his cock too much to hold off his climax any longer. "Ready?"

Tommy tossed back his head and cried out. "Oh, Mike, now, now."

He could feel Tommy's dick swell in his hand, and then Tommy came, back arched, mouth open, his body milking Mike's cock. Waves of pleasure, so intense they took Mike's breath away, flowed over and through him as he came deep inside Tommy. His fingers dug into

Tommy's hips as he held on tight, both of them jolted by the force of their orgasms.

Tommy fell forward, their slick skin meeting as they kissed. Mike returned his kisses, desperate to keep the connection, their bodies locked together as they rode out the last of it, their movements slowing until at last Tommy lay quiet on top of him, his body a welcome weight. Mike stroked over damp flesh, fingers curling through Tommy's hair, his cock still inside his lover.

Tommy lifted his head and smiled. "Wow."

Mike grinned. "Wow? That's all I get after that performance?"

Tommy's eyes gleamed. "I'll give you my ratin' later… when I get my breath back."

CHAPTER THIRTY

TOMMY HAD never been this happy.

He lay in Mike's arms, listening to the steady beat of his heart, Mike's body warm against his. They'd dozed off after making love, Tommy drifting into a deep, comfortable sleep. It was the first time in a week that he'd been able to sleep and wake refreshed. Mike's breathing was even, and Tommy had no idea if his lover was awake or asleep. He was too comfortable to move in order to find out.

Then Mike moved, stretching his lean body. He kissed the top of Tommy's head. "Hey there." His sigh stirred Tommy's hair. "You feel so good lying there."

Tommy shifted until he was leaning on Mike's chest, looking directly at him. "Feels pretty good from where I am too." He craned his neck, trying to see Mike's alarm clock. "What time is it?"

Mike reached over to the nightstand and picked up his watch. "Nearly five." Just then his stomach growled. "That's my body complaining about missing lunch."

"You didn't eat?"

Mike chuckled. "I had, er, other things on my mind, shall we say." He planted a big kiss on Tommy's head. "How about we get up and fix ourselves something to eat? Maybe a sandwich? Because I want to take you out to dinner tonight."

Tommy lay still, staring at Mike. "Dinner? Really?"

Mike laughed. "It's not like we're strangers to eating out, right? How many times have we had breakfast together at the diner?"

"Yeah, but dinner?" That felt different, more… romantic.

Mike's expression softened. "Yeah, I know what you mean. I want to take you to somewhere beautiful, romantic, with soft lighting and low music, where I can show off my gorgeous lover." His stomach forced out an even louder rumble, and Mike blushed. "But first things first. Kitchen."

"No shower?" Tommy loved it when they showered together.

Mike pushed him off and then reached over to slap his ass. "We can do that before we go out. Right now I need feeding." He got up off the bed and strolled naked out of the room. Tommy went to grab his briefs from the floor and then stopped, hand in midair. *It's just us.* He got up and followed Mike to the kitchen. Tommy stood in the doorway, resisting the urge to cover himself with his hands. Mike was at the sink, his firm ass dimpling as he moved. It was a lovely sight.

Mike paused in the middle of washing his hands, looked over his shoulder, and smiled. "Damn, you look good like that." He finished off his task and turned around so that Tommy could see his dick, half-hard and long. Mike glanced down and grinned. "That's *your* fault." He pulled a bag of bread from a cabinet and then opened the refrigerator. "What would you like on your sandwich? I got that sliced turkey you liked last time, swiss cheese, bologna...."

"Anythin' from that list sounds great. Can I do somethin'?"

Mike gave a nod to the fridge. "You can fill us two glasses with water. There's ice in the freezer."

Tommy went about his task. He couldn't get over how natural it felt to be naked in Mike's kitchen. It wasn't long before they were sitting at the dining table with their snack.

Tommy shook his head. "Well, this is a first. Naked lunch." He regarded Mike with narrowed eyes. "You do this a lot, don'tcha? Hangin' 'round the house, naked?" It wasn't something they'd done before. Tommy was used to watching Mike moving from bedroom to bathroom in the nude, but he began to get the feeling that only now was he getting to see the real Mike. It was a good feeling.

Mike chuckled. "Okay, you got me. I like being naked, all right? But I was thinking, seeing as you're gonna be here a lot more, you might as well get used to me in my natural state." He grinned, and then his expression grew more serious. "Look, just because I walk around with it all hangin' out doesn't mean you have to, okay? I could see when you walked into the kitchen that you weren't entirely comfortable." He gave a half smile. "Though the sight of you sure brightened up my kitchen."

Tommy's cheeks grew warm. "I... I guess it's somethin' I could get used to." He felt safe in Mike's house. Then he got to thinking. "What did you mean 'bout me bein' here more often? It's not like I can be here durin' the week. I got school." It saddened him how little time they would have together.

Mike sighed. "Yeah, I know. But I was thinking, maybe instead of staying with Ben on the weekends, you should come stay with me. If you want to, of course."

If he wanted to? Tommy beamed. "I'd love that."

"Though I should warn you. Staying here the weekend would mean Sunday lunch with my mom, who is dying to meet you, by the way."

That stopped him. "You're takin' me to meet your mom?"

Mike put down his glass of water and reached for Tommy's hand across the table. "Of course. She needs to meet the man I love."

A warm glow suffused Tommy's entire body. "Oh." The softly spoken syllable didn't convey even half the emotion that coursed through him.

"But for now, how about you come away with me this weekend? I could pick you up Friday night after class, and bring you back as late as we can Sunday. We could go to the coast, if you like. "

A whole weekend away with Mike. And he'd thought he'd never been this happy. "That sounds great." Then he paused. "But what about Woofs? Would you be able to get the time off?"

Mike winked. "Sure. I'll pull in a few favors. It shouldn't be a problem." He smiled. "And just so you know? The thought of spending a weekend away with you makes me really happy. I know it's only for a couple of days, but I think it'll be great. I'm sure we'll find some fun things to do."

Tommy didn't care what they did, as long as they did it together.

Mike got up from the table and took the plates to the kitchen, Tommy following. "Well, that filled a hole. I'm gonna make some coffee. You want some?" Tommy nodded. Mike started setting up his coffee machine. "We can always Skype during the week when you're at school, y'know."

The memory of their first Skype call sent heat rushing through Tommy. "Uh, okay."

Mike laughed. "And every call doesn't get to be like that first one, dirty boy. There was something I've been meaning to ask you about that. Your Skype address, TNewsome1995. Why that year?"

Without thinking, Tommy replied, "It's the year I was born." The words were out before he remembered.

Too late. Mike was staring at him, eyebrows raised. "Uh, Tommy? How old are you? Right this second?"

Well, shoot. "Nineteen," he said quietly. "I'll be twenty next month, though."

"Nineteen," Mike repeated slowly. "So I'm not dating a twenty-one-year-old student after all." He bit his lip. "Well, that explains the Cherry Cokes."

"Hey, I drink Cherry Coke because I really don't drink." *What must he be thinkin'?* "I'm sorry." Tommy's heart sank. "I didn't mean to keep it from ya. I was gonna tell ya about the fake ID, honest." He watched Mike's expression for some clue as to his reaction.

Mike crossed the kitchen floor and took him in his arms. "It's okay. At least I know now." He peered intently at Tommy. "But from now on, no secrets, okay? And that goes for me too." He kissed Tommy on the mouth. "I mean it, Tommy. I want you in my life, and I want us to last, so that means starting as we mean to go on, with us both being honest."

Tommy looked into his eyes and smiled. "I want that too. An' I promise, no more secrets." That earned him another kiss. The feel of Mike's dick against his thigh was a reminder of their state, and his shaft hardened. "Uh, would you mind if I put some clothes on?" Maybe he wasn't cut out to be a nudist. Not yet at any rate. Maybe with more practice.

Mike chuckled. "I tell you what. Let's both put on some clothes. It's just occurred to me that maybe we should go pick up your stuff before dinner. You might want a change of clothing."

He had a point. "Yeah, let's do that." Besides, he knew Caroline would want to know how things were going. He couldn't wait to see her face when he shared Mike's news. And then dinner out with Mike.

It was looking like it was going to be a great evening.

MIKE ALWAYS liked eating out at Joe's on Juniper. There were classier restaurants in Atlanta, true, but he loved eating outside with the colored lights sparkling in the trees, watching the people go by.

Tommy loved it, judging from the look of delight on his face. He kept looking up at the sparkly canopy above their heads and smiling. "This is so nice."

"I'm glad." Mike hadn't missed the looks from some of the restaurant's occupants. There'd been a few subtle double takes when someone had recognized him, but Tommy'd had his fair share of admirers too. Not that Mike was surprised. Tommy was well built and muscled, with a face that drew all kinds of attention to him.

Mike took Tommy's hand. "You happy?"

Tommy let out a sigh. "Yeah. Though it's makin' me feel greedy for more time with ya."

Mike felt the same way. In fact, he'd been thinking about that all afternoon. "So, you're in your second year?"

Tommy nodded. "I've been thinkin' 'bout doin' summer school, so I could end up doin' three years instead of four. Then there's another three years at the veterinary school on top of that."

Mike whistled. "A lot of studying." They'd discussed it before, but now it suddenly had more meaning. Now they were together.

"Yeah, but it'll be worth it at the end, if I get to be a vet." His expression sobered. "'Course, that means I'd have even less time with you in the summer." He let out another sigh and then seemed to shrug off his contemplative mood. "What about you? What you gonna do now you're not doin' porn anymore?"

"Keep working at Woofs. I've got enough put aside to be able to live on that." He took a deep breath and plunged ahead. "I figured I'd keep working 'til you graduate. Then I thought we might open a vet office." He waited for his words to sink in.

Tommy stared at him. "A... a vet office?"

Mike nodded, his gaze focused on Tommy. "Maybe somewhere a bit more rural, outside of Atlanta. Actually, I thought we could run it from somewhere close to our house." There, he'd finally gotten out what he'd been thinking about all that evening.

It felt as if the world stopped turning around them. All he saw was Tommy's face, his eyes wide, mouth open. "House? *Our* house?"

Mike tightened his fingers around Tommy's. "I was serious before, baby. I want us to have a life together. So—" He took a drink from his glass of white wine before speaking. "—I was thinking of selling my house, and—"

"But your house is great!" Tommy protested.

Mike smiled. "It's just a house, Tommy. I bought it as an investment, and as that, it's done just fine. It's worth a lot more than when I bought it." He chuckled. "A whole lot more. But it's not a home. I want to buy a place that's ours. Somewhere with space for horses, cows, dogs, chickens...." He laughed as Tommy's mouth dropped open even more.

"Well, you'll want to have some animals to practice on, right? And for that you'll need some space. I was thinking five to ten acres would be a good size."

Tommy stared at him. "You're serious, aren't ya?"

Mike nodded. "Been thinking about this all through dinner." He held up his hand. "Now don't start panicking. I'm not about to buy it this minute. But I can start looking. Maybe by the time you finish this year in June, I'll have somewhere for us to live that's ours." He smiled. "We can start making a home together."

"But... what about your job at Woofs?"

Mike shrugged. "I can stay at Mom's for the weekends. She'd love that. She'd love it even more if you came too." He tilted his head. "So how about it? Wanna live with me, baby?"

God, the light in Tommy's eyes was mesmerizing. "Yes," he said softly. "I'd love to." He shook his head. "This feels like a dream."

"A good one?"

Tommy's smile could've lit up the restaurant on its own. "Oh yeah, a really good one."

And with that, Mike felt as if his world had just clicked into its rightful position in the universe.

TOMMY SMILED to himself as he undressed for bed. He'd felt like he was walking on air since dinner. The day had brought one surprise after another. They'd spent the rest of the evening discussing Mike's plans. Tommy was still finding it hard to believe. Mike wanted to buy a house for them. He wanted to open a vet's office for Tommy. His words didn't leave any room for doubt in Tommy's mind.

Mike was serious about them having a future.

What a difference six months makes. At the end of September, he'd had a family who loved him. He had started to discover what it meant to be gay in Atlanta. A gay *virgin* in Atlanta. Now, here he was with his family having disowned him, but with a whole new family who cared for him. A boyfriend more than twenty years older than himself, a retired porn star, no less. And a future with Mike that stretched out before him, some of it tantalizingly out of sight as the road before them twisted and turned, but that was fine by Tommy. He was starting to like surprises.

Still, Mike's comment about no more secrets had gotten him thinking. Because he had a secret, one he hesitated to share, for fear of what Mike would think of him.

There was still so much he didn't know.

"What's on your mind?" Mike asked as he got into bed, pulling back the sheets for Tommy. "And don't tell me nothing, 'cause I know you too well."

Tommy climbed in next to him and lay on his side, facing Mike. "I… sort of have a confession."

"Oh?" Mike got comfortable. "Go on, I'm listening."

Tommy drew circles on the white sheet between them. "The day Ben showed me that video of you on the Internet? I told him I wasn't interested in porn. But—" He took a deep breath. "—that week, I… I might have watched a few of your videos."

"Oh." Mike studied him. "Just out of curiosity?"

Tommy nodded. "I couldn't stop myself. An' some of 'em were… interestin'." Mike looked like he was trying not to smile, and Tommy groaned. "Look, this is really hard for me, okay?"

Mike schooled his featured instantly. "Okay."

Tommy tried to breathe more evenly. "So I was watchin', an' I got a little confused."

"What confused you?"

"Well, I watched a few videos where you were… on top." Mike nodded, and Tommy pushed ahead. "But then I saw a couple where you were…."

"Bottoming?" Mike suggested.

Tommy gave him a grateful glance. "Yeah. An' what confused me was, I'd thought once you started, you know, havin' sex… you'd sorta chose your role an' then you stuck with it. But you were doin' both."

Mike smiled. "It's okay to ask questions, all right? And yes, it's true, there are some guys who bottom all the time and others who top. But then there are guys like me who are more versatile. Personally, I think I get the best of both worlds." He reached across the divide between them to stop Tommy's hand in its tracks and hold it. "But we're talking about you. So far you've only bottomed." He leaned closer. "Are you interested in doing something… different?"

Tommy regarded their joined hands. "Yes," he whispered. His cheeks felt like they were on fire.

"Baby, it's okay to have wants, needs. The great thing about being a couple is that we get to explore them together." Mike closed the gap between them and kissed him softy on the lips. "Do you want to know how often I've thought about having you inside me?"

Tommy jerked his head up. "Really?"

Mike nodded. "Oh yeah." And then he moved, shifting closer until their bodies were touching so Tommy could feel heat and hardness against his hip. Mike's gaze met his. "Yeah, that's how much I want it. You feel that?"

"Yes." His own cock was tenting the sheet, just thinking about it.

Mike slipped an arm over his waist and stroked his back. "God, I want you so much." He rolled onto his back, pulling Tommy with him. Reaching up, he cupped his face. "Make love to me?"

Tommy gave a soft moan and dropped his head to Mike's shoulder, nuzzling into his neck and kissing him. Mike wrapped his arms around him and then drew up his legs to wrap them around Tommy's waist. Tommy rocked against him, their already hard dicks rubbing against each other. He shifted until his cock was sliding in Mike's crease and Mike was making low, urgent noises, his legs pressing around Tommy's waist more firmly, his heels digging into Tommy's ass.

"Fuck, yeah," Mike groaned. "Want you." He moved faster, the heat between them escalating. "Let me suck your dick?"

Tommy pulled free of Mike's embrace and shuffled up the bed until he was straddling Mike's chest, his rigid shaft poking up toward his belly. Mike propped himself up on his elbows and eagerly licked the head, lapping up precome. Tommy clasped his hands around Mike's head and held him there while he thrust into Mike's mouth, slowly at first but gaining momentum as Mike took him deeper, groaning around the thick length. Then he gave the head a good, hard suck and Tommy cried out with sheer pleasure. He loved it when Mike sucked him off, but it felt too good. "You're gonna make me come at this rate," he gasped out.

Mike pulled free of him and grinned. "Not yet, you're not." He stretched out a hand to the nightstand, yanked open the drawer, and pulled out a condom and the lube. He thrust the lube into Tommy's hand. "Get me ready."

Tommy moved to kneel next to Mike and leaned over to kiss the head of his dick before running his tongue the length of it, licking over Mike's balls. Mike sighed with delight, and Tommy licked them again, knowing how much his lover liked it. He took one carefully into his mouth while he rubbed a slick finger over Mike's hole, pressing slowly into him, his pulse racing to feel Mike's heat tight around him. Mike pushed down, moaning when Tommy added a second finger.

"Now, baby, please?"

Tommy's fingers trembled as he covered his shaft with the latex and swiped his lube-slick fingers over it. Mike rolled onto his side, offering Tommy his ass, a position Tommy always loved whenever Mike fucked him. He curled up behind Mike and slowly pressed the head of his cock against Mike's entrance, while Mike grabbed hold of his thigh and held his leg aloft.

"That's it," Mike encouraged him. "Now push in, nice and slow. Let me feel you."

Tommy gently entered him, holding his breath as his dick was suddenly gripped by Mike's tight, hot channel. "Oh Lord, that feels...." It felt amazing. He began to slide in and out, his hand covering Mike's, holding his leg in the air. His hips moved awkwardly, and he had difficulty finding his rhythm.

"Stay in me, move with me," Mike demanded and rolled slowly onto his belly.

Tommy went with him, straddling his ass, plunging down into his tight hole.

"Oh." Tommy wanted to *move*. He began to thrust faster, not filling Mike entirely.

Mike turned his head to the side and tilted his ass higher. "Tommy, you're not gonna hurt me. Go hard if you want to. Just let go and fuck me." The last words sounded like he was begging.

Tommy pulled out and knelt up. Mike spread his legs wide, and Tommy sank back into him, pushing as far as he could go, until his hips were snug against Mike's ass.

"Oh God, *yes*, like that," Mike moaned.

Tommy pulled nearly all the way out and then thrust in, hard.

"Fuck, yeah, like that! Just like that!"

Tommy did it again, and this time Mike pushed back, slamming into him, his balls slapping against Mike's body.

"Now, baby, now. *Fuck* me!"

Tommy grabbed hold of Mike's waist and just let go, hips snapping forward, loud cries spilling from his lips as he punched his dick into

Mike's body again and again. Mike's harsh cries echoed around the bedroom, occasionally forming sentences, telling Tommy how good it felt, how he loved it… and that he loved Tommy. Between the two of them, they got a rhythm going, Mike pushing back to meet Tommy's thrusts, and it wasn't long before Tommy knew he was about to come. He dug his fingers into Mike's hips and buried his cock to the hilt in Mike's hole.

"Gonna come," he panted.

"Yes," Mike gasped. "Let me feel you."

Tommy sped up, the loud smack of flesh meeting flesh resounding. He came hard, falling forward to curve his body over Mike's while he pulsed into the condom. Tommy cried out against Mike's back, a joyous noise that burst out of him.

"Oh God, I can feel you coming." Mike dropped his head, voice hoarse. "That feels… so fucking good."

Then Mike's body tightened around Tommy's dick, and that was a whole new sensation.

He reached under Mike to stroke his cock, but one touch of his hand around the turgid length and Mike climaxed, hot come jetting onto the sheet below him. Tommy was shaking, tremors running through him, and he could feel Mike's body trembling under him. He clung to Mike, dick still wedged inside him, both of them shivering. Tommy couldn't speak. He closed his eyes and concentrated on the way Mike felt beneath him, the sounds of their breathing, harsh and erratic, the smell of come and sex that was so heady. Mike was hot and tight, wrapped around his cock, his body gripping Tommy like it didn't want to let him go.

Little by little he regained his composure, until he got to the point where he could breathe again. He kissed across Mike's shoulders and up his neck. Mike lifted his head and turned to meet his kiss, and Tommy breathed him in, not wanting it to end. When they finally parted, Tommy let out a low moan as his cock eased out of Mike's body.

"You were wonderful," Mike told him softly.

Tommy's heart soared at the words. "You felt amazin'." A sense of peace spread throughout his body in a soft, relentless tide, leaving him feeling calm. He rested his head against Mike's damp back. "We're *definitely* doin' that again."

And then he laughed as Mike's chuckle vibrated through him.

EPILOGUE

Late May

"MIKE, YOU don't have to do the dishes," Caroline protested. "That's what the dishwasher is for." She stood next to him at the sink as he piled the dirty dishes from lunch into the bowl already filling with hot, soapy water.

Mike chuckled and handed her the dishtowel. "Yeah, but it gives us a chance to talk. 'Cause you know Ben and Tommy won't be around if there are dishes to be done." He shook his head. "You should've seen Tommy's face when I told him there wasn't a dishwasher at the new house."

Caroline's face registered shock. "There isn't? What house doesn't have a dishwasher these days?" She peered at him. "Y'all have gone and bought a house out in the backwoods, haven't ya?"

He guffawed. "Just listen to you. Just like my momma. She complains about having to do dishes too. And for your information, yes, there *is* a dishwasher, but it was worth saying it for the sheer entertainment value."

Caroline swiped at him with the dishtowel. "You are just plain wicked, messing with that young man. I mean, c'mon, Mike, there are better things I can be doing with my time than washing dishes."

"And there are better things I can be doing with Tommy than washing dishes, if you know what I mean," he said, waggling his eyebrows. He knew Caroline well enough by now to judge how she'd react. As he'd thought, she blushed a little.

"I do believe that comes under the realm of TMI, Mr. Scott," she said, fanning herself with her hand. Then she chuckled. "Who am I kidding? The number of times I've walked in on you two downstairs and I didn't make enough noise to let you know I was coming." Her blush deepened. "Talk about giving a Southern lady an education."

Mike knew she was joking, although she had come into the living area once to find them on the couch. Ben had been out, and Mike was saying good-bye, only they'd gotten a little carried away. Thank God they'd kept their clothes on.

Caroline held out a hand. "Well, if you're putting me to work, pass me something to dry, why don't you?" Mike smiled and handed her a plate. "So, how is the house coming along? Does it need a lot done to it?"

Mike shook his head. "It's thirty years old and in really good condition." He'd fallen in love with the house the moment he saw it online, and when he'd shown it to Tommy, it was a done deal. They'd taken a trip out to Social Circle to the east of Atlanta to look at the house and its environs. It came with nearly six acres, plenty of land for their purposes. The house had been built in the middle of a forest. The views from virtually all the windows were of the cool green trees that surrounded it on three sides. There was a paddock and lots of space for Tommy's future menagerie. Better still, there was the possibility of a plot of land just down the road a ways, just right for a veterinary practice.

The house on River Cove Road couldn't have been more perfect.

"I'm sure gonna miss having Tommy around here." Caroline rubbed absently at the plate.

"Why'd you think we chose a house with five bedrooms? So that you could all come visit."

"It looked so beautiful when Tommy showed us the photos you took." She smiled. "He's grown so much these last six months."

"What? God, tell me he's finished growing!" Mike joked. He knew Tommy was sometimes a bit sensitive about being so much taller than him. Mike didn't mind. There was something about being held in Tommy's strong arms that made him feel completely safe and secure. Mike had always been the larger guy when it came to his exes, so it was a pleasant change.

Caroline chuckled. "You know what I mean, Mike! He's so much more... confident these days." She quieted for a moment. "Does he ever talk about his parents?"

"No." Mike took his hands out of the soapy water and leaned against the sink. "I tried, once or twice, to ask if he'd thought about getting in touch with them. He was adamant. Then I brought it up again when the house went through. I thought there might have been things back at his folks' house that he'd want with him." The memory made him smile. "He told me everything he needed was either at his dorm, your place, or standing right in front of him."

"Oh, that is so sweet." She took another plate from him. "It's been nice getting to know you these last months."

"Now that I'm no longer a porn star?" Mike said with a grin.

"Oh hush, you." Another swipe of the towel. "You know full well my problem with you was not your career—it was the way you hurt that boy by hiding it from him."

"I know. And like I said when we first met, I'm glad Tommy has you in his corner." Mike had become good friends with Caroline and Benny. A weekend didn't go by without spending some time with them and the kids. "You know, *you're* Tommy's family now, and that's not about to change. He'll still be staying in the dorm, unless he decides that he can live with the forty-five minute commute twice a day from Social Circle. And you know he and Ben will stick together." Thank God Ben had finally relaxed around Mike.

"So what are you doing with your time these days?" Caroline inquired. "When you're not working at Woofs, of course." She frowned. "Just how is this going to work, by the way? During the week, Tommy will be at school. On the weekends you'll be working. How are y'all ever gonna find enough time to be together?"

Mike sighed. "It's a logistical nightmare, is what it is. We've managed to sort out something, though. Mom said I can stay at her place on the weekends, which is great. When I told her there would be two of us, I thought she was gonna burst. She loves that boy." He was never going to forget her reaction when she met Tommy for the first time. She'd smiled politely and then dragged Mike into the kitchen under the pretense of looking at her leaking faucet. She'd stared up at him and mouthed, "Oh shit. He's a baby!" It hadn't taken her long to warm to him, however. By the end of that first Sunday lunch, she'd taken Mike aside, glared at him, and told him bluntly, "Don't screw this up, y'hear?"

"In answer to your question, I've been working on the house, getting it ready for when Tommy finished for the summer. He'd made up his mind not to do summer school this year, saying he'd rather spend the time at the house, with me."

Caroline froze. "He said that?"

Mike nodded. "Then I told him to remember the end goal. We'll have time enough together when he's finished his studies." He gave her a half smile. "Which was the right thing to say, I know, but damn, I hated saying it." Then he grinned. "Except Tommy hadn't done his research.

Sure, the summer session is two blocks of seven weeks, and yeah, he only gets a week or so before it starts, but he can do it online."

Caroline's grin matched his. "Oh, nice. Y'know, you might have given me an idea." She winked. "Ben needs to improve on his grades, after all."

Mike had to laugh at that. Ben was *so* gonna hate him for giving his mom the idea. "So I've told Tommy we're gonna have a regime. He has to get up early every morning and get his classwork done, and then the rest of the day is ours." Every minute they would get together was going to be precious, and Mike was going to make sure they got the most out of it.

TOMMY ENTERED the kitchen, Ben following behind. "That's the last of it," he told Mike. "All packed up an' ready to go." Everything he'd kept in Ben's apartment was now boxed or bagged up and thrown into the back of Mike's truck. They'd already cleared out the dorm room that morning. All of *that* was in the back of Tommy's truck. It was a weird feeling; all his worldly goods in two trucks. And with all the space at the house, he was sure he and Mike were gonna rattle around in there. Having said that, he hadn't seen the place since Mike had started moving all his things in. The sale of Mike's house had gone through fairly quickly, dovetailing nicely with the purchase of their new home.

Our new home. It still took some getting used to, especially when they went to look around the place. It had been so strange to walk around the beautiful house with its hardwood floors, its screened-in porch and long front veranda, and think that it could be theirs. And now he got to spend his summer helping Mike make it into their home.

Mike and Caroline looked in their direction and smiled. "Oh, you mean you were actually doing something?" Mike said with a grin. "And there was me, thinking you were avoiding clearing up after lunch." His eyes sparkled with amusement.

Tommy returned his grin. "Bite me."

"Now, now, boys." Caroline wagged her finger. "Play nice. Y'all are moving in together." She glanced at Ben. "There's lemonade in the fridge. Would you get it, please? I thought we could all sit and have a drink before Mike and Tommy leave. Oh, and go find your sister. She's probably talking to her friends on Skype in her room."

"Sure, Mom." Ben exited the kitchen in search of Bethany. Mike wiped his hands dry on a towel and came across to where Tommy was standing next to the table.

"You sure you've got everything?"

Tommy nodded. "Me an' Ben checked over the entire apartment three times. Besides, if I missed somethin', it's not like we're not gonna be here, right?" He sighed. "You're gonna keep my nose to the grindstone, aren't ya?" He couldn't complain. Working online was much better than attending classes, even if Mike made him stick to a timetable.

Mike's arms were around him in seconds. "Aw, I know it's tough, baby, but it's one summer. It's like I said. Get it all done early on so we get time for us. What did I say?"

Tommy grinned. "I know. I know. 'A few hours a day beats a week away.'" It was Mike's new mantra.

"And it means one less year in the long run." Mike peered intently at Tommy. "I know you're not happy about how little time we'll have once school starts up again, but we've talked about this."

"An' talked about it, an' *talked*…. Doesn't mean I have to like it." He knew Mike was right, of course. It wouldn't be forever. And part of him was pleased that Mike was thinking of the future. He gave Mike a flash of a smile. "Can't help it. I'm sorta old-fashioned like that. Y'know, movin' in together should mean we actually get to live together." He'd been thinking about that commute. Forty-five minutes twice a day was nothing. He could cope with that. Now all he had to do was convince Mike. Okay, so it would mean time he'd be spending in his truck and not on his studies, but on the plus side, he'd get to sleep in Mike's arms every night.

He couldn't see Mike arguing with that.

"I love that you're an old-fashioned kinda guy," Mike said with a smile. He stretched up and kissed the tip of Tommy's nose before taking his hand and guiding him to a chair.

"You two are so sweet together," Caroline said with a sigh. She sat at the table facing them.

"Where's Benson?" Mike asked.

"Playing golf at the club." Caroline's brow furrowed. "I asked him not to go, but he said it was the only chance he had to meet up with a couple lawyers who were in town. That man works too hard."

Ben and Bethany entered the kitchen, and Ben went to the fridge to retrieve the lemonade while Bethany fetched glasses from the cabinet.

"I was serious before, y'know."

Tommy turned to look at Mike. "About what?"

"Loving you being old-fashioned. It's the way you were raised. You have principles, integrity, respect. Do you know how rare those commodities are in a guy nowadays?"

Tommy stared at him. He didn't know what to say to such praise, especially in front of the others.

Mike nodded slowly. "This is what makes you so special, Tommy. This is why I love you. So remember, there is nothing wrong with being old-fashioned." A slow smile spread across his face, and Tommy was surprised to note how Mike's breathing quickened. "In fact, some occasions call for it."

Before Tommy could ask what that statement meant, Mike got up from his chair and knelt down in front of him.

"What are you doin'?" Tommy gaped at him. He could hear soft noises of surprise from the others.

Mike reached for his hand and held it, his gaze fixed on Tommy. "I'm taking a leaf out of your book and doing something a little old-fashioned. We're about to move in together, so I figured now was as good a time as any to ask you a question." He glanced up at Caroline. "Especially as your adopted mom is sitting there, watching us."

"Oh my." Caroline stared at him, her smile growing exponentially.

Mike returned his attention to Tommy. "So I'm here to ask you, Tommy Newsome, if you'll do me the honor of becoming my husband."

He was dreaming. He had to be.

"This is real, baby. This is me, asking you to spend the rest of your life with me. No, I'm not crazy. Yes, I know exactly what I'm doing. No, I don't care that you're only twenty. And yes, I do want an answer." He grinned. "Even if the answer is 'I'll think about it.'" He flushed. "Although I'd prefer an outright yes."

Tommy's heart was beating so strongly, he swore everyone in the room could hear it. And finally he found his voice.

"You really wanna marry me?" he whispered, unable to tear his eyes away from Mike.

"Oh God, yes." Mike shifted closer, his hand tightening around Tommy's. With his free hand, he reached into his shirt pocket. "I even have a ring." He held it up, a circle of polished silver.

It was the sight of the ring that made Tommy's heart soar.

"You… you've really thought about this, haven't ya?"

"Constantly. I bought this a month ago." Mike's eyes, wide and blue, were focused on him. "So, as you might imagine, I'm getting kinda nervous here, because—"

"Yes!" Tommy blurted out. "I'll marry you."

Mike visibly held his breath. "You said yes?"

Grinning, Tommy nodded. "I said yes." He couldn't resist yanking Mike's chain. "Your hearin' goin', Mike? This an age thing? Should I be worried here?"

Mike laughed. "You like living dangerously, don't you?" He made as if to put the ring back in his pocket. "So maybe I need to reconsider my—"

"Don't you dare." Tommy held out his left hand.

Caroline was laughing, Ben and Bethany too.

Mike placed the ring over the end of his finger and slid it into place. He leaned forward until his face was inches from Tommy's. "Love you. Need you. Want you in my life. Is that clear enough?"

Tommy smiled and closed the gap to kiss his fiancé on the lips. "Crystal."

That road snaking off into the future had just taken an interesting—and unexpected—turn.

Born and raised in the north-west of England, K.C. WELLS always loved writing. Words were important. Full stop. However, when childhood gave way to adulthood, the writing ceased, as life got in the way.

K.C. discovered erotic fiction in 2009, when the purchase of a ménage storyline led to the startling discovery that reading about men in love was damn hot. In 2012, arriving at a really low point in life led to the desperate need to do something creative. An even bigger discovery waited in the wings—writing about men in love was even hotter....

K.C. now writes full-time and is loving every minute of her new career.

The laptop still has no idea of what hit it... it only knows that it wants a rest, please. And it now has to get used to the idea that where K.C goes, it goes.

And as for those men in love that she writes about? The list of stories just waiting to be written is getting longer... and longer....

K.C. loves to hear from readers.

E-mail: k.c.wells@btinternet.com

Facebook: www.facebook.com/KCWellsWorld

Twitter: @K_C_Wells

Website: www.kcwellsworld.com

In the kingdom of Teruna, the red-cloaked Seruani teach the Terunans the art of love. Taken from their homes at seventeen to be trained, they are shunned as outcasts by society and considered the lowest of the low. So when Prince Tanish falls in love with the Seruan Feyar, the man who took his virginity and the only one to share his bed, he is not about to declare that love. No one can ever know, because the consequences would be too painful to consider for both of them.

When the king of Vancor visits Teruna, he promises that his son, Prince Sorran, will marry Prince Tanish to solidify the alliance between the two kingdoms, with the proviso that the virginal Sorran is instructed in the art of pleasing his husband-to-be. When Tanish's father chooses Feyar to be this instructor, the lovers decide Prince Sorran must be taught that this is to be a marriage in name only….

A resentful prince, unwilling to share his lover.

A resentful Seruan, unwilling to share his prince.

And the shy prince whose very nature sparks changes in the lives of all those around them.

Teruna is about to change forever.

www.dreamspinnerpress.com

John Wainwright is having a momentous day. To start off, he lands his first teaching job. Then his brother, Evan, and Evan's husband, Daniel, take him out to celebrate in Manchester's gay village. An encounter with a sexy man forces John to admit what he's been denying for too long—he's gay. His coming out proves he's supported and loved by his family and roommates. What more could a man want? There's just one small problem: John's dishy Head Teacher, Brett Sanderson, and John's gigantic crush on him. Too bad Brett is straight.

Brett Sanderson leads a double life. At thirty-three, he is the Head Teacher of a primary school. But for seven years now, during every school holiday, Brett has fled to Brighton, where he becomes 'Rob,' a man who has a different guy in his bed every night but has never had a relationship.

Once he's back in school, Brett is firmly back in that closet, until his newest staff member starts prying open the door. When John pulls out all the stops to get Brett's attention, neither man is prepared for the consequences.

www.dreamspinnerpress.com

Collars and Cuffs: Book One

Since the death of his submissive lover two years ago, Leo hasn't been living—merely existing. He focuses on making Collars & Cuffs, a BDSM club in Manchester's gay village, successful. That changes the night he and his business partner have their weekly meeting at Severinos. Leo can't keep his eyes off the new server. The shy man seems determined to avoid Leo's gaze, but that's like a red rag to a bull. Leo loves a challenge.

Alex Daniels works at Severinos to scrape together the money to move out on his own. He struggles with coming out, but he's drawn to Leo, the gorgeous guy with the icy-blue eyes who's been eating in his area nearly every night.

Leo won't let Alex's hesitance get in the way. He even keeps him away from the club so as not to scare him. And as for telling Alex that Leo is a Dom? Not a good idea. One date becomes two, but date two leads to Leo's bedroom… and Alex discovers things about himself he never realized—and never wanted anyone to see.

www.dreamspinnerpress.com

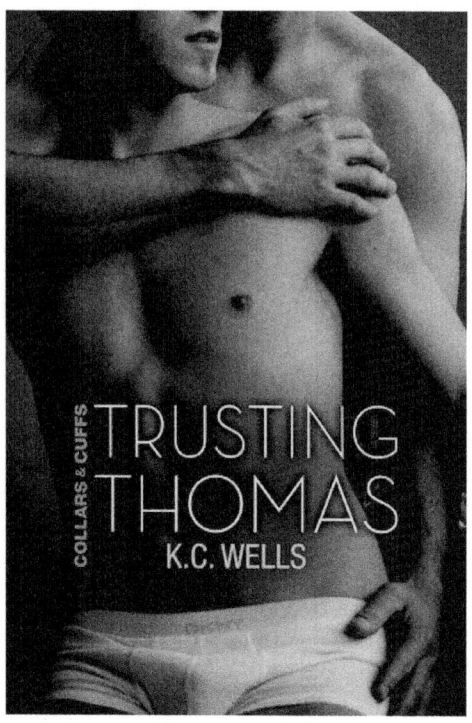

Collars and Cuffs: Book Two

Christmas is a time for goodwill to all, but Collars and Cuffs co-owner Thomas Williams receives an unexpected gift that chills him to the bone. A Dom from another Manchester club asks Thomas for his help rescuing an abused submissive, Peter Nicholson. Thomas takes in the young man as a favor to a friend, offering space and time to heal, but he makes it clear he's never had a sub and doesn't want one.

Peter finds Thomas's home calm and peaceful, but his past has left him unwilling to trust another Dom. When Thomas doesn't behave as Peter expects, Peter's nightmares begin to fade, and he decides he'd like to learn more about D/s life. A well-known trainer of submissives, Thomas begins to teach Peter, but as the new submissive opens up to him, Thomas finds he cares more for Peter than he should. Just as he decides it's time to find a permanent Dom for Peter, they discover Peter's tormentor is still very much a threat. With their lives in danger, Thomas can't deny his feelings for Peter any longer. The question now becomes, can Peter make it out of the lions' den alive, so that Thomas can tell his boy that he loves him?

www.dreamspinnerpress.com

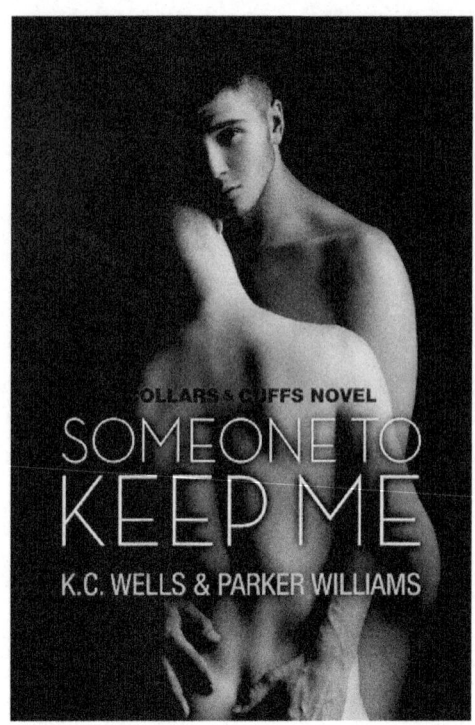

Collars and Cuffs: Book Three

Eighteen-year-old Scott Keating knows a whole world exists beyond his parents' strict control, but until he gains access to the World Wide Web, he really has no idea what's out there. In a chat room, Scott meets "JeffUK." Jeff loves and understands him, and when he offers to bring Scott to the UK, Scott seizes his chance to escape his humdrum life and see the world. But when his plane touches down and Jeff isn't there, panic sets in.

Collars & Cuffs favorite barman and Dom-in-training, Ben Winters, drops his sister off at the airport and finds a lost, anxious Scott. Hearing Scott's story sets off alarm bells, along with his protective instincts. Taking pity on the naïve boy, Ben offers him a place to crash and invites him to Collars & Cuffs, hoping his bosses will know how to help. Scott dreams of belonging to someone, heart and soul. Ben longs for a sub of his own. And neither man sees what's right under his nose.

www.dreamspinnerpress.com

Collars and Cuffs: Book Four

Recently returned to the UK after living in the States since he was eleven, Andrew Barrett is determined to keep busy and make a new life for himself. He works full time as a copywriter and strips at a club on Canal Street on weekends. But it still leaves him too much time to think. Then he finds the BDSM club, Collars & Cuffs, where at twenty-nine, he is their youngest Dom. Young doesn't mean inexperienced, however. All this activity keeps him focused with no time to dwell on the past. But the past has a way of intruding on the present.

It's been four long years since Gareth Michaels last set foot inside Collars & Cuffs. But when he finally summons his courage and steps back into his former world, he finds the man who drove him away is still a member, and what's more, he wants Gareth back. Two men in pain need the freedom they find in each other, but it takes another man's horrific plans to make them see it.

www.dreamspinnerpress.com

Collars and Cuffs: Book Five

The man who pimped Jeff may be in prison, but Jeff is still living the nightmare, selling himself to men and relying on pills to manage. Then he meets Scott, a young American man who could easily have been where Jeff is now. Scott's friends extend a helping hand to Jeff, and he grabs it.

Leo and Thomas bring Jeff to stay with Dom Damian Barnett until they can find him someplace more long-term. Still grieving from losing his sub to cancer two years before, Damian agrees to help. But when he glimpses the extent of the damage, Damian wants to do more than offer his guestroom. Jeff is not a submissive, but Damian can see he desperately needs structure in his life. It's up to Damian to find an answer.

He never expects that what he discovers will change both their lives.

www.dreamspinnerpress.com

Collars and Cuffs: Book Six

Anyone who frequents Collars & Cuffs knows Dorian Forrester is built for pain, including Dorian himself. But everyone has it wrong. For six years, Dorian's chased a feeling that remains tantalizingly out of his reach. Unteachable, Dorian can take anything and everything a Dom can throw at him. Still, it's not enough. Dorian needs… something more. Something he won't find at Collars & Cuffs.

Dorian's search takes him out of the safe environment he's known for years, out of his depth, and into a realm of deep, dark trouble.

Alan Marchant has been watching Dorian with interest for a while and knows there's more to Dorian than his label of "pain slut" suggests. When Dorian disappears, Alan and his friend Leo set out to find him. But the disoriented young man discovered cowering in a hotel room is not the Dorian they know and love. That Dorian is shattered. It's up to Alan to pick up the pieces and show Dorian there are better ways to fly.

They may be off on a new journey together, but their destination will rock them both to the core.

www.dreamspinnerpress.com

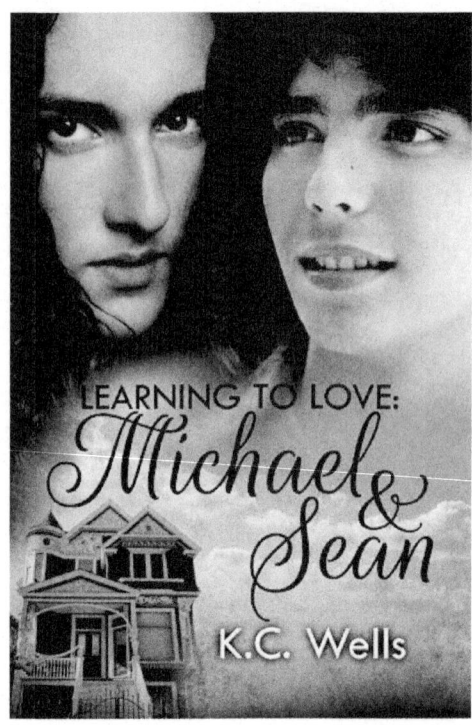

Learning to Love: Book One

Sean and Michael are best friends from the minute they meet and become roommates. But after supporting Sean in the wake of his brother's death, Michael finds himself questioning his sexuality and thinking about his roommate in a totally unexpected light. After all, he and Sean are straight—or so he thought. Suddenly Michael's not so sure any more. He turns to their gay housemate, Evan, for advice. Little does he know he's not the only one seeking Evan's help.

Michael and Sean are both thrilled to explore their newly discovered feelings for each other, but not everyone shares their enthusiasm. When the reality of homophobia intrudes on their academic and personal lives and threatens their happiness, the adversity should draw them closer. Instead, it drives a dangerous wedge between them and puts their relationship, their futures, and their health at risk.

www.dreamspinnerpress.com

Learning to Love: Book Two

Evan Wainwright's good relationship karma is paying off. After helping his friends, Sean and Michael, discover their sexuality—and each other—Evan meets the love of his life. Their new housemate, Daniel Collier, is everything Evan could want in a boyfriend. Now if Evan can just work out why Daniel panics whenever Evan tries to get close.

Daniel has finally met his soul mate. Evan is perfect for him—at least, he would be, if Daniel could find the courage to overcome his demons and leave the past behind. But his mental scars prove difficult to heal, and Daniel struggles with his heart, even though it tells him Evan is the one.

Life in the student house goes on despite the usual interruptions: a wedding, a trial for a hate crime, a gay couple with exhibitionist tendencies. Through it all, Evan and Daniel remind themselves they are meant to be together. But until Daniel trusts Evan with the secret that's tearing his family apart, "meant to be" is on hold.

www.dreamspinnerpress.com

Learning to Love: Book Three

When Chris Andrews gave evidence against the men who manipulated him into taking part in a homophobic assault, Josh Saunders was his rock, and his support gave Chris the courage to come out. Now that Chris finds himself sharing a house with Josh, he wonders where that strong, sexy guy has disappeared to. Chris wants him back—but he can't wait forever.

Josh has been attracted to Chris from the get-go, and the more time they spend together, the stronger the pull grows. But he needs to make sure Chris feels the same attraction, and not just gratitude. Josh bides his time, waiting for the right moment… and misses his chance when Chris starts seeing someone else.

Somehow Josh has to convince Chris they are perfect together. But first, he needs to figure out who has been sending Chris malicious letters, threatening him over the phone, and writing hateful slogans across their front door—and persuade his own ex, who seems determined to win Josh back, to get lost. In fact, Josh's life may depend on it.

www.dreamspinnerpress.com

Learning to Love: Book Four

One house, three couples, and one year left until their final exams….

Evan and Daniel want to take their D/s relationship to the next level. When Daniel suggests conducting a little research at a BDSM club, Evan is more than up for it. Trouble is, one of their housemates isn't happy about this.

Finances tighten for new couple Josh and Chris. Wanting to ease some of the pressure on Chris, Josh starts as an agency nurse. But tackling a heavy workload at medical school and working late-shifts leaves little time for the couple. Something's gotta give.

In Spain, Sean was diagnosed as suffering from migraines. But after the medications have no effect and he starts suffering from other complaints, he decides to get a second opinion without telling Michael. When Michael finds out, Sean's usually laid-back husband's reaction shocks everyone. But Michael needs to get his head sorted fast, because Sean needs his strength.

As their school career comes to a close and the one person who holds them all together starts to fall apart, the final exam is a true test of friendship.

www.dreamspinnerpress.com

Printed in Great Britain
by Amazon

29584501R00165